BOHEMIANS, BEATS AND BLUES PEOPLE

BOHEMIANS, BEATS AND BLUES PEOPLE

JIM BURNS

PENNILESS PRESS PUBLICATIONS
www.pennilesspress.co.uk

Published by

Penniless Press Publications 2013

ISBN 978-1-291-32093-0

Cover: Music shop window Tours, France – photo Ken Clay

CONTENTS

ACKNOWLEDGEMENTS

The essays and reviews first appeared in the following publications:

La Vie de Bohème, *New Society*, London, 27th April, 1967

Harry Kemp: The Tramp Poet, *Beat Scene 66*, Coventry, 2011

Beats, Bums & Bohemians, *Northern Review of Books* (on-line), 2012; *The Crazy Oik 15*, Warrington, 2012

This Quarter, *The Private Library*, Berkhamsted, Spring, 1970

Café Society, *Palantir 10*, Preston, December, 1978

Gilbert Sorrentino, *Beat Scene 51*, Coventry, 2006

In Praise of Booksellers, *The Penniless Press 2*, Preston, Spring, 1996

John Craxton, *Northern Review of Books* (on-line), 2011

Blues, *Prop 10*, Bolton, Winter, 2001/2

Contact, *Prop 6*, Bolton, Winter, 1999

Kurt Vonnegut's Jailbird, *Luciad*, Leicester, Summer, 1983

Things are not as they seem, *The Penniless Press*, Preston, Summer, 1996

The Indignant Generation, *Northern Review of Books* (on-line), 2011

The Masses, *Northern Review of Books* (on-line), 2011

The Great Fear, *Tribune,* London, 13th October, 1978

James T.Farrell, *The Penniless Press 15*, Preston, Spring, 2002

B.Traven, *Palantir 14,* Preston, April, 1980

Beats in Britain, *Beat Scene 47*, Coventry, Spring, 2005

How Far Underground? *Stand,* Newcastle, 1970/71

Pre-Beats, *Transit 12*, Coventry, Spring, 2003

Ted Joans in Paris, *Beat Scene 13*, Coventry, December, 1991

Gregory Corso, *Riverside Interviews 3*, Binnacle Press, London, 1982

The Floating Bear, *Poetry Information 14*, London, Autumn/Winter, 1975/76

Origins of the Beat Generation, *Palantir 18*, Preston, September, 1981

Evergreen Review, *Beat Scene 44*, Coventry, Winter, 2003

Kulchur, *Beat Scene 43*, Coventry, Summer, 2003

Jack Kerouac's Jazz Scene, *Palantir 23*, Preston, 1983; *The Review of Contemporary Fiction*, Elmwood Park, Illinois, Summer, 1983; *Transit 3,* Coventry, Summer, 1993

What's Your Song, King Kong?, *Jazz & Blues*, London, August/September,1971

The Names of the Forgotten, *The Penniless Press 4*, Preston, Spring,1997

Nica's Dream, *Northern Review of Books* (on-line), 2011, and *The Crazy Oik 13,* Warrington, Spring, 2012

The Hipster, *Jazz Journal*, London, July, 1968; *Beat Scene 64*, Coventry, Spring, 2011

Central Avenue Breakdown, *Comstock Lode 7*, London, Spring, 1980; *Blues & Rhythm 21*, London, July, 1986

Let the Good Times Roll, *Jazz and Blues,* London, February, 1972

My thanks to all the editors concerned and to Ken Clay and Joan Mottram

INTRODUCTION

This fourth collection of essays and reviews hopefully provides a useful and entertaining survey of various writers and others who might be said to slot easily into the category of bohemians. I have, admittedly, included some writers who perhaps wouldn't have welcomed being called bohemians. Kurt Vonnegut, Gilbert Sorrentino, and James T.Farrell, for example. But it can be argued that most writers have at least a touch of the bohemian about them, and only those desperate for respectability need to deny it. It may all depend on how you define a bohemian. It's a term that extends far beyond the popular conception of someone who has a free-and-easy life-style that has links, however tenuous, to the arts.

There are several essays dealing with little magazines. They seem to me to be essential to any study of 20th Century literature. *This Quarter, Blues*, and *Contact* between them say a great deal about the literature of the 1920s and 1930s if you want to look beyond the well-known. Likewise, *The Floating Bear, Evergreen Review*, and *Kulchur* offer insights into activity in the late-1950s and early-1960s. One of the pleasures of looking at little magazines of the past is that they have work by writers who never became famous or perhaps produced only a few poems or stories, but who nonetheless made a contribution to the writing of their time. I have to admit to not caring to spend too much time writing about successful authors. Lots of critics and literary historians already do that, so why should I bother? It's the "dusty side-streets" (as someone described them) that interest me.

The Beats are represented, as they were in the previous collections, though I've tried to keep clear of the better-known writers in that group. The essay about Jack Kerouac's jazz interests is an exception to the rule, but I think I can legitimately claim that there hasn't been extensive coverage elsewhere of the subject. As for Gregory Corso and Ted Joans, neither seems to me to have had too much attention in the past, though they were, at their best, two of the most entertaining poets associated with the Beats.

When writing about music over the years I've mostly focused on jazz, but one of the essays looks at rhythm 'n' blues in California in the late-1940s and early-1950s, and another develops the theme beyond the West Coast and touches on the early days of rock 'n' roll.

Since they were written a great mass of recorded material has been available and I'd probably have to take a different approach when writing them now. But I think that the essays as they stand still have some value in terms of the nature of the music and its social background.

The essays and reviews were written for a variety of publications, so there are variations in formats.

LA VIE DE BOHÈME

"Grub Street is as old as the trade of letters - in Alexandria, in Rome, it was already a crowded quarter; bohemia is younger than the romantic movement. Grub Street develops in the metropolis of any country or culture as soon as men are able to earn a precarious living with pen or pencil; bohemia is a revolt against certain features of industrial capitalism and can exist only in a capitalist society. Grub Street is a way of life unwillingly followed by the intellectual proletariat; bohemia attracts its citizens from all economic classes: there are not a few bohemian millionaires, but they are expected to imitate the customs of penniless artists. Bohemia is Grub Street romanticised, doctrinalised and rendered self-conscious; it is Grub Street on parade." - Malcolm Cowley, *Exile's Return.*

Bohemia, as Cowley makes clear, is as much a sociological as a literary phenomenon. Greenwich Village flourished during the boom of the 1920s, but the crash of 1929 soon put an end to the merry-go-round. Most artists pass through bohemia and a few actually stay there all their lives. Some continue to live what is, on the surface, a similar kind of existence even when they have no real need to do so. Preoccupation with one's work, or just a basic disregard for convention, can lead to nonconformity in dress and behaviour. Also, a man who is, in effect, self-employed does not have to give way to the social pressures which are felt by those who work in a large office. Nor must we forget that the words "artist" and "bohemian" go together in most people's minds, and the middle class - who are the main customers of the arts - are always ready to make exceptions for the unconventional (in life, not art) poet or painter. One might almost say that they expect nonconformity, and are disappointed when they don't get it. "How can you be a poet, you don't do anything 'different,'" someone once said to a friend of mine, and the word "different" was referring to his private life, not his poetry.

Bohemia thrives on coteries and cults, and consequently the genuine artists are invariably outnumbered by the hangers-on. Apart from the phoneys and opportunists and the people looking for kicks, bohemians are often those with the urge to create, but not the talent or energy to get their ideas into operation. In the 19th century Henry Murger, the first chronicler of bohemia, put it more bluntly when he said, "Bohemians are those for whom art is always a creed, and never a craft." Ephemera - little magazines, pamphlets, manifestos, and so on - are the literary expression of bohemia.

Murger was a would-be painter who turned to journalism out of necessity. In the 1840s, he began writing short stories of life in the Latin Quarter for a Parisian paper. Most of these were based on Murger's own experiences, or those of his friends, but they were romanticised enough to make their life seem reasonably attractive. Perhaps Murger needed to see it that way in order to stick it? The stories were popular, a book was published (*Scènes de la vie de Bohème*), made into a play, and Murger was a success. He promptly left bohemia.

His place was taken by a horde of young, would-be artists, who came to Paris searching for the comradeship, the fun, the girls and the inspiration, which they thought the bohemian life had. Murger, who knew what bohemia was really like (he died before he was 40 from the effects of his years among it), later wrote articles and novels which tried to portray bohemia as it really was, but the public continued to read his first book and bohemia was born.

The pattern of bohemianism was firmly established by 1900. Murger said that bohemia could not be found outside Paris; but the American who, in the 1920s, when asked to define the physical limits of Greenwich Village, said, "It has no limits, it's a state of mind," was nearer the mark. Bohemia springs up in various places - London, New York, Paris, Tangier, San Francisco, even in various provincial cities and towns - and it's easy to trace its developments in novels and other literature.

Each notable period of bohemianism has its chronicler, like Ernest Hemingway with his *The Sun Also Rises,* which delineates the activities of the expatriates in Paris in the 1920s, and Jack Kerouac, whose *On The Road* brought the beats to the fore in the 1950s. Nearly all of the best-known novels about bohemianism tend to see the life through rose-coloured glasses, despite an obligatory (the action, and characters, usually being based on fact) tipping of the hat to realism. Murger couldn't help making it seem basically cheerful; Hemingway invested it with a desperate, hard-boiled romanticism; and Kerouac saw it almost in religious terms. I find it curious that all three of the novelists I've mentioned had contemporaries who deal with much the same situations, but saw them from a more down-to-earth point of view. Champfleury wrote about Murger's bohemia, Robert McAlmon about Hemingway's, and John Clellon Holmes about Kerouac's beat world. I doubt, though, that their names mean anything to the advocates of bohemia. Apart from the quality of the writing, people will see only what they want to see, and what they want to see in bohemia is a world, and a way of life, which seemingly offers an escape from the standardisation and pointlessness of much middle-class life.

Bohemia flourishes as much as ever today, partly because of the encouraging economic circumstances (the squeeze doesn't squeeze this) partly because of the rising level of general standards of education. It's difficult - and not really all that useful - to define the actual physical boundaries of contemporary bohemia, as they tend to shift according to various social and economic pressures. Greenwich Village is now no longer the main bohemian centre in New York. The artists and the hangers-on have moved to the Lower East Side (known as the East Village), and already the building-up of a new image has started. The East Village has its own newspaper, and an astute journalist has already written a book called *The New Bohemia.* In England, where bohemia has never been as centralised as in America or France, one finds novels (those by Laura Del-Rivo and Cressida Lindsay, for example) which detail life in Notting Hill and such places.

Perhaps the true Bohemians in England are to be found in the provinces. Here at least, there is an intellectual proletariat of the kind Henry Murger knew. In *The Liverpool Scene* Edward Lucie-Smith says: "Banded together against the provincial environment, artists and writers exist as a single group, sharing one another's company, and also one another's ideas. If one wants to find a modern equivalent of Murger's in *la vie de Bohème* one has to look for it in Liverpool."

Liverpool apart, many provincial bohemias, are inhabited by those who have been educated to something better than they are currently doing, but who have been hampered by their working class backgrounds. At the same time, they have artistic aspirations, but not sufficient talent to put them completely into operation. As Murger and his friends did they produce their own magazines, or occasionally write for obscure publications, and they support themselves by becoming clerks, or postmen, or salesmen. A few are teachers. On the whole their world is as separate from the middle class cultural life, of the town as was Murger's from that of Paris. My own experience has been that most reasonably sized provincial towns have a small group like this, often centred around the local jazz musicians or the art school, and including a few part-time painters and poets, as well as the inevitable hangers-on. One can generalise too much, but it's also noticeable that, like Murger's bohemians, they tend to find their female partners amongst the working class girls of the area, though they're usually those who've had enough education to get them into a lower-grade clerical job.

I sometimes think that the idea of living in a definable community provides, even now, a substitute for the old village culture. The bohemian attitude to the arts often involves doing something which will entertain or stimulate the particular clique to which one belongs, this seemingly because of a desire to assert one's place in the community. This is particularly true of the provinces, where little effort is made to appeal outside the locality; those who feel they have more to offer either move on, or live outside the local culture. In conversations in the provinces it's not unusual to hear people refer to "Tom the painter" or "Jack the pianist," and so on. It's easy to read too much into this, but one can't help thinking of village life, with each person having his place and being known amongst his associates by his stated preoccupation (or occupation). I suspect that if we decentralised culture and administration more - so that provincial communities had another focus - the bohemian would lose some of his attraction.

HARRY KEMP: THE TRAMP POET

Writing about Harry Kemp some years ago William Brevda remarked that his "*Tramping on Life* is a precursor of Kerouac's *On the Road* in which Kerouac, like Kemp, is a tramp for the sake of his art. Kerouac takes to the road out of a sense of romance and in the spirit of youthful rebellion." Brevda also thought that Kerouac would have agreed with Kemp's idea that "wisdom was to be found more in the vagabond bye-ways of life than in the ordered and regulated highways." And he went on to point out that Kemp, like Kerouac, aimed for a prose style that would give the impression of speech and of the writer talking directly to the reader. In addition, *Tramping on Life* was similar to *On the Road* in the way that it dealt with actual events and used fictitious names to disguise the identities of real people.

So, who was Harry Kemp, the Tramp Poet as he was often called, and what was his role in the development of a bohemian tradition? He was born in 1883 in Youngstown, Ohio, though he grew up in Newark, New Jersey, birthplace of a later bohemian, Allen Ginsberg. As a boy Kemp read Byron and Whitman and became excited by the idea of becoming a poet. He also read Richard Henry Dana's *Two Years Before the Mast* and Josiah Flynt's *Tramping with Tramps*. When he was 17 he left home, made his way to New York, and signed on as a cabin boy on a ship heading for Australia. Once there he left the ship, tramped through Australia, and then got a job on a cattle-boat taking supplies to the troops fighting in the Boxer Rebellion in China. From there he worked his way to Manila and bummed around until the local authorities had a purge of young vagrants and shipped him back to America.

Some people might have thought that they'd picked up sufficient experience of roughing it by this time but Kemp, still anxious to widen his education, went on the road, hanging out in hobo "jungles" and hitching rides on freight trains. It wasn't all a romantic adventure, and he spent three months in jail in a small Texas town, though he claimed to have occupied his time usefully with studying and writing. When he was released he rode the rails across America and on arrival back in Newark attracted the attention of journalists, something that Kemp was to do throughout his life.

For the next few years Kemp moved around, spending time in Utopian communities where he encountered "rebels, eccentrics, pilgrims, literary wanderers like Richard Hovey and Bliss Carman." He was never averse to seeking publicity but he also had an idea that the "new bohemia" he was more and more involved with could lead the way towards what has been called an "innocent rebellion," which in Kemp's view would be poetical rather than political. He was, in some ways, almost forecasting what proponents of the "alternative society" of the 1960s wanted.

Kemp never completed what might be called a formal education. He bluffed his way into being enrolled at Kansas University, while at the same time ensuring that the local paper would announce his arrival with the headline: "Tramp Poet arrives. Kansas enrols Box-Car Student." He was starting to publish poetry so he fitted neatly into the sort of semi-mythical role of the "hobo who reads Homer; the anti-intellectual intellectual; the man of action who is a man of spirit." I've listed just a few of the descriptions accorded to Kemp by his biographer but I think they get across the idea that he was the kind of writer who can provide good copy for journalists. But I don't want to suggest that his reputation rested solely on the publicity he got. He could write and in a poem called "Experience" he used a long-lined style, probably derived from Whitman, to describe what he'd done. It's not unlike Ginsberg, too, in the way that it kicks off each stanza: "I have camped in California by the shoreward-heaving sea/And I've walked Manhattan's pavements all night long." Other poets, like Carl Sandburg and Arturo Giovannitti, often adopted a similar format but Kemp seems to have used it fairly early, if not consistently.

After four or five years in Kansas, where he admitted to "desultory classroom effort," interspersed with work on farms, Kemp drifted to New York in order to establish himself as a poet. He couldn't keep out of the news, though, and an affair with the wife of Upton Sinclair, author of the famous novel *The Jungle*, got a lot of attention. By 1912 he was settled in Greenwich Village and his first books were starting to be published. Kemp had a knack for hustling money out of publishers for future projects while he also produced poems and stories and articles for various magazines. He was never really a radical from a political point of view and it was said that he wrote a proletarian poem, "The Factory," so he could impress an attractive female who belonged to Emma Goldman's anarchist group. Not everyone appreciated his poetry, and one newspaper described him as "a hatless and hairy scrivener...a worthless shiftless devil, who believes Bohemian life accords with his artistic temperament." Leaving aside the quality of Kemp's poetry, most of which was fairly conventional in its technique and content, the way in which he invited scorn does remind me of some newspaper reports of the Beats when they first came to the attention of the press.

Kemp had arrived in Greenwich Village at an opportune moment. The area was packed with writers, artists, intellectuals, political activists, and bohemian characters, and as Floyd Dell put it: "It was a beautiful year, a year of poetry and dreams, and of life renewed and abundant. We were all full of ideals, illusions, and high spirits. We were young and the world was before us." For Kemp it was the perfect setting. He could write his poems, romanticise his situation, pursue any number of young women, drink, and generally indulge himself. It was a period of great social and political ferment and the Wobblies (the Industrial Workers of the World) were involved with major strikes which were supported by many Greenwich Villagers. It's said that Kemp, if he got involved, "was there more for love of excitement and the spectacular than for love of the masses."

American entry into the First World War in 1917 meant that the "poetry and dreams" Floyd Dell had referred to were soon overshadowed by a national mood which frowned on anyone not following a pro-war and patriotic line. Kemp had published a few poems in *The Masses*, the radical magazine suppressed by the government when America started sending troops to Europe, but he wasn't left-wing enough to cause the authorities to consider him worth prosecuting. His interests tended to be directed to his own writing and the little theatre company he had founded. In 1920 a collection of his poems, *Chanteys and Ballads: Sea Chanteys, Tramp Ballads and Other Ballads and Poems*, brought him some success and went part way towards convincing critics that he could write poems that were colourful, well-constructed, and at their best convincing from the point of view of persuading the reader that the poet wasn't just writing about subjects he'd only experienced from a distance. When Kemp wrote, "I've decked the tops of flying cars/That leaped across the night," he was describing what he'd done during his hoboing days.

His *Tramping on Life*, described as "an autobiographical narrative," was published in 1922 and proved to be popular, its vivid account of Kemp's early wanderings appealing to both critics and readers. Some careful editorial advice had persuaded him against including too many of his poems in the narrative and he managed to establish a style that, as William Brevda put it, " tries to break through artifice and to sound like actual speech." The words "are not so much read as heard." It's a description that could easily apply to *On the Road*. Perhaps flushed with success Kemp decided to visit Paris where numerous American writers had congregated. He wanted to promote his "League of Bohemian Republics," a theory that envisaged all the bohemian communities uniting: "When the earth is salted with bohemianism and the army of bohemians is so strong that the world will recognise its power will come the real revolution which will overturn bolshevism and capitalism and shock the people into thinking and understanding." Again, it's relevant to draw parallels between what Kemp said and some of the more fanciful statements in the "underground" publications of the 1960s and even relate Kemp's ideas to social theories advocated by Ginsberg, Gary Snyder, and others.

On a more downbeat level when Kemp got married in 1924 his wife understood that "she had a husband to support." His aversion to doing anything other than writing or taking part in various schemes to publicise his bohemian theories was well known. The marriage didn't last too long and when his wife left him she said: "Life was not dull with Harry. You never knew quite what was going to happen next," but then she added: "It couldn't have gone on, it was too fantastic."

More Miles, a second instalment of Kemp's autobiographical novel, was published in 1924, though it didn't turn out to be as popular as the earlier book. There were suggestions that the public mood was changing and people were less inclined to find his bohemianism as entertaining or able to shock or surprise. The same sort of thing happened when interest in Kerouac and the Beats began to decline after the initial response lost its impetus.

In the late-1920s Kemp moved to Provincetown and life in a small shack on the edge of the sea. He continued to write and to drink, and even had a couple of novels published in the 1930s, though neither made any sort of impact either in terms of critical acclaim or sales.

One of them, *Love Among the Cape Enders*, used his experiences among the bohemian community in Provincetown and most of its characters could easily be identified as based on real people Kemp had encountered. After the 1930s, though, he slid from sight, at least as far as most people were concerned. He drank heavily, self-published a few slim books, tried to publicise various schemes, and somehow survived, often thanks to friends who looked after him. He still had his shack but also had an apartment he was allowed to use on a rent-free basis. A description of it says a lot about his situation: "Kemp's apartment, with its one light bulb and a smoky oil stove, was dark and smelly. There were books and magazines everywhere, and what space remained was a virtual corridor. Kemp's desk was piled two feet high with papers."

William Brevda says that "Harry's drinking in these final years was rough and crude - besotted, sullied, crawling crude," and that his more concerned friends tried to persuade other visitors to bring food rather than alcohol when they came to see him. But one night someone gave him a jug of wine and the following morning he was found to have suffered a cerebral haemorrhage. He died on August 8th, 1960. He had known that he was getting close to the end of his life, anyway, and had requested that he be cremated and his ashes scattered over the dunes in Provincetown and in Greenwich Village. It was claimed that he had been working on a history of Greenwich Village and had accumulated around a thousand pages of notes for it, but it's doubtful if the project ever got anywhere near a publishable manuscript.

I often wonder if Jack Kerouac had read any of Harry Kemp's work or knew anything about him. I think Allen Ginsberg would have been aware of him, partly because Kemp had been published alongside Louis Ginsberg, Allen's father, in magazines and anthologies, but also because Ginsberg had a sense of bohemian history. But he probably wouldn't have been too impressed by Kemp's poetry. It was mostly conventionally tidy but often quite sentimental. Most of the poems are forgotten now, though short pieces like "A Poet's Room, Greenwich Village, 1912," and "Street Lamps, Greenwich Village," have some period atmosphere and charm. And "The War They Never Fought," with its satirical comments on bankers, businessmen, and politicians, still has an edge. As for Kemp's prose, *Tramping On Life* is worth looking at for its picture of hobohemianism.

NOTES

There are references to Harry Kemp in standard histories of American bohemianism, such as Albert Parry's *Garrets and Pretenders: A History of Bohemianism in America* (Dover Books, New York, 1960); Allen Churchill's *The Improper Bohemians* (Cassell, London, 1961); Robert E. Humphrey's *Children of Fantasy: The First Rebels of Greenwich Village,* John Wiley, New York, 1978). A few of his poems are in *Echoes of Revolt: The Masses 1911-1917*, edited by William L. O'Neill (Quadrangle Books, Chicago, 1966) and *The Greenwich Village Reader*, edited by June Skinner Sawyer (Cooper Square Press, New York, 2001). A section from *Tramping On Life* was included in *Marginal Manners: The Variants of Bohemia*, edited by Frederick J. Hoffman (Row, Peterson & Company, New York, 1962). The best overall survey of Kemp's life and work is William Brevda's *Harry Kemp: The Last Bohemian* (Bucknell University Press, Lewisburg, 1986).

BEATS, BUMS AND BOHEMIANS

These three novels were first published in 1961 and they all deal with lives lived on the fringes of society in the 1950s. The title of the series they appear in - "Beats, Bums and Bohemians" - sums up the kind of people they focus on, though their links to an older Soho bohemianism might incline the pedantic to wonder if "Beats" really applies in a couple of cases. There were Beats around in the late-1950s, and the word itself was often a substitute for bohemians, but colourful and/or oddball characters didn't just arrive in Soho after Jack Kerouac and Allen Ginsberg became well-known. Roland Camberton's *Scamp*, an earlier title from New London Editions, can be mentioned as throwing light on the subject in fictional form, and *The World is a Wedding*, an autobiography by Bernard Kops, tells in part about his induction into the community of misfits in Soho: "The regulars included the would-be poets, the sad girls from Scotland, the artists without studio or canvas." And he refers to Iron Foot Jack, the "King of the Bohemians," and Iris Orton, "A strange girl with a cloak, who was a beautiful poet." I remember seeing some of her poems in *Jazz & Blues* around forty years ago when I was writing for the magazine, so she was obviously still around then, but like so many poets she's since been forgotten. *Jazz & Blues* was edited by Albert McCarthy, himself an old Soho bohemian with roots going back into the 1940s.

I've mentioned *Jazz & Blues* because Terry Taylor's *Baron's Court, All Change*, the book that might have some sort of Beat linkage, has a fair amount of jazz content and points to the importance of the music as a kind of escape from the routines of working and lower middle-class lives and the dull and dispiriting nature of the jobs available to intelligent, but not academically qualified young people. John, the hero of the novel, has an interest in spiritualism, though it becomes clear that it too is a means of finding something that doesn't tie in with the conformity of the wider society. It's at one of the spiritualist meetings that he encounters Bunty, an older woman, who is also there because it offers an alternative to conventional involvements. As she says: “There's a hundred different paths to travel that have nothing to do with crying babies, football pools, watching the tele, and Saturday night at the local.” Bunty introduces John to abstract art, alcohol, and some tentative sexual adventures, but at the same time his jazz interests take him into the world of cannabis, or "charge" as those in the know called it. Several other names are also used and I suppose it's inevitable that, as well as its virtues as a novel, *Baron's Court, All Change* has a great deal of sociological interest. There were never all that many books, either fact or fiction, that talked about the kind of people who frequented jazz clubs where modern jazz was played in the 1950s, which is one reason that I read Terry Taylor immediately his book was published in 1961. It referred to experiences when listening to the music that I could identify with. John says that his introduction to bebop came through hearing *Bebop Spoken Here*, a track recorded by Tito Burns in 1949. It was around 1950, when I was fourteen, that I first heard this record, and though I suspect that more-aware enthusiasts may have considered it a commercialised version of the real sounds it seemed to me to sum up an attitude of wanting to stand apart from the square world.

John is soon a committed user of cannabis and is drawn into selling as well as using it. He and a friend are soon supplying many of the musicians they admire, but John objects when the friend wants to expand their business into dealing in heroin. A couple of junkies are described in the novel and their dependency is shown as contrasting with the benign influence that cannabis supposedly has. The partners have been using the home of an acquaintance, Miss Roach, to hide their supply of drugs, though she's not aware of this fact. When the police raid her flat she's left to take the blame because she has a previous conviction for possession of cannabis. John seems to be having a crisis of conscience as the novel ends, but it's not clear if he'll tell the police that Miss Roach is innocent. He has been portrayed as behaving responsibly in other circumstances, particularly with regard to his sister, so the reader is left guessing about what will happen.

As I said earlier, *Baron's Court, All Change* has documentary value, and jazz historians may find it of interest. A few names of real people are mentioned, such as Phil Seamen, a legendary British drummer and notorious junkie, Kenny Graham, Sonny Stitt, and Charlie Parker, and Miss Roach has a cat she calls Wardell Gray. Other musicians have fictitious names, though it may be possible to identify the real people behind them, if that's what you like to do. For me, it's enough that Terry Taylor evokes the period and the atmosphere so well. True, some of the slang now sounds so dated that it's almost cute, but most slang is like that.

At one point in Terry Taylor's novel his hero is in a Soho coffee-bar and describes it as a place "where the strangest mixture of human beings gathered to fix up deals that never materialise, to talk about their painting and writing and a whole gang of other things, but I'm afraid they talk more than they create." It's a description almost echoed in Laura Del-Rivo's *The Furnished Room* when the central character, Beckett, goes into a Soho cafe and reflects on the kind of people he'd fallen in with when he moved to London: "He had found writers who did not write, painters who did not paint, petty thieves who were so unsuccessful that they were always scrounging the price of a cup of tea, and pretty girls who turned out to be art-school tarts with dirty faces."

Taylor's hero has ambitions, if only to break away from suburban existence, and his activities as a drug dealer might point to an attempt to establish a role for himself in the circles he'd chosen to move in. But Beckett is a drifter, a man without any real aim in life. He works as a clerk but hates it and hasn't the energy or motivation to move on to something more interesting or challenging. He's not necessarily a bad person and helps an old man who is being harassed by some Teddy Boys. He also has some regard for his mother. But an encounter with a disgraced ex-officer leads to him considering whether or not to get involved in a plot to murder an old lady for her money. Beckett, with his mixture of Catholic guilt and existentialist doubt, needs to do something that will force him to face up to reality. He wants to feel something beyond doubt and disbelief because, as he says at one point, "disbelief is the opposite of freedom, because it paralyses action at the root."

The Furnished Room, like *Baron's Court, All Change*, is full of small details that create the atmosphere of the 1950s. It's a world of brown ales and pubs that close at 3pm. When Beckett invites a girl back to his bedsit he has to ask her to talk quietly because he's not supposed to have visitors after 10.30pm. And he says: "I want to find a place without a landlady on the premises. I detest the whole race. The constant pettiness and prying, the complaining notes pushed under the door." After Beckett walks out of his job he drifts around, has desultory affairs with a couple of women, and eventually agrees to kill the old lady.

The kind of quasi-philosophical discussions that Beckett has with the old man he helped and with the slightly sinister ex-officer are the sort of thing that Harry in Colin Wilson's *Adrift in Soho* likes to engage in. It's perhaps not surprising that Laura Del-Rivo was, in the 1950s, a member of a group that clustered around Wilson. I would guess, though I could be wrong, that he had some influence on her writing. Wilson's own novel is about yet another unsettled young man who samples the Soho scene. The difference is that Harry has no desire to become a king-pin around the jazz scene, nor is he as depressed and aimless as Beckett.

It's true that, like John and Beckett, he's at odds with the world of humdrum jobs and conventional people, but he's determined to become a writer and is far more intellectually inclined than the others. Harry understands from the beginning that the bohemian life he encounters in Soho may have its charms, and can be entertaining, but it's not likely to lead to producing anything of great value. His immersion in it is just a short episode on a longer journey. It was Arsène Houssaye, the 19th Century French writer, who said that he was suspicious of literary bohemians because he saw them as only passing through and looking for material to write about. And it isn't to Colin Wilson's discredit if I say that his book often gives that impression. It's an intellectual exercise, albeit one with a light touch and some humour. John and Beckett are contemptuous of the non-productive bohemians they encounter, whereas Harry is amused by them.

The world of literature and learning is a constant throughout *Adrift in Soho* and names like T.S.Eliot, Dostoevsky, Nietzsche soon crop up. There are also references to Count Basie, Stanford White, Sir Thomas Beecham, and Charles Boyer. Harry is an autodidact and likes to immerse himself in a world of culture where one thing leads to another. When he finds his way to bohemian dives in Soho he encounters a self-proclaimed anarchist, Robert De Bruyn who sells him a book by Lautréamont, and is introduced to Iron Foot Jack and other characters. I'm sure that many of them would be easily recognisable to anyone who frequented Soho in the 1950s, or who knows something of the literature of the period. The people Harry talks to are not the types found in *Baron's Court, All Change*, nor in *The Furnished Room*. They often seem to be from an older category of bohemians.

I was reminded of John Gawsworth, at one time a poet with at least a minor reputation but who declined into drink and a shambling existence around Soho and elsewhere. I doubt that many people know his poetry, and I've only read it in a couple of anthologies, but he had been rated enough in his day for a *Collected Poems* to be published by Sidgwick & Jackson in 1949. He also edited *Poetry Review* for a time and was said to be knowledgeable about the literature of the 1890s. Gawsworth (his real name was Terence Ian Fytton Armstrong) also wrote fantasy and horror stories and knew M.P.Shiel, who bequeathed him an island in the Caribbean that he supposedly owned. Gawsworth liked to see himself as the King of Redonda and was given to bestowing titles on friends and acquaintances, especially those who plied him with liquor. There's an entertaining, though perhaps also sad account of a visit that Gawsworth paid to the St Ives poet Arthur Caddick in the Winter 1972 issue of *The Cornish Review*. Caddick was not averse to a drink himself but he struggled to cope with Gawsworth's alcoholic eccentricities. Interestingly, there is some useful information about him in *All Souls*, a novel by the Spanish writer, Javier Marias.

Have I digressed too far from considering *Adrift in Soho*? Not really, because I wanted to mention Gawsworth as an example of the sort of bohemians around Soho when Wilson got there in the pre-Beat days. His book is full of characters like Gawsworth. Harry meets a man who describes himself as a "Babouvian," which he explains is a follower of Gracchus Babeuf, "one of the earliest and greatest of the socialist thinkers." Later, there's a reference to "two drunken homosexual painters," who, when mentioned a second time, are described as "Welsh." But it doesn't take much imagination to guess that they're based on the two Scottish Roberts - Colquhoun and MacBryde - who were well-known around Soho in the 1940s and 1950s.

Harry has a dream of establishing a "community of artists" who would pool their resources and support each other. But he lodges in a tumbledown Notting Hill house where a variety of would-be poets and writers live, and soon realises that their main aim is to avoid having to work. He comes to the conclusion that "avoiding work costs more energy than a straightforward job." While sampling the bohemian scene he's met an out-of-work actor who has explained his philosophy of bohemianism, and though Harry has been interested by what he's seen and heard he knows he can't possibly remain in that situation: "I could never live according to James's 'philosophy of freedom.' For better or for worse, I am a bourgeois." Harry has realised the truth in what Tambimuttu, another Soho regular of the post-war years, told Julian Maclaren-Ross: "If you get Sohoitis, you will stay there always day and night and get no work done ever."

Adrift in Soho ends on a more-positive note than the other two books under review. Harry helps an artist, Ricky, who is the one talented person in the Notting Hill house, to construct a barrier to his studio so that the shiftless bohemians hanging around in the rest of the property will not keep invading his space and stopping him working. Harry feels a sense of satisfaction at the thought that Ricky has accepted him as understanding why it's sometimes necessary to go to extreme lengths to assert one's needs for privacy and time to work.

I can't end this review without referring to the context in which the three books were first published. 1961 was very much a time when books and articles by and about bohemians, Beats, and other outsiders seemed to abound. The Beat explosion of the late-1950s was partly responsible, but I'd guess that rising affluence and the loosening of the social restrictions that shaped life in the 1950s also helped. The 1960s didn't really start until 1963 or so, and the kind of "underground" scene often dominated by pop music was not much in evidence before that. But something was stirring. I've had a quick look along my bookshelves and there are books, all published around 1961, that point to the interest in the bohemian lives of artists and writers. To name a few of them, Robert Baldick's *The First Bohemian:The Life of Henry Murger*; Allen Churchill's *The Improper Bohemians*; Ned Calmer's *All the Summer Days*; Louis Vaczek's *The Troubadour*; Lawrence Levine's *The Great Alphonse*. I'm sure I could find more if I looked hard enough. Bohemianism was in the air, and Soho, St Ives, Montparnasse, and Greenwich Village, not to mention North Beach in San Francisco, were the places to head for.

And the writers now? Taylor, Del-Rivo and Wilson are all still alive. A note tells us that Wilson lives quietly in Cornwall with his 30,000 books. He's written over 100 himself on a variety of subjects. Laura Del-Rivo also carried on writing but supported herself with a market-stall in Portobello Road. Terry Taylor never published anything after his first book, though there was a "lost" novel and another that remains unpublished. He had a somewhat colourful life, being at one time the lover of the photographer Ida Kar. An exhibition of her work at the National Portrait Gallery in 2011 included photographs of Taylor and Laura Del-Rivo. I was delighted to read that, in more recent years, he ran a sandwich shop in Rhyl.

BARON'S COURT, ALL CHANGE by Terry Taylor
New London Editions. 205 pages. £9.99. ISBN 978-1-907869-27-3

THE FURNISHED ROOM by Laura Del-Rivo
New London Editions. 245 pages. £9.99. ISBN 978-1-907869-14-3

ADRIFT IN SOHO by Colin Wilson
New London Editions. 214 pages. £8.99. ISBN 978-1-907869-13-6

THIS QUARTER

This Quarter first appeared in the spring of 1925 and was edited by Ethel Moorhead and Ernest Walsh. The initial issue was published in Paris, and the second (dated Autumn-Winter 1925-26) - still edited by Walsh and Miss Moorhead - in Milan. Walsh died in 1926 and Miss Moorhead then moved to Monte Carlo, the editorial address of the third issue (Spring 1927). After a lapse of almost two years Miss Moorhead published the fourth number in 1929.

During the Walsh/Moorhead era the magazine was printed wherever convenient, i.e. by local printers in Paris, Milan and Cannes. Each of these issues contained approximately 300 pages (size 9 x 5.1/2 inches) and was bound in soft, coloured paper covers. The first issue was priced at $1, but this was increased to $2 with the second number. This meant, for instance, 9s for the bulky third issue if bought in England, which may seem rather a lot considering the general level of wages and prices then.

Edward Titus assumed control of the magazine with the first issue of the second volume in 1929, and edited it until its demise with the fifth volume in 1932. He reduced the average number of pages per issue to between 180 and 200, but retained the format and priced the magazine at $1.25 or 5s. It's worth noting that the Black Manikin Press sign was incorporated into the cover design.

This Quarter was distributed in Canada, England and the U.S.A., as well as in France (in the latter country it was, of course, mainly aimed at the English and American expatriates). The London bookseller, F. B. Neumayer, was the principal English agent.

*****

'Little magazines are of two kinds, dynamic and eclectic. Some flourish on what they put in, others by whom they keep out. Dynamic magazines have a shorter life, and it is around them that glamour and nostalgia crystallises. If they go on too long they will become eclectic although the reverse process is very unusual. Eclectic magazines are also of their time, but they cannot ignore the past nor resist good writing from opposing camps. The dynamic editor runs his magazine like a commando course where picked men are trained to assault the enemy position: the eclectic is like an hotel proprietor whose rooms fill up every month with a different clique.'[1]

The 1920s saw the birth of numerous little magazines, many of them of the dynamic variety. As the expatriates drifted to Europe their views were put forward in the pages of publications which were sneered at by the literary establishment of the day, but which are now recognised for what they were: the pollinators of the writing and art of a new generation. *This Quarter* was, in its first few issues, the epitome of the approach found in the dynamic magazines of the period, and an air of romance surrounds these early days and many of the people who were then active. When the magazine changed hands towards the end of the 1920s, and a less-committed editor was at the helm, it lost some of its impetus - although the quality level was just as high - and consequently the later issues have tended to be overlooked in literary histories. In its own small way the magazine, during its brief lifetime, represented the best of both the dynamic and eclectic styles, as well as providing a map of the changing fashions of the 1920s.

Ernest Walsh, who with Ethel Moorhead edited the first two issues of *This Quarter*, was a young poet who had gone to Paris to die. It sounds rather romantic, and in keeping with the image of the so-called 'Lost Generation', but was in fact the harsh truth. Sylvia Beach said of him: 'Ernest Walsh... knew that he had only a few months to live and he had decided to come to Paris to spend the time remaining to him among the writers he admired.'[2] Injuries sustained in a plane crash had affected Walsh's lungs and he was suffering from tuberculosis; one can see a myth starting, and Walsh's appearance on the expatriate stage added to it even further. He was something of a character and, as Ernest Hemingway described him, 'dark, intense, faultlessly Irish, poetic and clearly marked for death as a character is marked for death in a motion picture'.[3] He came to an arrangement with Ethel Moorhead - 'Though she was a good many years older than Walsh, they had a liaison which would have tempted any libertine. She allowed him all the freedom to which virilia is entitled'[4] - and together they planned the first issue of *This Quarter*. Walsh was much impressed by Ezra Pound and the magazine kicked off with a dedication to him: 'This number is dedicated to Ezra Pound who by his creative work, his editorship of several magazines, his helpful friendship for young and unknown artists, his many and untiring efforts to win better appreciation of what is first rate in art comes first to our mind as meriting the gratitude of this generation.' Oddly enough Pound himself did not contribute to the first issue - it seems he was asked but failed to respond - but James Joyce, Ernest Hemingway, Richard Aldington, Robert McAlmon and others, were in the pages of the bulky, book-size magazine.

The determined anti-political tone of *This Quarter* - Walsh said: 'You cannot make a literary journal out of a political journal, because beer and wine don't mix'[5] - was evident not only in the editorial statements but also in the choice of work. In the second issue, for instance, Walsh printed Gertrude Stein, Hemingway - the short story 'The Undefeated' - Pound, Joyce, Kay Boyle, Morley Callaghan,[6] and some of the once well known, but now almost-forgotten writers of the 1920s, Emanuel Carnevali[7] and Robert McAlmon[8] amongst them. McAlmon published in most of the best magazines of the period, but his writing, though honest and vigorous, was rarely developed; it is significant that he seems to have had extracts from several unfinished - or at least unpublished - novels printed in the 1920s and early 1930s, and he was noted for his failure to apply himself to his craft. He is remembered now as being the man who ran the Contact Press, which published books by Stein, Hemingway, William Carlos Williams and others.

Walsh was, by this time, a very sick man and he died in October 1926.[9] The third issue of *This Quarter* had been delayed because of his illness, and when it eventually appeared (in the spring of 1927) it was edited solely by Ethel Moorhead and was dedicated to Walsh and Emanuel Carnevali. Miss Moorhead - who, Edward Dahlberg recalls,[10] had been active in the Suffragette movement in England - was almost as impassioned as Walsh in her attitudes towards life and art, and she caused something of a scandal by withdrawing the dedication to Pound which had been a highlight of the first issue. As with most literary squabbles the reasons behind the act were many and varied, but briefly it would appear that Pound had upset Miss Moorhead - and Walsh, when he was still alive - by demanding an exorbitant fee for some of his work and also by treating Walsh's poetry in an offhand manner. It is difficult to determine just who had offended whom, and how, in fact, because the piece entitled 'Ezra Pound and *The Exile*', in which the Moorhead/ Walsh case is laid down, does ramble a bit.

The literary wars aside, however, it was a good number. There was a large section devoted to Walsh's work - both poetry and prose - as well as tributes to him from Kay Boyle, Eugene Jolas (connected with the famous magazine *transition*) and others. Walsh's poetry was not exceptionally good but it did have some connection with his insistence that 'The writing of literature is the writing of speech and the writing of speech is the putting forth of ideas and emotions'. His prose tended to be loose and emotional, and had the sound and intensity of a sick and angry man. Walsh could leap from the personal - bitter references to his own illness - to the general - 'Children are, up to a certain age, free un-tampered intelligences. Then education begins and organised education is the fourth-rate product of third-rate minds' - to literary criticism in the form of hurling insults at the establishment for its failure to recognise the genius of Walsh's contemporaries (or at least those of them he liked). Of course, one can view this latter trait as being typical of the members of any clique, and one's suspicions tend to harden even more when one finds John Herrmann - another now-forgotten writer - praising Walsh and McAlmon, whilst Walsh boosted Herrmann, and McAlmon published his novel, *What Happens*. I do not think it was quite as bad as it seems - Herrmann, for instance, spent very little time on the expatriate scene - but it does show how vulnerable to attack these people were.

McAlmon's story in this issue - yet another extract from a novel which did not ever appear - was a rambling affair, full of the best - the obvious desire to set down only what he had personally experienced - and the worst - the sloppy writing and the irrelevance of much of the material - of his work. The following passage is typical:

'No, no', Alaric answered quickly, not wanting a cluster of black children around him when he landed from the motor-boat. Their sick eyes upset him; their clutching paws, should he give one a coin, would make his whole body seem to itch. The desert quality had its fascination, the Nile, the mud village, the moving picture of palms, hills, dun sand, and eternally sprouting black figures on the Nile bank, pleased him; gave him an impression of removed, two-dimensional actuality of life that nevertheless seemed unreal, or only a dream reality. The Koran was all these children were taught, but he need feel no resentment for that. It gave him no greater sense of the ghastly futility of life, ultimately, than he had felt in London, and in New York, amongst highly educated, but terribly wearied people.'

McAlmon would continue for pages in this vein, and his dialogue was clearly almost straight reproduction of conversations he himself had taken part in on his travels. Much of what he had to say was of interest, but he ruined the effect in fiction by his refusal to edit his work. Morley Callaghan, Patrick O'Rourke, Picabia, A. S. J. Tessimond (a young English poet then living in Birkenhead - the editors must not have been completely averse to work from outside the magic circle of expatriates) were also contributors to the third issue of *This Quarter*. It is interesting, too, to look at the advertisements for other publications of the period - *New Masses, transition, Double Dealer, The Calendar*; the names of McAlmon, Herrmann and many more are listed there as well.

Ethel Moorhead edited the magazine for one more issue - amongst those in its pages were Edward Dahlberg, with a portion of the novel later published under the title *Bottom Dogs*,[11] and Robert McAlmon, with a long chunk of his epic poem 'North America, Continent of Conjecture' - but then decided to throw in the towel. She disappeared from the literary scene after this, and Edward Dahlberg summed her up when he said: 'She was a guerrilla fighter of letters, and when she thought she had finished what she set out to do, she dropped from sight, just as Carnevali, McAlmon, and John Herrmann had done.'[12] Luckily, Edward Titus offered to continue *This Quarter*.

Titus was a different type of person altogether to Ernest Walsh and Ethel Moorhead. A keen bibliophile, he had opened a bookshop in Paris and also ran the Black Manikin Press, which brought out books by, amongst others, Mary Butts and Ludwig Lewisohn.[13] He was of the opinion that the expatriates needed correct business methods in the operation of their magazines and presses, and as a result he was often dismissed as being a mere businessman, that most hated of animals amongst the bohemians. The fact that he was married to Helena Rubinstein did not help, either, but in all fairness it must be pointed out that Titus had a genuine interest in the arts in general, and in new writing in particular.

Titus conveniently took over with the first number of the second volume. In doing so he managed to start another literary war by taking a few shots at the famous *transition* manifesto which had stated: 'The plain reader be damned.'[14] Max Eastman and Harry Crosby - the latter a regular *transition* contributor and another of the romantic figures of the era[15] - were indulging in a battle of words about the philosophy implied in the various statements in the manifesto, and although Titus did not really come down in favour of either side he did say that clarity was sometimes necessary. After that the war hotted up slightly, and Titus at one point noted that transition, if written backwards, reads 'no it isn art'.

His more catholic tastes were at once apparent, and Herbert Read, D. H. Lawrence - the essay 'Pornography and Obscenity' - Allen Tate, Liam O'Flaherty and T. F. Powys turned up in the first issue under his guidance. In the second issue a few of the expatriate crowd - McAlmon and Edwin Lanham (now best known for his mystery stories) - were included, and Morley Callaghan - who contributed a short-story - tells an interesting tale about how he came to be in this *This Quarter*. Titus, despite his activity, had never met such people as McAlmon and Hemingway - Callaghan makes a comment about the possibility of anti-Semitism amongst the Paris crowd but I would guess that Titus's social status, and the natural clique-ishness of the expatriates (a revealing example of this is McAlmon's admission that he knew very few French writers, despite living in France for several years) were responsible for his lack of contact with the American contingent - and was consequently very interested when the Canadian writer introduced him to McAlmon. During the course of their evening together a couple of local characters happened to enter the bar where they were drinking, and Titus, listening to Callaghan and McAlmon argue about the two, suggested they should each write a story on the subject which he would publish in the next issue of *This Quarter*. Callaghan relates[16] how McAlmon ended the evening in a drunken state, so he either forgot about the story, or - more likely - just never got around to it. Callaghan did, though, and his 'Now That April's Here' is a neat description of the types who hung around the fringes of the expatriate world.[17] Whether McAlmon's story - 'Court Reporting Office' - in this issue of *This Quarter* was accepted on its merits (it is very rough and ready), or whether Titus took it instead of the story McAlmon never produced, is impossible to say.

One of the other contributors was Sisley Huddleston, an English journalist who was familiar with most of the writers and artists - English, American and French - in Paris.[18] It is perhaps a comment on Titus's tastes and contacts that someone like Huddleston - who wrote such novels as *Mr. Paname* ('a charming romance laid against the Bohemian background of the Latin Quarter in Paris', to quote the jacket) in which characters with the names Ernest Intheway, Ezra Ounze and Gertrude Stoll figure[19] - should be printed in a supposedly avant-garde magazine. Huddleston knew his Paris, and was a decent journalist, but he was hardly the most stimulating of creative writers.

Titus kept *This Quarter* going into the 1930s - Samuel Putnam assisted him - and added to his impressive list of contributors. Robert Penn Warren, William Carlos Williams, William Gerhardi and Ralph Cheever Dunning - the latter yet another ill-fated poet who flared brightly and briefly[20] - were all in *This Quarter* at one time or another. There was, too, an increasing interest shown in European writing. Roger Vitrac's play 'The Ephemera' was printed, as were small anthologies of new work from Italy, Russia and other countries. Despite the devotion to art for its own sake, the magazine was bound to reflect some of the social and political turmoil of the time. Proletarian literature was represented by an excerpt from James T. Farrell's *Studs Lonigan*, and some of the editorial comments touched on events in Europe. Titus himself seems to have been quite liberal minded - though with a tendency to say 'a plague on all your houses' when faced with a situation where people were choosing sides - but the following (not by Titus, it should be noted) has a doubtful air about it: 'There is no such thing as intellectuals who live their days outside the common working life of the nation, but all, at one and the same time - soldiers and blackshirts, populace and artists - are bound together in the common lot, in triumph and in peril'. This is quoted from an Italian paper of the time and the rather ambiguous comment: 'If this is true, it is something for any nation to have accomplished', is added. One can imagine what Ernest Walsh - a great champion of the individual - would have said to quasi-political propaganda like that.

Titus once remarked: 'We have had no "platform", no "program" ', and this was true enough of the issues he edited. It was also, no doubt, the reason why the magazine lacked the Moorhead/Walsh fire when it was under his direction. Qualitatively speaking, *This Quarter* was as good with Titus as it had been with Walsh and Miss

Moorhead, but the latter pair - and the people they championed, McAlmon, Herrmann, Kay Boyle, Carnevali, et cetera - represented a state of mind, one that was for a period typical of Montparnasse (even if some of the people mentioned, and others like them, didn't live there). One can see the limitations implicit in their attitudes towards both life and art - the number of failures in the latter is significant - but it is hard not to admire their sincerity and enthusiasm. Likewise, it is difficult not to admire the early issues of *This Quarter*, and at the same time neglect those published by Titus. Both deserve to be given attention, however, and credit for what they did, not for what we think they should have done.

REFERENCES

1. Cyril Connolly, 'Fifty Years of Little Magazines', in *Art and Literature*, Vol. 1 (Lausanne, March 1964), pp. 95 - 109.

2. Sylvia Beach, *Shakespeare and Company* (Faber & Faber, London, 1960), p. 147.

3. Ernest Hemingway, *A Moveable Feast* (Jonathan Cape, London, 1964), p. 106.

4. Edward Dahlberg, 'The Expatriates: A Memoir', in *Alms For Oblivion* (University of Minnesota Press, Minneapolis, 1964), p. 52.

5. Quoted in a brief but interesting survey of *This Quarter* in Albert Parry's *Garrets and Pretenders: A History of Bohemianism in America* (Dover Publications, New York, 1960), p. 337.

6. See Callaghan's *That Summer In Paris* (MacGibbon & Kee, London, 1963), pp38-39

7. See the *Autobiography of Emanuel Carnevali*, compiled and prefaced by Kay Boyle (Horizon Press, New York, 1967).

8. McAlmon is a particularly fascinating figure but it is only in recent years that he has received the attention he deserves. For further details see *Robert McAlmon: Expatriate Publisher and Writer*, by Robert E. Knoll (University of Nebraska Press, Lincoln, Nebraska, 1959); *McAlmon and The Lost Generation: A Self Portrait,* edited by Robert E. Knoll (University of Nebraska Press, Lincoln, Nebraska, 1962); *Being Geniuses Together*, by Robert

McAlmon (Secker & Warburg, London, 1938). This latter - a rare collector's item now - has been revised by Kay Boyle (who added chapters of her own memoirs of the 1920s) and re-published by Doubleday & Co., New York (1968). Collectors of curiosa might like to note that four of McAlmon's stories were published in a cheap paperback under the title *There Was a Rustle of Black Silk Stockings* (Belmont Books, New York, 1963). The text of the stories appears to follow that of the Contact Press *Distinguished Air* (*Grim Fairy Tales*), in which three of them first appeared, and it would be interesting to know why the paperback publisher decided to issue the book. McAlmon, most of whose books appeared in limited editions, would no doubt have had a sardonic comment on the publicity he was getting after he died.

9. Kay Boyle's novel *Year Before Last* (Faber & Faber, London, 1932) is a fictional portrait of Walsh's last days. For a factual account see Miss Boyle's contributions to the later edition of *Being Geniuses Together.*

10. Dahlberg, op. cit., p. 52.

11. *Bottom Dogs* was first published by Simon & Schuster, New York (1930) and later re-issued by City Lights Books, San Francisco (1961).

12. Dahlberg, op. cit., p. 54.

13. Ludwig Lewisohn's *The Case of Mr. Crump* was published by Titus in 1926. The first complete edition to be made available in England appeared in 1968 when Constable & Co. Ltd., London, distributed copies of an American edition published by Farrar, Straus & Giroux, New York, in 1965.

14. See Malcolm Cowley's *Exile's Return* (The Bodley Head, London, 1961), pp. 275-277, for information on the signing of the manifesto.

15. Cowley, op. cit., pp. 246 - 88.

16. Callaghan, op. cit., pp. 102-7.

17. Callaghan's 'Now That April's Here' is included in his collection, *Stories 1* (MacGibbon & Kee, London, 1962).

18. Huddleston's *Bohemian Literary and Social Life In Paris* (Harrap & Co., London, 1928) contains references to Walsh, Titus and numerous other writers of the period.

19. Huddleston, *Mr. Paname* (Thornton Butterworth Ltd., London, 1926).

20. Hemingway, op. cit.,pp. 123-7. Some of Dunning's work can be found in Ezra Pound's magazine *The Exile*, issues 2 (Pascal Covici, Chicago, 1927) and 3 (Pascal Covici, Chicago, 1928).

CAFÉ SOCIETY

"Bohemia," according to Malcolm Cowley, "is Grub Street romanticised, doctrinalised, and rendered self-conscious; it is Grub Street on parade." It's a statement with a fair amount of truth in it, though it tends to simplify the differences between the two locations (or states of mind). As Cowley went on to point out, Grub Street (which was an actual street in London until it was renamed in 1830) comes into operation wherever there is a chance of earning a living, no matter how precarious, from writing, whereas Bohemia is a revolt against certain features of industrial capitalism. In Grub Street the kind of writing one does isn't really important; one hacks out what one has to. In the London of the 18th Century the inhabitants of Grub Street were, according to Johnson, "writers of small histories, dictionaries, and temporary poems," and it was from this kind of description that the term "Grub Street" came to be applied to the ephemeral productions of literary hacks. As the Augustan satirists also made clear, the term was used to refer to the style of life that the hacks followed out of *necessity*. I stress the "necessity," because it is this which, in many ways, distinguishes Grub Street from Bohemia. People live in Grub Street because they *have* to, in Bohemia because they *want* to. That's a generalised definition, of course, and there is clearly an overlap from one way of life onto the other. But I suppose there is a basic truth in the notion that Grub Street writing may involve the writer in handling material he has no real commitment to (as with the 17th Century hacks who churned out stuff for political groups or private individuals on request, and in return for specified amounts), whereas one imagines the Bohemian writing out of a sense of dedication. The concept of the poet starving in his garret, but refusing to compromise himself, stems from this aspect of the difference. It is, essentially, a concept that has its origins in the Paris of the 1840s, and its most popular portrayal in Puccini's opera *La Bohème.* But one should never forget the overlap of interests I referred to. For example, the book which launched Bohemia into the general public consciousness was based on stories written to make money for their author so he could buy time to concentrate on what he thought of as his more serious work. It is this kind of contradiction which often makes it difficult to know where to draw lines when documenting the history of Bohemia.

The difficulties are apparent in Steve Bradshaw's *Café Society*, an uneasy, though interesting attempt to provide an account of "Bohemian life" from the London of the 17th Century through to the Greenwich Village of the 1960s. The problem seems to be that the subject is so wide-ranging (and I'm not just thinking of the lines of demarcation between Grub Street and Bohemia) that unless one fixes on a specific aspect of it there's a tendency to be sketchy. *Café Society* often falls into that trap. Most students of Bohemia have particular eras and areas that attract them more than others, and Bradshaw is no exception. Had he concentrated on his favourite periods of Bohemian history he would, I feel, have produced a better book.

Bradshaw tries to put a framework on his subject by insisting in his introduction that he's essentially only interested in café life, but his case is weak, and throughout the book he constantly weakens it even further by moving out of the cafés whenever it suits him to do so. There would be nothing wrong with this, of course, if he hadn't tried to lay down some rules, but to keep breaking them merely adds to the uneasiness with which he seems to have approached the whole subject. Likewise, he explains away his failure to deal with some significant aspects of Bohemia (the Dadaist movement, for example) by saying that he hasn't tried to be objective in his choice of periods and places. That again might be acceptable if it weren't for the fact that he sometimes can't offer a very convincing testimony for the choice he has made. His final chapter is typical of this drawback, and has the appearance of being knocked together to enable the publishers to use Bob Dylan's name on the cover of the book, so that they'll hopefully attract some of the pop-music audience. One could also be cynical and suggest that, as Bradshaw himself has worked in the pop field, he could knock out a quick chapter which wouldn't involve the research needed to deal with literary aspects of the same period.

Moving on to Bradshaw's basic reasons for writing his book, there is, I think, a good point made when he says that contemporary life, despite its constant encouragement of collective activity, can't offer a worthwhile parallel to Bohemian café society, with its spontaneity: "Nowadays if you have no taste for official institutions it is hard to know where to find people with your own interests. Of course there are many thousands of colleges, professional bodies and institutes which have been set up to cater for this need. And yet it is hard for most people to feel any excitement about vast organisations, formal social gatherings or self-enclosed bodies that are barred to the public." In other words, as official organisations have grown so has Bohemian life declined. There perhaps doesn't seem to be a need for people to get together to discuss things, formulate plans for little magazines, arrange their own exhibitions, and so on. It's all done at the local arts centre or college, with professional administrators organising everything. And while this, and the general growth in higher education facilities, no doubt has its beneficial side, it can and does lead to conformity. Academics and arts administrators may like to think of themselves as enlightened when compared to the man in the street, but within their own society they establish very orthodox frameworks of interests and opinions. They're also usually operating in a career structure, something which would appear to be very opposite of what Bohemianism stands for. In the sense that he worries about the question of the institutionalisation of artistic activity, and expresses a vague feeling that something is missing now that there aren't Bohemian communities of any consequence, Bradshaw is on the right track. But *his* history of Bohemianism isn't always likely to convince a doubtful reader that he's missing anything of real value.

He kicks off with the London coffee-houses of the 17th and 18th Centuries, and paints a lively, interesting picture of the life which revolved around them. He makes the worthwhile point that the art of the periodical essay, as conceived by Steele, was intended to reflect the kind of topics discussed in coffee-houses, and the way in which they were approached. He also quotes Addison: "It was said of Socrates that he brought philosophy down from heaven to inhabit among men; and I shall be ambitious to have it said of me that I have brought philosophy out of closets and libraries, schools and colleges, to dwell in clubs and assemblies, at tea-tables, and in coffee-houses." In many ways this section is one of the most valuable in the book. Bradshaw is happy with his basic material, and although his coverage is necessarily sketchy, he does make a few good points. But one might be forgiven for wondering what it all has to do with Bohemianism? As I said earlier, the line between Grub Street and Bohemia isn't always a clear one, but insofar as there was a Bohemia in London at the time we're speaking of it would probably be better located in the areas inhabited by the now-forgotten hacks who were pilloried in Pope's *The Dunciad.* Bradshaw rightly says that these types would most likely have been shunned by the relatively affluent and genteel frequenters of the coffee-houses, but I would guess they might very well have been at home in the Parisian Bohemia that Henry Murger knew and used to formulate the myth of Bohemianism as a way of life. The poverty, low-life, loose morals, and sometimes minor criminality, mixed with hack writing and high hopes, were expressions of both the Grub Street of 18th Century London and the Bohemia of 19th Century Paris. That the respectable eventually triumphed in England, and the Grub Street hacks mostly sank from sight by the beginning of the 19th Century, whereas Bohemianism began to flourish in France, may say a lot about the differences between the two countries, and the characteristics of their inhabitants. It might have been interesting had Bradshaw spent a little more time discussing the real Grub Street types like Ned Ward, Tom Brown, Edmund Curll, and all the others who are to be found discussed in studies of 17th and 18th Century literary London, such as Philip Pinkus's *Grub Street Stripped Bare* and Pat Rogers' *Grub Street: Studies in a Subculture,* neither of which are listed in Bradshaw's bibliography.

A brief chapter in *Café Society* tries to chronicle the existence of an 18th Century café life in France, with those in Paris in particular seen as hotbeds of the unrest which eventually resulted in the French Revolution. But again, one tends to think that Bradshaw is trying too hard to convince his readers that the life in and around the cafés was necessarily Bohemian as opposed to just generally lively. Writers and political activists gathered in them, it's true, but the circumstances of the time may just have determined that this happened. It was, after all, a fairly easy way for anyone with a cause to find a ready-made audience.

However, it is in the 1830s that we begin to notice the first authentic signs of Bohemia as we know it today. It's interesting to consider what brought about the formation of this society within society. And why did it happen in France and not England? The economic factor is important, but one has also to take into account national characteristics. Joanna Richardson, in her book *The Bohemians: La vie de Bohème in Paris, 1830-1914*, maybe summed it up when she wrote: "The Frenchman is naturally more inclined than the Englishman to accept the Bohemian way of life, to countenance its idleness, frivolity and passionate intensity....The Frenchman, by his nature, is more inclined to indulge in café life, to prolong intellectual conversation. He lacks the matter-of-factness of the Englishman." If that is a correct analysis then it may also explain why the Grub Street hacks disappeared as British society became more controlled and "matter of fact" with the developing industrialisation of the late 18th and early 19th Centuries. The kind of shiftless life they represented was hardly likely to be looked on kindly by a society which admired hard work and thrift, and although there was a 19th Century Grub Street it was, as George Gissing's *New Grub Street* makes clear, a dismal place (I'm not, of course, referring to a specific location) largely inhabited by struggling middle-class writers for whom respectability in both life and literature was important.

If the economic factor was influential in Britain then the same was true of France. Economically the French lagged behind many of their European neighbours in the early 19th Century. The process of developing factory production, and the gradual dwindling of old crafts, took longer, with the consequence that its impact was spread out over a greater period and helped create something of a minor displaced class. This was largely made up of the sons of small shopkeepers and craftsmen. Better educated than their parents these young men looked with distaste or disinterest on the prospects available to them if they followed in the family traditions. Their educations had often opened their eyes to the heady world of Romantic literature and art, and the events of the early 1830s (in both art and politics) seemed to promise a new society. They drifted to the large towns and cities (Paris in particular) where they hoped to obtain suitable employment and, assuming their aims were artistic ones, to become famous. But there were insufficient jobs to go round. Had a situation existed where industry and commerce were booming, and had their background been different, they probably would have found steady employment as salesmen, clerks, managers, commercial artists, solicitors, accountants, and so on, but they found instead that they were in a vacuum. Their talents, if they had any, were only likely to enable them to scuffle along on occasional earnings from working as part-time teachers, minor clerks, hack journalists, and the like. An intellectual proletariat had been born, a declassed group which related neither to the middle-class or the growing industrial working-class or the peasantry. It was this group, along with the poverty-stricken Parisian art students they inevitably mixed with, that were soon nicknamed Bohemians, a term that seems to have come into use in the 1830s. The French had previously used it to describe gipsies (who they thought originated in the old Central European province of Bohemia), and the seemingly feckless way of life of the would-be writers and artists put them in the same category as the perennial wanderers. Bradshaw at least picks up on this point, even if he doesn't give a convincing account of the causes of the birth of the intellectual proletariat I've discussed above. Reading *Café Society* one would imagine that the Bohemians just suddenly appeared one day in the 1830s.

By the 1840s the Latin Quarter had become known as the home of the Bohemians, and it was in 1845 that Henry Murger wrote the first of the short stories which would later be collected in *Scènes de la vie de Bohème.* Murger actually had ambitions as a poet, and the stories (based on the escapades of himself and his friends) were written primarily as a means of making a little money. They were reasonably popular, but it was only when Theodore Barrière helped adapt them for the stage that they attracted widespread attention. Two years later, in 1851, they appeared in book form, and Bohemia was officially on its way. It is from that date that one can trace the popular conception of the Bohemian writer and artist. Balzac and Gautier may have referred to Bohemians in the 1830s, and there had been a minor play, *Les Bohémiens de Paris*, performed in 1843, but Murger was the man who effectively established Bohemia and the Bohemians as having some definable qualities, at least to outsiders. Whether many of the originals of Murger's characters saw themselves as participating in a way of life that others would envy is a matter for debate. Hunger, debt, disease, and death were commonplace among Murger's friends and associates, and although his stories seemed to play down that side of things they were, in fact, accurate and even bitter. The point is, though, that they were thought of as dealing with a desirable life-style. After Murger people went to Paris to become Bohemians. Murger and his contemporaries may have had one foot in Grub Street and one in Bohemia, but *Scènes de la vie de Bohème* virtually set up Bohemia as a separate province.

Bradshaw immerses himself and us in the café world of mid-19th Century Paris, but he's sometimes a bit shaky with his facts and a bit breathless in his desire to pack in as many anecdotes as possible. Sometimes the facts of the anecdotes are even wrong, as when he repeats Hemingway's mistaken story about Baudelaire walking around the Left Bank with a lobster on a leash. It wasn't Baudelaire, it was Gerard de Nerval, and he was actually seen walking through the gardens of the Palais Royal with a lobster on a pale blue ribbon. He claimed that lobsters were serious, peaceful things which knew the secrets of the deep and, unlike dogs, didn't bark. Another mistake is describing Murger as the son of a painter when his father was in reality a tailor who doubled up as the concierge of an apartment block in Paris. Bradshaw may be thinking of the painter Jean-Baptiste Isabey, once one of Napoleon's favourite artists, and an inhabitant of the apartments Murger's father was responsible for. It's a sloppy mistake, especially considering that Bradshaw's bibliography includes at least two books which could have given him the correct facts.

Away from facts, Bradshaw is reasonably accurate about the way in which Murger's book romanticised the lives of the Bohemians, despite his sticking fairly closely to the actual details, including their deaths. Their existence was often harsh. Government grants, welfare services, and the like, were few and far between in 19th Century Paris, if they existed at all. Murger himself died at the age of thirty-eight, worn-out from his early years struggling to exist in the garrets and cafés of the Latin Quarter. Even Puccini's *La Bohème*, romanticised enough to make it palatable to the bourgeoisie, retains some idea of the way in which Murger and his friends lived. The death of Mimi isn't all that far removed from the reality of the death of Lucile Louvet, Murger's one-time mistress. She died from tuberculosis at the age of twenty-four, and was buried in a pauper's grave. The nature of the illness is evident in *La Bohème*, even if it does have Mimi passing away in a garret instead of a hospital.

As the 19th Century developed so did the variants of Bohemia. Bradshaw's next three chapters skip through the Parisian cafés frequented by the Impressionist painters, cross the Channel to have a quick look at the early days of the Café Royal in London, and then dart back to France to find out what Verlaine and Rimbaud got up to. It's all fairly well-worn ground, and Bradshaw doesn't come up with anything startlingly new, either in the way of anecdotes or analysis. The main problem is his desire to pack in as many names as possible, so that they seem to tumble over each other in the breathless style that Bradshaw's prose has. If you have dozens of references to people and places pushed into short sentences, which in turn are grouped into short paragraphs, which are then assembled into short chapters, the final effect is of an enthusiastic, but never discerning writer attempting to convince his readers that he knows his subject, but doesn't want to be thought of as taking it or himself too seriously. Maybe it's Bradshaw's journalistic background that's the problem (so many contemporary journalists seem to feel it necessary to trivialise everything), but his approach can be irritating. There's an uneasiness about it, and it rather reminds me of Englishmen in pubs and their determination never to be serious for more than a couple of minutes at a time if the subject of the arts crops up. We end up with desultory conversations, "matter of factness," manufactured jokes or anecdotes, and a flippancy which intrudes each time anyone looks dangerously near digging below surface level.

There's more uneasiness, as the book progresses. "There was never any real Bohemia in the coffee-houses of Vienna," Bradshaw says, and then fills sixteen pages with names and anecdotes. One gets the feeling that the opportunity of shoving in references to Wittgenstein, Freud, Kraus, and even Hitler (who led a bohemian existence in Vienna for a brief period) was too good to miss. In actual fact, the Vienna of those days was a lively and interesting place, and he neatly quotes Martin Esslin on this: "If the coffee-houses in the city centre were swarming with philosophers and poets, political theorists and social visionaries, the innumerable beer-halls and wine-taverns of the outer suburbs were filled with half-educated imitations of these brilliant figures, who brooded over their beer, producing the wildest pseudo-philosophies." In some ways those "half-educated" types can be seen as in a direct line from some of the inhabitants of the original Grub Street and Murger's Bohemia. But Bradshaw never develops, or even opens themes such as that, though one can see the consequences of the pseudo-philosophies in events like the various uprisings after the 1914-18 War. In Munich, for example, a short-lived revolutionary government, which included a number of poets, would-be philosophers, and general Bohemians, was nicknamed "The Coffee-house anarchists." Bohemianism has never been limited purely to the arts, and there have always been exchanges of ideas between the artists and the political activists of both the Left and the Right.

The final days of the Café Royal are fairly boring unless you want to read all the well-worn stories about Lawrence being sick on the table-cloth, Aleister Crowley not paying his bill, and the Sitwells bitching with everyone. Talented people frequented the place, it's true, along with the oddballs like Crowley, but the English bourgeois mentality dominated too much for it to ever be a real Bohemian hang-out. Bradshaw is more at home with the Parisian Bohemia of Utrillo and Modigliani, and his chapter on that includes one of the best anecdotes he uses in his book. It concerns an incident in the Lapin Agile, a cafe frequented by Apollinaire, Picasso, Max Jacob, and others:

"Sometimes strangers would wander into the café. One night a man dressed like a sailor in a reefer jacket and red scarf sat listening to a conversation about Gauguin and foreign travel.

'In Tahiti,' he interrupted, 'it rains all the time and the women are dressed in oilcloth.'

Max Jacob decided to test his credulity. 'There is an alarm clock on top of every mountain in Switzerland,' he said.

'It is quite possible,' replied the stranger politely.

'And do you realise how far they carry cleanliness in Holland?' asked the novelist Pierre MacOrlan. 'I assure you that in some places it's far from rare to meet smokers walking out of saloons with their pipes so they can empty them beyond the city limits.'

'Why not?'

The wilder the stranger's own stories became, the more they were inclined to believe them. It was only later they found out he was a farmer who had never left France. 'His why not,' wrote Francis Carco, 'took our breath away by its phlegmatic indifference and superior tone. But after all, why not? The man was right. Since the flower girls of Gauguin's Tahiti were only a myth, anything was possible! One could let the imagination run wild...' "

It's a nice anecdote, though not one likely to have much appeal to Englishmen who pride themselves on their "matter of factness."

It will probably have been noticed that Bradshaw has largely limited his survey to France and England, apart from his brief trip to Vienna, and it strikes me as odd that he's almost completely ignored American Bohemianism. There is a long tradition of it, and it is well documented. Such books as Albert Parry's *Garrets and Pretenders* and Emily Hahn's *Romantic Rebels* offer wide-ranging accounts of the various characters who've enlivened American Bohemias, and there are numerous books dealing with individuals, specific places, Bohemian magazines, and related matters. New York, San Francisco, Chicago, and New Orleans have all had noted periods when Bohemianism flourished, and although Bradshaw might argue that his café society brief precluded a coverage of these places there is evidence to show that cafés, as well as bars, were an essential part of American Bohemias. The fact that American cities were cosmopolitan places, because of the large numbers of immigrants, would alone have ensured that European customs and habits were in evidence.

There is a chapter on the expatriate Bohemia (largely American, though not exclusively so) of Paris in the Twenties, but it suffers from holding to the myth (beloved of journalists) that most of the people around Montparnasse at that time were fakes, failures, or layabouts. As in any Bohemia there were, no doubt, examples of all three types, but one need only look at such magazines as *This Quarter, Transatlantic Review*, and *transition* to realise that a lot of the expatriates were working hard as editors or writers. The list of achievements by writers who spent time in Paris is impressive, as a glance at the bibliographies in such books as George Wickes's *Americans in Paris: 1903-1959* and Hugh Ford's *Published in Paris: American and British Writers, Printers, and Publishers in Paris, 1920-1959* will easily demonstrate. Harry Crosby, for example, may have been a rich playboy, but he also wrote quite a lot (not all of it good, but some of it interesting), and published many other writers in the Black Sun Press series. He rates a single, disparaging reference in *Café Society.* Bradshaw's uneasiness keeps surfacing all the time. He appears to be interested in the people he mentions, and yet seems to have the need to run them down and belittle their talents. It strikes me that it's basically the same kind of attitude I mentioned earlier (the fear of being thought of as serious), and in this case comes through almost as a re-assurance to the average reader that, although he may have written a book about writers and artists, Bradshaw is really at heart a good, matter-of-fact Englishman and shares the bourgeois attitude that Bohemians are nothing but a bunch of skivers and scroungers.

There are some more shaky facts, too, in this chapter. Bradshaw refers to John Reed's *Seven Days That Shook The World* as the classic account of the Russian Revolution. I don't want to be pedantic, but Reed actually reckoned it had taken the Bolsheviks ten days to shake everyone else. Then Bradshaw says that Robert McAlmon was editor of *This Quarter* and, as such, first publisher of Hemingway. McAlmon never edited *This Quarter* (he was an occasional contributor to it, but the editors were Ernest Walsh, Ethel Moorhead and, later, Edward Titus) and in any case Hemingway had published in other little magazines (*The Double Dealer, Poetry Chicago, The Little Review*, etc.) before he appeared in *This Quarter* in 1925. It is a fact that McAlmon's Contact Press published Hemingway's first book, *Three Stories and Ten Poems*.

The treatment of McAlmon in *Café Society* is typical of Bradshaw's misrepresentation of the activities of the personalities he discusses. McAlmon was not the most disciplined of writers or publishers, just as he was not the most disciplined of men. He drank heavily and frequented the cafes far more than was good for him as either man or artist. But he ran Contact Editions (which published William Carlos Williams, Hemingway, Mary Butts, Gertrude Stein, and others), and wrote a large amount of prose and poetry himself, some of which is still worth reading. Bradshaw's account makes it appear as if McAlmon was little more than an irresponsible drifter rather than a writer and publisher whose activities were admired by Ezra Pound, Kay Boyle, and others whose opinions count for something.

It's interesting, I think, that Bradshaw quotes Hemingway's journalistic pieces for the *Toronto Star Weekly* almost in admiration for his wisdom in noting how the Bohemians wasted their days. But what was Hemingway doing other than pandering to the prejudices of the paper's readers, as well as possibly providing them with a subconscious re-assurance that their own lives were the really worthy ones? It was the same kind of cheapjack performance that has often typified journalists' observations of Bohemia, and one is tempted to ask whether envy isn't at the root of it. Most journalists never achieve anything as worthwhile and lasting as the works of art produced by many people who could be described as Bohemians. I recall an article which appeared in *The People* in 1960 in which Jack Kerouac, Gregory Corso, and Allen Ginsberg were attacked, and yet I doubt that the person who wrote it ever produced a book comparable to their various novels and collections of poems. In

Hemingway's case, he did prove himself as a writer, but the fact that he once worked as a journalist isn't convincing proof that every hack has the seeds of greatness in him. On the other hand the failures of Bohemia have often turned out something of value before they've succumbed to idleness, drink or poverty.

If Bradshaw is weak on American Bohemias, he's totally silent on the British one that existed in the Thirties and Forties, and which is perhaps best dealt with in Julian Maclaren-Ross's *Memoirs of the Forties*, and in some of the first-rate short stories in *Nine Men of Soho*. There are other books, too, such as Nina Hamnett's *Is She A Lady?* and Derek Stanford's recent *Inside the Forties*, not to mention Ruthven Todd's lively memoir in the catalogue for the exhibition held at the Parkin Gallery in 1973 under the title "Fitzrovia and the road to the York Minster." That reference will, of course, indicate that it was a Bohemia fairly well centred on pubs, but there were cafés and restaurants which were frequented by the talented people mentioned in all the items I've listed. Tambimuttu, Dylan Thomas, Nicholas Moore, Alex Comfort, Charles Wrey Gardiner, and W.S. Graham are just a few of the names that spring to mind, along with their outlets in print such as P.L. Editions, Poetry London, and Grey Walls Press, One of the best accounts of the war-time period is Robert Hewison's *Under Siege: Literary Life in London, 1939-45*, a splendidly-documented coverage of people and events. As Hewison remarks at one point, "Released from the inhibitions of peacetime, men and women felt the urgency of living for the day, and the pleasures of the day, when time to enjoy them was short." Which is, surely, an ideal recipe for Bohemianism? A Bohemianism that took people in and out of the services, but which was, because of that fact, possibly livelier and more open than anything that had previously existed in this country since the 18th Century. Probably the last fling of what might be called conspicuous Bohemianism was the Beat movement of the Fifties and early Sixties, though Bradshaw effectively ignores it. But insofar as it established centres of activity (North Beach in San Francisco, Venice West in Los Angeles, and a revitilisation of parts of Greenwich Village) it was well in the Bohemian tradition. And, for a time, there did exist a kind of café society. The July 1959 issue of *Playboy* ran a feature on "The Coffee Houses of America," in which it said that "An old European custom with a new American accent has taken hold on both Coasts." Fred McDarrah's photographs in *The Beat Scene* (complemented by his record of the New York art scene in *The Artist's World*) captured some of the activity for posterity, and Bill Manville's *Saloon Society* followed Murger in using the ups and downs of Bohemian life as the basis for its stories. Rather than deal with the Beat scene, however, Bradshaw chooses to offer us a sketchy chapter which primarily tries to show Greenwich Village Bohemia as the province of folk-singers like Bob Dylan, Joni Mitchell, and Phil Ochs. They were around, but were only a part of the total activity. John Gruen's books, *The New Bohemia* and *The Party's Over Now* give a far broader picture of the scene, ranging from poets like Ginsberg and Frank O'Hara, to painters such as Franz Kline and Jackson Pollock, experimental theatre activists Julian Beck and Judith Malina, and a whole host of other writers, painters, actors, musicians, and hangers-on. No mention either in Bradshaw of satirists such as Mort Sahl or Lord Buckley. Or of the "Happenings" which were often staged in cafés. Al Hansen's "Incomplete Requiem for W.C. Fields" was first staged at the E-pit'o-me Coffee House, which was operated by three neo-plastic painters, Don McAree, Larry Poons, and Howard Smythe. Other coffee-houses, such as Riker's or The Chuck Wagon (which, depending on your taste, may or may not be as romantically named as Parisian cafés) were well-known hang-outs for writers and artists. And what about the poetry readings held in places like Les Deux Magots, The Tenth Street Coffee-house, and The Café Le Metro?

In San Francisco, such cafés as the Coffee Gallery and The Co-Existence Bagel Shop were popular meeting places for the local Bohemians. One of them was, in fact, the scene of an incident which deserves to go down in Bohemian history generally, because it was, in its way, just as romantic as most of the events (such as Malcolm Cowley's arrest after assaulting the owner of the Rotonde in the Twenties) that Bradshaw chronicles. The Negro poet Bob Kaufman got involved in an argument with a policeman, and was eventually arrested. During the course of the argument the guardian of law and order stamped on Kaufman's foot, and it was later found that the nail of his big toe had to be removed and an abscess beneath it drained. Kaufman went one better than Cowley, too, and while he was in custody wrote a sequence of "Jail Poems" which soon appeared in the magazine *Beatitude*. This is the kind of thing that the legends of Bohemia are properly drawn from, and not the meanderings of a handful of singers.

British Bohemia of the Fifties and Sixties wasn't as varied and lively as its American counterpart, but it did exist. To name just a couple of examples, there was a place called the House of Sam Widges where the London Beats hung out in the early Sixties, and the Liverpool poetry renaissance was partly built on activities in coffee houses and similar places. One of Roger McGough's early poems is, in fact, called "Café Portraits." All this is ignored by Bradshaw, perhaps because it's now unfashionable for London-based journalists to consider what goes on (and went on) in the provinces. But it's more than probable that had *Café Society* appeared ten years ago it would have automatically included a chapter on the British "underground" of those days. As Edward Lucie-Smith remarked in the Sixties, "If one wants to find a modern equivalent of Murger's *Vie de Bohème*, one has to look for it in Liverpool." And it's worth considering the suggestion that many of the poets, artists, musicians, and what have you, who were active then were, in more ways than one, an intellectual proletariat rather similar to the one Murger knew. Like his Bohemians they were alienated from the working and lower-middle classes because of their education and interests, but at the same time could not fit into the established middle-class set-up which controlled the media, the academies, etc. So, for a time at least, they formed a subculture, although some of them were eventually absorbed into the establishment culture, again like Murger and many of his friends.

Throughout *Café Society*, including the flimsy Epilogue, there's a constant tone of "Things ain't what they used to be," a parading of comments by writers and others that Bohemia is dead or dying, or now only inhabited by failures and phoneys. But almost everyone looks back on his own experiences as somehow being better than those of younger generations. The pub we frequented ten years ago is never as good as it was - the jukebox is louder, the beer isn't as good, the place is full of kids. What are complaints by middle-aged writers, looking back on their Bohemias, but variations on the same theme? True, it's possible today to argue that increasing institutionalisation has maybe taken away the need or the impulse to establish Bohemian communities. Young writers go to colleges or universities, and then often become teachers, arts administrators, and the like. Older ones drift into the academies or the media. Definable Bohemian areas (where writers and artists lived and mixed together) have broken down under this kind of pressure. And what might be called the formalised freedom of academic Bohemia is no real substitute. Economic factors, too, have had their effect. Property development, vast rehousing schemes which have pushed people into the suburbs, inflation, almost permanent high unemployment, are just a few of the things which have made cheap living difficult. It seems to me that, wherever I go, I meet people who reflect, often wistfully, on the days when the older parts of cities (and these parts were usually central) had lots of cheap flats, and when there were always a reasonable number of part-time or temporary jobs that allowed one to earn enough to get by on, and yet still have time to write or paint. Are they just being nostalgic, or are things actually worse than they were fifteen or twenty years ago? After all, some kinds of Bohemian communities do exist today, even if they do tend to be small and scattered. Maybe it's that we always assume that Bohemia will have a literary base but we've failed to keep up with changing attitudes towards books, magazines, and similar outlets. If so, then we'll inevitably look on current Bohemias as lacking. However, I don't want to fall into Bradshaw's trap of assuming that Bohemia is dead - his wilful ignorance about the Fifties and Sixties shows that he may have a subconscious wish to see it buried - so let me close this review of his untidy book by suggesting that it's perhaps never a fixed place anyway, and is where you find it. Who knows, a new Bohemia may be just around the corner. And maybe Hippolyte Havel, old anarchist and Greenwich Village Bohemian (as well as the model for Hugo Kalmar in Eugene O'Neill's play *The Iceman Cometh*) had it right when, asked by a middle-class lady to define the boundaries of his Bohemia, he replied, "It has no boundaries. It's a state of mind."

Café Society: Bohemian Life from Swift to Bob Dylan by Steve Bradshaw. Weidenfeld & Nicolson.£6.95.

GILBERT SORRENTINO

Gilbert Sorrentino was probably best known as a novelist who wrote books that can never have been said to appeal to a mass audience. They were not easy to read and Sorrentino expected his readers to be as familiar with a wide range of subjects as he was. But it's often forgotten that he had an important role in the development of new writing in America in the late 1950s and early 1960s. Sorrentino was born in Brooklyn in 1929 and was educated in local schools. He attended Brooklyn College for a year before entering military service. When he was discharged he began to write a novel and poetry. He returned to Brooklyn College in 1955, "for want of something better to do," but never graduated. However, he met some other students who were also keen to establish themselves as writers, among them Sam Abrams and Hubert Selby. They decided to publish a mimeographed magazine which would feature their own work and that of other writers they could contact. The magazine was to be called *Neon.* The first issue featured work by Sorrentino, Abrams, John Richardson, and a couple of Australian poets who had been recommended by Ezra Pound, who had responded to a letter that Sorrentino had written to him. It's perhaps an indication of the small audience for new writing that only 250 copies of *Neon* were produced. Some were placed in three specialist bookshops in New York, a few went to City Lights in San Francisco, a number sold by mail, and the rest given to contributors and friends.

But things were happening in America, and Sorrentino soon discovered a little world of new writers, magazines, and small presses that were coming to life in the mid 1950s. He read *Origin, Black Mountain Review, Chicago Review*, and similar magazines, and came across poems by Ginsberg, Corso, McClure in other publications. When the second issue of *Neon* appeared it included Hubert Selby's first published story, *Home For Christmas*, and poems by Paul Goodman. Years later, Sorrentino recalled that Selby paid for this issue and that it sold out, largely because of the poem that William Carlos Williams contributed to it.

"Everything seemed to be happening at once," Sorrentino said in retrospect. The circulation of *Neon* increased and poems began to pour in, many of them from Southern California. There were problems getting the magazine printed (only the first issue had been mimeographed) and Sorrentino wasn't too happy when the third issue came out, partly because it seemed to him "unfocused" in terms of the writers he'd used. He realised that it was better to select work from the New York area, or at least from poets he was put in touch with as one writer recommended another and Sorrentino, reading a variety of magazines, picked up on who he thought was producing the most interesting new poems and prose. It was during this period that he got to know the work of Paul Blackburn, Robert Creeley, Fielding Dawson, Joel Oppenheimer, and Max Finstein, and began to use their poems and stories in *Neon*.

The *Neon* network spread further when Sorrentino contacted Louis Zukofsky who then advised him to get in touch with Lorine Niedecker, Cid Corman, and Robert Duncan. Many of these people were published in the fourth issue of *Neon* in 1959. The front cover had drawings by Fielding Dawson who had also done the cover for the fourth issue of *Yugen*, a magazine edited by Leroi Jones. As both came out around the same time they were displayed side by side in some bookshops in New York. Anyone who has edited a little magazine can tell you about the difficulties experienced with raising money (sales never match the production costs), finding reliable printers, and arranging for copies to be distributed. Sorrentino struggled constantly with such problems. The third and fourth issues of *Neon* had been printed on the West Coast, but that meant that it was impossible to keep a close check on what was happening and that the cost of having the printed copies shipped to New York cancelled out any savings made on the printing. Because of the delays between each issue of *Neon,* Sorrentino arranged for a small, cheaply produced publication, *Supplement To Now*, with work by Selby, Creeley, Charles Olson, and Jonathan Williams, to be sent free to subscribers. He had plans for a fifth issue of *Neon*, with poems by Michael McClure and Ron Loewinsohn, but the usual problems with money and printers stopped him going ahead with it. Eventually, in 1960, *Neon Obit* (clearly the final issue) saw light of day thanks to a friend of Sorrentino helping out with the finances. Leroi Jones, Fielding Dawson, and Charles Olson were in its pages, and the issue sold out almost immediately, possibly because interest was picking up in the new writing. But it's useful to note that only 300 copies were printed. The likely audience for a little magazine was still small.

Sorrentino's involvement with little magazines didn't end when *Neon* closed down in 1960. The first issue of *Kulchur* had appeared in the same year and Sorrentino met its editor, Marc Schliefer, and began to write for the magazine. By the time the fourth issue was published in 1961 he was the guest editor and the range of writers he used (they included Paul Goodman, Walter Lowenfels, who had been with Henry Miller in Paris in the 1930s, Edward Dorn, and Hubert Selby writing under the name of Harry Black) pointed to his wide range of interests. They were, perhaps, too wide to suit the publisher of *Kulchur*, Lita Hornick, and Sorrentino eventually moved away from editorial duties on the magazine. I've written a short history of *Kulchur* in an earlier issue of *Beat Scene* (number 43, Summer, 2003) so won't say much here apart from to refer to the lively essays and reviews that Sorrentino wrote for it.

To insert a personal note, I recall writing to Sorrentino early in 1964 after I'd read his *Remembrances Of Bop In New York, 1945-1950*, in *Kulchur*. It was a wonderfully evocative memoir of what it was like to have grown up in the period concerned and to have been a young fan of the new music, which was, according to Sorrentino, his "entrance into the general world of culture." I'd had a similar experience when I first encountered modern jazz in England around 1950, and told Sorrentino how much his article had interested me. I got a friendly reply in which he told me about hearing Red Rodney with Gene Krupa's band in 1945. And he also commented on the sad situation in New York in the early 1960s, with many jazz musicians out of work and doing other jobs: "Allen Eager runs a garage here in New York, George Wallington works in his father's air-conditioning store, I saw J.R. Monterose playing for 5 bucks and coffee in a little trap on Second Avenue." I'd also mentioned reading some of Sorrentino's poems in magazines, and he sent me a copy of *The Darkness Surrounds Us*, his first collection, and said that another book, *Black And White*, was due from Totem/Corinth Press later in 1964.

I've focused on Sorrentino's participation in the early days of the *New American Writing* of the 1950s and early 1960s (he worked as an editor for Grove Press at one time) because that seems to me to tie in with much of what *Beat Scene* covers. But he did, of course, go on to make a name for himself as a novelist. His first novel, *The Sky Changes*, was published in 1966 and was a relatively straightforward account of the break-up of a marriage during a trip across America. I say "relatively straightforward" because Sorrentino increasingly experimented with form, and I have to admit to a limited taste for his later work. *Steelwork* (1970) was a lively, if episodic look at life in Brooklyn in the 1930s and 1940s and was readable enough, but I struggled with *Splendide Hotel* (1973) and what some people say is his masterpiece, *Mulligan Stew* (1979), left me floundering. I'm not offering any sort of critical commentary on these books, simply saying that I found them difficult to deal with, and I'm well aware that others rate them highly. But they were never likely to make Sorrentino into a best seller, and in later life he reluctantly moved to California and held down a teaching post at Stanford University. He died on the 18th May, 2006.

Someone once referred to Gilbert Sorrentino as a "maverick," and it was an apt description. Although he was closely involved with the new writing of the 1950s and 1960s, and knew many of its practitioners and helped promote a wide range of writers, he was never identified with any particular group. He wasn't a Beat, he didn't go to Black Mountain College, he was not of the New York school. He was, as his books (novels, poetry, essays) made it clear, very much his own man.

IN PRAISE OF BOOKSELLERS

Not too long ago a friend told me about an evening he spent in a pub with some young poets. One of them had recently had a collection published and it had been reviewed in the *TLS*. The poet spent the whole time wanting to discuss in detail what the review had said and why, and she clearly had little interest in any conversation that might revolve around books generally or anything else other than her own work. My own experience over the years is that this is sadly typical. These days I don't mix much with poets and I don't care to, and some of the best conversations about books and writers that I've had have been with publishers and printers and booksellers. And it occurs to me that these people have often done far more for literature than any number of minor poets with yet more mediocre books that simply add to the catalogue of mostly-unread publications.

I was put in mind of this when I read an obituary of Barry Hall. I wonder how many poets will know who he was? For the record, he was behind Goliard Press, which, in the 1960s, printed and published books by Elaine Feinstein, Charles Olson, Aram Saroyan, and others. Hall wasn't only publishing books, he was helping to bring work by the people mentioned to the attention of an insular British audience. He had spent a year in San Francisco in the early-1960s and as a consequence was friendly with many of the poets and painters identified with the San Francisco Renaissance. He didn't only print for Goliard, he produced books for Bernard Stone's Turret Press and Stuart Montgomery's Fulcrum Press, including the first edition of Basil Bunting's *Briggflatts.*

Later in the 1960s, Goliard operated under the Jonathan Cape umbrella as Cape Goliard, with Hall including Neruda, Ginsberg, Paul Blackburn, and Gael Turnbull in his list. I recall with pleasure a beautiful edition of Ginsberg's *T.V.Baby Poems*, and well-produced editions of Turnbull's *Scantlings* and John Wieners' *Nerves*. I don't suppose the young poet obsessed with her review in the *TLS* will have heard of most of these writers, but they were and remain well worth reading. Hall obviously loved their work and getting it into print wasn't simply a job for him. Like many of his kind, when he thought that he'd done what he'd set out to do he walked out, went to America again, and then to Kenya, where he died in October, 1995.

I mentioned that Hall produced books for Bernard Stone, and I am reminded of the many times I've browsed in the various bookshops he had over the years. I say "had" because he sadly closed down his operations, ill-health and the massive costs of running a specialist shop in Central London finally combining to defeat him. He had a shop in Kensington Church Walk in the early-1970s, moved to Floral Street in Covent Garden, then to Lamb's Conduit Street, and finally to Great Queen Street. I think I have the sequence right. But wherever he was the shop was always open house to writers, publishers, little magazine editors, and others, and Bernard was never slow to open a bottle of wine or pour out a glass of vodka, no matter what the hour. He was always also good for a conversation about books. He had readings in his shops and they were sometimes near-riotous affairs, with drunken poets sliding down piles of books and Bernard watching it all with an amused eye. His shop was stocked with small press publications, little magazines, and off-beat editions, not to mention some rare old books. He published poets, too, in his Turret series, and I wonder if he ever got the thanks he deserved? Too many poets often take the view that editors and publishers are there for their benefit. A friend who edited a magazine once asked a poet he'd published if he'd approach a bookshop in his area to see if they'd stock the magazine. The poet was indignant and refused on the grounds that he was a creator and it certainly wasn't his job to do the dirty business of selling the magazine.

Bernard Stone wasn't the only one who tried to make bookselling more than a mere commercial occupation, and Barry Miles for a time ran Better Books in Charing Cross Road as an outpost of the small press and little magazine movement of the 1960s until the owners (Zwemmer's) got tired of the low profits and the high level of oddball characters hanging around the place. He then opened up Indica Books in Southampton Row and that was an equally exciting location to pick up the latest books and magazines from American and British presses, as well as material linked to the historical continuity of modernism. It's curious how so many of today's young poets have little or no real awareness of this continuity and instead work mostly within a British (sometimes even just English) framework. Indica became famous as the "underground" scene of the 1960s developed and the newspaper-format *International Times* moved the spotlight away from literary concerns. The pop hordes moved in with, to my mind, disastrous results, though Indica continued to be a shop worth visiting.

Compendium Books opened up in the late-1960s, with the indefatigable Nick Kimberley ensuring that its stock of poetry and avant-garde writing was always up-to-date. There simply wasn't anywhere else carrying such a range of material for those who didn't think that the mainline bookshops had it all. Kimberley opened up his own shop, Duck Soup, in a little alley off Red Lion Square and tried to maintain it as somewhere to obtain the unusual. I'm just pulling out memories, of course, when naming these shops, and there were others. And I'm also concentrating on places I personally visited from around 1960 onwards. Someone ought to write a book about the famous bookshops which have, over the years, acted as centres for literary activities. A few, such as Sylvia Beach's Shakespeare and Company in Paris and Lawrence Ferlinghetti's City Lights in San Francisco, have become well-known through being identified with specific groups. Shakespeare and Company was home to the 1920s expatriates like Hemingway and Robert McAlmon and will always be associated with the original publication of Joyce's *Ulysses*. Ferlinghetti's shop, which opened in the 1950s, attracted the San Francisco writers, including the Beats, and also became the centre for the City Lights publications, which included Ginsberg's *Howl.* But what about David Archer's shop in Parton Street, London, which, in the 1930s, was where the young British modernists gathered? George Barker, David Gascoyne, Charles Madge, and Dylan Thomas, met there, and the shop acted as a base for Roger Roughton's surrealist-influenced magazine, *Contemporary Poetry and Prose*. Archer is a virtually-forgotten figure now, mentioned only in memoirs of the 1930s and the Soho bohemia of the 1940s, but he did the essential work of running a bookshop when it was needed and helping to get new writers into print.

I could go on listing. What about George Whitman's rambling Shakespeare and Company (same name but not the same location as Sylvia Beach's shop)? But I think of so many which, selling new books, or second-hand books, or a mixture, have provided what I think of as one of the essentials of a civilised life. I was recently introduced to someone working in Waterstone's and his name stirred a faint memory of the Trent Bookshop in Nottingham, shortlived, I seem to recall, but somewhere to find poetry and experimental literature, and at some point in the 1960s, they ran a weekend festival at which Roy Fisher, Jon Silkin, G.S. Fraser, Jonathan Williams, and many more, appeared. The man who effected this introduction was Geoffrey Clifton, who had a fine theatre and cinema bookshop in Manchester which was the haunt of writers and actors and academics. You could talk to him about books and what was in them. His shop closed when the local council decided to increase the rent by 100%, this at a time when they were supposedly promoting the city as home for a Year of Drama and around the corner from the threatened bookshop were some well-furnished offices staffed by smooth bureaucrats engaged in the process. It seemed typical of the times to close down an excellent specialist bookshop while pumping more money into an ever-expanding bureaucracy.

Bill Butler had a bookshop in Brighton many years ago and got himself prosecuted by the local police, who took exception to some of the modern literature he stocked though nearby shops openly displayed racks of girlie-magazines. Another bookseller, Larry Wallrich, who then had a first-rate second-hand shop near the British Museum, published a large collection of poems and prose to raise funds for Butler's defence and got contributions from Michael Hamburger, Thom Gunn, Ginsberg, Ferlinghetti, and a number of other contemporary writers. Despite the support the case broke Butler's back as a bookseller and he closed down, which is presumably what the authorities wanted. It's easier to turn a blind eye to pornography than it is to tolerate the unusual. As for Larry Wallrich, who had been at the Phoenix Bookshop in New York when it was a centre for poets, he later moved to Toronto and carried on his trade there. Larry was a great friend of Jim Lowell, who opened the Asphodel Bookshop in Cleveland in the 1960s and pushed not only the local poets but also the work of British and American moderns generally. In 1988, the 25th anniversary of Lowell's start in the bookselling trade, a number of American writers, including Robert Creeley, got together to publish a tribute to him, something too few poets do for those who promote their work. But then as a poet once said to me, and without a trace of irony in his voice, "when I'm famous you'll be able to say that you helped me get started." I prefer the Jim Lowells of this world. He still continues in business, though with a mail-order catalogue and, if you can get to his house in rural Ohio, a one-time garage packed with shelves of great books from past and present.

The names continue to roll. Harold Briggs, who ran a bookshop in New York called Books 'n' Things, and had been around since the 1920s, supporting himself in the depths of the Depression by hunting down second-hand books in obscure places, and who was an expert on little magazines, avant-garde presses, and literary criticism. He had himself published poems in magazines and they showed how he had an awareness of what went on in the world and not just in his own head. As his friend Harry Roskolenko, who also appeared in avant-garde and left-wing publications, said much later: "Harold and I hated every aspect of fascism, in and out of books. Today, using a more contemporary form of rhetoric-in-action, there are poets who salute it, unconsciously, in their mindlessness and malice." When Briggs died, around 1970, an editor named Marvin Malone produced an issue of *The Wormwood Review* mostly about him, knowing that people like Briggs had made a contribution to literature, not only as poets but as booksellers or whatever. Malone is the kind of editor who does know these things. Another issue of his magazine was devoted to Jon Edgar Webb, a writer, editor, and publisher, who, in the 1960s, brought out *The Outsider* from New Orleans, labouring with a hand press and producing three issues before he and his equally-dedicated wife, Louise 'Gypsy Lou' Webb had to leave town and move to Arizona, where they published a beautifully-designed double-issue which was largely concerned with the work of Kenneth Patchen. The Webbs also published a book by Charles Bukowski at a time when other publishers didn't want to know about him. They were old-style bohemians with a love of traditional jazz and modernist verse and suffered ill-health, poverty, and other mishaps, while publishing *The Outsider*. A note in the final issue tells how they pawned everything, apart from the printing press, a table, two chairs, and a bed, to raise money for the magazine. It's a world away from poetry competitions and those poets who calculate everything in terms of how they'll benefit from it.

But I'm moving into a world of little magazine editors and that requires a separate article. In this one I wanted to mention Barry Hall and then talk about a few bookshops, though there have been other printer/publishers whose activities need to be documented. The bookshops, and the people who ran them, are rarely, if ever, remembered, and over the years they've provided me with more pleasure and interest than most other activities. In a world where they are increasingly under threat from indifference, commercial pressures, and changing fashions in taste, they ought to be treasured. Browsing around the shelves, finding something of value (and I don't mean that in a financial sense), and perhaps having a conversation with the bookseller, strikes me as much more satisfying than listening to the self-centred complaints of a poet whose work will probably be forgotten in five years time.

JOHN CRAXTON

There is in *Penguin New Writing* 35 (1948) a small selection of photographs under the heading, *Portraits of Contemporary British Painters*. Eight artists are included: Robert Medley, John Craxton, John Minton, Robert Colquhoun, Robert MacBryde, Keith Vaughan, Lucien Freud, and Leonard Rosoman. There's no doubt that Freud is the one whose reputation prospered and whose work has been internationally acclaimed. Several of the others died relatively early and, it's probably true to say, never achieved their full potential due to a variety of personal circumstances. Minton and Vaughan committed suicide and the two Roberts declined into drink and near-destitution. Freud apart, I suspect that few people, other than those with an interest in British art of the 1940s, will know much about most of the others, though biographies have been written about Minton and Vaughan and the two Roberts. But it's almost 25 years since a major exhibition, *A Paradise Lost: The Neo-Romantic Imagination in Britain 1935-1955* (Barbican, 1987) and Malcolm Yorke's book, *The Spirit of Place: Nine Neo-Romantic artists and their times* (Constable, 1988), drew attention to their work .

John Craxton appears in Yorke's book and was prominently displayed in the Barbican show. And he survived until he was 87 and died in 2009, perhaps because, while always taking his art seriously, he tended to believe that "life is more important than art," and he spent a lot of time indulging his liking for food, wine, travel, conversation, and the like. There have been suggestions that he spent too much time on these things with the result that his work suffered.

Craxton was born in 1922 in London to well-off parents who had artistic connections (his father was a pianist, musicologist, and Royal Academy of Music professor and his mother the daughter of an art publisher). Ian Collins describes their home as "a chaotic haven" and full of "warm bohemian disorder." Craxton from an early age had an interest in art and after encouragement by the art teacher at one of the schools he attended he had work exhibited at a London gallery when he was 11. When he was 14 he went to Paris where he saw Picasso's *Guernica*. Years later he said: "There's not a line wasted or out of place. And there was no sense of brushwork; I was already aware of the false admiration of 'beautiful passages of paint.' You shouldn't be aware of the construction. The point is the emotional impact." It's interesting, though, that Craxton doesn't seem to have had any kind of response, emotional or otherwise, to the general situation in Europe at that time. As Collins puts it: "the pain, politics and propaganda of a deeply troubled continent passed him by."

One thing becomes clear from the account of Craxton's life: he was always fortunate in the sort of people he knew. His family connections put him in touch with various people in the world of the arts as when his mother persuaded Eric Newton, art critic of the *Manchester Guardian*, to look at his portfolio of drawings. Newton suggested that he apply to the Grosvenor School of Modern Art, but he was turned down because he was considered too young to look at nude models. A friend then persuaded him to go to Paris where the restriction didn't apply.

In Paris he was befriended by a Russian family whose daughter had been a visitor to his parent's home in London. Jacques Milkina was a portrait painter and he encouraged Craxton to focus on "the crucial role of drawing and the importance of getting the colour harmonies right in ensuing paintings." By the time Craxton returned to London war clouds were gathering, though again he doesn't appear to have paid too much attention to events outside his own sphere of activities. He enrolled for drawing classes at the Westminster and Central art schools, and accompanied a family friend on field trips to country churches. Drawings from this period show him to be influenced by Paul Nash and "depicting dead, split and toppled trees." And there's a pen and ink illustration of the ruins of Knowlton Church, a place Craxton described as "a set for an M.R.James ghost story."

It was in the early-1940s that Craxton met Peter Watson, who was to play a significant role in his life for some years. Watson, a wealthy patron of the arts, was "a collector of beautiful things and brilliant young men, and was the perfect connector for John." He showed him drawings by Samuel Palmer and Craxton "took these revelatory images as touchstones for his own times and nature." A comparison of Palmer's "Valley thick with corn" from 1825 with Craxton's "Poet in Landscape" from 1941, both reproduced in the book, shows how much he was influenced by the earlier artist. He had never heard of Palmer before seeing the drawings Peter Watson had but knew at once that he had encountered someone special. It's relevant to note that he was also deeply involved with William Blake's work, both poetry and painting.

Craxton was faced with conscription in 1941 but was eventually rejected for military service. His 1942 "Dreamer in Landscape," has a man closing his eyes and "blotting out a claustrophobic world of twisted and tortured trees and rampant foliage eerily lit by a sickle moon." It's not hard to accept that it represented Craxton's attempts to escape from the ugly wartime world around him. He later said that "Poet in Landscape" and "Dreamer in Landscape" were derived from Blake and Palmer and were "my means of escape and a sort of self-protection...I wanted to safeguard a world of private mystery and I was drawn to the idea of bucolic calm as a kind of refuge." Both were illustrated in *Horizon*, a significant publication at that time, and helped to focus attention on Craxton.

He may have been trying to stand aside from a London dominated by the effects of war, but being someone never averse to socialising he frequented the pubs and clubs of Soho, mixing with Colquhoun and MacBryde and becoming friendly with Lucien Freud, though they eventually fell out. But for a time they shared a studio, thanks to Peter Watson, and Craxton did say that his time with Freud had its advantages: "He made me scrutinise. I gave him confidence. We respected our diversity. And nobody bothered us - we could just get on and paint." A meeting with Graham Sutherland also had an effect, as did an encounter with John Piper. Ian Collins states: "John Craxton greatly admired the way in which Piper's modernist sensibility had been mobilised from abstraction to record an architectural heritage menaced or destroyed by war." Other factors were at work, with Craxton reflecting some aspects of surrealism so that he was thought ideal to illustrate a book of poems by Ruthven Todd, a poet associated with the "New Apocalypse" group. Craxton's "private world of mystery and allegory" was not exactly surrealistic but neither was Todd's poetry.

Craxton said of wartime London: "Everything was narrowed down to practically nothing. In Soho there was the French pub and the Swiss House - which I liked because they were talking pubs - and the Golden Lion where sailors were picked up." He noted that a few galleries were still open and that he sometimes frequented the Coffee An' which was "a rough house with porno-erotic pictures on the wall and an incredible range of customers: intellectuals, draft dodgers, people looking for a pick up." The war also had a restrictive effect on the supply of art materials available, though Craxton, again thanks to family contacts, managed to get hold of a supply of Ripolin household enamel paint which gave his paintings a brighter colour.

The artists that Craxton was mostly associating with have generally been linked to the Neo-Romantic movement. The term had originated in Paris in the 1920s but by the 1940s it was being used to describe "certain members of an otherwise disparate group of British artists tied to the appropriated tag in the 1940s by writer and surrealist artist Robin Ironside. He bagged it for an art that was personal and contrasting with the doctrinaire geometrical abstraction of the 7 & 5 Society under Ben Nicholson. In the rigours of war and its aftermath, the title came to cover a sense across the arts of escape from a world of anxiety into an insular landscape protected by history, myth and fantasy." Craxton was never convinced that Neo-Romantic made sense as a term - "You're either Romantic in spirit or you are not," he said - but he did know Keith Vaughan, John Minton, Michael Ayrton, and others, though he wasn't always necessarily impressed by them. He thought that Ayrton was too full of self-importance and described him as "the last barrage balloon in London that never got taken down."

Several of Craxton's lithographs were used in *The Poet' s Eye*, an anthology edited by Geoffrey Grigson, who also wrote a 1948 monograph, *John Craxton; Paintings and Drawings*, publication of which was financed by Peter Watson. But there was a problem in the post-war years in that Craxton's work was sometimes said to be "too bright, charming and decorative," perhaps because he was too busy enjoying life to get down to the necessary sustained effort that could result in significant creativity. Wyndham Lewis was of the opinion that he produced "a prettily tinted cocktail that is good but does not quite kick hard enough."

The ending of the war allowed Craxton to travel, first of all to the Scilly Isles where, Collins says, "John found valuable resources for a series of dark landscapes already begun in Welsh pictures. Primary yellows, blues, reds and greens against black were taken from the banded colouring of tarred fishing boats and worked into luminous Miro-like compositions." Thanks to Peter Watson he visited Paris and then went to Switzerland where a show of his work had been arranged at a gallery in Zurich. Athens followed, again thanks to

Watson's influence, and he was represented in British Council exhibitions alongside Matthew Smith, Graham Sutherland, and Ben Nicholson. He certainly appears to have been something of a Golden Boy in the way that his career was advanced through the well-connected.

It was the Mediterranean that was to become Craxton's base for most of the rest of his life. He went to the island of Poros where "he could live cheaply and freely" and gain inspiration from "the intensity of Aegean light." The design and colour in some of his paintings are reminiscent of the work of the ill-fated Christopher Wood. In due course Craxton settled on Crete where he painted pictures of Greek boys and sailors and produced landscapes which utilised "double and triple lines in pigment." They also displayed his liking for Byzantine art. I have to admit that when looking at the examples of Craxton's work from this period I have the feeling that they lean towards the decorative, no matter how pleasant they are in their form and colour. It's a feeling I also experienced when I visited the Craxton exhibition at Tate Britain earlier this year (2011).

Ian Collins narrates how a Craxton exhibition at the Whitechapel Gallery in London in 1967 "drew a chilly response from critics - many now in thrall to American abstract expressionism and the cool, satiric gloss of pop art. A journey towards playfulness, sensuality and pattern - and love in a hot climate - was noted and resented." This reaction tied in with Craxton's expulsion from Greece when the military junta came to power. He was suspected of espionage, largely because he liked to frequent sailors' bars where, it was suggested, he was fishing for naval secrets. He then travelled widely to North and East Africa, the Canary Islands, Kenya, Tunisia, Morocco, and Lanzarote. Often in financial difficulties he accepted a commission to decorate a harpsichord for the Scottish Baroque Ensemble and collaborated with a potter on a range of domestic ceramics. Collins refers to his "final fifteen years - when he was often locked in what he called 'procraxtonation' – two vast unresolved paintings, and variants on them, often blocked his easels." He did occasionally have paintings in the Royal Academy summer exhibitions, and when he died in 2009 he was "making some of his best drawings for years, with Greek birds, trees, rocks and ravines in black ink soaring above the Tippex white."

Was John Craxton a major artist? The answer has to be "no," though he was often a very good one. His early work reflected the circumstances in which he found himself, with wartime restrictions on movement and freedom of expression shaping his thinking. The later work is usually much more colourful and entertaining to look at, though it sometimes lacks depth. It seems to have lost some of the mystery - the enigmatic quality that he mentioned - when he settled on the Greek islands. Did he fritter away his talent in return for easy living?

Someone who knew him said: "He was having fun and living doing what he loved," which sounds like an ideal way to get along and something that most people would settle for. But it's not necessarily a guarantee of achieving anything truly remarkable in the arts. Real achievement may depend on a willingness to give up other things in order to concentrate on essentials. Craxton's art perhaps lost the cutting edge of his early promise when he decided that Greece and hedonism were his priorities. Or it could be that he'd realised that he was never likely to fulfil that promise and so settled for a highly competent but stylised art that would appeal to people with romantic or nostalgic notions about the Mediterranean.

Ian Collins has written a book that looks fondly on John Craxton's output as an artist. It is beautifully illustrated and well-documented. And if it may not convince anyone that he was a painter of the first rank it should draw attention to him as someone who was highly-skilled and often produced work that, if not always memorable, was usually pleasurable to look at.

JOHN CRAXTON by Ian Collins, Lund Humphries. 184 pages. £35.
ISBN 978-1-84822-0690-0

BLUES

In February, 1929, a precocious young poet by the name of Charles Henri Ford launched *Blues:A Magazine of New Rhythms* from a small town in Mississippi. Despite his distance from the main centres of literary activity, Ford was aware of the latest developments in writing and, partly because of this awareness but also thanks to his friendship with Kathleen Tankersley Young, he managed to get his magazine off the ground in a way that firmly demonstrated his commitment to the experimental. Young was a slightly older poet, already published in little magazines, and she was in touch with Parker Tyler, who was active in Greenwich Village circles and was destined to play a part in later issues of *Blues*.

The first issue had only twenty-eight pages, but Ford and Young got contributions from a variety of modernist poets, including Eli Siegel, whose *Hot Afternoons Have Been in Montana* had aroused controversy (and been much lampooned) when it won a major poetry prize in 1925. His poem in *Blues* was less controversial, being a fairly routine free-verse piece, but it suited the tone of the magazine. Other contributors included Louis Zukofsky, Norman Macleod, Herman Spector, and Joseph Vogel, all of them linked to the literary Left. It's interesting that they applied modernist techniques to their work, something which, a few years later, was often frowned on by communist cultural commissars when "socialist realism" came to the fore. There was also a short poem by Robert Clairmont one of those unusual characters who, if no longer remembered for his poetry, has a place in histories of American bohemianism. He'd taught a rich businessman to swim, and years later was astounded to hear that he'd been left half a million dollars in the man's will. Clairmont increased this amount by investments during the boom years of the 1920s, and was known as The Millionaire Poet. He also had a reputation around Greenwich Village for his generosity and his wild parties, but lost all his money when the Stock Market crashed in 1929.

Some of the same names appeared in the second issue of *Blues*, though Ford also persuaded Ezra Pound and William Carlos Williams to send some prose. Pound's page was a mini-manifesto, with lines like "Government for utility only," but Williams, ever a friend to little magazines, wrote a piece stating his belief in the principles of modernism: "At least inversions of the sentence seem finished. At least 'poetic' diction should not be tolerated. We have at least learned to speak plainly in verse. At least one can say clearly what he means without necklaces of adjectives to half us with their 'nuances.' Lofty thoughts certainly ought to be finished now as material for a poem." Whether all the poems in *Blues* could be said to "speak plainly in verse" is another matter, but that wasn't the point. Ford placed one of his own poems in this issue, and it's an interesting example of a long-lined, semi-lyrical experiment, and perhaps points to his later involvements with surrealism.

Blues was coming out on a monthly basis, with between twenty-five and thirty pages per issue. And it was slowly attracting new contributors. Kenneth Rexroth, who was to go on to be the grand old man of American non-establishment writing until his death in 1982, made his first appearance in print in the third number, and the way in which little magazines and their editors inter-connected was highlighted by the publication of work by Alfred Kreymborg, editor of *The American Caravan*, a book-size annual of new writing, and Eugene Jolas famous for starting *transition*, one of the great expatriate magazines in Paris. Ford, of course, had poems in *The American Caravan* and *transition,* though I don't think this necessarily suggests that he and Kreymborg and Jolas were simply doing each other favours. More likely the small world of little magazines and avant-garde writing inevitably meant that people submitted material to the same outlets. A glance at the notes on other contributors to *Blues* finds the same magazines mentioned all the time - *The American Caravan, New Masses*, *transition, The Dial,* etc.

Little magazines sometimes take a few issues to get into their stride, and the fifth began to show a wider range of contributors and styles. James T. Farrell, who would soon establish himself as a major American novelist with his *Studs Lonigan* trilogy, provided a short story well in the manner of his hard-boiled accounts of broken lives. There were contributions, too, from a couple of writers who later got caught up in politics. John Herrmann had spent time in Paris (his novel *What Happens* had been published there by Robert McAlmon's Contact Editions), and was active as a writer and member of the American Communist Party. His novelette, *Big Short Trip*, a subtle account of the effects of the Depression on middle-America, won a Scribner's prize, and he published another novel, *Summer Is Ended*, which was praised. Herrmann was connected to the Ware group in Washington, and it was later alleged that its members had passed official documents to Communist Party contacts. Alger Hiss, whose case attracted much attention in the 1940s and 1950s, was said to have links to the Ware group. Herrmann doesn't seem to have published much after the 1930s, and in the post-war period he moved to Mexico to avoid being questioned by the FBI about his 1930s activities. Alongside him in *Blues* was Harry Roskolenkier, later known as Roskolenko, a poet who was in the Trotskyist movement in the USA in the 1930s. He later abandoned poetry and wrote short stories and travel pieces, as well as a colourful autobiography, *When I Was Last on Cherry Street*. As a contrast to Herrmann and Roskolenkier there was Harry Crosby, another Paris expatriate who, with his wife Caresse, founded the Black Sun Press. Crosby, a rich man's son, was keen to push experience to its limits, and dabbled in drugs and sexual excess, as well as drinking heavily. He wrote a mixture of poetry and prose which contained lines like: "Abominable dead harbour of the past. You are the poison Satan urges me to drink. I smell the stench of your wharves even to this day. Your coils of rope are serpents ready to strike." At his best, he could achieve a semi-hypnotic flow, as in *House of Ra*, in the sixth issue of *Blues,* where the sun shines on everything, including "on the ladies' chemises plain, on the ladies' nightgowns plain, on the ladies' pyjamas plain, on the ladies' drawers plain, on the ladies' chemises silk," and so on for several pages. Crosby achieved notoriety in December 1929 when he and a society woman died in a joint suicide pact in a New York hotel.

Gertrude Stein ("George and Genevieve Geronimo with or with whether they thought they were with whether. They thought that they with whether"), Laurence Vail, Kay Boyle and Walter Lowenfels, all of them with Paris links, were in the sixth issue, and each was well in the modernist camp. Boyle was represented by a poem, though her main literary achievements were to be as a novelist and short-story writer. Her novels, *My Next Bride, Monday Night*, and *Year Before Last,* all explore the expatriate experience in various ways. Walter Lowenfels was another of those writers who specialised in experimental verse and favoured left-wing politics. He was from a well-to-do background, but chose to live in Paris, where he was in Henry Miller's circle. He appears, as the effusive Jabberwhorl Cronstadt in Miller's *Black Spring*. Lowenfels returned to the USA in the 1930s, gave up writing poetry, and worked for the Communist Party for many years. It was only in the 1950s, when the American Communist Party was falling apart and people like Lowenfels were being hounded by the FBI, that he started writing poetry again. He never regained his old standing, but his early work was highly regarded by the international avant-garde and was widely published in England and America.

Parker Tyler, who had kept in touch with Ford by mail, had become an associate editor by the time the seventh issue came out in the Autumn of 1929, the monthly publication schedule having been abandoned after the July number. There were more pages (forty-six) and the range of contributors was still widening. One of the fascinations of looking at old magazines is the opportunity to discover a whole world of now-forgotten poets. What happened to Harold Anton, Forrest Anderson, and James Henry Sullivan? Their work utilised the standard free verse techniques of uneven lines and loose associations, and though not bad was hardly memorable. It was, in other words, much like most poetry at any time. Other writers, such as William Carlos Williams, Kenneth Rexroth, Paul Bowles, and Edouard Roditi, were destined to last a little longer. And so was Erskine Caldwell, then finding his way into the literary world by placing his stories in *Blues* and similar publications. He would soon become famous for shocking the public with novels like *Tobacco Road* and *God's Little Acre*. Lionel Abel, writing poetry in 1929, was a leading New York intellectual in the 1940s and 1950s, writing for magazines such as *Partisan Review* and *Dissent.* This issue of *Blues* also had a short, experimental prose piece by Edgar Calmer, described as a Paris-based newspaperman. He was still around in the the 1960s, when he wrote a lively but conventional novel, *All The Summer Days*, about his expatriate period.

Ford moved to New York early in 1930, encouraged to do so by Parker Tyler, who was reasonably established as a poet, book-reviewer, and poetry performer who appeared alongside Maxwell Bodenheim, Eli Siegel, and other Greenwich Village celebrities. *Blues* began to slow down from that point, with only two more issues appearing in Spring and Autumn, 1930. Both maintained the usual standard, though without any major surprises. There was an appearance by a young British poet, Sidney Hunt, who seems to have been one of the few on this side of the Atlantic to be interested in what *Blues* was doing. He said in a letter from London: "Of the revolution of the word and the dream let loose there is little here." His own poem, July 5th, 1929, was a bright, semi-surreal workout which, if typical of what he wrote, must have made him an isolated figure in Britain. For issue nine, William Carlos Williams was asked to write a commentary on contemporary poetry and he lamented the lack of substance in much of what he read. He added: "I swear I myself can't make out for the life of me what many of them are talking about, and I have a will to understand them that they will not find in many another."

Writers who later became well-known in other fields were again in evidence. Harold Rosenberg would become a noted critic, supporting the abstract expressionist painters, and a major voice in New York intellectual circles. And Ben Maddow, a radical poet (in both technique and politics) in his younger days, went on to work in left-wing documentary film-making, moved to Hollywood to write scripts (he contributed to *Intruder in the Dust* and *The Asphalt Jungle)*, and was blacklisted in the 1950s when the film industry purged itself of communists.

It's worth noting at this point that when Ford and Tyler met in New York they commemorated their subsequent adventures in a novel, *The Young and Evil*, in which they, and others like Kathleen Tankersley Young and Herman Spector, were portrayed in thinly-disguised fictional form. Considered too daring to be published in America or Britain it eventually appeared in Paris in 1933 under the imprint of Jack Kahane's Obelisk Press. It was re-issued by the Olympia Press in Paris in 1960, but was only published in Britain in 1989 when the Gay Men's Press brought out a new edition.

The ninth issue of *Blues* gave no indication that it was the last, but Ford sailed for France in 1931, anxious to meet Gertrude Stein, Djuna Barnes, and the rest of the Paris community. He continued to write poetry, as did Parker Tyler, though Tyler increasingly turned to film and art criticism. Kathleen Tankersley Young died in 1933, a possible suicide. *Blues* was very much a magazine of its time, determined to promote the new and the different. That so many of its contributors made a mark in the literary world, or moved successfully into other areas, indicates that its editors were alert to talent. Even the forgotten writers often had something worthwhile to say. And if some of the contents now seem to have the dated air that experimental work can acquire with the passing of time then it should be remembered how exciting it was when it first appeared in print.

CONTACT

Little magazines start and stop for a variety of reasons, and it's interesting to look at their backgrounds and find out why they were founded and how they foundered. The case of *Contact*, which was born and died in the same year, is especially intriguing.

It's necessary to go back to the 1920s when a magazine called *Contact* was edited by William Carlos Williams and Robert McAlmon from an address in New York. It survived for four issues, and used work by Marianne Moore, Ezra Pound, Wallace Stevens, and others. McAlmon then moved to Paris, retained the name for his publishing venture, and published a fifth number of the magazine. But this early version of *Contact* is not the one we're concerned with. In 1931, two New York booksellers, David Moss and Martin Kamin, took over McAlmon's Contact Editions stock. They also suggested that he revive the magazine, and though McAlmon initially expressed interest he soon decided that it wasn't the right time for another literary review. By 1932, he'd lost faith in small, experimental magazines, and thought that the atmosphere of the 1930s called for something different. Williams Carlos Williams was interested, however, and asked Nathanael West to help him edit the new *Contact*. Williams' love of little magazines was well-known, and he thought of them as all being a part of one continuing magazine which spotlighted the real worthwhile writing of the time.

Nathanael West had struck up a friendship with Williams after the older writer had recommended that Contact Editions publish West's first novel, *The Dream Life of Balso Snell.* West was living in New York and working as a hotel manager, a position which enabled him to accommodate, often free of charge, some of his needy friends, including Edmund Wilson, James T. Farrell, and Dashiell Hammett. He was, like Williams, enthusiastic about little magazines, and both wanted a publication which would continue the tradition of the avant-garde reviews of the 1920s, such as *This Quarter*, *Broom*, and *transition.* But, as Williams wisely observed, they represented "the originality of our generation thoroughly free of an economic burden." In 1932, probably the worst year of the Depression in America, with millions unemployed and the homeless and hungry haunting the streets, an avant-garde literary magazine seemed irrelevant. Williams, in his editorial in the first issue, acknowledged this, but affirmed his belief in the necessity and value of good writing, especially when economic and political concerns drew attention away from it.

The booksellers, Moss and Kamin, were the publishers of *Contact*, with Williams and West responsible for editorial matters, but the arrangement would turn out to be less simple than that. However, the first issue appeared in February, 1932, and had over one hundred pages. Williams, West, and McAlmon took around thirty-five of these, perhaps because attracting material for a first issue isn't easy. Williams took the editorial pages to defend the decision to launch a little magazine in hard times, grabbed several more for a spirited analysis of the avant-garde magazine tradition, and featured his story, *The Coloured Girls of Passenack -Old and New*. McAlmon's contribution was one of his better stories, *It's All Very Complicated*, a dry tale of an American lesbian arriving in Paris and drifting into the expatriate world that revolved around the bars of Montparnasse, with occasional trips to sample Berlin's seamier side. Alcohol, drugs, and sexual deviation, were central to some of McAlmon's writing (one of his books was subtitled *Grim Fairy Tales*), and his sardonic tone emphasised the oddball nature of his characters. Nathanael West was already working on *Miss Lonelyhearts*, which would be his second novel, published in 1933, and a chapter from it followed McAlmon's story. What all three prose pieces had in common was a use of the colloquial to tell a story.

Williams' belief in "the American grain" possibly inclined him to look favourably on Charles Reznikoff's *My Country 'Tis of Thee,* which was a minor reworking of old court records highlighting a propensity for violence. Williams himself would include factual documents in his creative work, as in his long poem, *Paterson*. And his interest in popular culture was spotlighted by the piece that the Mexican artist, Diego Rivera, wrote about Mickey Mouse, "one of the genuine heroes of American art in the first half of the 20th Century." There was also a witty Hollywood sketch by S.J. Perelman which fitted West's demand for "an American superrealism" to stand against European surrealism. West, of course, later wrote one of the great Hollywood novels, *The Day of the Locust*, to promote a bizarre picture of the place. E.E. Cummings, Louis Zukofsky, and Parker Tyler, supplied most of the poetry in *Contact*, with Cummings mocking the aims of magazine editors in his humorous, *Let's start a magazine.*

There were indications of the way things were going in the literary world in several of the advertisements in the second issue of *Contact*. Another little magazine, *Contempo*, indicated that it was planning a special issue devoted to "proletarian literature," which would be edited by Mike Gold, one of the American Communist Party's leading spokesmen on cultural matters. And there was a full-page advertisement for *The Left: A Quarterly Review of Proletarian and Revolutionary Art*, which was printing writers like Jack Conroy, Sol Funaroff, and Albert Halper, who would be acknowledged as producing work that dealt with contemporary concerns from a radical point of view. But *Contact* continued to follow a non-political line in that its contributors rarely, if ever, referred to specific political problems or solutions. What the prose in *Contact* aimed for was a natural American style of story-telling, in which the colloquial played a strong part and regional matters came to the fore. Erskine Caldwell's story, *Over the Green Mountains* was located in Maine and dealt with rural types. Nathan Asch, son of the famous Jewish writer, Sholem Asch, contributed a story set in Texas. Robert McAlmon and Charles Kendall wrote about experiences in Mexico. And Julian Shapiro's *The Fire at the Catholic Church* had a travelling salesman encountering religious rivalry in a small town. All of these pieces utilised a direct, matter-of-fact approach. The editors had said that "*Contact* will attempt to cut a trail through the American jungle without the use of a European compass," and stories such as these seemed to do just that.

The second issue of *Contact* had appeared in May, 1932, and the third came out in October. One of its brightest stories was Julian Shapiro's *Once in a Sedan, Twice Standing Up*, which Williams had initially been reluctant to use because of its provocative title. It concerned a New York lawyer getting caught up in a country case which involved a local preacher who had seduced a young girl. Shapiro later wrote under the name of John Sanford, and is still alive and publishing. He has never become well-known, but has a high reputation in American non-establishment literary circles, and Black Sparrow Press have published several of his books. The rest of the prose in this issue was equally interesting. Erskine Caldwell's *Mama's Little Girl* was a bleak story of an abortion, and James T.

Farrell's tough *Jo-Jo* was about the downfall of a sad drunk. Farrell was a political activist, being linked to the Communist Party for a time and then the Trotskyists, but he didn't believe in loading his fiction with obvious political statements. One of the longest contributions was John Herrmann's *Charley Weiman*, a flat, but readable narrative of a young American's adventures in Germany in the immediate aftermath of the First World War. It painted an intriguing picture of how someone from a German-American background viewed the people he'd been told to think of as enemies. With the preponderance of prose (probably West's choices, as he rather than Williams seemed to be doing most of the editing) the short poems by Yvor Winters and Louis Zukofsky which were included in this issue almost got lost.

A fourth issue was planned, but Martin Kamin, one of the booksellers backing *Contact*, told Williams and West that he wanted them to put together an issue devoted to communist writers. He had, in fact, been pushing for this for some time, but the editors had ignored him. Kamin kept demanding that they invite contributions from Gorky, Mike Gold, and other American and foreign writers. In his view, good writing was synonymous with political commitment of a left-wing variety. Or, to be more exact, of a communist nature. And with many American writers turning left, the time seemed right to push *Contact* in the same direction. Both Williams and West had some sympathy with left-wing ideas, but didn't think that the magazine ought to be a vehicle for writers who simply came out with politically-correct statements. A falling out with Kamin was inevitable, and when it came it led to *Contact* closing down. It had foundered on the rocks of politics, and its three issues were almost the last fling of the 1920s type of little magazine, with its devotion to good writing and experimentation. The 1930s were darker years and, as Robert McAlmon foresaw, they had no place for a publication like *Contact*.

KURT VONNEGUT'S JAILBIRD

"Labour history was pornography of a sort in those days, and even more so in these days. In public schools and in the homes of nice people it was and remains pretty much taboo to tell tales of labour's suffering and derring-do."

Those words occur near the beginning of Kurt Vonnegut's *Jailbird,* his superbly ironic novel about the life of William F. Starbuck, supposed oldest and least-known of the Watergate conspirators. Vonnegut himself says them in relation to some comments about a character in the book based on Powers Hapgood, a Harvard man who, because of his strong sympathies with the working-class, went to work in the coalfields and was an activist in the miners' union. He was such an activist - and a left-wing one - that John L. Lewis, then Kingpin of the United Mine Workers, at one point had Hapgood and other "reds" barred from office. Later, however, during the great union drives of the Thirties Hapgood operated as an effective and experienced organiser for the Congress of Industrial Organisations (C.I.O.), the blanket body set up to bring the lessons of industrial unionism home and get American workers (or as many of them as possible) into unions which would steer clear of the pitfalls of craft unionism. There's a whole dynamic period of American union activity referred to when Vonnegut merely mentions someone like Hapgood. The industrial versus craft unionism debate was carried on vigorously in labour circles from the early part of the century, with early advocates of Industrial unionism being the famed Wobblies (I.W.W. - Industrial Workers of the World, and note, it is Industrial and not International Workers as even some of the best reference books have it.)

In his introduction Vonnegut refers to having met Hapgood as well as to an incident he heard about and which histories of American labour document. In the Thirties Hapgood helped organise a strike against RCA in Camden and was arrested and imprisoned. 5,000 angry strikers converged on the prison, and the nervous police chief decided that discretion was the better part of valour and turned Hapgood loose. Direct action with a vengeance. That particular strike was actually called by the United Electrical, Radio and Machine Workers of America, a fact which is not without some

relevance to Vonnegut's book. He has Starbuck - an old radical, albeit of a largely arm chair kind - refer to a volume called *Labour's Untold Story* by Richard O. Boyer and Herbert M. Morals, an edition of which was published by the United Electricians Union. Just to fill in a little more detail, the United Electrical was a radical union which came out of the Second World War as a major force in American industry, having almost 500,000 members (many of them obviously in key jobs) and a leadership heavily influenced by Communists. Both Government and management saw it as a threat, and the onset of the Cold War was a heaven-sent opportunity to carry out a drive designed to rid the United Electrical (and other unions) of left-wingers.
Patriotism was the name of the game, of course, but it wasn't just a coincidence that management welcomed the reduced bargaining power that repression helped bring about. The story of the anti-left campaign - and it was effective - is told in David Caute's massive study of American domestic anti-communism, *The Great Fear*, and in Bert Cochran's *Labour and Communism*. Anyone interested might also profitably refer to Clancy Sigal's *Going Away*, a "novel" which is a kind of political *On The Road* with the narrator driving across the United States and meeting up with fellow-victims of the blacklist. Which brings us back to Vonnegut. In his book Starbuck falls foul of the Un-American Activities committee and. has to testify before it. *Jailbird* hints at this tradition of American radicalism from the Twenties to the Thirties. It's a period that has been increasingly written about in recent years. To take a couple of current examples, Jane Foster's *An Unamerican Lady* and Lillian Hellman's *Scoundrel Time,* we find the latter in particular arousing impassioned responses in *Encounter* and elsewhere. That the subject - Thirties leftism, Forties war and Cold War, and Fifties blacklisting - can still get the emotions going can easily be seen from Miss Hellman's comments and, for example, Sidney Hook's reflections on them, as printed in *Encounter.* Sidney Hook, now there's a name ... but I digress. Still, I ought to mention that memoirs of the Thirties by both Edmund Wilson and Malcolm Cowley have just appeared in print. And glancing through a pile of recently-published American books I see that there are volumes by old labour organisers and Party members. One is even called *The Romance of American Communism*, and reading the interviews in it one can understand why Starbuck and his contemporaries felt the way they did, even if they were often more

liberal than left deep down at heart.

I think what Vonnegut is getting at is the dedication and sincerity of many of those organisers and activists, and their total belief (which may seem naive to us now) in the rightness of their cause and its inevitable victory. There was a sense of moral outrage at the state of the world behind their beliefs and actions, and Vonnegut himself displays some of it in his comments on the Sacco and Vanzetti case. At this point I pause to wonder how many people know anything about Sacco and Vanzetti? Maybe I'm mistaken, or perhaps I've mixed with too many friends with similar interests, but it seems to me that at one time lots of people in this country, as well as America, had heard of them. Two Italian anarchists, a shoemaker and a fish-peddler, they were charged with attempting to hold up a wages truck. At the time - the Twenties - the general feeling in labour and liberal circles was that they had been framed. And whatever the truth of the matter they certainly should never have been convicted on the basis of the evidence presented against them. But as Starbuck points out when telling their story, the judge, at an earlier trial which was probably arranged to establish a criminal past for Vanzetti, remarked "This man, although he may not have actually, committed the crime attributed to him, is nevertheless morally culpable, because he is the enemy of our existing institutions."

Of course, some local readers might think that the American setting of the Sacco and Vanzetti injustice somehow makes it irrelevant. People didn't think that way in the Twenties. I'll refer you again to that book, *Labour's Untold Story*, page 234, where a footnote lists headlines from just one issue of the *New York Times* in April 1927. Protests were pouring in from Britain, 50,000 people paraded in Sweden, police had to protect the American embassy in Berlin against demonstrators, there were strikes in Argentina. And more of the same kind of activity in Russia, Denmark, France, Norway, Uruguay, Poland, Holland, Paraguay, Belgium, and Canada. Not just individuals involved, either, but thousands of working people protesting against the injustice experienced by two of their own kind.

The kind of dedication that Vonnegut, either directly or through Starbuck, sees in people like Hapgood and Sacco and Vanzetti had its parallels here. Reading a little pamphlet recently I came across references to Wobblies active in Liverpool in the Twenties and Thirties. The pamphlet in question is called *Liverpool 1921-22,* it's by a man called George Garrett, and it's an excerpt from an unpublished autobiography of life on the dole and in the ranks of the working-class activists of the time. I mention it because it's very much in the mould of "Labour's suffering and derring-do" as Vonnegut has it. It was said of Garrett, who'd been a sailor, wandered the States (which is where he joined the Wobblies), and worked on the docks, when there was any work to be had, that he was "Christlike, so marked by suffering, so free from bitterness, so generous to those who persecuted him. Blacklisted, imprisoned, almost starved, miserably clad; he yet speaks and acts like a Christian gentleman." That was the opinion of Canon Raven of Liverpool Cathedral. In *Jailbird* it's mentioned that Powers Hapgood, when asked by a judge why a man of his background and education should devote his life to union work, replied, "Because of the Sermon on the Mount, sir."

Like Vonnegut, I tend to think that you're not likely to find Garrett and Hapgood and their kind discussed in the homes of nice people or taught in many schools, though what they did was probably as relevant to most people's lives as anecdotes about kings and queens and stories of famous wars. Maybe I ought to slip in a quick chorus of "Should I ever be a soldier 'neath the Red Flag I would fight," but that might be thought of as going too far in this day and age. It occurs to me, too, at this point that some of you may be wondering, after my reference to Wobblies active in Liverpool, whether the organisation was not primarily American. Well we are talking about *Jailbird*, which is an American novel, but if the American-British connection with the Wobblies needs to be taken further than my reference to George Garrett then it's worth mentioning Tom Mann, James Connolly, James Larkin, and other British and Irish labour leaders who had links with the I.W.W., and whose ideas were centred around syndicalism or industrial unionism. Or why not read Charles Ashleigh's picaresque autobiographical novel, *Rambling Kid*, or George Hardy's more-formal, but equally-interesting autobiography, *Those Stormy Years*. Both Ashleigh and Hardy were English-born, became I.W.W. members in America, were eventually deported back to Britain, and later joined the Communist Party, as did many of their ex-colleagues in the States.

Vonnegut doesn't talk much, if at all, about the Wobblies. His story, insofar as it looks to the past, mainly mentions the Twenties and

Thirties, and by that time the I.W.W. was a spent force as a major organisation. Hammered into the ground by Government repression from 1917 onwards, torn by internal factional fights, and suffering from serious organisational defects that limited its effectiveness as a union (which is what it really set out to be), the I.W.W. slid into relative obscurity after the early-Twenties. It still had members, many of whom were active during the C.I.O. organising drives, strikes and sit-ins of the Thirties, but its previous all-embracing influence on labour activists, intellectuals, writers, and artists petered out. The Communist Party more or less took over the role that the Wobblies had performed prior to 1920 insofar as providing a focal point for radical activity was concerned. And it's still a highly-complex and debatable argument whether or not Communist influence didn't destroy a whole free-wheeling tradition of American radicalism. The problem with the Communists was their often blind dedication to the Party line, and in particular to the idea of Russia as a guiding light for all radicals. The Wobblies, on the other hand, whilst hardly nationalists, always had a very American tone to their revolutionary activity. I have already mentioned that they attracted recruits in Europe - and in the British Isles they chiefly found support in cities such as Liverpool, Glasgow, and Birmingham, and from amongst Scottish, Irish, and Welsh labour activists - but the one place where the I.W.W. made an impact outside America was Australia, a country with a young history, a large immigrant population, and frontier conditions often not much different than those found in the United States. Wobbly influence was strong in Australia, especially amongst miners and transient workers, though it was most likely the gospel of direct action rather than any larger syndicalist or industrial unionist theory which appealed to those people. Australian Wobblies often displayed a militancy that went far beyond even that of their American counterparts. The organisation was in the vanguard of the anti-conscription campaign that sprang up in Australia during the Great War, and some of its members were prepared to go to extreme lengths to make their point. Take the story of Tom Barker. He was a British-born Wobbly who was sent to prison for "prejudicing recruiting." Some of his fellow-Wobblies promptly resorted to "sab-cat" methods to obtain his release. The "sab-cat" was Wobbly slang for the black cat which symbolised sabotage, and though American Wobblies were usually careful to claim that their ideas of sabotage were limited to such things as lightning strikes, slowing down on the job, and so on, the Australians weren't quite as fussy. A series of fires occurred in shops and industrial premises, the general message being that they'd continue as long as Barker was in prison. He was released nine months before his sentence was due to terminate. You can read all about this - and about other Australian Wobbly capers (one was a mad scheme to destroy the economy by printing counterfeit money) - in Ian Turner's *Sydney's Burning*.

Just to round off the Barker story. He was eventually deported from Australia to Chile, the British authorities refusing to take him because, among other things, he'd insulted the King. In later life, though, he did get back to London, where he became a Labour councillor and Lord Mayor of St. Pancras. He may have been comparatively mellow, but still had flashes of his old spirit. It was Barker who ran a red flag up over St. Pancras Town Hall in 1958, thereby putting elements of the British press into a state of near-hysteria, and at the same time no doubt having a quiet chuckle to himself. "Derring-do" was never any the worse for having a sense of humour linked to it.

However, perhaps I shouldn't digress any further? Why did Vonnegut's *Jailbird* lead to all this? After all, he doesn't say all that much about it in the book. But to me it's a sign of a good writer when his implications can trigger off a series of reflections in the reader's mind. *Jailbird*, without flag-waving or tub-thumping, suggests, in a subtle way, a world that's largely lost to us now. Dedicated labour leaders and activists, poets with genuine social consciences. Vonnegut quotes from an imaginary (I think) poet, Henry Miles Whistler, writing about the death of a child on a picket line. It isn't all that far from reality. And it at once reminds me of a couple of generations of now-forgotten American poets : Lola Ridge, Sol Funaroff, Orrick Johns, Arturo Giovannitti. The latter is a name to conjure with. Associate of the leading Wobblies in their heyday, flamboyant organiser, editor of labour newspapers, and a poet of real talent. Some of his poems deserve to be revived. "The Walker" is a fine prison poem, "When the cock crows" and "The Senate of the Dead" are vigorous protest pieces. I'd guess that Allen Ginsberg - growing up in a household with a mother who was a Party member and a father who had at least left-liberal sentiments - was as familiar with poets like Giovannitti as he was with Blake or Smart or

Whitman. I'm talking now about an overlooked tradition of American populist poetry. Carl Sandburg and Vachel Lindsay might be remembered, but who has ever heard of William Vaughn Moody or Mike Gold? You won't find much about them in academic histories, but Kenneth Rexroth's idiosyncratic, but fascinating *American Poetry in the Twentieth Century* is a good guide to these forgotten poets.

I wanted to talk about Hutchins Hapgood, too, because Vonnegut refers to him in passing as one of Powers Hapgood's uncles. Hutchins Hapgood mixed in that American bohemia of the early part of the century that spilled over into the world of radical politics, and some of his books - *The Spirit of Labour* and *Types From City Streets* - reflect his interests. But I think I'd better call it a day. I've only approached *Jailbird* from one angle, and an admittedly specialised-interest angle at that, but as I suggested earlier the fact that it did provide the platform for my comments points to the strength and variety of Vonnegut's writing.

THINGS ARE NOT AS THEY SEEM

I have, over the years, been a casual fan of crime novels. Not the kind beloved of English readers, with elderly ladies solving mysteries in quiet villages, but rather the American variety, with hard-boiled private eyes walking down some mean streets. But even that description doesn't really say what I like, the private eye novel being almost a genre in itself. I suppose what I'm mostly talking about are the so-called "pulp" novels, largely produced in the 1940's and 1950's (though with their antecedents in the 1930's) in response to the demand by paperback publishers for books which could be cheaply produced and mostly sold outside normal bookshop outlets. Some authors in this field did, it's true, cross boundaries and their works were seen as literature by literary people. Raymond Chandler, Dashiell Hammett, and Ross Macdonald spring to mind in this respect, but I doubt that most of the other writers, usually publishing directly into gaudy paperbacks, were ever written about by "serious" critics. One of the few early attempts by a well-known critic to look at some of the hard-boiled, tough-guy, call them what you will, novelists was Edmund Wilson's *The Boys in the Back Room,* published in 1941, and dealing, in part, with James M. Cain, who wrote *The Postman Always Rings Twice*. Horace McCoy, author of *I Should Have Stayed Home,* and Richard Hallas, whose *You Play the Black and the Red Comes Up* has one of the most evocative titles there is. It almost sums up what happens in a lot of the books and, also, in the films which later became categorised as film noir. Wilson referred to such writers as "the poets of the tabloid murder," and they did seem to be re-shaping the kind of stories that cropped up most days in newspapers. There were others like them, most of them now forgotten and sometimes unfairly so. James Ross wrote a bleak novel called *They Don't Dance Much*, which is not only about crime but presents as well a picture of Depression days in small-town America. And Edward Anderson's *Thieves Like Us* has much to recommend it for its portrayal of 1930's situations.

Edmund Wilson clearly selected a few of the better writers when writing his essay, and much the same has happened when critics have turned their attention to the "pulp" novelists of the late 1940's and the 1950's. A few names crop up regularly and it's difficult to locate information about the lesser-known (though not necessarily lesser-talented) writers, which is why Woody Haut's *Pulp Culture and the Cold War* (Serpent's Tail, 1995) is such a valuable book. It doesn't try to be all-inclusive, and its title indicates a specific period (roughly 1945 to 1960) that engages the author's attention, but it is well-documented and deals with writers mostly outside the standard framework of literary criticism. I'm not reviewing Haut's book, simply drawing attention to it as a useful and provocative source of information.

I said earlier that many "pulp" novels were produced to meet a demand for cheap paperbacks but, as Haut makes clear, quite a few of the writers tried to create something worthwhile when dealing with description, character-development, suspense, and psychological depth. They also, whether by accident or design, often reflected the mood of the times. Not too many dealt directly with politics, though Mickey Spillane's *One Lonely Night* stands out as a bizarre exception ("They were Red sons-of-bitches who should have died long ago ....."), if not a particularly well-written one. William McGivern's *Margin of Terror* also touches on anticommunist paranoia, and he may well have been genuinely anticommunist himself but, as a "pulp" writer, he also knew how to ride on the 50's Cold War bandwagon. *Margin of Terror* is not one of his best books, with its stereotypical American hero saving a beautiful girl from the dastardly Reds, but it reflected (and perhaps also fed) the unease of the period. Uneasiness is a key factor in many "pulp" novels, just as it is in more literary novels. (Sloan Wilson's *The Man in the Grey Flannel Suit* is an example) and in sociological studies (see David Riesman's *The Lonely Crowd*) from the 1950's. There is a constant feeling that all is not well and that, below the surface of "normality," lies the possibility of breakdown. People are trapped in cobwebs of intrigue, middle-class respectability is threatened, and assumed values soon break down under pressure. "Pulp" novelists were not the only ones to see things this way, and studies of Hollywood films of the postwar years frequently point out how they often involve similar ideas.

As an aside, one of the fascinating things about more than a few of the writers (of both "pulp" novels and movies of the film noir style) was their link to the political left. A glance through the credits of classic film noir productions will bring to light names such as Albert Maltz, Abraham Polonsky, Clifford Odets, and Robert Rossen, all of them with one-time membership of the Communist Party noted in their FBI files. As for the "pulp" writers (and some of them worked in Hollywood, as well as writing novels), Jim Thompson had been a Party member in the 1930's and Vera Caspary, author of *Laura*, a classic crime novel and film, had also belonged somewhere along the line. William Lindsay Gresham, who wrote the weird *Nightmare Alley*, had served with the International Brigades in Spain, and Dorothy B. Hughes, whilst not a communist, was sympathetic to left-liberal causes. Her novel *The Fallen Sparrow* has a Spanish Civil War veteran at its centre. There may be nothing highly significant in all this, though I suspect that, for some of the writers, the world of the crime novel was not only a way of earning a living but also allowed them to offer a critique of society at a time when they sometimes found it difficult to get more orthodox socially-observant books published. Ed Lacy's books often seem to me to make social commentary a part of the story, especially in a book like *Harlem Underground*, where references to race politics and general social trends are worked into the text.

Left-wing or not (and I'm not claiming that most of them were) these writers knew how to tell a story. Gil Brewer wrote over fifty novels and around five hundred short stories, with admittedly variable results. But the short, but effective *13 French Street* deserves to be remembered. A middle-class man, with a good job in a museum and a safe marriage about to take place, goes to visit an old war-buddy and finds himself sucked into a whirlpool of murder as his friend's wife exerts her baleful influence. Women, it needs to be said, mostly represented two basic types in "pulp" fiction. They were either faithful and true or they were femmes fatales. Again, there is a parallel with film noir, and it says something about the uneasiness that men felt about the place of women in postwar society. They were threatened by their growing assertiveness, which, in books and films, often came out as negative in intent and result. But leaving this aside, what is impressive about Brewer's book is its compulsiveness as matters build to their inevitable climax. And Brewer could also write short, but highly effective passages which set the scene for what was about to happen and highlighted the contrast between the surface calm and the storm that was brewing:

"Church bells tolled a solemn recollection of timeless Sundays spent in an apathy of occasional prayer tokening an afterward of roast chicken and mashed potatoes, stuffed stomachs and shirts, groaning couches and the geometric disarray of thick newspapers among the wailing havoc of snores, wet diapers, clanking kitchen sink, or the shade-drawn sedate parlours where through rich cigar smoke they mumbled ritualistic weekly histories of business and how Oscar got drunk last night at the hotel bar. As I drove up Main Street people were congregating in front of the churches and it was a nice autumn Sunday for death."

Now it's obviously true that for every *13 French Street* there were twenty and more "pulp" novels that were thoroughly routine when it came to dialogue, character-development, and anything else you care to mention. A reader wanting to find decent writing in this field had to be prepared to pick and choose carefully. Even an interesting writer, such as Gil Brewer or William McGivern, had his off-days. But it is worth looking for the good stuff. McGivern's excellent *The Crooked Frame*, to pick out one book from his output, has much to recommend it. Set in the world of "pulp" magazines it adroitly exploits the standard plot of a man waking up from a binge to find blood on his clothes and a dawning suspicion in his mind that he may have killed someone in an alcoholic blackout. McGivern manages to sustain the tension with a neat mixture of little twists in the plot and wicked office politics, showing his skill as a writer as he does so. It's noticeable how many of these books involve characters with a drink problem. Fredric Brown's *The Screaming Mimi* kicks off with a broken-down reporter stumbling drunkenly through the night and finding himself caught up in a murder hunt. And Kenneth Fearing's *Dagger of the Mind*, set out in an artists' colony and with some sly references to artistic manners and morals, also has a drunk as its central character. Fearing was himself an alcoholic, as was Jim Thompson, whose books are awash with booze.

Thompson was, incidentally, a fascinating character. He had belonged to the IWW and, later, the Communist Party, and had worked at a variety of jobs, as well as turning out a string of novels, several of which are not easily categorized as crime stories, though that's the way they were published and are described in bookshops. Thompson drew on his own experiences for background material, as in *South of Heaven* which is set in the Texas oil field of the 1920's. He had worked there and amongst his acquaintances had been Harry "haywire" McClintock, an IWW organiser and singer who later worked in radio and was reputed to be the composer of hobo songs such as *"Hallelujah, I'm a Bum"* and *"Big Rock Candy Mountain."* Thompson told friends that reading Marx while working in the oil fields had been a turning point in his life, and some of his early writings, in a 30's proletarian style, revolved around the exploitation of labour. By the time he came to write *South of Heaven* in the 1960's, he had severed his links with organized politics, but his writing still had an edge when it came to describing conditions amongst the transient workers hired to lay gas pipe-lines and brutalised by their struggle to stay alive. Thompson's books have attracted some interest in recent years, partly thanks to film-makers who have seen his work as suitable for adaptation to the screen, so *The Grifters, The Killer Inside Me*, and many of the other novels he produced for the "pulp" market of the 1950's are easily available. The revival of interest had also brought about the re-publication of his earlier novels, *Now and on Earth* (1942) and *Heed The Thunder* (1946), neither of which is a crime book. If anything, they reflect his roots in the Depression years.

I mentioned Ed Lacy and *Harlem Underground*, which is about a black cop struggling to defuse tension created by both white racists and black militants. A previous Lacy book, *Room to Swing* had featured a black private detective and was thought to be one of the first to do so. And Lacy, whose work was included in an anthology of short stories by Afro-American writers, was described as black, but was, in fact, Jewish American. Under his real name, Len Zinberg, he had written radical novels in the 1930's and early 1940's. His awareness of the problems faced by blacks comes through in his books, and *Room To Swing* is prefaced with a quote from Thomas Jefferson: "The mass of mankind has not been born with saddles on their backs, nor a favoured few-booted and spurred ...." The point is, though, that Lacy worked within the "pulp" framework, whatever social comments he made in passing, and he was good at what he did. Like Gil Brewer he knew how to set a scene:

"It was just another ordinary and dreary bar on Amsterdam Avenue in that part of New York City called Washington Heights. Why it was named Grand Cafe, nobody seems to know. It had neither gaudy neon lights nor air-conditioning, and the small screen TV perched in one corner was the same set it had been when TV was a novelty."

That's the opening of *Visa to Death*, and Lacy carries on

documenting the ordinariness of the place and its clientele and then introduces a double killing. The main story itself is interesting and involves some shady wartime deals which corrupt their protagonists and follow them into civilian life. Lacy was another writer who had been a Communist Party member, so his crime novels may well have allowed him to continue earning a living while offering at least some observations on the way that money, power, and the pressures of capitalism affected people. And he did it without preaching.

I am conscious that I have been jumping around with what I've said in this piece and I've certainly not tried to assess the books concerned in a systematic way. As I've said at the beginning, I am a casual fan of crime novels and I just keep an eye open for "pulp" novels as I browse in second hand bookshops and pause at market bookstalls. Picking them up cheap is part of the fun. And I make mistakes and realize I have started reading a dud. But they can yield up good writing and stories that grip the imagination. Charles Williams's *The Hotspot* (originally called *Hell Hath No Fury*) has a terrific twist in its tale with the "hero" caught in a web that will enable him to live in material comfort but will also involve him in a totally soulless existence. William McGivern's *The Big Heat* and *Odds Against Tomorrow* are well written and both play on 50's problems and paranoias (crime creeping into the suburbs, racism, etc.) and Steve Fisher's *I Wake Up Screaming* concerns a Hollywood writer accused of murder and hounded by a slightly insane policeman. Fisher worked in Hollywood and the book has some sharp things to say about the studio system and its injustices. I make no claims for these books being great literature, but it seems to me that quite a few of them are much better written than many "literary " novels which were coming out in hardbacks and being reviewed in the right places. It's rather like Jim Thompson said when asked about writing: "There is only one plot - things are not as they seem". Or, to put it another way, you can't judge a book by its cover.

THE INDIGNANT GENERATION

Some years ago, around the mid-1990s, there was something of an upsurge of interest in the writers and artists of the Harlem Renaissance, the movement usually characterised as relating to the 1920s. Glancing at my bookshelves I can see several anthologies published, or re-published at that time, and I have a memory of at least one large art exhibition. Lawrence P. Jackson says that the Renaissance started in 1924 and then "collapsed as the economy ground to a halt in the early 1930s and unemployment and breadlines became common American realities." But the fact of a movement coming to an end doesn't mean that individuals stop writing and, in any case, new writers appear despite, or perhaps because of, the economic situation.

By the mid-1930s there was a new generation of writers and intellectuals on the scene, many of them influenced by Marxism and with a tendency to "see the racial problem in economic terms." The number of black graduates rose but employment problems continued even when the economy showed signs of recovery. Blacks with degrees still had to be content with menial jobs if they managed to find work. And, as Jackson puts it: "The unemployed black writers, artists and activists were making a beeline for the political parties and artistic clusters on the left wing." Socialists and communists were not a new breed among blacks in the United States, and black intellectuals had "cut their teeth during the 1910s on the giant issue of the delegation of the resources of society, the kind of leadership group needed to begin the redistribution of power and the involvement of the rank-and-file." He mentions a group mainly made up of West Indians in New York which included Claude McKay, whose *Home to Harlem* and *Harlem Glory* point to his radical leanings, including his involvement with the Industrial Workers of the World. McKay published poetry, novels, and other writings, and though often critically acclaimed his "reward for all of this was to live hand-to-mouth for his entire adult life."

McKay always had a deep suspicion of communism, even if he did sometimes work alongside communists, but there's no doubt that, for many other blacks, the American Communist Party had a significant role in their activities. As so often happened, communist policy and tactics were dictated by Moscow, and the "Black Belt thesis" held that "Negro Americans were an oppressed nation, sharing a common land, heritage, and culture, and that American blacks deserved the right to self-determination and their own national territory." Maps were produced which showed the areas that blacks should control. Was this ever a realistic proposition and likely to appeal to the mass of blacks in the United States? It hardly mattered when Stalin gave his approval.

For writers the communists were important because of the existence of the *New Masses* and the John Reed Clubs that were established in many towns and cities. *New Masses* had always been sympathetic to blacks from its inception in 1926. I have a somewhat tattered copy of the December 1926 issue which contains four poems by Langston Hughes, a report on conditions in various parts of the South, and an advertisement for *Fire*, "a quarterly devoted to the younger Negro artists," edited by Wallace Thurman, a leading black writer. Jackson says that, "*New Masses* was an excellent example of the sort of radical democratic possibility available to black writers in the 1930s." As for the John Reed Clubs, they were based on the kind of literary studios for worker-correspondents created by Prolecult in the Soviet Union. New York and Chicago had the largest clubs and their purpose was both educational and agitational. When Party policy dictated in 1928 that the class war should be taken into every aspect of culture, the slogan "Art is a Class Weapon" emphasised opposition to notions of "art for art's sake." The Chicago club had a mixed membership, including the white novelist Nelson Algren and the black writer Richard Wright. *Left Front,* a magazine funded by the John Reed Clubs, published some of Wright's early poems. He was later to break with communism and, in 1950, contributed to a notable anti-communist anthology, *The God That Failed*, but in the 1930s he was a dedicated member of the Party and believed that a union of blacks and whites could be forged to oppose capitalism. Wright's *American Hunger,* which only saw complete publication in 1977, is a fascinating account of this period of his life.

Party policy changed again in 1934 and the Clubs were dissolved, along with many of the little magazines they had started. Proletarian writers, black and white, were usually unknown and little published, and they were discarded in favour of "a broader coalition that could accommodate already established artists; this new coalition became known as the Popular Front." Few black writers could lay claim to being widely known, but Langston Hughes did have credibility with the Communist Party. He'd spent a year in Russia in the early-1930s and had a publishing record stretching back well into the 1920s. And he was popular with whites. His work had become increasingly radical and was regularly featured in *New Masses*. By 1934 he was president of the League of Struggle for Negro Rights, a communist-front organisation that, according to Eugene Lyons in his 1941 book, *The Red Decade*, had Earl Browder, William Z. Foster, Gil Green, and Clarence Hathaway, all of them members of the American Communist Party, on its council. Lyons thought that Hughes was "stronger in heart than in mind," and "accepted the shadow of communist phrases for the substance of reality." He also went on to suggest that the League never really meant much to the Negro masses, "attracting largely careerists and black bohemians." Hughes's radicalism tapered off in later years, and Saunders Redding, writing about a 1962 conference in Kampala that both he and Hughes attended, remarked on the fact that Hughes avoided reading any of his radical poems and didn't join in the discussions about anti-imperialist revolutionary activity.

In 1935 the New Deal programme established the Federal Writers' Project which aimed to provide work for at least some unemployed writers, though there were always arguments about who qualified as unemployed or as a writer. Leaving aside the differences of opinion the Project did offer employment to a number of black writers, among them Sterling Brown and Richard Wright. Brown produced some work for a guidebook to Washington that Jackson describes as "among the most arresting analyses of an African American urban community, from privies to lace curtains, ever written." He was also involved with interviewing ex-slaves, "arguably the most important research undertaken by the entire Federal Writers' Project", and invaluable to scholars studying the history of slavery.

Richard Wright was hired by the Chicago branch of the Project as a field reporter for the state guidebook, though he also benefited from having time to write a novel. Other black writers on the Project included Willard Motley, who later made a name with the novel *Knock on Any Door*, and Frank Yerby, who also succeeded as a novelist but with potboilers that had white heroes and heroines cavorting in the old South. Prior to success with *The Foxes of Harrow* and *The Vixens* Yerby had contributed to little magazines but had grown tired of earning little and reaching only a small audience. It's easy to dismiss a writer like Yerby but, as Jackson points out, his "apparently innocuous historical romance had the capacity to touch an audience that a 'professionally liberal' book might never have reached. Yerby used the pulp narrative to present without pleading the common sense arguments in favour of ending racial segregation."

Jackson performs a useful service by devoting a great deal of attention to Chicago in the late-1930s. Writers like Arna Bontemps, Frank Marshall Davis, William Attaway (author of a social-realist novel, *Blood on the Forge*, which focused on working conditions and racism in the steel mills around Pittsburgh) and Margaret Walker were active in the city, though the most successful was Richard Wright. His *Uncle Tom's Children* (1938) and *Native Son* (1940) were critically acclaimed and commercially popular, at least when compared to books by other blacks. The four stories in *Uncle Tom's Children* revolved around racism and, as one critic put it; "In each story, the main character experiences a traumatic event that takes him or her from childhood innocence to hardened militancy." *Native Son* was an even bigger success, though Wright had to agree to a certain amount of editing and censoring to make it acceptable to the Book-of-the-Month Club readership. Even so, it was remarkable that a novel as hard-hitting as *Native Son*, with its stark message of racial divisions and their consequences, could be made available to a wide audience.

Native Son also had a political effect: "The new breed of young blacks - exposed to college, seeking Marxism and relationships with Communists but not in awe of them, highly critical of white liberals and the traditional black middle-class, and violently impatient with segregation - converted *Native Son* into a catalyst for political organisation." Jackson points out that Ralph Ellison, then a "young Marxist radical, decided that Bigger's 'indignation' - the violent eradication of the idea of moral and ethical justification in favour of Marxist 'necessity' was Wright's paramount achievement." The entry of America into the Second World War found white liberals like Archibald MacLeish attempting to persuade black newspaper editors to play down calls for racial equality so as not to rock the boat during wartime. Young black writers were still pushed towards left-wing publications or obscure little magazines if they wanted to see their work in print. A significant publication was *Negro Quarterly* which Jackson says "was largely shaped by Communists," though it disagreed with the Party's policy of soft-pedalling on demands for an end to segregation in the armed forces. *Negro Quarterly* struggled to attract readers and wartime paper shortages also affected its capacity to maintain a regular publication schedule.

Young black writers didn't hold with curtailing their calls for racial equality and instead saw the war as an opportunity to push their demands even harder. After all, wasn't it meant to be a war for democracy and against fascist ideas of racial superiority? Chester Himes, not long out of prison, and already published in *Esquire* and *New Masses*, wrote an article in which he said: "Now, in the year 1942, is the time; here in the United States of America, is the place for 13,000,000 Negro Americans to make their fight for freedom in the land in which they were born and where they will die. Now is the time and here is the place to engage and overcome our most persistent enemies. Our native American fascists." It was enough to start the FBI keeping a check on his future activities.

The Communist Party, or people with links to it, still played a part in getting black writers into print. Edwin Seaver had worked for The League of American Writers, a front organisation, and the *Daily Worker*, and in 1944 he edited the first *Cross-Section*, a large anthology with a definite left-wing slant and contributions from several black writers, including Richard Wright, Langston Hughes, Ralph Ellison, and Carl Ruthven Offord. What Jackson says was obvious from the work by black writers was that the kind of consensus between blacks and white liberals that had typified the 1920s and 1930s was breaking down: "By 1944 the fiction writers were imagining black identity in the same terms that Horace Cayton had predicted - one that did not rely on white liberals." Cayton was a black activist in Chicago who encouraged people to look to their own communities for support rather than relying on white liberals. Like Chester Himes he attracted the attention of the FBI when he questioned why blacks should be fighting in a war that would only benefit whites.

Jackson states that by 1945 it was obvious that a second "Renaissance" was in sight. Wright, Ellison, Ann Petry, Gwendolyn Brooks, Robert Hayden, the critic Saunders Redding, and many more, were being published regularly and given serious attention. One problem that arose, though, was that as the war ended and an anti-communist mood began to build up, writers displaying what could be called un-American tendencies were looked on with suspicion. Discussing some events at the writers and artists retreat at Yaddo, Jackson remarks that "few blacks outspoken on racial issues were invited as guests." When Chester Himes's *Lonely Crusade*, his novel about politics and prejudice in an aircraft factory, was published in 1947 it got some unfavourable notices because it seemed to be sympathetic towards communism, or at least didn't show communists as simply evil characters bent on destroying the American way of life. Jackson thinks that readers "would not gravitate to a book that showed Communists as wise liberators," and he adds that the book sold poorly. Some of Himes's fellow-writers thought he'd made a mistake by publishing his novel at a time when the "Red Scare" was mounting in intensity.

Newer black writers were less directly-political than their immediate forerunners. Willard Motley's *Knock on Any Door* was certainly written in a social-realist style but its central characters were white and its theme was one of social reform of the kind that would solve the problem of juvenile delinquency. It had a good liberal message and, perhaps not surprisingly, was picked up by Hollywood and turned into a powerful film. The book sold reasonably well and it's interesting to note that Motley was assumed to be white until his photograph appeared in newspapers and magazines.

Another writer who began to surface in the post-war years was James Baldwin and he started to make a name for himself with reviews in *New Leader, Commentary*, and *Partisan Review*, publications that were inclined more to the centre than the left. They certainly weren't the kind of magazines most young black writers would normally be associated with. Jackson also mentions Anatole Broyard as another black who managed to enter the world of prestigious intellectual journals, but he is something of a special case in that he could pass for white and usually tried to do so. Baldwin was dark-skinned but knew how to turn white sympathy to his advantage, according to Jackson. He had been a member of the Young People's Socialist League and a Trotskyite, but it's doubtful if radical politics were ever his main interest, and he soon distanced himself from writers like Richard Wright and Ralph Ellison with his article, "Everybody's Protest Novel," which ended with an attack on Wright. In Jackson's view Baldwin said that "wallowing in bitterness and indignation was flawed because it led to violence and self-destruction, either of the black self, of the black people, or of the American nation."

Baldwin and other black writers moved to Paris, where the city seemed to offer an environment largely free from racial prejudice, though they soon learned that it was only their American passports that ensured they weren't harassed too often by the police. They couldn't help noticing that other coloured residents were treated differently, particularly when the Algerian War of Independence started. Baldwin, Chester Himes, Ralph Ellison, Richard Wright, William Gardner Smith, and others, were all in Paris at one time or another. Interestingly, the early-1950s saw the publication of what Jackson refers to as "four key works of African American highbrow modernism," namely Ralph Ellison's *Invisible Man*, Ann Petry's *The Narrows*, Gwendolyn Brooks's *Maud Martha* and James Baldwin's *Go Tell It On The Mountain.* And he claims: "These works, all of them major achievements in narrative form and psychologically complex black characters, would signal the successful acceptance of blacks into American life."

Richard Wright's *The Outsider* was also published in the early-1950s, though Jackson says that "the public never warmed to it," and he relates the response to it to that which greeted Norman Mailer's *Barbary Shore,* which he describes as "trying to work through the communist-capitalist-existentialist morass and using elements of detective fiction as well." With anti-communist hysteria at its height (black writers in Paris were convinced that their conversations were being reported to the CIA) it wasn't a time for any kind of book that didn't seem to adhere to conventional notions of politics. The American Communist Party was starting to fall apart as its members were hounded, lost their jobs, and in some cases went to prison. Its influence on black writers was in decline, though a few still gave it their support. Lloyd Brown, author of the 1951 prison novel, *Iron City*, pointed out that white liberals were quick to distance themselves from communism in the Cold War atmosphere of the 1950s, "while glossing over the actual hard work that had been conducted by the Communist Party in defending black rights and black lives since the 1930s."

As the 1950s developed new black writers got their novels published. Jackson brings in Herbert Simmons, whose *Corner Boy* he describes as "a gritty novel of black urban life," in which Simmons "graphically revealed the institutionalisation of narcotics and gang violence in urban America." New black poets appeared, among them Ted Joans, Bob Kaufman, and Leroi Jones, all of them linked to the

Beat movement. And James Baldwin continued to produce important books, including *Giovanni's Room*, set in Paris, and *Another Country*, which moved to New York and especially Greenwich Village. In an interesting aside, Jackson says that Seymour Krim, who had written a couple of provocative essays about white attitudes towards blacks and his own experiences in Harlem, "was nearly a double for the character James Baldwin would name Vivaldo in the 1961 novel *Another Country*." Jackson's discussion of Krim, Norman Mailer's *The White Negro*, hipsters, and the whole question of how and why many whites wanted to identify with black experiences and life-styles is well worth reading.

There are a few minor errors in this book. A sentence is repeated on page 182, and elsewhere Eugene McCarthy is confused with Joseph McCarthy. Norman Podhoretz's famous attack on the Beats, "The Know-Nothing Bohemians," comes out as "No Nothing Bohemians." And Jackson seems shaky when he touches on jazz. Charlie Parker died in 1955, not 1956. He gets Thelonious (as in Thelonious Monk) wrong several times. And he refers to "Duke Ellington and his band's great soloist voice on the trumpet, Roy Eldridge." I don't think Eldridge was ever a member of the Ellington orchestra, certainly not on a regular basis, and it's probably true to say that he became best known to many jazz fans for being featured with the white bands led by Artie Shaw and Gene Krupa.

Minor quibbles apart, *The Indignant Generation* is a splendid book, succinctly argued and packed with information about writers, books, magazines, and organisations. Jackson provides some useful critical comments on various novels, short stories, and poems. And he rightly indicates how the American Communist Party played a significant role in getting black writers into print, even if its influence wasn't always completely benign.

THE INDIGNANT GENERATION: A NARRATIVE HISTORY OF AFRICAN AMERICAN WRITERS AND CRITICS, 1934-1960
by Lawrence P. Jackson, Princeton University Press.579 pages.£24.95. ISBN 978-0-691-14135-0
Distributed in the U.K. by John Wiley & Sons Ltd.

THE MASSES

There is currently (April, 2011) an exhibition at the National Gallery in London called *An American Experiment: George Bellows and the Ashcan Painters*. And there's an excellent small book accompanying the exhibition, but nowhere in it is it mentioned that Bellows, and his contemporary, John Sloan, were for a time closely associated with the radical magazine, *The Masses*. Neither the exhibition or the book claim to be comprehensive surveys of Bellows and the Ashcan group, so there is perhaps a good reason why that episode in their lives is left out. But the book under review does focus attention on the material that Bellows and Sloan contributed to the magazine.

Rachel Schreiber describes *The Masses* as a "small-run journal published in New York City between 1911 and 1917," which seems a rather low-key description but she then says that it "was an exceptional magazine produced during an exceptional decade." It was started by Piet Vlag who ran the restaurant at the Rand School of Social Science, a socialist establishment which aimed to "educate workers and raise class-consciousness." Vlag persuaded many of the writers and intellectuals who came into the school to contribute, even though he couldn't pay them. *The Masses,* like many political and literary publications, never sold enough copies to make it a profitable venture and its use of graphics kept production costs high. According to Schreiber it always depended on outside donors who were often "wealthy philanthropists who were sympathetic to socialism and enjoyed *The Masses'* exposés." Neither the bohemians on the editorial board, nor the philanthropists, liked to have details of the funding too well-known so that their standing in their respective communities would not be affected.

The years prior to the First World War were a time of social ferment. Eugene V. Debs had received almost one million votes when he stood for the Presidency, the I.W.W. was flexing its muscles, and unions in New York were organising strikes among the large immigrant workforce in the city. There was a general feeling that the time was ripe for change. Needless to say, there was opposition to change, especially among business leaders, conservative politicians, and others with a vested interest in maintaining the status quo. But many writers and artists were inclined to support socialist ideas, and when *The Masses* appeared it pulled in writers like Max Eastman, Floyd Dell, John Reed, and Mary Heaton Vorse, and artists such as George Bellows, John Sloan, Stuart Davis, and Robert Minor .

It needs to be noted that it was not a theoretical journal, no matter how much it wanted to promote socialism. Schreiber describes it as "idealistic," but makes it clear that it was "humorous, literary, and journalistic," and she quotes Floyd Dell as saying that it "stood for fun, truth, beauty, realism, freedom, feminism, revolution." Humour was a key factor in the magazine, especially in the visual work. I don't think there is any doubt that it's the drawings that have retained their interest over the years. Irving Howe once pointed out that "not much of the political writing in *The Masses* has worn well," whereas the art work can still pack a punch. There was a drawing by Boardman Robinson (it's not in Schreiber's book) of two working-class women talking. One asks the other why she's celebrating and is told that her son is being released from prison. He was sentenced to ten years but has been given three off for good behaviour. "Ah," says the first woman, "I wish I had a son like that." There's humour there, though some might claim that it's of a patronising kind. A darker humour comes through in K.R. Chamberlain's drawing of an obviously upper-class couple watching soldiers marching off to war, and the woman saying, "It checks the growth of the undesirable classes, don't you know." I've read some of the poetry that was published in *The Masses* and very little of it still has energy or relevance.

Schreiber states that "the muscular male appeared regularly in political cartoons that supported labour rights," and that in the anti-war cartoons he "served as the iconic and symbolic ideal for the might of the working-class." That "might" was seen as a contrast to the supposed weakness of the ruling class, and in the illustrations bosses were often shown as bloated while younger well-to-do types come across as effete and indolent. These were all stereotypes, of course, and in the case of representations of the working-class they could almost lend themselves to confirming suspicions about workers being "brutish, unintelligent, and prone to violence." But artists liked to play on ideas of working-class muscularity as compared to middle and upper-class flabbiness. There's a wonderful drawing by George Bellows, "Superior Brains: The Businessman's Class," which has a group of skinny or overweight, but clearly out-of-condition businessmen, being put through their paces by a trainer. It's effective and very funny, but really no more true than idealised drawings of supposedly fit and healthy workers.

One of Schreiber's main points is that mostly male figures appear in cartoons of industrial situations. And, of course, men did play a dominant role in heavy industry and many of the service industries, as well as in strikes. But women were heavily represented in the garment trades in New York and in the mills of New England and Massachusetts. In many ways, however, the artists tended to accept the idea, also believed by their supposed opponents, that "the normative worker was male," and that a woman's role should be mostly domestic. Schreiber says that "Unionists and other labour advocates took it for granted that men should be the primary wage earners," and she points out that, in fact, "the realities of working-class life" meant that everyone in a family (husband, wife, older children, the elderly) often had to contribute when possible. Women did do domestic work and look after children but they also had to do piecework in the home or work in sweat shops. There are a few drawings of women in these circumstances reproduced in the book and they mostly show them as worn-out and downtrodden. This was probably an accurate portrayal of their circumstances and it contrasted with the frequent images of working-class men towering over cringing bosses. Or there was Robert Minor's picture of "labour's lawyer," a giant fist punching its way into a courtroom and terrifying everyone there.

Minor was one of the most forceful of the artists linked to *The Masses*. It's significant that he and Art Young were overtly political artists and, unlike Bellows, Sloan, and others, did not also produce what might be called conventional (in the sense of non-political) work for the art market. And it's a fact that, once they lost contact with *The Masses*, Bellows and Sloan were no longer involved with direct social and political commentary. Schreiber notes that Robert Minor did produce work which focused on women's role in industry but that little of it got into *The Masses*. Was this because the editorial board "favoured the gendered distinction of active male working figures to passive female victims"? Perhaps not, though she does think that "the editors emphasised a visual strategy that elevated the muscular male working-class figure to heroic status in order to further their political aims, leaving female workers within the space of representation to serve only as symbols for the adverse aspects of industrial labour."

One of the most striking illustrations shows a large capitalist (easily identifiable by his top hat and coat tails, not to mention the grim expression on his face) pointing to an empty cradle and shouting "Breed" to a woman standing nearby. In the background is a gloomy factory with hordes of workers pouring in while large black clouds hang menacingly overhead. The clouds symbolise war (the word is actually printed among them). Schreiber has a neat discussion of this drawing by Art Young, but I couldn't help thinking that her idea that it is a "depiction of (male) workers and soldiers as dispensable fodder for industrial gain" may be pushing the gender analysis a bit too far. It may sound like nit-picking but I think I can see some female figures in the crowd, and Art Young would have been well aware that women worked in large numbers in mills and elsewhere and were just as much "dispensable fodder for industrial gain," as well as being affected by war. But I don't want to quarrel with Schreiber's general view that the role of women was often overlooked or underplayed in *The Masses*.

The suggestion that women should breed tied in with worries about eugenics prevalent at the time. The mass immigration policies that had led to an influx of people from Russia, Eastern Europe, Italy, and other places led to claims of "race suicide" as birth rates among white middle-class American-born women declined. *The Masses* satirised these fears by questioning how people with large families living in deplorable conditions could be expected to raise healthy children. Art Young's "Hell on Earth" pictured a mother with three young children in a hovel while the father (not at all a sturdy-looking type) stares in despair at a pile of bills falling off a small table. Young liked to tag on captions and this one read: "Questions for Eugenists: In an atmosphere of worry and fear, how can children be developed physically and morally?" Of course, some people would ask why the working-class had children if they couldn't afford them, but this was a time when birth control methods were known about but were still frowned on because they would, it was said, encourage women to be promiscuous. The notorious Anthony Comstock and his Society for the Suppression of Vice attempted to limit the circulation of information relating to contraception and other matters. *The Masses* supported Margaret Sanger in her work and frequently attacked Comstock. There are three illustrations (one by George Bellows, two by Robert Minor) which lampoon him, but one of the sharpest comments on what happens when proper forms of birth control aren't available was K.R. Chamberlain's "Family Limitation - Old Style," which shows a woman about to drop a baby into the river.

Artists in *The Masses* were fervently anti-war and Schreiber has some interesting comparisons to make between their views and those expressed by illustrators in more-conventional magazines. While Robert Minor drew an officer looking at a massive but headless man and saying, "At last a perfect soldier!", and Art Young showed a tough-looking worker confronting a capitalist and asserting that, having done the fighting, the workers would now take over, the suffragist magazine, *The Woman Citizen*, had covers which hammered away at the idea that if women played a key role in the war effort (they were called "Win-the-war-Women") by working in factories, on the land, or even just knitting, they would earn the right to vote. The women in these pictures were usually pretty, neatly-dressed, and if in a domestic setting shown only with one healthy child. It would seem that there was only a single-issue involved, that of getting the vote, and that otherwise there was an acceptance of the traditional female roles, with women only going outside them when an emergency arose. A K.R. Chamberlain drawing in *The Masses* suggested what would really happen once the war was over and men attempted to dominate again.

The editors of *The Masses* had never been totally in agreement about how political its art work should be, and not all of the illustrations were as didactic as some of those I've mentioned. John Sloan's "The Return from Toil" is simply a picture of a group of tidily dressed working-class girls walking arm-in-arm and seemingly having a good time. And the same artist's "The Bachelor Girl" can be taken as a positive statement about a woman living independently, though that may be a form of social comment, not all of society thinking it right and proper that women should be able to act in that way. With regard to illustrations that didn't fit into the political category there was a mocking little rhyme in circulation:

They draw nude women for *The Masses*
Thick, fat, ungainly lasses –
How does that help the working classes?

But it's undeniable that social and political commentary was a priority for most of the artists, as it was for the writers, and once America entered the First World War in 1917 trouble was almost inevitable. Draconian laws restricting free speech came into force and were cited by the Post Office as the reason for refusing to deliver copies of *The Masses* to subscribers and that added to the problems it had been having for some time with distributors who refused to place it on bookstalls because of its anti-war sentiments. Some of its contributors (George Bellows was one of them) deserted the magazine. And then the Government decided to prosecute some of the editors for allegedly conspiring to obstruct recruitment and enlistment in the armed forces. Two trials took place and both resulted in hung juries. Art Young was the one artist to appear in court, along with the writers Max Eastman and Floyd Dell, and even though they walked free the magazine was effectively at an end.

As I mentioned earlier, it's the illustrations in *The Masses* that have survived best. Just look at the Robert Minor drawing on the cover of Rachel Schreiber's book. It's called "Pittsburgh," and is a comment on the use of militia to suppress a strike. A worker is impaled on the bayonet of a rifle held by a lunging militiaman, and Schreiber refers to the "forceful crayon strokes and deep contrasts between the dense black marks and the white page." Its power is still evident. She also describes it as a "striking example of the dynamic, powerful images of the muscular male workers that had become standard fare by the time of its publication in *The Masses* in August, 1916," so it helps support her general thesis about the "workings of gender and the role of images in activist practices" early in the 20th Century. She presents her case efficiently, though at times I couldn't help thinking that, given the period they lived in, the artists couldn't help portraying men and women, and their respective roles in society, in certain ways. Hutchins Hapgood, a writer who shared many of the same interests with the writers and artists of *The Masses* (see his *Types From City Streets*, with lively illustrations by Glenn O. Coleman, an artist associated with the Ashcan group) later wrote an autobiography called *A Victorian in the Modern World*, and that title perhaps points to the crux of the problem, which was that they were living at a time when old and new values were often in competition for the attention of creative people and this led to inevitable contradictions in their attitudes and activities.

Gender and Activism in a Little Magazine is a fascinating book and is largely free of the worst forms of academic jargon. Rachel Schreiber has not tried to tell the whole story of the rise and fall of *The Masses*, and though she does sketch in the backgrounds of the leading artists who contributed to the magazine it is necessary to turn to other books for information about their activities and those of more artists who are referred to. Her lengthy bibliography will easily provide the relevant information. I ought to add that the book is well illustrated throughout.

GENDER AND ACTIVISM IN A LITTLE MAGAZINE: THE MODERN FIGURES OF THE MASSES by Rachel Schreiber

Ashgate Publishing Ltd. 182 pages. £60. ISBN 978-1-4094-0945-8

THE GREAT FEAR

McCarthyism is, of course, the term we use to describe the kind of witch-hunting and blacklisting associated with the anti-communist purge in America during the early fifties. It's a common fallacy to assume that Senator Joseph McCarthy launched the purge, and that when he eventually fell from grace his vicious practices disappeared with him.

David Caute's massively documented survey of anti-communism during the Truman and Eisenhower administrations makes it clear that McCarthy was merely a product of the hysteria his name now represents, and that it flourished both before and after his brief reign.

There had been anti-radical drives in America prior to 1945 (most notably just after the first world war), and during the thirties there were smear campaigns about alleged communist influence on New Deal policies. But the mood of the times was then against any mass display of anti-communism. Even so, we need only look at a book like Eugene Lyons' *The Red Decade* (published in 1941) to see how the ground was being prepared for a purge. Its lists of suspect individuals and organisations must have helped nourish the phobias of future witch-hunters. Once the second world war ended, and the Soviet Union was increasingly seen as the enemy, the mood in America changed. By 1947 events in Europe and Asia had created a feeling of disillusionment with the hopes and promises of the war years. And the Republicans, anxious to reassert themselves after 14 years of domination by the Democrats, were only too willing to exploit the rumblings of discontent for all they were worth.

American businessmen were calling for a blacklist of communists as early as 1946, Left-wing writers were investigated in Hollywood in 1947, and in the same year President Truman ordered security checks on all federal employees. He needed to counter Republisan charges that he was soft on reds, and also raise enthusiasm for his foreign policies. And though it was communism abroad that was the real threat, it was easier to get tough with the supposed communist threat at home.

Not that the American Communist Party was very strong - but it was an obvious target. Curiously enough it seemed that, as its influence declined, so hysteria about it increased. A few genuine spy cases didn't help matters, and when the Korean war broke out in 1950, and the communist conspiracy appeared to be in full swing, the hysteria came to a head.

Investigations began into the activities of certain social workers, teachers, civil servants, writers, industrial workers, actors, seamen and others whose connections were suspect. At the same time members of the press, the academies, the entertainment business and the judiciary thought it expedient to let it be known that they weren't prepared to tolerate dissidents in their organisations.

The results were witch-hunts and blacklists, often helped by House Un-American Activities Committee hearings, but frequently needing little more than innuendo, references to events years before, unsubstantiated accusations and implications by association, to trigger them off. Evidence of radical literature in their possession was enough to get some people fired and blacklisted.

David Caute thoroughly covers the pathetic stories of careers cut short, broken marriages and even suicides, as pressures built up. There were failures of nerve by establishment liberals who ought to have known better and risked more, and acts of defiance by ordinary people who just got tired of being pushed around and fought back. There were also the minor officials who took a delight in denying a disabled war veteran assistance because he'd been named as a communist, or cancelling a widow's pension because her late husband had been under suspicion, or refusing benefits to the unemployed if they'd been sacked for political reasons. True, many of these decisions were reversed when taken to court, but in the meantime people had suffered. And there were wives insulted and refused service in shops, families harassed out of their homes, children beaten up at school - all because opportunist politicians, and elements of the press, were drumming up a frenzy of fear and mistrust.

One of the most interesting sections in *The Great Fear* is that dealing with the effects of the purge on the trade unions. One might have expected them, at least, to have made some kind of a stand - especially when activists who had served the unions well during the organising drives of the thirties were being hounded. But, with a few honourable exceptions, they backed down, even to the extent of carrying out their own purges to assure the authorities of their loyalty.

Management, of course, thrived on the situation. It was a heaven-sent opportunity to get rid of militants, to split unions, and to ensure that company puppets were in positions of power. And it could all be done in the name of patriotism.

David Caute, rightly I think, stresses that America did eventually overcome the Great Fear. Some people had kept their nerve all along, others recovered it after brief retreats into the convenience of silence. And it would be foolish to pretend that the purge was anywhere near as bad as the kind of thing carried out by Stalin. But it did affect thousands of lives, as well as help spread a blanket of conformity over much of the country. And its impact on some aspects of American society - such as the union movement - was far reaching enough for it to be still felt today. *The Great Fear* chronicles a sad time in American history, but it's good that Caute has brought his committed and informed mind to bear on it. We need to be constantly reminded of how easy it is to whip up hysteria, and of how much damage it can do when it inevitably gets out of hand.

THE GREAT FEAR by David Caute, Secker & Warburg, London, 1978

JAMES T. FARRELL

Writers frequently suffer from the vagaries of fashion and it's not unusual for a novelist to be forgotten within a few years of his death. In James T. Farrell's case it would seem that the collapse of his reputation has been almost complete, and it's probably only in a few universities, mostly in the United States, that his name now evokes any interest. And yet, at one time, his novels and short stories were easily available in both hardback and paperback editions and he was often mentioned alongside Wolfe, Hemingway, Steinbeck, Faulkner, and other leading American authors. That Farrell's standing has declined so much is curious and invites at least a brief examination of his work.

He was born in Chicago in 1904, the son of a teamster and a domestic servant. His parents were too poor to provide for him and when he was three he went to live with his grandparents, who were relatively better off. Farrell's environment during his childhood was that of the Irish-American ghetto, and although he did not personally experience great material poverty he was in a position to observe it, and its effects, at close quarters. It would be wrong, however, to assume that his observations persuaded him that simple economic factors were responsible for what he found lacking in the lives of his relatives, friends, and neighbours. Farrell was keenly aware of the spiritual and intellectual poverty which affected even those who were in reasonably comfortable circumstances.

During his schooldays on Chicago's South Side he was lucky enough to encounter teachers who encouraged his interest in literature. He graduated from high school, did some routine jobs, and studied at the University of Chicago, then noted for the strength of its sociology department. But Farrell never completed his university courses and preferred instead to follow his own leads. He hitchhiked to New York and worked as a clerk for six months while studying assiduously and writing. He had, someone once said, "embarked on a fierce regimen of reading and writing, in and out of school, from which he never subsequently deviated." Murray Kempton, who knew Farrell in the Thirties, described him as "the best-educated young writer of his time," his auto-didacticism taking in not only literature but also history, politics, sociology, philosophy, and other subjects.

A year in Paris in the early-Thirties further helped Farrell broaden his range of interests.

By the mid-Thirties he was established on the American literary scene. He had started to write his *Studs Lonigan* trilogy, closely based on his youthful experiences and observations, in 1929, and the first part, *Young Lonigan*, appeared to acclaim in 1932. *The Young Manhood of Studs Lonigan* followed in 1934 and *Judgement Day* in 1935. Farrell even managed to publish another novel, not linked to the Lonigan series, in 1933, along with short-story collections in 1934 and 1935. His articles, stories, and reviews were regularly published in magazines like *Pagany, Dynamo, Story, The New Masses*, and *The American Mercury*.

Farrell had what was once described as a "modest but significant political collaboration with the Communist Party, especially in cultural activities," in the early-Thirties, though he was never actually a Party member. In 1935 he was invited to give a paper at the First American Writers' Congress, a communist-organised event, and chose to talk about the short-story, referring favourably to left-wing writers like Nelson Algren, Ben Field, and Whittaker Chambers, the latter still a struggling communist author and only later to become famous for the part he played in the downfall of Alger Hiss. But Farrell's relationship with communism was at an uneasy stage. He had begun to question Party control of creative projects and was increasingly critical of writers like Jack Conroy and Clara Weatherwax, who were seen as stalwarts of the proletarian novel, and Clifford Odets, whose plays were praised by *The Daily Worker*. Matters came to a head in 1936 when Farrell's *A Note on Literary Criticism* was published. This was a book-length attack on the way that communist critics expected writers to respect formulas laid down by the Party. Farrell's ideas were not dissimilar to those of Trotsky, in that he dissented from the notion of a proletarian culture and firmly stated that a creative artist had to follow his own dictates and not those of cultural commissars.

Trotsky's name was not mentioned in Farrell's book but the communist press took issue with his theories and activists such as Isidor Schneider and Michael Gold went into print to denounce Farrell and point out how he was deviating from the Party line. Not surprisingly, he soon aligned himself with the American Trotskyists of the Socialist Workers Party. This involvement was to last until the mid-Forties, when Farrell slowly but surely shifted to the right, though not excessively so. By 1948 he was a firm supporter of the Marshall Plan for the reconstruction of Europe and was quoted as saying, "Only American wealth and power stands in the way of Stalinist expansion." To be fair, he never became the kind of one-time left-winger who cried mea culpa for his past affinities, nor did he name names and indulge in the vicious anti-communist rhetoric of the McCarthy years.

In 1973 Farrell said, in the introduction to his *Judith and Other Stories*: "I have attempted to create out of the life I have seen, known, experienced, heard about, and imagined, a panoramic story of our days and years, a story which would continue through as many books as I would be able to write." It's a good description of what he did do and it points to his concern to make his fiction relevant to the times he lived through. He often conceived his novels as part of a series, as with the three that tell the story of Studs Lonigan, five that explore the life of Danny O'Neill, and three outlining the activities of Bernard Carr. In the late-Fifties he started a new series, *A Universe of Time*, and had completed the twelfth book in it just a few weeks before he died in 1979. Many of the same people, sometimes under different names, appear in Farrell's fiction, and he himself is there as Danny O'Neill, Eddie Ryan, and, partly, as Bernard Carr. But he wasn't simply a writer using thinly-disguised autobiography and he shaped his material to suit his purposes. It's true that some of his books can almost be used as guides to certain events, an example being *Yet Other Waters*, the third novel in the Bernard Carr trilogy. Farrell's intention had been to trace the fortunes of a young writer coming to New York in the Thirties and facing the twin perils of Stalinism and commercialism. At the novel's centre is a conference clearly based on the 1935 American Writers' Congress, and a comparison with the historical record will show that Farrell only lightly fictionalised certain characters and events. In the novel an intellectual called "John Keefe" delivers a speech in which he asks for the term "Proletarian literature" to be replaced by "People's literature" and is promptly condemned by a Party activist named "Jake." In real life it was Kenneth Burke who made the speech and Joseph Freeman who attacked him, Party policy being to still support the idea of proletarian writing. Popular Front ideology, would later change that. A proletarian novelist, Pat Devlin, makes a speech in the novel and says, "There is more of the vigour of proletarian literature in a strike leaflet, however crudely written, than there is in all the style and pseudo-erudition of a college graduate's painful course from the saints to the Revolution," which Bernard Carr takes to be an attack on him. Devlin was based on Jack Conroy, who actually said, "a strike bulletin or an impassioned leaflet are of more moment than the three hundred prettily and faultlessly written pages about the private woes of a gigolo." Farrell and Conroy never did get along and fact became fiction when Farrell decided to use the feud in a novel.

The same themes were worked and re-worked in many of Farrell's writings, and he seemed anxious to record how authors and intellectuals were corrupted by too close a contact with communism and with commercialism, both leading to mediocrity. His final book, the posthumously published *Sam Holman*, has a main character based on Herbert Solow who passes through various phases, from fellow-travelling with the communists, to alliance with the Trotskyists, and finally a job on Henry Luce's business magazine, *Fortune*. It may be that this aspect of Farrell's writing is of interest only to cultural historians of the New York intellectual world of the Thirties and Forties, but it could also be that the ideas he was dealing with - political and commercial corruption of values - never really lose their relevance. Farrell always tried to hold out against any activity which he thought would endanger his principles, and in the Fifties, when his books weren't selling and he was almost destitute, he refused to take teaching posts or turn his hand to any kind of writing simply to make money. He said, "I began writing in my own way and I shall go on doing it. This is my first and last word on the subject."

If the kind of political fiction I've referred to does have its limitations then it may be that Farrell's reputation will have to rest on the novels and stories which deal with Studs Lonigan, Danny O'Neill, and the Irish-American world of Chicago in the first thirty or so years of this century. His rites of passage explorations move around this landscape, recording everything in vivid detail. And, contrary to many assumptions, it's not necessarily the slum neighbourhoods which are described. When he later wrote about how he had conceived *Studs Lonigan*, Farrell was careful to point out that he had deliberately set the book in a relatively-affluent area where people had steady jobs and owned their own houses, so that he could avoid a kind of vulgar economic determinism which would make Stud's downfall easily explainable. He was enough of a Marxist to suggest that the onset of the Depression hastened his decline by wiping out his savings and destroying his job, but he said that personal failings had started the slide as Studs drank, gambled, ran with gangs, and generally gave himself up to the life of the streets. What Farrell was getting at was the way in which social conformity - the pressure to go with the crowd, agree with the group, and subjugate the sensitive side of one's personality in favour of a rough macho image - could destroy an individual. When he wrote his Danny O'Neill novels, which roughly parallel Studs Lonigan in their time-sequence, his central character found a way out of the restrictive cultural environment, just as Farrell himself had done. The world he described may be a specific one, and its surface details consequently dated, but the situations evoked are still very real today.

Criticisms of Farrell's work have often focused on his need to record everything and the way in which this can get in the way of the story. Malcolm Cowley once alleged that "Farrell's life work ....is not a work of invention or combination or construction, as with other novelists, but an immense labour of recollection," but this perhaps overlooks the care with which he shaped what he remembered into fiction that could be compelling in its intensity.

He was not just an old-fashioned naturalist and had read James Joyce and other modernists so that he knew how to use interior monologues and dreams and the intermingling of the personal life and the life of the streets. In his best work the details are an integral part of the narrative and emphasise how the characters respond to their surroundings and are, in turn, affected by them. It can't be denied that Farrell could sometimes be a clumsy writer, nor that his earnestness could occasionally turn ponderous, but he got close to achieving what he set out to do in terms of writing "a panoramic story" of the times he lived through.

NOTES

Most of Farrell's books, over fifty of them covering novels, collections of stories, poetry, essays, literary criticism, and other matters, are now out-of-print. An exception is *Studs Lonigan*, a paperback edition of which was published in 1993 by the University of Illinois Press. The same press also published a selection of short fiction under the title *Chicago Stories* in 1998. Both books have useful introductions and listings of Farrell's books.

Farrell's *A Note on Literary Criticism* was reprinted in 1992 by Columbia University Press and has an informative introduction by Alan Wald. Wald also wrote a book, *James T. Farrell: The Revolutionary Socialist Years* (New York University Press, 1978), which provides a fascinating survey of Farrell's political involvements and how they were reflected in his novels and short stories. I've not mentioned individual stories in my article but many of them do touch on political events and personalities and, like the novel, *Yet Other Waters*, provide fictionalised portraits of various writers and activists. It's easy to recognise them if one has a basic knowledge of left-wing American politics of the Thirties and Forties.

A Paris Year: Dorothy and James T. Farrell, 1931-1932 by Edgar Marquess Branch, published by Ohio University Press, 1998, is a detailed account of Farrell's year abroad, using diaries, letters, and other materials, and again showing how he turned all his observations and experiences into fiction.

B. TRAVEN

The "mystery" of B. Traven seems to have been solved by Will Wyatt and Robert Robinson in a BBC TV programme, a transcript of which was printed in *The Listener* for the 4th and 11th January, 1979. Traven was B. Traven Torsvan, Hal Croves, Ret Marut, and Herman Albert Otto Maximilian Feige, born in Swiebodzin, Poland. He was probably a few other people along the way, including Richard Maurhut, author of an anti-war novel published in 1916. The information that he was Feige was, essentially, the net result of the BBC researchers' investigations, most of the other information having been tossed around over the years by earlier trackers on the Traven trail. But the programme did offer a good account of Traven's life, or at least as much of it as is known about. It clarified some of the existing details, and it helped dispel a few myths, most notably the one about Traven somehow being an illegitimate son of Kaiser Wilhelm II. But then Traven himself probably only encouraged a belief in that notion in order to keep people guessing. It was, after all, well in keeping with his overall philosophy. "If you do not wish to be lied to," he wrote, "do not ask questions. The only real defence civilised man has against anybody who bothers him is to lie. There would be no lies if there were no questions." If it is pointed out that there was one occasion when he did give his real name - when questioned by the police in London in 1923 - then one can reply that, being on the run from the German government under the name Ret Marut, he perhaps found it convenient to use his real identity in the circumstances. Telling the truth can sometimes be as useful as telling lies.

However, without in any way wishing to denigrate the BBC programme, I think it is fair to say that it didn't take us much closer to a clear picture of what made him tick. That aspect of life he kept to himself to the end, other than in the way it was outlined by his writing. Again, this was in line with his philosophy. The man, he said, wasn't important. It was the books that counted.

With this in mind it's interesting to consider how his literary reputation stands at the moment. His books - one or other of them at least - are always in print somewhere in the world, and an upsurge of interest in the United States in recent years resulted in reprints of most of his novels. But one suspects that few people in the British literary world - especially that part of it dominated by academics - know much about Traven as a writer. They may have come across his work if they've moved in left-wing circles, though this is perhaps truer of the Continent than the British Isles. In this country he seems to be looked on as some kind of superior adventure writer rather than as a provocative novelist with an idiosyncratic, but sustained social and political position. Of course, Traven doesn't fit into a neat category, nor are his books of the kind that would engage people whose experiences and interests rarely stretch outside the literary. Picaresque stories, they heave with life as it is lived at the lower levels.

Which isn't to say that they suggest that it is in any way nobler, better, or cleaner there. On the contrary, they are clear in their implications that it can be brutish and mean. But perhaps the concerns are clearer?

One of Traven's earliest books, *The Cotton-Pickers*, has just been re-issued in a new translation, and it's interesting to compare it to the first British edition, published in 1956. There have always been problems about exactly how Traven's books were written and translated. The subject is far too complicated to delve into here, so I'll merely refer to the 1956 edition (translated by Eleanor Brockett) in relation to the new one, translated by Traven's widow, Rosa Elena Lujan. It could be assumed that the latter's relationship with Traven would enable her to have the specialised knowledge necessary to understand his style, but this clearly doesn't automatically follow. Traven was often secretive with her, so much so that he once told her that he had no knowledge of German despite the fact that she had seen him typing in that language!

From an admittedly brief comparison I'd be inclined to the view that, although both versions contain faults in terms of not always ringing true in English, there is little between them from the point of view of readability. There is a compelling quality about the basic story, and the overall tone of the writing, which more than makes up for the occasional lapses of the translators. What is noticeable is the difference in which the two editions are put together. The 1956 edition contained forty-two, often short chapters. The latest one has only twenty-five, some of the shorter ones having been linked.

Leaving aside the stylistic questions the book still reads well. It was first published, in German, as Der Wobbly, a pointer to the fact that the main character in it - an American called Gales - occasionally mentions the I.W.W. (Industrial Workers of the World - Wobblies, as they were nicknamed) in a sympathetic manner.

And throughout the novel there is a general tendency towards the anarcho-syndicalist theories of the Wobblies. The I.W.W. Songbook had the slogan "To fan the flames of discontent" on its cover, and it is, perhaps, no coincidence that, wherever Gales works, a strike occurs. When this is pointed out to him by one of his employers he replies, innocently, "It's not my fault if men get dissatisfied and want something better. I never say anything to such men. I keep mum, and let others do the talking. So it beats me, everywhere I go people say I'm a Wobbly, a troublemaker." An ironic sense of humour was another Wobbly characteristic.

It is interesting to speculate on how Traven managed to pick up the I.W.W. ideas in order to write *The Cotton-Pickers,* and have it published in Germany in 1926, bearing in mind that he couldn't have arrived in Mexico before 1923. There have been suggestions that he possibly didn't experience the events he describes, and that they were passed on to him by an American he met. Unlike some theories about Traven's work this one is worth considering seriously. A combination of someone else's experiences and a writer's own observations are not unusual in fiction. And the I.W.W. references could be explained by such a situation. Traven may have met an American Wobbly after he'd arrived in Mexico. Many Americans drifted into the country in the Twenties in search of work or adventure. Some had been there since the early days of the Revolution, and had even participated in it. The I.W. W. was still an influential organisation in the early Twenties, despite the rise of the Communists, friction amongst the Wobblies, and the attacks on its members by the American authorities. So, the use of Wobbly ideas in Traven's book doesn't seem to me to be all that surprising, particularly when one considers that few, if any fully-rounded theories are actually referred to at length. What the Wobblies were good at was expressing the natural resentment of the underdog, and on the whole it is this kind of attitude that comes through in the book. One suspects that Gales may know much more than he cares to admit, but that he finds it useful to disguise it beneath a rough-and-ready exterior, and this again would tie in with rank-and-file feelings among the Wobblies. A mixture of hard-reading and hard-living was not all that unusual, with Shelley, Marx, Nietzsche, and a multitude of political tracts tucked in with the essentials that transient workers took with them.

The general principles of the I.W.W. were also partly drawn from French and Spanish anarcho-syndicalist sources, and the organisation maintained contact with people like Tom Mann, one of the leading British exponents of syndicalism. There was, prior to the First World War, a large amount of interest in syndicalist schemes throughout Europe, so Traven, as Ret Marut, would have been familiar with them before he even got to Mexico. His anarchist sympathies when he was Marut were well-known, and he was a participant in the ill-fated Munich Revolution of 1918/19, which involved socialists, communists, anarchists, syndicalists, and others. That his general background would have led him to consort with Wobblies in Mexico is not surprising, though there is no evidence that I know of to indicate that he was ever a member of the organisation. But its basic philosophy would clearly appeal to him because Traven could never be described as a communist or a socialist. His own attitudes were derived from anarchist doctrines, especially those of the individualist anarchist variety. The 19th Century German philosopher Max Stirner was his spiritual father. And Stirner (admired in some anarchist circles, though criticised in others) was thoroughly attacked by Marx and Engels in *The German Ideology.*

Personally, I'm not inclined to think that the statements made in *The Cotton-Pickers* ever add up to much more than the kind of grass-roots philosophising one can hear at union meetings, or whenever a bunch of disgruntled workers get together. I do not say this in a derogatory manner. It is precisely because Traven can put across this type of statement so effectively that his books survive. Had they been full of more-obviously intellectual theorising they would, I feel, have faded into obscurity long ago. But their mixture of powerful narration and down-to-earth comment has an obvious appeal. One can understand that much of what is said is anti-capitalist, but when I read in a Traven book, "Sing Sing...is the residence of all New Yorkers who get caught. The rest have offices on Wall Street," I am reminded not so much of Marx, but of my father saying something very similar when, as a child, I walked with him past the local prison and asked him about the people inside it. And my father was not a well-read man, nor an overtly politically-conscious one. But he had grown up in Liverpool in the early part of the century, and had gone to sea in 1911. What he had absorbed was, I suggest, drawn from the general social consciousness of the working-class life of that period, when syndicalism, socialism, trade unionism, and the like were espoused on street corners. No doubt Marut had picked up similar ideas during his wanderings as an impoverished actor in the Germany of the pre-1914 era. He was obviously something of an intellectual, albeit a bohemian one, but I think sufficient of the street-corner style got through to him so that he could see it as the natural expression of ordinary people, and thus make his characters seem genuine when he started writing as Traven.

That there is still a fair amount of confusion about Traven's basic philosophy is evident from James Naremore's introduction to the screenplay of *The Treasure of the Sierra Madre.* In his otherwise valuable comments he refers to Traven's "conscious" Marxist ideas. Now it's easy to accept that it is possible for someone to have Marxist ideas without being a professed Marxist, but it needs to be noted that if Traven's opinions on certain matters were similar then they were probably so through coincidence, and not because of any formal studies, or an overall philosophical position. I've already mentioned that Traven was not a communist or a socialist, and George Woodcock, writing about Michael Baumann's book on Traven (*T.L.S.*, 27th August, 1976) said, "there is no shred of communism or socialism in the generally understood sense in any of the novels." This seems to me to be true, even if some people find it unpalatable, just as it is true that, to quote Woodcock again, the libertarianism that pervades them "is of the extreme individualist kind."

It happens to be a fact that Traven wrote largely about working people, peasants, and down-and-outs, and seemingly operated in the area of fiction that usually gets labelled "proletarian." But he was reputed to have himself said that this was "pure accident," and that he had just happened to have come across more of that type of person. From the point of view that he often dealt with the struggle of peasants against authority he can be easily quoted to illustrate a socialist message. But the reader is deluding himself if he thinks that this is the complete picture. Scattered around his books are comments that hardly square with a portrait of a man who thought the working-class and its organisations beyond reproach: "They are more patriotic than the Kaiser's generals ever could be, and more narrow-minded than a Methodist preacher's wife" (*The Death Ship*); "Unions exist for a good reason: both capital and labour need them... When adequately paid and decently treated, this army is eager to fight any system that threatens their liberty to work for capital. In this way, unions are the best mates that capital ever had." (*The White Rose*). And when workers are vindictive, nasty, or opportunistic it is not suggested that they are like that because of the immediate problems of the capitalist system. It is human nature that is at fault on a grand scale, and though the smashing of the system is a necessary step in the direction of a better society it will only be a first step. A massive change of consciousness must follow if the old problems are not to appear again in a new disguise.

There are, it is true, what could be called Marxist ideas in *The Treasure of the Sierra Madre.* Take the following, for example:

"The discussion about the registration of their claim brought comprehension of their changed standing in life. With every ounce more of gold possessed by them, they left the proletarian class and neared that of the property holders, the well-to-do middle class. So far they had never had anything of value to protect against thieves....Those who up to this time had been considered by them as their proletarian brethren were now enemies against whom they had to protect themselves. As long as they had owned nothing of value, they had been slaves of their hungry bellies, slaves to those who had the means to fill their bellies. All this was changed now. They had reached the first step by which man becomes the slave of his property." Still, this kind of analysis is one that was (and is) shared by anarchists and Marxists alike. It is the solution to it that brings out the differences in their philosophies.

When John Huston wrote and directed the film version of Traven's book he changed elements of the original story in order to make it easier to handle, and also to fit in with certain Hollywood conventions. There are asides and digressions in the novel which were completely dropped from the film, and Traven's firm anti-capitalist, anti-clerical tone was largely smoothed over. Traven never seems to imply that, had the men not fallen out amongst themselves, they could have been successful and led happy-ever-after lives. It is always implicit in his story-telling that, no matter what the results of the expedition, their attitudes would be affected by becoming property owners. And, one is led to think, affected for the worst. Huston's version, though direct in its suggestion that gold can corrupt, constantly hints at the possibility of future happiness if the men will only be reasonable with each other. It is a shift of emphasis that reduces Traven's political parable to a fuzzy moralising acceptable to Hollywood and the audience it aimed at.

In some ways, though, the film is tighter, and it has an overall sense of foreboding that isn't always evident in Traven. It is, in that sense, more psychologically based. There is an interesting contrast, too, in the way in which the entry and exit of a fourth prospector is handled. In the novel Lacaud drifts into the camp, is looked on suspiciously, but helps fight off some bandits, and generally seems concerned more with his own plans than with what the others are up to. He adds variety to the story and helps illustrate how the gold has affected the three men by making them distrust all strangers. Because of the type of person he is - a wandering loner, always hopeful about what tomorrow will bring - his appearance also allows Traven to reflect on human nature. In the film, Cody (as Lacaud is renamed) wants to share in the group's operation, and the others are prepared to kill him rather than accept this proposal or allow him to leave with an idea of what they've discovered. The problem is solved when Cody is shot in the bandit attack, an event which allows Huston to indulge in a degree of sentimentality suggesting, through the discovery of a letter on the body, that the three prospectors are lacking or missing something in life by not having the home connections that Cody had. It's a device clearly aimed at the cinema audience, whereas Traven was less sentimental. He never gives an indication that the men could be doing anything other than what they are doing.

Huston's film does have a grittiness that gives it honesty and, despite my reservations, its general lack of sentimentality makes it stand out from others of the period. As Naremore points out there is little or no use of the landscape for a softening effect, and the almost-obligatory introduction of a woman into the story is largely bypassed; Huston did hint at it by having the younger of the prospectors say, at the end of the film, that he's going to look up Cody's widow. The major part of the action is shown through close-ups of the dirty, unshaven faces of the men, and by a concentration on their dishevelled appearance.

And the performances Huston got from the actors helped build up the feeling of paranoia and inevitability that pervades the expedition from the start. It would be impossible to deny that Huston's script was responsible for the impact of the film. Whatever changes he made in Traven's story, whether ironing out the narrative or mellowing the social criticism, it still stands as a piece of craftmanship in its own right. And it is well worth having it available in book form.

The re-appearance of *The Cotton-Pickers,* and the appearance of the film script for *The Treasure of the Sierra Madre*, should help bring Traven to the attention of a new generation of readers, as well as providing pleasure for those who were already familiar with his books, but had, perhaps, been unable to obtain recent editions of them. There are few writers who can tell a story so powerfully, and make relevant political points, without reducing their capacity to be popular. The identity of the man may not be in any doubt, but the discovery of his real name will not in any way detract from his achievements. It is, as he himself said, the books that matter.

NOTE: The script of *The Treasure of the Sierra Madre* is one of a series of book editions of Warner Bros. screenplays. Others now available include *The Jazz Singer* and *Mystery of the Wax Museum*, with *High Sierra, The Adventures of Robin Hood*, and others to follow. Each contains the complete screenplay (including material dropped from the final version of the film), together with an informative introduction, some stills, and notes.

A collection of Traven's stories, *The Kidnapped Saint*, has been published as a companion volume to *The Cotton-Pickers.* As well as several stories it contains a memoir of Traven by his widow, a translation of some work produced by him when he was Ret Marut, and an interesting article on Marut's career between 1916 and 1922.

THE COTTON PICKERS by B. Traven. Allison & Busby, 1979

THE TREASURE OF THE SIERRA MADRE. Screenplay by John Huston, based on the novel by B. Traven. University of Wisconsin Press, 1979

BEATS IN BRITAIN

There were no British Beats but there were people in this country interested in what the Beats were doing, and who thought that their writings ought to be brought to the attention of British readers. In this short article I want to look at a handful of little magazines which attempted to introduce work by Kerouac, Ginsberg, Corso, Burroughs, and others, and to consider the opposition that, in some cases, they ran into. It needs to be kept in mind that although *On The Road* and some other Kerouac books were easily available here around 1960, and it was possible to find *Evergreen Review* and some City Lights publications in a few specialist bookshops, much new American writing was only just starting to break through the cultural barrier. And the Beats generally were often looked on with suspicion. BLAME THESE MEN FOR THE BEATNIK HORROR, screamed a headline in *The People,* a widely read Sunday newspaper, in August 1960, and beneath it were photos of Kerouac, Corso, Ginsberg, and Burroughs. Reactions to the Beats in literary circles were not quite as sensational but they often adopted a dismissive tone. In such an atmosphere, it was an adventurous editor who decided to give the Beats space in his magazine.

Michael Horovitz and David Sladen launched *New Departures* in the summer of 1959, and Sladen said: "I believe in the avant-garde of all ages; and the need to move with the times but not necessarily in step." And they gathered together a strong group of writers, many of who were then among the avant-garde. Samuel Beckett and Piero Heliczer were present, but the name that stands out in connection with this survey was William Burroughs, and he contributed a couple of short pieces revolving around junkies. I always did prefer to read Burroughs in short doses and there's still something exciting about the language and rhythms of the work that appeared in magazines around this time. Much of it later formed part of his novels, of course, but the impact often seemed much greater when it was read in a fragmentary way. The following issue of *New Departures* (a double combining 2 and 3) came out in 1960 and included poems by Robert Creeley, Corso, Ginsberg, and Kerouac. I'm focusing on the Beats but it's relevant to point out that Horovitz (David Sladen seems to have disappeared - what happened to him?) saw their work as part of the international avant-garde and also featured material by Eugene

Ionesco, Adrian Mitchell, and others. It wasn't a case of going overboard for the Beats but instead recognising that what they were doing could be viewed alongside adventurous writing from Britain and Europe. Horovitz has kept *New Departures* going in one form or another over the years but this account ends with the fourth issue in 1962 which was a "Jazz and Poetry" special with Creeley and Corso but also a large amount of space devoted to the expanding *New Departures* live performances in which Horovitz and Pete Brown played a leading role.

New Departures started its life in Oxford, though soon moving to London, and *Gemini* was also Oxford linked with an editorial address at New College. It's the Summer 1960 issue which is of interest here, largely because it contained a special section devoted to San Francisco poets. Bob Kaufman took pride of place with six poems and was, in fact, the strongest contributor. I doubt that anyone now remembers the others, like Alan Dienstag, Richard Gumbiner, and William Morris, except as names that crop up in one or two old magazines. None of them seem to have had any staying power as writers, unlike Kaufman whose best work is still worth reading. There was a poem by Gregory Corso in *Gemini* but it was not part of the San Francisco supplement.

Moving north to Edinburgh provides an interesting story, *Jabberwock* was the official publication of the Edinburgh University Renaissance Society, and the editorial in the issue for 1959 was a statement by Alex Neish saying that he was resigning because other people opposed his interest in what was happening in the United States. Neish made a general attack on the Scottish literary scene and said it was dominated by "middle-aged conformist hacks," whereas the Americans offered a glimpse of what was new and exciting. His final gesture as an editor was to print what must have been one of the widest selections of new American writing to have appeared in a magazine published in Britain. Ginsberg, Snyder, Corso, Whalen, Creeley, Kerouac, McClure, Burroughs, and Olson were all featured and a few eyebrows must have been raised at the references to sex and drugs in some of the material, even if they were, by today's standards, very mild. But I suspect that hostility was also aroused by the forms used. The Beats and others often returned to the modernist tradition that had been largely overlooked in the 1940s and 1950s. The sight of poems that didn't rhyme or even scan in a conventional manner and which roamed across the page probably annoyed many readers.

Alex Neish's determination to promote the new Americans alongside a few Scottish writers he considered interesting (Edwin Morgan, Ian Hamilton Finlay) led him to start his own magazine, *Sidewalk*, in 1960. Ginsberg, McClure, and Charles Olson were in the first issue, alongside French writers, and reading the magazine now wouldn't incline anyone to think that it represented anything unusual. But the atmosphere in Scotland in 1960 was such that *Sidewalk* was attacked from all sides. The most vicious onslaught appeared in the *Glasgow Evening Times* which had a headline reading ALONG THE SIDEWALK TO THE GUTTER and a report advising readers not to buy the magazine or allow it into their houses.

Sidewalk managed to stumble into a second issue with stories from Burroughs, Creeley, and Michael Rumaker, but the usual problems of money and distribution, plus the opposition the magazine had encountered, forced Neish to discontinue it. He published a few things of his own in magazines in the 1960s but then drifted into obscurity.

It might be useful to mention another Scottish encounter with prejudice against new writing which occurred in 1963. *Gambit* was a university magazine edited by Bill McCarthur who decided to use work by Burroughs and Alexander Trocchi. But he resigned when attempts were made to censor the contents, and he started *Cleft.* Only two issues came out, in 1963 and 1964, but Burroughs, Norman Mailer, Gary Snyder, and Michael McClure were printed along with forward-looking Scottish and European writers. I recall meeting McCarthur at a literary event around this time but, like Alex Neish, he disappeared after the 1960s.

I'm not trying to cover all the appearances by American Beats and related writers in British publications during this period. I've written elsewhere about how magazines such as *Migrant* and *Satis* featured Bukowski, Ed Dorn, and others, and put British and American writers in touch with each other. The handful of magazines I've covered were those which, rather than printing an occasional American, published quite a few of them in each issue.

The last publication I want to look at is *Outburst,* started by the English poet, Tom Raworth, in 1961. In the first issue he spotlighted

Creeley, Fielding Dawson, Ed Dorn, Snyder, Olson, and Denise Levertov, alongside some local poets like Pete Brown and Michael Horovitz. Like other British editors, Raworth didn't just print Beats but also picked up on a wide range of new American poetry and prose.

Ambition often outstrips achievement in the world of little magazines and the second issue of *Outburst* didn't appear until 1963, and it had a note on its back cover appealing for subscribers and hinting at financial problems. Ginsberg was there (he seems to have been everywhere in those days), as were Corso, Whalen, Paul Blackburn, Leroi Jones, and Douglas Woolf, a lively novelist and short-story writer who is, I would guess, mostly forgotten now, though in the 1960s he was in several important anthologies of new American writing.

Tom Raworth never did get another issue of *Outburst* into print, though he went on to become a leading British avant-garde poet. But the two issues that were published provided an impressive range of experimental writing. It may seem strange that a handful of little magazines, most of them with very limited lifespans, can appear so important in retrospect, but as someone who was around at the time and got them as they appeared, I can testify to how valuable they were. Some writers (the four named in that shock-horror piece in *The People*) were becoming well-known, but many of the others were not widely published in Britain. The little magazines gave us an opportunity to read their work and discover new names. And that is what true little magazines are for. Their editors are often overlooked when histories of literary movements are written, but the contributions they made deserve to be recorded and remembered.

HOW FAR UNDERGROUND?

'I am used to thinking of the writer, then, as a man who stands at a certain extreme, at a certain remove from society. He stands over against the commercial culture, the business enterprise, the whole fantastic make-believe world which some people would like us to believe is the real world. Of course it can't be that for the writer.'[1]

Twenty or so years ago I set my beret firmly on my head, got out my dark glasses, tucked a copy of Charlie Parker's *Stupendous* under my arm, and stepped out into the weird and wonderful world (or so it seemed to my young mind) of the underground. Of course, I didn't know I was doing just that - there was then very little fashionable appeal in the idea of an underground (a term never used in those days, incidentally, though I suppose those of us who were, consciously or not, discontented with society did adopt a kind of life-style) - which just goes to prove how different things were from today's souped-up scene, with every kid over the age of ten having the idea thrown at him from all angles by the con-men of the mass-media.

Despite its faults - and the curious bop/beat/bohemian world I tagged along with over the years had more than its share of cranks, nuts, and phonies - I always did feel that a non-establishment area had more to offer. After all, any experience that leads you to Paul Goodman, Kenneth Rexroth, Roy Fisher, Edward Dahlberg (just a few names, selected at random) can't be bad. It's odd, though, how the underground idea has developed, and how - if I may voice the suspicions of a soured and ageing (by hippie standards I'm practically written-off) mind - it now represents as much of a threat as a promise. Let me define my terms. From a literary point of view I was weaned on the little magazines of the late fifties and early sixties (I was a late starter, not getting involved with writing until after my discharge from the army in 1957). They were my guides and I took them seriously. Even allowing for the natural feeling of excitement resulting from my own initial involvement with something new I do think there was, in the upsurge of activity in 1957-62 (to set a rough frame on it), often a genuine response along the lines referred to by Rosenfeld. Agreed, those people who had been functioning in that manner all along found it amusing - and sometimes irritating - that they were suddenly the centre of attraction, and quite a few of the lesser lights who popped up were quick to exploit the publicity of their position for all it was worth. Still there was an overall feeling of a rejection of the money society's values, and a healthy interest in possible alternatives. I'm not claiming any great significance for much of the activity. If you want to see how silly some of it was borrow a copy of *The Beat Scene*[2] and flick through it. How quaint the photographs often are - get me, Ma, I'm a bohemian! But it was the golden age of innocence compared to what the Hippies inflicted on us. I don't want to waste any space by detailing the already well-known history of the Hippies and my main intention is to determine what effect they could have on the little magazine world and those writers who choose to function in it. As a social movement the underground has deserved a lot of the criticism levelled against it - personally I find it hard to feel a great affinity with people who take pop music so seriously (and don't get me wrong - I've no built-in antagonism to good, rocking pop; Wynonie Harris has been belting it out on my record-player for years) - and the American poet Charles Plymell (by no stretch of the imagination a member of the establishment) surely hit the nail on the head when he dismissed the mass Hippie culture in the following words: 'Hippies make me sick. Tim Leary makes me sick. I say Turn on, Tune in, Drop Tim. I say drop all the fucked up generation of upper middle-class teenagers pouring into Psychedelphia. They are the hippies who have read about the "underground" in *Life-News-week* et al. They are the starlets of their own mindless ego, trying to blow the mind of the square world. They have not dropped out of culture because they had to, like many, somewhere in a forgotten American dream, they have dropped out to follow the scenes advertised in mass media and to put on their beads and devour it with all the likeness of a Madison Ave. businessman. Their mod clothes are being bought with the same war machine blood money as the Brooks Bros. suit.'[3]

I've spent a fair amount of time hunting through underground (I'm using the word in its popularized sense) publications of one kind or another and I've been struck by the almost total absence of creative writers. There are a few in the U.S.A. - Richard Brautigan, perhaps; Ken Kesey, although he hasn't published anything recently - but on the whole Mailer, Burroughs, Kerouac and Ginsberg are invoked and all of these people basically belong to an earlier era. In this country you can add Trocchi - like Kesey, however, he's a non-producer these days - and maybe Jeff Nuttall. Burton Wolfe, a sympathetic chronicler of the Hippie scene, mentions that Michael McClure and Lenore Kandel are often spoken of as being in the fold but that both were in their mid-thirties and reasonably established when the cult began, and goes on to say: 'In the field of the arts, which ought to have been the most fruitful area of endeavour for hippies, there is little evidence of real accomplishment. Except for their music, a frequent criticism in the press to the effect that hippies have not created any distinctive art forms is substantially true. Certainly, they have not created a new form of literature. All of the new writing that has been done by hippies is in styles that are many years old. The same holds true for the subject matter.'[4] And Lawrence Lipton, perennial supporter of dissident social or artistic movements, struggled hard to make a case for the new 'wordcraft' when he focused on it[5] but could only come up with two new names - Willard Bain (*Informed Sources*) and Ishmael Reed (*The Free-Lance Pallbearers*) - neither of them of vast importance.

The truth of the matter is that the underground accent is on journalism or on a kind of spontaneous verbal creativity. As Seymour Krim said of a group of underground personalities: 'They are all writers, radicals, activists, and all have very quick and creative minds. But when I say they are writers I should qualify that and say WORDMEN, because the self-imposed isolation of writing as opposed to performing in public, Doing their Thing before an audience they can actually see responding to them, has come to seem to them like what Abbie (Hoffman, the Yippie leader) would call 'Masochistic Theatre'. Why jerk yourself off when you can ball? I can hear John (Wilcock, underground journalist and editor) or perhaps Ed (Sanders, poet, publisher, rock musician) say, why artificially lock yourself in a room when the action is on the unpredictable and chance-ridden streets? Why sanctify the written word when it grows stale by the time you put it down (let alone get it printed) compared to the immediacy of the spoken one?' [6] Now there is a degree of meaning in this. The equation of the creative act - writing a poem, say - with masturbation, and the joys of intercourse with the turmoil of the streets, has a half-truth built into it. The only snag is that it doesn't take into account the fact that a writer's seed, once on the page, hopefully impregnates someone else's mind not just now but in the future as well. And it probably reaches more minds - and in a less suspect atmosphere - than the outpourings of the 'wordmen' involved in street activity. I'm not condemning such activity, only suggesting that it is no substitute for art. I'll grant that behind the anti-literature stance of the activists there is probably a deep pro-life feeling, but I do think that the stance may also represent a demand for instant-pleasure and instant-success. And although I'll no doubt be accused of advocating the W.A.S.P. ethic of work and suffering being good for you if I say that the pleasure principle isn't necessarily the best one to operate on, I'll chance it. I certainly don't think a serious writer ought to take it - or the instant-success principle - as his guide. As the underground has gained momentum in recent years - and the anti-literature trend has built up too - there has been a marked decline in the number of good little magazines. Oh yes, they do still exist but you have to go a long way to find them and most tend to be the longer-established publications. There seems to be little of the drive that spawned many of the fine magazines (*Outburst, Sidewalk, Big Table, Nomad, Between Worlds*, the early issues of *Evergreen Review*) of ten or fifteen years ago. Or rather the drive has been diverted into other channels. But, say my underground acquaintances, what about all the weekly/ fortnightly/ monthly newspapers - or near-newspapers - we have now. There are plenty of these, who can deny it? Unfortunately, they don't offer much scope for the creative writer, though there are probably opportunities within them for journalists.

It may be of value to deviate slightly at this point and take a closer look at one of the underground papers. I've chosen the *International Times,* daddy of all such publications in this country, and the issue in question has 28 pages and the names of Trocchi, Burroughs, and Ginsberg across the front cover.[7] There are two pages devoted to this trio (nothing of importance from any of them, unfortunately), one to the Chicago conspiracy trial, one to a plea for a 24 hour city, one to an article on pollution, nine to pop music, and the rest to a mixture of cartoons, reviews, letters, advertisements, and brief reports on arrests, raids, etc. The news pages, it should be noted, also contain a fair amount of advertising matter. What is significant about the whole paper is (a) the sloppiness of the presentation - if any of the writing is good there is certainly no editorial conception of the possibility of it being enhanced by the layout - and (b) the refusal to explore any subject in real depth. With few exceptions - the piece on pollution is one of them - we are given pop journalism of the kind you get in the *Daily Mirror,* though the writing in the latter is usually clearer, more to the point, and less likely to be scattered with childish expletives. What both papers particularly have in common is their pretensions to seriousness - the *Mirror* tries to kid us with Royalty, *International Times* with pop stars - and significance, whereas really the layout, not to mention the writing, works against the reader getting to grips with the words. One wonders if this is deliberate. For example, what would a close analysis of the following (from an interview with John Lennon) produce? Lennon was asked about his meeting with Aage Rosendal Nielsen and replied: 'Well, we changed them a lot and they changed us as well. The changes went on with Aage. I don't know what they were into before, but they're certainly into something else now, like he's writing this book called *Violent Education* and it ends up like peace. I think he held his views, his manifestations verbally and mentally is a damn sight different from what it was.' Fair enough, I've pulled that out of context but even so what does it mean? One is inclined to ask how Lennon knows that 'they're certainly into something else now' if he doesn't know what they were 'into before', but as most underground thinking seems to be done to a background of ear-splitting, mind-numbing pop the simple logic of this will probably not sink in.

As for the ideas in *International Times* - and any new movement of any kind ought to have ideas (well, that's what I was taught to believe anyway) - I'll content myself with a few words about the 24 hour city article because this does in many ways typify the false reasoning about social or economic problems that pervades most underground thinking. In places it reads like one of the 'it was all fields when I was a lad' brigade reminiscing: 'Before the war trams used to run all night. Prior to 1939 the normal service continued to about 1.30 when there was a break till 5.00 a.m. However, during the night there was a tram service on the same routes which was used mainly for mail but which passengers could use. The last tram left Canonbury for Stoke Newington at 1.20 a.m., the normal service now stops before midnight.' That's right, and you could post a letter and it would be delivered the same day, and you didn't have to wait to see your Doctor before they brought in this National Health nonsense, and . . . well, you've heard it all before (the last time, personally, from a local Tory councillor). No-one bothers to say how many unemployed we had before the war - forcing people into taking badly paid jobs with lousy conditions, so that it was easy to operate things like all-night services - and no-one bothers to explain who would run the services now. It would be the real economic underground, of course; the lower paid workers; the immigrants; the people who haven't the skill or education or right social background or colour to get them into good jobs. There are other points, too, and I hate to be an old fuddy-duddy and raise them but it would be nice to have some answers. I mean, how many factory workers want 24 hour cities? Let's face it, kids, it isn't the middle-class who live in the town or city centres and have to put up with buses trundling up and down their streets and waking their kids. It's those lower-paid workers and immigrants. 'Damn and blast, why do they have to exist?'

One other noticeable thing about the underground press is that it operates on a very narrow front. There are signs that some local papers are interested in community problems, and this to me is an ideal function for such publications, especially if they can manage a reasonable distribution and focus attention on matters ignored by the 'official' press (and there's endless scope, as a brief glance at English provincial dailies will show). But pop tends to rule the roost in too many of the publications and though John Wilcock's recommendation for a successful formula - 'a mixture of pot, art, politics, religion, sex, humour and revolution' - might set the general pattern, there is little endeavour to make it of more than surface interest. Few of the papers have any in-depth reporting - *Rolling Stone*[8] is an occasional exception - and too much emphasis is placed on interviews, presumably because they seem to exemplify the value of spontaneity and the spoken word as opposed to the written. The trouble is that many of the interviewees are hardly the most intelligent or articulate of people.

The accent on instant-news, and the basic falseness of the positions, limit the value of the underground in so far as the serious writer is concerned. So where does he survive? It has been suggested that little magazines ceased to have any true function as the avant-garde declined as an identifiable entity. The commercialization of much avant-garde activity, the introduction of paperbacks (and especially of such magazine-pocketbooks as *New World Writing* and *New American Review*), has perhaps limited the role of the little magazine but it does seem to me to still have an important place in the literary/social set-up. As Isaac Rosenfeld put it: 'The little magazines were part of the image of garret poverty and obscurity. Now they survive, but survive with a certain opulence (Rosenfeld was referring to the magazine-pocketbook type of publication) that threatens to crush them. Surely the specific idea of the little magazine, just as the specific idea of the avant-garde, gets lost in such a translation. And that idea was of a perhaps small but vigorous and very vital, active, and conscious group which knew fairly well the sort of thing it stood for even if it had no specific program and whether or not it had any political allegiances.'[9] It is the latter part of Rosenfeld's statement that interests me because it does sum up what I've suggested throughout this article, i.e. that the real underground (and I hate to use the term in this context because of its current connotations) is comprised of a small body of poets, writers, social critics, what have you, who refuse to be sidetracked by mass-media cooked-up questions, whether they stem from the pop underground or from the establishment press. They may not have a specific programme but, as Rosenfeld suggested, they do know the sort of thing they stand for. It is only in the little magazines - literary or political or both - that such a group can survive, even though they may occasionally find a home in the underground (current sense) papers and even with paperback publishers. The Penguin anthology of underground poetry, *Children of Albion*, had at its best more to do with this kind of underground than with the 'flowers, hash and polymorphous free love' some of its critics chose to associate it with.[10]

Charles Bukowski has a funny poem, called 'The Underground',[11] in which he expresses some of the misgivings a man like himself (and he's one of what I would call the genuine underground) feels when faced with aspects of the contemporary scene:

then I went to the bar next door and
bought 3 more packs of beer
when I got back they were talking Revolution
so here I was back in 1935 again,
only I was old and they were young, I was at least
20 years older than anybody in the room
and I thought, what the hell am I doing
here ?

But of course we're here whether we like it or not, and it's as well to acknowledge that the underground does have things to offer. One can admire its liveliness,[12] its courage - particularly in the U.S.A. where the forces of reaction tend to crack down harder than they do here - its initiative, its often genuine honesty. And it sometimes deserves support from people like myself who, one way or another, have had connections with the underground in the past but can't always come to terms with it in the present. Certainly, as the backlash gathers speed - and I don't think there's any doubt that it is - there's every need for writers to be prepared to stand up to the reactionaries, though I still insist that they must maintain their own individuality and integrity. From a literary point of view the hippie concern for an involved form of writing could provide some good lessons for little magazine editors. There is a tendency for our magazines to offer, not an outlet for the serious writer wanting to work out his ideas in a sympathetic and stimulating atmosphere, but an ivory tower, a refuge, for the writer wanting to play the literary game. This is not the same as Rosenfeld's writer standing 'at a certain extreme, at a certain remove from society'. There is a growing body of work - Mailer's *The Armies of the Night*, Frank Conroy's *Stop Time*, Frederick Exley's *A Fan's Notes,* maybe Norman Podhoretz's *Making It*, some of Tom Wolfe's writing, Fielding Dawson's *An Emotional Memoir of Franz Kline* and certainly, I think, James Drought's *The Secret* (I can't think of any British writers to add to the list, though Ray Gosling's *Sum Total* might fit in) - which points the way towards an involved (not to be confused with committed in the political sense) and imaginative non-fiction, even though some of the books mentioned masquerade under the guise of fiction. To quote Seymour Krim again: 'I believe the ex-novelist, the new communicator that we can see already in the early and various stages of his making should speak intimately to his readers about these fantastic days we are living through but declare his credentials by revealing the concrete details and particular sweat of his own inner life; otherwise he (or she) will not have earned the right to speak openly about everything or be trusted.'[13] Krim's work - as typified by some of his essays in the brilliant *Views Of A Nearsighted Cannoneer* [14] - is amongst the best of this new genre, and it's significant that much of it was printed in the little magazines in the late fifties and early sixties.

Editors here would do well to encourage similar excursions by our writers - the essay-length piece fits both writer and editorial requirements and is highly suited to this form - because I would guess that they will prove to be influential and effective means of transmitting ideas about contemporary society. Only the little magazine would seem to offer the writer a chance to use this style and still have time to work out his ideas in his own way, and without coming under pressure to meet a deadline - 'we don't want it good, we want it tomorrow', to use A. Alvarez's neat phrase - or cater for the kind of feeble audience attracted to the underground newspapers. The latter may make all the noise but it's essential that the real underground continues to speak to those willing to listen to it.

Notes

1. Isaac Rosenfeld. 'On the Role of the Writer and the Little Magazine', *Chicago Review Anthology* (Cambridge University Press, London, 1959).

2. *The Beat Scene* (Corinth Books, New York, 1960). Edited by Elias Wilentz.

3. Charles Plymell. 'Open Letter to Editor of International Times, London', *Open Skull 1* (San Francisco, 1967).

4. Burton H. Wolfe. *The Hippies* (Signet Books, New York, 1968).

5. Lawrence Lipton. 'Robin The Cock & Dopeyduk Doing The Boogaloo In Harry Sam With Rusty Jethroe and Letterhead America,' *Cavalier*, New York, April 1968.

6. Seymour Krim. 'Should I Assume America Is Already Dead?', in *Shake It For The World, Smartass* (Dial Press, New York, 1970).

7. *International Times,* London, 27th February-13th March, 1970.

8. See, for example, *Rolling Stone 43*, London, 4th October, 1969, which has a long, well-documented survey of the Underground Press in general.

9. Rosenfeld. Op. cit.

10. *Children of Albion: Poetry of The Underground in Britain* (Penguin Books, 1969). Edited by Michael Horovitz. Interested readers may care to refer to my 'Underground Poets: A Reply From The Northern Line' (*Ambit 42*, London, 1970) which attempted to answer some of the criticisms levelled against the anthology.

11. Charles Bukowski. *The Days Run Away Like Wild Horses Over The Hills* (Black Sparrow Press, Los Angeles, 1969).

12. For those who don't care to plough through the various underground newspapers there are three anthologies which collect some of the more interesting writing: *Some of IT,* Knullar Ltd., London, 1969), edited by David Mairowitz; *The Hippie Papers* (Signet Books, New York, 1969), edited by Jerry Hopkins; *Notes From The New Underground* (Viking Press, New York, 1968), edited by Jesse Kornbluth.

13. Krim. 'The American Novel Made Me.' Op. cit.

14. Krim. *Views of A Nearsighted Cannoneer* (Alan Ross, London, 1969).

PRE-BEAT

There are a few novels that are usually mentioned as forerunners of the Beat concerns that came to the fore in the late 1950s. Kerouac's *The Town And The City* (1950), John Clellon Holmes's *Go* (1952), and William Burrough's *Junkie* (1953) are obvious examples, and Chandler Brossard's *Who Walk In Darkness* (1952) and *The Bold Saboteurs* (1953) can also be included in the list. Some people would additionally point to Nelson Algren's *The Man With The Golden Arm* (1949) and others might suggest Herbert Gold's *The Man Who Was Not With It* (1956). All of these books dealt with, in one way or another, the interlocking worlds of bohemianism, jazz, drug addiction, and what were usually seen as social groups outside the conventional framework acknowledged by most people. There are no doubt similar novels that could be mentioned and in this short piece I'll look at three which are not often talked about in this context.

George Mandel's *Flee The Angry Strangers* (1952) dealt with the Greenwich Village scene, though Mandel did more than just highlight the lives of painters, poets, and other bohemians. His characters have arrived in Greenwich Village from a variety of starting points, ranging from Camden to the Pennsylvania coalfields and beyond, and while there are would-be writers and artists among them they are not all aiming at that status. For some the one common factor is junk and the book's central female character, Diane, slowly descends into addiction to a background of bebop and a kind of nihilistic philosophy in which the square world is dismissed. She hangs around a cafeteria packed with people not unlike herself, and one of her companions describes it as "packed with dope fiends and philosophers, prostitutes and poets, artisans and hoods, darlings, dreamers, derelicts and every American variety of displaced person, all together in a debris of Babel, which some conciliatory side of him had defined as fundamental human affinity." Later, when Diane is fully hooked and part of a group which sees addiction as a way of challenging the moral authority of the wider world, she becomes something of a philosopher herself: "Junkies and derelicts and poets who needed to learn about life - somehow convinced that life and pain were synonymous - came to sit around her, and she dressed in black as often as she could to convince everyone as though she were a voice from old graves, with nothing to gain for herself, with a preachment of nothing to offer them at all. Quit painting, she told artists; throw your books away, she told students from the university east of the park. 'Come sit in the Cosmopole,' she invited inhabitants and tourists alike. 'You don't need anything in this world. Only poverty is holy.'"

What Mandel called the Cosmopole Cafeteria in his novel was based on the Waldorf Cafeteria, as he made clear in a memoir, *Bohemia Lost*, published in *Gent* in October, 1957. Mandel looked back on his time around Greenwich Village and the characters he'd known, like Joe Gould and Maxwell Bodenheim. It was Gould who was reputed to have compiled an oral history of the world, though it probably existed more in his imagination than in reality. His major accomplishment, apart from getting drunk, was to disrupt parties by flapping his arms and squawking like a seagull, thus earning the nickname, Professor Seagull. As for Bodenheim, he had been a prolific poet and novelist in the 1920s and 1930s before he succumbed to drink and became notable for hawking his poems around Greenwich Village bars to raise money for his next bottle. He met his end in a squalid apartment, murdered by a man who had tried to seduce Bodenheim's wife.

George Mandel never claimed that his novel was a forerunner of the Beat sensibility and, in fact, he went into print to deny it. A talented cartoonist, he published a very funny book, *Beatville U.S.A.* (1961), which neatly satirised some of the more extreme manifestations of the Beat lifestyle. In his introduction he pointed out that he was sometimes called "a member of the Beat Generation because certain commercial anthologists called my first novel Beat." And it's true that Mandel was included in *Protest: The Beat Generation And The Angry Young Men* (1958), one of the first anthologies to publicise the Beats. But as he pointed out: "I happen to be a graduate of what, for want of a less preposterous term, might be called the pre-Beats."

Mandel's novel used some of the hip slang of the period (he later recalled that his publisher tried to persuade him to add a glossary to his book, reasoning that, in 1952, few people would be familiar with the terms used by junkies, jazzmen, and their associates) and it also occasionally crops up in Bernard Wolfe's *The Late Risers* (1954) which focuses on Times Square and some of the people around it. To be fair, Wolfe's book is not too concerned with bohemians and concentrates more on what the jazz singer Babs Gonzales referred to as "hustlers and hat-box chicks," meaning seedy show-business types, press agents, gossip columnists, night-club employees, and the like. *The Late Risers* almost veers between Damon Runyan and the bleak Ernest Lehman stories that were used as the basis for the savage film, *Sweet Smell Of Success*. But Wolfe brought his own kind of fast moving storytelling to the subject and also displayed a more than passing awareness of radical politics. This was not surprising because, in the late 1930s, he'd been in Mexico as one of Trotsky's bodyguards and later wrote a novel, *The Great Prince Died* (1959), partly based on his experiences. Wolfe's style in *The Late Risers* was meant to capture some of the surface freneticism of his characters and their way of talking in a smart streetwise manner, but he also made serious points about politics and race-relations. One of the most interesting characters is Movement, a Negro whose favourite reading is Herman Melville's *The Confidence Man* and who has learnt how to survive in a hostile white world: "Now when an especially enterprising member of my ethnic group ventures out into the white world, because it is so colourful to him, he endeavours to make friends. The most efficient way to make friends is to show up on the fronts of their eyes as you already exist behind them. That way you show you are not a trouble maker and do not want to upset anybody in his set habits."

A later Bernard Wolfe novel, *The Magic Of Their Singing* (1961), did deal more directly with Greenwich Village, hipsters, jazz musicians, Beats, and related types, but by that time any number of novelists and journalists were writing about these things, though not many of them were as witty and intelligent as Wolfe in painting a picture of lives lived on the fringes of society.

The clash between the values of most people in the 1950s and those of the bohemians was dealt with in R.V. Cassill's *A Taste Of Sin* (1955), a novel published directly in paperback form and so missing the kind of critical attention that Mandel and Wolfe might have had. But there is a tale behind *A Taste Of Sin* which relates to the Beats. The *Protest* anthology included a Cassill short story, *Fracture,* which had originally been published in *Epoch* magazine in 1952 and in which a conventional middle class couple have their lives disrupted by a bohemian drifter. As the editors of *Protest* said, whereas once bohemians were just seen as colourful oddballs, Cassill's story hints that "the square is no longer certain. Suddenly the rebel without a cause has assumed a new role, one fraught with urgent meaning and danger." What wasn't mentioned in *Protest* was that Cassill had developed his story into the novel, *A Taste Of Sin*, and shown how the suggestion of disturbance in the relationship between the husband and wife does develop into a real rift when the husband gets too involved with the bohemian and his young girlfriend.

This theme of relationships and values falling apart under pressure occurs in more than one of Cassill's books, though *A Taste Of Sin* is the one in which the pressure is felt from a bohemian source. Cassill was a curious writer who produced more than twenty novels and numerous short stories, and who was able to move easily from hardback fiction to pulp novels with titles like *Lustful Summer* and *The Wife Next Door*. It could be that some of his pulp novels, especially *Night School* and *The Wound Of Love*, were as good as what he thought of as his "serious" fiction. His major work, *Clem Anderson* (1961), did have a few bohemian scenes set in Paris and New York as it followed the ups and downs of a writer's life, but although it was praised when it first came out it's virtually forgotten now. Cassill's links to the Beats centred on his story in *Protest* and he let it be known that he didn't really welcome the association. In his article, *An Experience Named Greenwich Village,* in the March, 1963 issue of *Cavalier,* he took a somewhat laconic look at the romance of Bohemia. He was obviously familiar with its history, and the magazine described him as a "longtime villager," but when he referred to "the San Remo where Bodenheim sold poetry worse than Ginsberg's for the cheapest juice," he was stating where he stood on the question of Beat writing.

Mandel, Wolfe, and Cassill were not Beat writers but they sensed that something was happening culturally and they thought it was worth writing about it. In this way they touched on experiences and concerns that Beat writers also dealt with in a somewhat different manner. It's instructive to read all of them.

TED JOANS IN PARIS

A warm day in Paris and I walk into Shakespeare and Company and there's Ted Joans. I haven't seen him since 1978, when we were both reading at the Berlin Literature Festival, and we shake hands and reminisce about that event and talk about what has happened since. Ted always seems to be on the move and he tells me that he's due to visit Rome, Vienna, Budapest, and Bratislava later that month, though he'll return to Paris. It's his base, or at least one of them. Winters he spends in Timbuktu.

Later, we sit outside the Café Le Rouquet on the Boulevard Saint Germain, which is where Ted Joans can be found most afternoons when he's in Paris, and where he even has mail delivered. He introduces me to James Yates, an active 85 year old black veteran of the International Brigades whose book, *Mississippi To Madrid*, tells a colourful story of hoboing adventures in Depression America and war in Spain. Meeting interesting people is the kind of thing that happens when you're with Ted, and he's a mine of information about what is going on in Paris and elsewhere, pointing me in the direction of art exhibitions, handing me leaflets and notes about events, and giving me addresses of people I might want to meet. We discuss the marvellous André Breton show at the Pompidou Centre and that leads us to Ted's own taste for surrealism, something which is obvious from his work. It was Breton, in fact, who said that he was "the only Afro-American surrealist," and it's easy to understand why. Ted Joans is a painter as well as a poet and is steeped in the art and literature of the surrealist movement.

It's a pleasure to be with him and I think about his writing, which I've known for over thirty years. He was featured in such influential anthologies as *The Beat Scene* and *The Beats*, but also satirised the Greenwich Village scene in his book, *The Hipsters,* which was described as "a mixture of Dali, Ernst and Kerouac stirred up in a surrealist stew." His collection of poems, *Afrodisia* and *Black Pow-Wow: Jazz Poems*, came out in the USA towards the end of the 60s and Calder & Boyars published *A Black Manifesto In Jazz Poetry And Prose* in this country in 1971 and *Black Pow-wow* a little later. Copies can still be found in bookshops like Compendium in Camden Town. There was also a pamphlet, *Sure, I Really Is,* from the surrealist specialist John Lyle in 1982, though this seems something of a collector's item now. A new book, *Wow: Selected Poems Of Ted Joans*, is due to be published by Handshake Editions, Paris, in 1991. The man I'm talking to is clearly something of a Beat legend, companion to both Charlie Parker and Jack Kerouac in 50s New York, and one of the liveliest members of the movement. But although Joans got along with the Beats he never gave up his devotion to André Breton and the surrealists, nor to the leading black writer, Langston Hughes. Jazz was also a major influence on Joans, a one time trumpet player himself. I recall that at the Berlin Festival he wore a T-shirt bearing the slogan, "Jazz is my Religion," and that when he read his poems he gave them an infectious swing. The beat in his work was the beat of jazz and it went well with his outspoken statements about the way black people are often treated. The anger came through (his own father was killed by whites in a 1943 Detroit race riot) but it never lapsed into incoherent rage. He was once quoted as saying, "I'm too intelligent to be anti-white. I'm just pro-me, which is black." And it's true that his poems have an understanding and humour which balances out the bitterness they may contain when he's being directly social or political.

It seems apt that I've met up again with Ted Joans in Paris, that city of infinite possibilities. He's obviously at home there, his surrealist spirit thriving not only on its historical aspects (surrealism was/is an international movement and yet Paris has been its headquarters all along) but also on its café life and its general role as a literary and artistic centre. He keeps the Beat spirit alive, too, in his work and the way in which he approaches life. Poetry and the whole process of opposing conformity are important factors in his thinking.

It occurs to me to ask him when he was last in Britain and he says it was some years ago, though now that a certain lady is no longer our Prime Minister he thinks he'll soon make another trip across the Channel. He speaks with anger about what he sees as the sad effects the Thatcher and Reagan years had on their respective countries.

A few weeks after our meeting, when I was back in England and Ted had returned from his reading tour, I had a postcard and a letter from him, both written in his idiosyncratic style and full of interest and enthusiasm. Getting something in the mail from him, like an unexpected meeting in Paris or reading some of his poems, is the sort of thing that can make a day seem brighter. Let's hope that his new book will soon be available to entertain and instruct us.

GREGORY CORSO

Yes, now that I am older
the old of my youth are dead
and the young of my youth are old
Wasn't long ago
in the company of peers
poets and convicts
I was the youngest for years
I entered prison the youngest and left the youngest
of Ginsberg Kerouac Burroughs ... the youngest
And I was young when I began to be the oldest
At Harvard a 23 year old amongst 20 year olds

That excerpt from Gregory Corso's poem, *Feelings on Getting Older*, points to one of his constant preoccupations: his own situation in the world. The poem sets up a question - what is it like to grow older? - and then answers it, rhetorically, with a series of reflections on various aspects of the process. Childhood, his experiences in prison, at Harvard, as one of the leading Beat poets. And in the way he handles his experiences there is still much of the puzzled urchin groping for answers to the confusion he sees and feels. It is, perhaps, this confusion that often impels Corso to take a less than considered look at the world when operating outside the poems. In a discussion involving Allen Ginsberg, Peter Orlovsky, and Corso, not to mention various members of the audience, which took place at Salem State College in 1973, Corso constantly disagreed violently with the others about their notions regarding the problems of living and learning. "You're all gonna drop dead. There ain't nothing to learn. That's the fact," he said, "You're gonna get old and drop dead, man. That's what the fuck's gonna happen to you."[1]

It is this kind of public behaviour which has tended to type Corso as one of the last of the genuine Beats, someone straight out of the Fifties image of the movement, and more akin to Kerouac and Cassady than to the later Ginsberg or Orlovsky. In Gary Snyder's words: "Gregory really probably is the last of the Beatniks in that sense in that he's manifesting the same style that he manifested in the Fifties. It's a matter of style."[2] The same could be said of his poetry

- which, if the comparatively little he's published in recent years is anything to go by, has hardly altered - in tone, content, style - since the late-Fifties. This is not necessarily bad. Many jazz musicians, for example, stay within a framework they establish early in their career, and yet still manage to extract things of value from it. And, on the other hand, there are poets who seem to be always trying to "make it new," but who never actually produce much of lasting quality. Corso can, at least, claim to have written some poems that stand the test of time. And I would go so far as to suggest that one poem, *Marriage*, stands with Ginsberg's *Howl*, and a handful of other Beat works, as archetypal. If nothing else does, it should ensure that Corso has a place in literary history.

But let me begin to look in a little more detail at aspects of his life and work. He was born in 1930 in Greenwich Village of American-Italian parents. They were, however, somewhat shadowy figures, and by the time he was eleven he was in an orphanage. After that, he experienced the children's observation ward at Bellevue Hospital, and then, when he was sixteen, prison. The events surrounding his arrest and conviction have been referred to in accounts of his activities, and Corso covers them again in the interview, so I'll not repeat them here. It was during his three years in prison that he began to take a more-serious look at his life, and the world around him, and he also began to read in a wider area than he'd previously moved in. The now-famous (in Beat legend) dedication in his second book, *Gasoline*, is relevant: "I dedicate this book to the angels of Clinton Prison who, in my 17th year, handed me from all the cells surrounding me, books of illumination." When asked, many years later, what kind of books he was referring to, Corso replied: "They were really dumb-ass books to begin with. There was Louis Beretti, first of all, Henderson Clarke wrote all those books about Little Italy, gangster books. That was what convicts read. All right. Now the smart man was the man who handed me *Les Miserables*. And you know who did that? Me. When I went to the prison library, I looked at that fat book and I knew what miserable meant. I was 16.½. When I said they passed me books of illumination, I meant they handed me something else, not the books. Yeah, there was a guy who had a beautiful standard dictionary and I studied every fucking word in that book. 1905. This big, it was. All the archaic, all the obsolete words. That's illumination, I guess."[3]

After leaving prison Corso met Allen Ginsberg in what he once referred to as a chance meeting in a bar. He had already written some poems, and showed them to Ginsberg, who then introduced him to other members of the Beat fraternity, such as Kerouac, Burroughs, and John Clellon Holmes. This is not the place to outline a history of the movement, but it does need to be stressed that Corso did only meet up with the others in 1950. From that point of view he doesn't figure in such fictionalised accounts of the early years as *Go*, *The Town and the City*, or *On the Road.* Those books primarily dealt with events between 1944 and 1950. Likewise, what I've mentioned about Corso's life prior to 1950 - the family (or lack of it), limited formal education, prison, etc. - will immediately make clear that he had a different attitude than the others. They, in their various ways, had been, or still were, involved in aspects of the social system, even if their life-styles and involvements tended to alienate them from middle-class concerns. But Ginsberg, Burroughs, Kerouac, and Holmes had experienced the educational set-up, to varying degrees, and as a consequence had some awareness of literary history. Ginsberg's knowledge of European as well as American poets and writers is well-known, and Kerouac could claim some familiarity with the works of Céline, Spengler, Joyce, to pull just a few names out of the bag. With Holmes we have a man who was politically aware as well. And this sophistication could be extended to someone like Carl Solomon with his interest in dadaism and surrealism, and to the whole shifting mass of young New York writers the Beats mixed with in the fifties. This isn't at all surprising as most literary movements tend to be made up of people who have had a reasonably extended formal education. Hence their acknowledgement of literary history, of styles, and of the advantages and disadvantages of maverick behaviour. It was one of the better aspects of the Beat movement that it did incorporate some writers who were self-educated - Corso, of course, and Ray Bremser and Bob Kaufman - and generally managed to do so without being in any way patronising. The reference to Bremser is deliberate in that he, like Corso, had a proletarian background which included a spell in prison. And again, like Corso, he had a highly-individual sense of language which perhaps derived from an informal education in which each item tends to be seen in isolation, so that it is as logical to use the style, imagery, and grammar of, say, the English Romantic poets as it is to attempt to write in a consciously-contemporary manner. Of course, a counter-argument can be set up by pointing to Ginsberg, whose work has involved stylistic acknowledgements to Whitman, Blake, Christopher Smart, and I suspect a whole gaggle of mostly-forgotten populist poets like Vachel Lindsay, Arturo Giovannitti, and Mike Gold. But Ginsberg knew precisely what he was doing in choosing to write that way. Corso, I would guess, didn't, and the fumblings of his early verse point to his not being too clear about what he wanted to do, and how he wanted to do it.

Corso has recalled that his first poems weren't always greeted with enthusiasm by the people Ginsberg introduced him to. Holmes thought he used too much "green armpit imagery," a term that the novelist has explained elsewhere as describing poetry which seemed to self-consciously strive for semi-surreal effects.[4] And Mark Van Doren suggested that Corso wrote too much about his mother. It's difficult to know how accurate these criticisms were because the poet's early work was mostly lost when a suitcase containing his manuscripts was mislaid in a Greyhound Bus terminal. But one poem from this period seems to have survived to be included in *The Vestal Lady on Brattle*, Corso's first book:

Sea Chanty

My mother hates the sea,
my sea especially,
I warned her not to;
it was all I could do.
Two years later
the sea ate her.

Upon the shore I found a strange,
yet beautiful good;
I asked the sea if I could eat it,
and the sea said that I could.
- Oh, sea, what fish is this
so tender and so sweet? -
- - Thy mother's feet - was its answer.

I must admit that, on the evidence of the poem (Corso did once say that another from *The Vestal Lady on Brattle* also dated from his early period, though I've been unable to decide which one), it is easy to understand what both Holmes and Van Doren were getting at. The form is slack, the diction alternates uneasily between the conversational and the archaic, and the imagery is contrived. It's a young man's poem, and especially a young man with a mind full of ideas derived from life and literature, but unshaped by any kind of formal application.

Following some brief wanderings Corso drifted to Cambridge, where he hung around the Harvard campus, attending classes unofficially, reading voraciously in the library, and writing. Encouraged, both intellectually and financially, by some of the students he knew, and with poems appearing in publications like *The Harvard Advocate* and *i.e.*, Corso put together a small collection which was published as *The Vestal Lady on Brattle*. It's interesting to look at a few of the poems in this volume from the point of view of how they demonstrated his concerns, and his stylistic leanings at the time.

The first thing that strikes one is that the poems are, when compared to much of his later work, built up in short lines. Someone once asked Corso if he was then working to a concept of "projective verse," and his reply not only set the historical record straight, but also indicated how he saw his own poems from that period:

"I didn't know anything about projective verse, Mr Olson and the Black Mountain people until Ginsberg introduced me to it - and when the heck was that? That was pretty much late - No, I never pondered too deeply on that. The first book, it's very awkward, a green book, just ideas trying to come out. Lots of it literary, conglommed together; and I cut out lots of fat. I thought in those days that poetry is a concise form, built like a brick acropolis."[5]

(For the record, anyone curious about Corso's attitude towards the writers of the Black Mountain school of poetry should look at his short poem, *For Black Mountain*, in *Yugen* 4 - Corso says, amongst other things, that "the incomplete idea/is the new destruction" - and Gilbert Sorrentino's sharp response in the following issue).

Generally speaking, the poems in *Vestal Lady* rarely have much to recommend them in terms of form. It is the content that claims and holds the reader's attention. Insofar as construction is concerned they are competent on the whole, but only in the way that any young would-be poet could be competent, i.e. by operating within already-established boundaries. There is, after all, little of technical interest about the following:

Let us love a thing together once
A thing vermilion

The plain is wide and many colors
Lie beneath the chestnut tree

Let us go there
You shall be my bride

I want to run vermilion through your hair

Called *Thoughts on a Japanese Movie* the poem is mildly entertaining, but hardly of lasting quality.

Elsewhere in the book one finds a mixture of similarly bright but essentially slight fragments, some green armpit imagery, excursions into a social milieu and argot then considered unusual, one or two down-to-earth sketches, and an occasional flight of fancy that gestured towards developments in Corso's later work. It was clearly a collection by a man wending his way through various moods, unclear as to what he wanted to settle on, and as a consequence coming up with incomplete poems and ideas. But there are good things. A bleak little poem, *Greenwich Village Suicide*, unpretentiously hints at the loneliness that is often the lot of those moving to areas like Greenwich and finding little or no satisfaction in a life on the fringes of the arts. *The Horse was Milked*, a poem seemingly about a junkie taking a shot, has effective lines, and succeeds largely because of them, and its terse rhymed couplets:

Then he rubbed and shook and yanked his hair,
and vomited air, nothing but air.

Or there is an attempt at a word picture of Coney Island in which the description moves into the semi-surreal:

Night dips into an empty soda bottle, and the joke wears off.

and:

flick on their neon-mockery of the stars
(noontime for the crab!)
thumbtacking their feet upon the sandy roof

The latter lines in particular seem to incline towards the kind of language used in later Corso poems. They perhaps aren't as imaginative, as joyous in their irreverent toying with both sound and meaning, but the feeling is definitely there. The reader can sense that something is being worked towards.

However, one of the most-successful poems is a fairly straightforward account of a service held in New York for the then recently dead Dylan Thomas. Its quiet portrayal of the scene - the bartender from the White House lounging outside the tavern to watch the mourners, the way in which two people guide the widow firmly to a pew by means of hands sliding under her arms, the disappearance of the mourners, and the fact that kids are playing ball in the street outside the church - adds up to a poem which is both moving and well-written.

From the same period as *Vestal Lady* stems a short play of Corso's which was produced by students at Harvard in 1955, and the text of which appeared in *Encounter* in 1962. Witty, fast-moving, the play revolves around a busload of people on their way to San Francisco. Amongst them are a tourist, a poet, a hipster, an Indian, Beauty, a college girl, and a middle-class liberal lady. Not a great deal happens, to be honest, as the poet gets drunk, bewails the state of the nation (people don't buy little magazines, he says, and that's the problem), and others agree, disagree, and skirt around each other. When the play was published in *Encounter* Corso made a large claim for it by stating that it "documents, predates anything ever written about the Hipster and hip talk, the Square, and the advent of San Francisco's 'poesy rebirth'." In the sense that, having been written in 1954, it clearly predates the upsurge of popular interest in such subjects, which tended to get underway in 1957 after *Howl* and *On the Road* made their impact, Corso maybe had a point. But there had been references in writing to hipsters and hip talk well before 1954 as, for example, Anatole Broyard's article, "Portrait of the Hipster," which was printed in *Partisan Review* in 1948. Corso was nearer the mark when he pointed out that his play, by treating the whole thing as farce, was certainly different to the post-1956 celebrations of Hip which in Mailer-esque fashion tried to read significant ideas into it. This tendency to take a farcical view of matters was typical of Corso, and was, I suspect, part of a defensive mechanism derived from both personal and cultural influences. Reminiscing about prison life,

Corso stressed that he survived because "That's where I learned to be funny in life. Because I made them laugh, I was protected. Humor was a necessary survival condition when I was in prison."[6] And one wonders if the tendency to see large issues in terms of farce wasn't also a way of surviving an intellectual world he felt at odds with?

It has been suggested that some aspects of Corso's use of language in several of his early poems demonstrate his interest in Shelley. If so, it was an awkward influence in that the language seemed to hold back a complete expression of what Corso was thinking. But the liking for Shelley, though frequently referred to, appears to have had more to do with life-style and social attitudes rather than literary style. Asked at various times about Shelley, Corso has acknowledged his interest, but whilst accepting the Romantic links he has pointed out that they were with "German romantics, not English. That's when I got into the whole megalactic shot, and into thinking of infinity and what is finite."[7] His enthusiasm (and that is, I think, the right word) for Shelley, although undoubtedly genuine in its appreciation of the poems, had much to do with the way in which the Romantic poet flouted convention, dedicated himself to poetry, and was a leading light of a group of brilliant individuals. "Shelley was a sharp daddy; oh, he's beautiful. I mean Byron couldn't stand up to him, none of them could, stand up to him, when he was going good."[8]

Literary gossip is not my concern in this piece, but those interested in the events of the early and mid-Fifties can pick up references to Corso, under the name of Raphael Urso, in Kerouac's *The Subterraneans* and *Desolation Angels*. He wandered to Mexico, the West Coast, Europe, and in Paris in 1957-58, as he recalls, "things burst and opened, and I said, 'I will just let the lines go and not care about fat'. I figured if I could just go with the rhythms I have within me, my own sound, that that would work, and it worked."[9] A little of the release referred to managed to creep into a few of the poems in his second collection, *Gasoline*, which came out in 1958 in time to place Corso fully in the Beat hierarchy, and so ensure him a fair amount of publicity. A long poem, *Ode to Coit Tower*, may seem the extreme example of "letting the lines go," but it is perhaps too self-consciously experimental, and the lines are sustained by effect rather than natural energy. Much better is a poem like *Visions of Rotterdam,* with its famous (or infamous, if one believed a muckraking report in *The People* in 1960) lines:

Two suitcases filled with despair
    arrived in Rotterdam

or the fine poem, *Uccello*, which brilliantly sets up a word picture of the great battle scene, and also brings in Corso's own desire to be part of the event:

how I dream to join such battle!
a silver man on a black horse with red standard and striped
    lance never to die but to be endless
    a golden prince of pictorial war

If still uneven in terms of style and level of achievement, *Gasoline* did have enough good poems for its author to be taken seriously. Besides those mentioned, sharp vignettes such as *Mexican Impressions, Italian Extravaganza*, and *Birthplace Revisited* testified to his alert, but still-innocent eye, almost as if he was still the New York street kid alive with a need to observe what was going on around him, and finding it strange, exciting, and exhilarating. *Birthplace Revisited*, in which the poet imagines going back to the area where he grew up, and which neatly plays around with the cinematic conventions of gangster films, ends where he puts paid to his enemy, the past:

I walk up the first flight; Dirty Ears
aims a knife at me ...
I pump him full of lost watches.

Which relates to something Corso wrote in an article called "The Time of the Watches:" "One thing an old philosoph con told me on my second day there became a wrist watch around my soul. He said 'Son, don't you serve time, let time serve you', and that's just what I did."[10] This obsession with time - and a fascination for the past which is evinced in many of Corso's poems also points to it, as does his recurring thoughts about death - is a major theme in his work, and one which can be seen operating in his need to set up rhetorical questions about the nature of things, his own mortality, and similar concerns. It's also evident in the wistfulness of his reminiscences of childhood:

How happy I used to be
imagining myself so many things -
  Alexander Hamilton lying in the snow

shoe buckles rusting in the snow
pistol shot crushing his brow

It's a disjointed view of time (history) which sees it as a series of colourful events rather than a continuous process, and which, with its suggestions of the poet imagining himself into all the parts, stresses the need to know, and to understand. The poem it's taken from, *How Happy I used to Be*, was printed in Corso's third book, *The Happy Birthday of Death*, published in I960. Although some of the poems appear to date, at least stylistically, from pre-1957, the collection was notable for containing such items as *Marriage, Clown, Power*, and *Bomb*, all poems in which Corso set up the subject and then toyed around with it, asking himself questions, part-answering or rejecting them, throwing in asides, occasionally letting his imagination slide into the light fantastic. But it was, I think, the fact that he was dealing with easily-identifiable subjects in each case that enabled him to pull off the feat of both entertaining, and instructing the reader. *Marriage* is possibly the most successful, its mixture of humour, wistfulness, and genuine concern sustained by a freely-moving line, and a relaxed but precise use of language. The first two lines set the pace:

Should I get married? Should I be good?
Astound the girl next door with my velvet suit and faustus hood?

Having asked the question, Corso immediately takes off into flights of fancy about meeting the parents:

When she introduces me to her parents
back straightened, hair finally combed, strangled by a tie,
should I sit knees together on their 3rd degree sofa
and not ask where's the bathroom?

then the wedding:

O God, and the wedding! All her family and her friends
and only a handful of mine all scroungy and bearded
just waiting to get at the drinks and food

and then the honeymoon:

All streaming into cozy hotels
All doing the same thing tonight

which leads Corso to think it might be better to defy convention, and become a mysterious figure who acts as a subversive influence:

O I'd live in Niagara forever! in a dark cave beneath the Falls
I'd sit there the Mad Honeymooner
devising ways to break marriages, a scourge of bigamy
a saint of divorce -

But he imagines what it would be like to have a young wife waiting at home for him, to have children, to astound the neighbours with mad prophecies. He shifts from the mundane to the bizarre, perhaps knowing all the time that it is his love of the latter that will always prevent him from settling down in a "normal" manner to establish a home and family. Once that thought occurs, however, he's faced with the alternative - loneliness:

Because what if I'm 60 years old and not married,
all alone in a furnished room with pee stains on my underwear
and everybody else is married! All the universe married but me!

It is the indecisiveness that gives the poem its humanity, and it does have much in common with the poet's obsession with time. Although Corso has spoken in his poems of feeling that his life is directed by something beyond his control, one does often suspect that he thinks it may be out of control.

The poem *Power* seems to me to be basically about the desire to have the means to control one's own destiny, albeit it has also been seen as suggesting other things. But although Corso does range far and wide over aspects of power, he stresses the personal viewpoint:

Power
What is Power
A hat is Power
The world is Power
Being afraid is Power
What is poetry when there is no Power
Poetry is powerless when there is no Power
Standing on a street corner waiting for no one is Power
The Angel is not as powerful as looking and then not looking
Will Power make me mean and unforgettable?

Despite some memorable lines - "Standing on a street corner waiting for no one is Power," for example - the poem isn't completely successful, and Corso, to my mind, was happier with *Marriage,* or with the short, but delightful *Poets Hitchhiking on the Highway* which operates within a limited framework that Corso could handle confidently. Instead of trying to bite off and chew a big subject he took a simple scene of two poets trading nonsense phrases, and transformed it into a celebration of imagination and humour, and of being alive to all the possibilities of life and language. And all that without posturing.

It was around this time (I960) that Corso wrote his only published novel, *The American Express*, a fairy-tale of sorts which, with illustrations by the author, told a story of the odd events when "the great ship *Here They Come*" sets sail with a passenger-list of eccentrics. Awaiting the arrival of the ship is Detective Horatio Frump, whose comments on time are worth quoting. Asked when the ship will arrive, he replies:

"Hard to say, gentlemen. A boat like that doesn't run on time, that is, not on time as we know it."

"Word has it there might be something other than humans on board, Mr Frump."

"We know the boat has left, and the boat, if all permits, will arrive. Therefore it is my belief that whatever departs must arrive."

"Can you be clearer, Mr Frump?"

"Well, in a relative sense nothing starts and nothing ends. But for humankind things do start and end. Man, unlike the universe, is beginning with end. He is born into that which always was and he dies from that which always is. The boat will come into what always was and what always will be. It is my firm belief that the passengers aboard are determined to disembark with the sole intent to change things somewhat. They do not like the idea that they depart and arrive. They too would like to be without beginning without end, just like the universe, gentlemen."

After various adventures the passengers depart on the ship *There They Go*, leaving Frump to "rest awhile and resume his work after the ship has left. He was certain that the force he was after was not going to depart on that ship." Interestingly, Corso had published what was said to be the first chapter of *The American Express* in the *Transatlantic Review* in 1960, though the piece concerned didn't actually appear in the book itself. Called *Detective Frump's Spontaneous and Reflective Testament*, it was a long incantation of joy to just about everything, and had something in common with certain of Corso's poems. But it is his introduction to the piece which is of relevance in this context:

"*Detective Frump's Spontaneous and Reflective Testament* tells no story, nor is it meant to. Yet its meaning to the story to create for Frump a state in which he can find no wrong, and so hold love and sympathy for all things - Frump is the Force who sees all things as excusable because they are, and who sees all things as GOOD and GRAND, except one, his adversary, the Anti-Force, who he sees as a terrible downright WRONG, and can find neither love nor sympathy for him. Frump excuses even condones! murderers, warlords, dictators, plotters, rapists, pimps, in short, he atones every imaginable crime - his only concern is to ferret out and destroy his Anti-Force. Now who can this Anti-Force be who is so much more terrible than any imaginable crime? If Frump hails all man and all things, how then can he not hail his 'foe'? His Anti-Force, by the way, is a man. Thus this novel is but a repeat of that classical theme, man's noble and victorious search for that 'evil' which besets all man."

Of course, it's easy to see that what Frump is trying to ferret out and destroy is the Anti-Force within himself. Like God, or Power, it is all within man, and in fact one of the characters in *The American Express* at one point says: "What's all this nonsense about looking for Power outside yourselves. It's in YOU!"

It is clear from histories of the movement that, like other Beat writers, Corso was particularly active in the 1957-1962 period. (My framework is designed more for usefulness than strict definition, but the peak years of the Beats were, I believe, in the timespan indicated). A fourth book, *Long Live Man*, came out in 1962, and collected some of his recent poems. Again, the preoccupations with time, death, and decisions stand out. As one of the shorter poems says:

Every man is free
Be he in chains or at sea

And another poem, *Friend*, astutely remarks:

Sometimes I scream Friends are bondage! A madness!
All a waste of INDIVIDUAL time.

The extent of Corso's wanderings are also reflected in the book, a long poem, *Greece*, being its hinge, if not its strongest point. But elsewhere, places like London, Venice, Germany, and Morocco are mentioned, sometimes in a manner that smacks more of notes towards a travel book than poems of any sustained vision or even alertness, Perhaps the life-style didn't lend itself to settling down to work at the poems?

After the early-Sixties Corso's life and creativeness seem to have been affected by personal problems, and by an awareness that the general situation was changing. In his own words, "A lot was changing in 1964. The bombs were falling down, the whole thing with Vietnam was starting. Kennedy was dead, there was this slow, gradual coming to what you've got today. Which is: One Big Suck. That's what the whole thing is. Everything just went tumbling. Haven't seen anything built up."[11] From a personal point of view, Corso had tried marriage, and teaching at SUNYAB. His marriage failed, despite what were, according to reports, his sincere attempts to conform. As for teaching, he lost his post when he refused to sign a loyalty oath. This oath, a legacy of the McCarthy years, required anyone working for the university to declare that they were not, nor had they been, members of the Communist Party, or if they had they were dutifully repentant. Corso never had been political in the formal sense, and he certainly hadn't belonged to the Party, but he delayed signing, and then decided to refuse on principle. According to Bruce Cook, who discussed the incident with Corso, he said: "Well, I was teaching a course on Shelley. Imagine that. Of all the people who wouldn't sign a loyalty oath it's Shelley."[12]

So, a silence descended in terms of book publication, although a few poems came out in magazines. (It needs to be mentioned that, in the interview, Corso refers to other reasons for the non-appearance of collections in the period referred to). The late-Sixties were the days of the Hippies, student protest, and the build-up of opposition to the war in Vietnam. Corso's old friend Ginsberg thrived on the era, but Corso himself seemed more confused than anything. Asked in a 1973 interview if he was "detached from the whole war thing," he replied, "Yes, completely ... the whole thing in Vietnam has just lost all meaning, legendariness. Whereas the Vietnamese, no matter how much they are being bombed they've got something to go for."[13] Which seems a sober enough remark. In the 1973 Salem State College discussion, however, he first of all sympathised with the suggestion that Kerouac had turned his back on Vietnam: "He was poor, simple, human bones. No wonder he turned his back on it. That beautiful man would never hurt a - He's the only man I know in life who never hurt a soul." But as Ginsberg and Orlovsky continued their questioning of Kerouac's attitudes, Corso (most probably exasperated), was reduced to snarling, "Those Gooks had to go," a remark which Ginsberg probably summed up accurately when he said, "Here you hear alcohol talking."[14]

That Corso did, however, have a genuine understanding of Kerouac's basic impulses - confused as they may have been on the surface - is evident from his long eulogy, *Elegiac Feelings American*, written in 1969, and dedicated to the late-novelist. In it Corso not only pays tribute to Kerouac, and laments his passing, but also laments the seeming failure of the American Dream:

All we had was past America, and ourselves, the now
America, and O how we regarded that past!
And O the big lie of that school classroom! The
Revolutionary War ... all we got was
Washington, Revere, Henry, Hamilton, Jefferson,
and Franklin... never Nat Bacon, Sam Adams,
Paine... and what of liberty? was not to gain
liberty that war, liberty they had, they were the
freest peoples of their time; was not to lose that
liberty was why they went to arms - yet, and
yet, the season that blossomed us upon the scene
was hardly free; be there liberty today? not to
hear the redman, the blackman, the youngman
tell.

The poem succeeds not only because of its intensity of language and imagery, but also because Corso keeps the statements in check. The fact of his constantly bringing the reflections back to Kerouac seems to remind him that his main purpose is to eulogise a friend, and whilst clearly saying other things he doesn't try to make too-large comments on life and death. In fact, the vision is largely social, and Corso appears happier with it than with the philosophical. It can be placed alongside two other poems in the book, *The American Way* (which dates from 1961) and *America Politica Historia, In Spontaneity*, both of which discuss the condition of the country, and Corso's own feelings about it. They each make the statement that he considers himself "nationalistic," though he later stated, "That's not my true feeling. I really didn't understand what that meant, and thought of the poet as the universal being. Being nationalistic about something is being geographical."[15]

The poems in *Elegiac Feelings American* were drawn from a ten year period, 1959 to 1969, and although a few of them are slight, and should never have been put into a collection, the overall impression was healthy enough, and in 1970 the title poem alone gave one hope that Corso would be more active. But silence descended again unless one counts a few interviews, and occasional short poems and drawings in little magazines and the like. It has only been in the past two years or so that Corso has re-surfaced, as witness some readings in England, the interview, and a short piece in *The Guardian* in which W. J. Weatherby seems to have caught him in an optimistic mood.

At the beginning of this piece I quoted from a poem in Corso's unpublished (at the time of writing) collection, *Herald of the Autochthonic Spirit*. It appears to stress the confusion that continues to proliferate as one gets older. Reading it, I was reminded of a scene in the Arthur Penn film, *Night Moves*, where the detective, attempting to reassure a young girl, tells her that he understands how life can seem disturbing, mixed-up, and unpredictable. But, he goes on to say, "Let me tell you, when you get to 45, you'll realize it's no better." Elsewhere in *Feelings on Getting Older*, Corso plaintively recalls:

When I was young I knew
        but one Pope
        one President
        one Emperor of Japan
When I was young nobody ever grew old
or died The movie I saw when I was ten
        is an old movie now
        and all its stars
        are stars no more

And in another poem, *Bombed Train Station, 80 Killed*, he sombrely writes:

Life has changed/*La Dolce Vita* has soured
and there's a big hole now
where children of vacation played

Life has become afraid of time and places
Who knows where or when
a suitcase will be laid?
Who knows what masks
bombers wear beneath their faces?

The language is bleaker, the vision similar, as if the events and experiences of twenty years had taught Corso that life isn't always the same, that treating it as farce doesn't change it, and it can get worse. In some ways he had always known this, of course, as witness his comments in a letter, published in 1963, in which he discussed poetry and religion:

"It takes an awful lot to live in the world as a poet, I don't care how certain a man may be of what he is, I always look people straight, I stand before them, eye to eye, and I know that no-one can be at all very certain, life is such that we can only believe and hold to our beliefs, uncertainty is what life is, reality is ever changing, it isn't immutable, it doesn't hold what was yesterday is so today, so then the poet too is ever changing, if it be truth he is at, then he cannot stick to his guns, that is why I admit contradiction, I am contradictory because I am of life and life is contradictory."[16]

I've tended to look at Corso's poems largely from the point of view of what they're saying, and I've not said much about his technique, other than to refer to the change which occurred when, around 1957/58, he decided that he should let his lines run loose and often long. Frankly, I've never thought that he was a very skilled or original technician, and his most successful poems have been either the fairly simple, short sketches, such as *Italian Extravaganza* or *Of One Month's Reading of English Newspapers*, or the longer *Marriage* and *Elegiac Feelings American*, where the conversational style has been sustained by Corso's closeness to the subject-matter. His originality has been more obvious in his use of language, his overall vision, and his humour. But at his best he's managed to combine these factors into poetry of real and lasting value. And if only a handful of his poems survive then he will have achieved more than many other poets whose work, though skilled, essentially says little of any consequence. To quote Carolyn Gaiser, Corso "has a talent for feeling. Although his poems impulsively avoid the limitations of rhyme and metre, they show, at his best, the sure control of a poetic intuition."[17] Or, in Corso's own words in the poem, *Getting to the Poem*:

I write poems from the spirit
for the spirit
and have everything

NOTES

1. 'Discussion following poetry reading April 1973, Salem State College', *Gone Soft,* Vol.1. No.3, Spring 1974, page 23.

2. 'Gary Snyder: An Interview by James McKenzie', *The Beat Diary,* 1977, page 143

3. 'Gregory Corso: An Interview by Robert King', *The Beat Diary,* page 4.

4. See the Introduction by John Clellon Holmes to *Neurotica*, Jay Landesman Ltd., 1981.

5. 'An Interview with Gregory Corso', *Unmuzzled Ox*, 1973 Unpaginated.

6. Corso Interview, *The Beat Diary*, page 12.

7. Corso Interview, *Unmuzzled Ox*. Unpaginated.

8. Corso Interview, *The Beat Diary*, page 19.

9. Corso Interview, *Unmuzzled Ox*. Unpaginated.

10. Gregory Corso, 'The Time of the Watches', *Cavalier*, December, 1964, page 94.

11. Corso Interview, *Unmuzzled Ox*. Unpaginated. ;

12. Bruce Cook, *The Beat Generation*, Scribners, 1971, page 144.

13. Corso Interview, *Unmuzzled Ox*. Unpaginated.

14. Salem State College Discussion, page 29.

15. Corso Interview, *Unmuzzled Ox*. Unpaginated.

16. Gregory Corso, 'An Open Letter on Poetry and Religion', *The Aylesford Review*, Vol. 5, No.3, Summer 1963, page 123.

17. Carolyn Gaiser, 'Gregory Corso: A Poet, the Beat Way' in *A Casebook on the Beat*, ed. Thomas Parkinson, Thomas Y. Crowell Company, 1961, page 272.

FLOATING BEAR

"*Bear* Number One, what I remember about it. We printed 250 copies. Our mailing list was just two pieces of paper with names scribbled on them, 117 names that we had gotten out of our address books. Painters, poets, dancers, those folks, and mostly from New York. It was February 1961 and how it came about was that the year before A.B.Spellman and I decided to do a magazine called *The Elephant at the Door*. One of the first manuscripts we got was from Russell Edson and he called it *The Horse at the Window*. (There seem to have been a lot of animals around at the time.) Then, when it came to the point where A.B. had to reject his first manuscript, he decided that he didn't want to be an editor because he couldn't reject anybody. I just put all the manuscripts in a file drawer and forgot about it, and the next year Leroi came up with the idea that we should do a newsletter that would go out free to writers. Then came the question of a name. Half kidding, I suggested calling it *The Floating Bear*, which was a boat Winnie-the-Pooh made out of a honey pot. It had a characteristic I was really fond of: 'Sometimes it's a Boat, and sometimes it's more of an Accident.' To my surprise Leroi liked it, and so it became *The Floating Bear, a newsletter.*"

I've lifted that from the fascinating introduction, adapted from taped interviews with Diane Di Prima, which is tagged onto a facsimile edition (fully annotated and indexed) of *The Floating Bear,* a mimeographed newsletter which ran from 1961 to 1969 mostly under Miss Di Prima's able guidance. I say "mostly" because Leroi Jones was involved with the first twenty-five issues, and a few guest-editors -John Wieners, Bill Berkson, to name a couple - also got in on the act somewhere along the way. But Miss Di Prima was, I would guess, the driving force once the publication got started. To be strictly accurate, I suppose it would be true to say that *The Floating Bear* lasted until 1971 because in the Summer of that year there was an issue of *Intrepid* which appeared under the title, "The Intrepid-Bear issue," and which used some of the manuscripts still held by Diane Di Prima when she suspended operations with the thirty-seventh issue.

In the introduction Miss Di Prima mentions that the balance in the issues she co-edited with Jones was achieved because of their different ideas about what was good and interesting. As she says, "He was involved with our thought, our investigation into what we were and what our stance was in relation to society and the world outside. He liked strong, politically aware poetry, and a lot of prose and criticism, I reacted more intuitively to what I read - didn't always "understand" the poems I was into." She also refers to the fact that Jones had some experience in the magazine field, his own publication, *Yugen,* having started in 1958. (It died in 1962, incidentally.) In fact, much of the material published in early issues of *The Floating Bear* had originally been submitted to Jones for *Yugen.*

The first few issues of *The Floating Bear* were mimeographed at Larry Wallrich's Phoenix Bookshop in New York (Wallrich now operates a first-rate specialist book service in London), and distribution was as casual as Miss Di Prima implies in her introductory comments quoted above. The newsletter was not sold through bookshops - a number of copies were given to Wallrich in return for his assistance with the production of the early issues - and anyone asking for a copy got one, and whatever back issues were available. But if the production and general distribution were almost-deliberately casual the contents indicated that the editors were anxious to get their publication to the writers that mattered. Creeley, Dorn, Olson, O'Hara, McClure, Oppenheimer - they're all represented in its pages. It needs to be stressed at this point that *The Floating Bear* was not a magazine as such. Like *Migrant* in this country, it was devised as a means of putting writers in touch with each other, and a way of getting things into "print" quickly so that they could spark off a response and, hopefully, create the right atmosphere for creative work.

1961 saw seventeen issues of *The Floating Bear*, 1962 issues eighteen to twenty-six, 1963 issues twenty-seven and twenty-eight. The balance were scattered over the 1964-1969 period. That the energy behind the newsletter - and the need for it - were essentially to be found in 1961 and 1962 is obvious, and not all that surprising. Personal matters play a part in these things, of course, and it's significant that Jones dropped out after issue twenty-five, and that Miss Di Prima moved around a little after 1962. But "personal matters" are often a reflection of trends in the larger society, and the middle and late-Sixties saw the rise of the Black Power movement, a build-up in student politics, and the advent of the hippies and flower-power. The intense literary activity of the 1957-1962 period gave way to social concerns, and an esoteric newsletter perhaps seemed less relevant.

It would be wrong to suggest that *The Floating Bear* represented any particular school or style. There were magazines around at that time which did aim at pushing particular theories - certain publications connected with the "deep image" poets spring to mind, as do those of the "New York school" - but *The Floating Bear* had no fixed policy other than a loose dedication to the new and/or modern. After all, any publication that features Burroughs, Creeley, Olson, Kerouac, Ginsberg, Lamantia, Selby, Carl Solomon, Joel Oppenheimer, McClure, Gilbert Sorrentino, Stuart Perkoff, and John Wieners, not to mention literally dozens of others, many of them unknown outside their own circles, can hardly be said to be restricting its pages to a clique. The approaches to poetry represented in it - and despite a certain amount of prose the newsletter's principal achievements were in the poems it used - were many and varied, and even a summary knowledge of the American non-establishment scene of the Sixties will suffice to allow readers to accept my statement that many of the people mentioned had widely-differing views about the writing of poetry. Or prose for that matter. In this connection it's interesting to read Gilbert Sorrentino's comments on his fellow-writers in issue thirty.

It was inevitable, I think, that the quality of the contents varied a great deal. Some of the poems now seem to be merely fashionable exercises, others, I suspect, were published because they were by friends of the editors (the guest-editors appear to be most guilty in this respect), and a number must have been just bad choices resulting from the need to make instant decisions and get the newsletter out. But this is all understandable, and acceptable if one allows for the stated purpose of *The Floating Bear*, i.e. to serve as a newsletter that would keep writers in touch with each other and create a climate of activity. It was a useful publication to have around at the time it first appeared, and this excellent re-print is a fascinating guide to much of what was liveliest and most interesting in American poetry ten or fifteen years ago.

The Floating Bear, a newsletter. A facsimile re-print, published by

Laurence McGilvery, P.O.Box 852, La Jolla, California 920J7, U.S.A. Available in the United Kingdom through Larry Wallrich, 25 Whitehall Park, London N19 3TSC Price: £12 (hardcover) and £8 (softcover). It should be noted that an edition with a bound-in *Intrepid* "Intrepid-Bear" issue is also available, price £14 (hardcover), and £10 (soft-cover)

ORIGINS OF THE BEAT GENERATION

"We define neurosis as the defensive activities of normal individuals against abnormal environments. We assume that human beings are born non-neurotic, and are neuroticised later. We do not agree that it is the measure of social intelligence and psychiatric health to adapt to, and rationalise for, every evil. We do not subscribe to the psychosomatic fashion of throwing the gun on the corpse and the blame on the victim. We give space to the description of the neuroses with which human beings defend themselves from an intolerable reality. But it is with this reality that we are primarily concerned.

Neurotica is the first lay-psychiatric magazine. It is our purpose to implement the realisation on the part of people that they live in a neurotic culture and that it is making neurotics out of them. The practitioners have their own journals. *Neurotica* is for the patients - present and future."

Those words are from the editorial in *Neurotica 5*, published in 1949, and they define, as well as anything, the aims of the magazine. Or perhaps it's better to say that the contents of the magazine defined its aims, and that the editorial referred to offered a summary of them.

But let me outline the essential details of the history of *Neurotica* before I look at the contents. It was founded in St Louis in 1948 by Jay Landesman, a man described by John Clellon Holmes (in *Nothing More to Declare*) as having a "Pop Imagination." By that Holmes meant Landesman "refused.....society's categorical choice of either remaining an aesthete or becoming a vulgarian. For any and all evidences of a unique and unconventional point of view interested him, and he looked for these evidences in junk shops, movie houses, and newstands (wherever his own quirky eye led him) as well as in bookstores, art galleries, and theatres." Landesman published issues 1 to 4 from St Louis, 5 from Stamford, 6 to 8 in New York, and then handed over the magazine to Gershon Legman for a 9th and final number in 1951. Legman, it needs to be said, had contributed a great deal to the magazine before becoming its editor. That brief synopsis of the magazine's lifespan does not indicate how much of a focal point it was for a variety of contributors and readers who comprised what might be said to have been an intellectual "underground." (One hates to use the word "underground" these days because of its immediate links with the phoney, over-publicised scene of the Sixties; Legman's pamphlet, *The Fake Revolt,* is the best illustration of how one member of a real "underground" saw through the falseness of the later one). Holmes makes it clear in his introduction, however, that a spirit of camaraderie did exist, and that there was an overall feeling of being part of a group which stood in opposition to (even if loosely) many of the social and cultural aspects of the period.

Of course, looking through the contents now it may seem, especially to anyone under the age of thirty-five, or even forty, that there is little surprising about much of the material. After all, articles about psychiatry, sex, popular music, comic books, and the like, have been the staple fare of even a widely-available weekly like *New Society* in recent years. But if one uses one's imagination, and tries to look into the recent past, then it ought to be possible to understand why *Neurotica* did seem so unusual and adventurous in 1948. It's true to say that similar areas were being explored in specialist publications, but usually as precisely that - specialist subjects - and often with no obvious appreciation of possible connections with other matters. *Neurotica* tried to bring together writers and their interests in a way that pointed to a continuity of relevance. And, of more importance, it did it in a manner that was then unusual in that it tried to popularise subjects which were considered esoteric.

For what it's worth, too, I'd like to suggest that, even if not consciously, *Neurotica* was a way of speaking against the mood of conformity brought on by the onset of the Cold War. In Eric F. Goldman's *The Crucial Decade and After: America 1945-1960* the following comments are made: "The shocks of 1949 loosed not only a sweeping anti-Communism, but a tendency to denounce anything associated with the different or disturbing as part of a Communist conspiracy. With the end of 1949 many an American was attacking Sigmund Freud in the same breath with his denunciation of Alger Hiss... People were beginning to use the word 'intellectual' as if it meant some compound of evil, stupidity, and treason." My suggestion is in no way designed to imply that *Neurotica* was political (or if it was, that it was committed to a specific position), but rather to indicate that, as Goldman makes clear, political events had influenced wider social attitudes to a degree where a publication of its kind could be seen as challenging the status quo.

It's worth referring to one minor item which has relevance to the points raised in the preceding paragraph. *Neurotica 6* had a little section called "Anti-Psychiatrica" which utilised material from newspapers, and in which the following appeared: "The Psychoanalytic infection has corrupted American culture very deeply...there cannot be any intellectual advance in our country today without a determined philosophical struggle to destroy the paralysing obscurantism of psychoanalysis wherever it pollutes our social and cultural life."

That was published in a 1949 issue of *The Daily Worker*, and it may have been indicative of the way in which American Communists - then an embattled and dwindling group - were still desperately trying to demonstrate that they were good, wholesome types at heart, though no doubt more-substantial reasons (the basic clash between Freudianism and dialectical materialism, for example) also played a part in determining Communist attitudes. Whatever the reasons, one can't help but draw some ironic humour from the fact that the Party was attacking Freud at the same time that, if Goldman is correct, many Americans were equating his theories with the supposed evils of Communism.

Still, such matters are not really my concern, and my aim in pointing to them has been to give an idea of the kind of social and cultural climate in which *Neurotica* operated. It seems to me that any worthwhile magazine ought to be at least partially aware of such questions, and as I mentioned earlier, there does appear to have been a general agreement amongst at least some of the contributors that they were going against the grain.

But who were the contributors, and what were their concerns? The first issue, published in 1948, contained a lengthy piece by Rudolph Friedmann which established the tone of many of the later essays and articles. Concerned with problems of sexuality, and attacking the repressive nature of society (British in particular, it should be noted), it was written in an imaginative rather than a purely factual style, so that the reader got, in effect, a creative view of "The End of Feeling," as the piece was called. An equally lively and important contribution from Friedmann appeared in the second issue. With this he launched a savage attack on the purge against prostitution which, in the late Forties, was carried out in London and other major cities. What is especially intriguing is that, at times, one might almost be reading something by William Burroughs: "Another detective never brought his arrests back to the station. He disposed of their bodies by nibbling at them with rat-teeth, spitting indigestible pieces of skin down the street drain. Every little man would like to be a police spy with rat-teeth...."

What Friedmann was hitting out at was the kind of repressive little-man morality which the post-war Labour Government unfortunately often seemed to represent: "The Labour Party as the party of the working class and the lower middle class has gone beyond unconscious life and become the party of conscious death, and the enemy of all that is erotic and exotic.....A city without prostitution is a city without culture; the city has regressed into a village ruled not by life but by the Methodist Labour Party peasant. Historically the coming to power of the Left represents not the birth, of new life but the attempt of degeneration to be reborn through repression." Friedmann's writing throws up numerous provocative ideas like that, and not all of them are necessarily limited by being about events in 1948 or so. I suppose one could fairly argue that all political parties are now parties of (and with policies designed to cater for) the working class and lower middle class, and that, as a consequence, they're all tainted with the little man morality, albeit that morality may have altered some of its views on certain aspects of sexuality. It would be interesting to know what Friedmann, if he's still alive, would make of today's attitudes.

The second issue of *Neurotica* was particularly strong on articles, and had what I feel was one of the most valuable items it ever published. William Krasner's "The Psychopath in our Society" wasn't the first analysis of the psychopathic condition, but it was an early attempt to take the investigation beyond medical boundaries and into what might be called general social areas. Krasner's thesis was that psychopaths were far more numerous than most people imagined - like any label of its kind the term invites ideas of madmen, whereas psychopaths can seem as sane as anyone else - and that society tolerated, and even rewarded them when they fulfilled socially useful roles. Ruthlessness in business is, for example, often held to be a virtue, the policeman who breaks the rules to supposedly uphold the law is condoned, the sportsman who goes all out to win, no matter how, is seen as justified. All these activities, and others such as war, the arts, and politics, present ample opportunities for the psychopath to operate, and be not only protected, but even admired. But as Krasner pointed out:

"No nation or culture consisting wholly or even largely of psychopaths can long survive. The psychopath is a disruptive, parasitic, immoral influence, and any group, while it may for various reasons support and even honour him, must fundamentally rest on a firm economy and on a great mass of hardworking responsible people to exist; and in direct proportion to the extent that he is tolerated, that his attitudes find support in the culture pattern, to that extent it is an unhealthy society."

Words that, some people might think, could say a lot about contemporary Britain and its problems.

There were other indications of *Neurotica* concerns in the second issue, namely an article about the social milieu of bars and taverns, and a story, "Tea for Two," by John Clellon Holmes which was, in his own words, "an experiment with the language of jazz written before I had dug Bird, Diz and the full thrust of bop." Reading it now tends to bring out its slightly strained air of being "with it," as they used to say, but I suppose it was a brave attempt to capture a mood or life-style at the time it was first published.

The Holmes story does, I think, demonstrate that most of the poetry and fiction published in *Neurotica* was less convincing than the articles and essays. The tone of the "creative" work was frequently over-consciously modern, with jerky, experimental prose and semi-surreal poems full of contrived imagery. Holmes admits this in his introduction, and it would have been less than honest to have overlooked saying so.

I don't want to write a complete survey of the contents of each issue. But it is worth mentioning that Gershon Legman grabbed a major part of the third with a piece on "The Psychopathology of the Comics." Legman, pictured by Holmes as a "combination of crank, gypsy scholar and pamphleteer, intellectual spelunker and journeyman-philosopher," was as influential as Landesman in terms of directing the preoccupations of the magazine, and his *Neurotica* contributions were forerunners of his books such as *Love and Death, The Fake Revolt, The Rationale of the Dirty Joke*, and the *Horn Book*, all of them provocative, idiosyncratic publications. Legman's biting prose hit out at everything and everyone:

"Does anyone notice that in radio and television we now see happening what was sworn would never happen: fantasy bloodlust spilling over into fact, with prize-fights, wrestling matches, football and ice-hockey - once rough competitions, now holocausts of berserk bone-crushing while televised millions wet their pants - authors thrown to critics, contests in abuse and blatherskite under the name of comedy, spot-news broadcasts from the foot of the electric chair, paid sadistic quizmasters cracking the whip over fumbling quizzes, their trash-filled brains reeling between avarice and insult, audience-humiliation programmes (under the guise of confessionals and giveaways) capitalising on mayhem and sado-masochism in the nth degree, with the payoff to the victims in refrigerators."

Neurotica always ran a small section of classified ads, most of which, one suspects were concocted by the editors. And a warning at the head of the column ought to have dissuaded anyone from taking them too seriously: "*Neurotica* does not assume any responsibility for anything that happens to anyone who answers any of its ads." Despite this, an appeal in the fourth issue from a young lady keen on the works of the Marquis de Sade, and wanting to meet a man interested in Sacher-Masoch, drew a batch of bizarre replies, many of which the editors gleefully printed in the following number.

Young New York writers like Anatole Broyard, Chandler Brossard, and Allen Ginsberg made their appearance in the sixth issue. (Readers might profitably refer to Brossard's novel, *Who Walk in Darkness*, for a fictionalised view of the milieu they worked in). Ginsberg's offering was an early, short version of the nonsense-poem which later became popular in Beat circles under the title "Pull My Daisy." It's interesting, too, to note that there was another item which has been incorporated into the annals of the movement. Carl Solomon's "Report from the Asylum" was an essay on his experiences when undergoing treatment, and was reprinted in the *Protest* anthology in 1957. For the record, Solomon also contributed to issues 7 and 8.

The ninth saw Legman in complete editorial control, and contained a statement which indicated that he wasn't interested in receiving fiction, poetry, or literary criticism. It was also mentioned that the anti-analytic jitters prevailing in America had "taken a definite turn for the worse. " Whether this was one of the reasons for *Neurotica* failing to appear again is impossible to say, though Legman's bias towards psychoanalytic problems was evident. Holmes reckons that it foundered "on the reefs of penury and the national apathy of 1952." and that's possibly as accurate a summing-up as we're ever likely to get.

I've referred to only a fraction of the contents of the five-hundred plus pages which made up the nine issues, and it will be obvious that they contain much more of interest. For the curious there are, small oddities - a poem by Leonard Bernstein, an effective story about junkies by Larry Rivers (now best known as a painter, but with past involvements with both writing and jazz), material from Marshall McLuhan, Kenneth Patchen, Lawrence Durrell, and Wallace Markfield. Looking at names such as these the reader might wonder why *Neurotica* is referred to as "The authentic voice of the Beat Generation," but it is the tone of the magazine as whole which made it, as the blurb say, "a breeding ground for the ideas and style that were to set Kerouac on the road and Ginsberg howling." And from a point of view that sees the Beats in the late Forties and early Fifties as part of a cultural "underground" rather than, as some woolly-minded enthusiasts think, the whole of it, this claim seems reasonable. Not all of the work published in the magazine matched up to its high aims, but that it did use much of value is proved by the fact that it has been reprinted in full thirty years later. How many little magazines does that happen to?

John Clellon Holmes's involvements with the Beat movement are common knowledge, but he's always interesting to read because of his range of interests, and his capacity to make the past come alive and take an objective look at it. And this interview is well constructed. Let me quote a short passage. Holmes was asked about his war experiences when he served in the Hospital Corps:"Anti-fascist though I had been since 12, the experience ended war for me. Fifty boys of my own age died while I watched, helpless to help. A hundred more were crippled forever, and no June night would promise them anything but bitterness. I feel a solidarity with them still. I've never written about any of this, except glancingly. War-memories encourage romanticisation, and my paltry-few would be demeaned by that approach, being mostly visceral, having to do with the simple frailty of the body, and the hard facts of the scarred future."

What a pleasure it is to read something like that from an interview.

Perhaps the answers to the questions were written down, or if spoken, tidied up for publication, but whatever the method it's certainly more satisfying than the kind of recorded interview where the transcript reproduced every pause, broken sentence, interrupted thought, and repetition.

Leaving aside the technical aspects of the interview it's very interesting to see Holmes talking about the war years because it is often forgotten, especially by recent devotees of the Beats, that the Forties were of key importance in terms of shaping their attitudes. In this respect his comments on jazz are worth noting:

"My only unachieved ambition, aside from a subtler understanding of work I've already done, is to play bop piano - to feed chords to brilliant soloists, to comp like Dodo Marmarosa or Al Haig or any of ten thousand who play funky and know the changes. At one point in late 1948 I measured my intellectual and artistic evolution by the fact that I stopped going to Nick's and Jimmy Ryan's and moved to the Three Deuces, Birdland and Bop City."

He develops this theme to mention - inevitably - Charlie Parker, and again one can't help wondering if newcomers to the Beat saga truly understand the influence Bird had in terms of providing an example and supporting the impulse to create art of one kind or another. Kerouac's respect for Parker is well known, and other writers like Ted Joans, Robert Creeley, Ginsberg, Corso, and Gilbert Sorrentino have testified to his stature. I mention this not to suggest that anyone not of the generation that grew up with Parker's music can't comprehend Holmes, Kerouac, etc. - to do that would be to limit the range of their writing unfairly - but more to propose that an understanding of the movement does rest largely on an awareness of what it drew from jazz.

Elsewhere, Holmes refers to the possibility that much of his work deals with "homelessness, rootlessness," and goes on to suggest that a lot of Beat writing generally "is about the feeling of being refted from home, useable past, and the tradition, the sense of continuity, which bolster both." And there is, perhaps, a link here to his idea that he sees "no reason any longer why writers should have to compartmentalise their work in their own eyes. I, at least, refuse to do so. I write poetry, essays, travel pieces, fiction, and criticism. I paint in acrylics. I keep journals. I make eccentric films. It's all part of the same flow." It seems to me that there could be something in the notion that the "flow" is what replaced the home, past, tradition, etc. referred to by Holmes. Think of the "flow" in the movement of Kerouac's *On The Road*, for example.

There is much more in *Interior Geographies* that it would be useful and valuable to quote, but the interview is best read in its entirety. It adds up to one of the most perceptive documents of its kind on Holmes, and the Beats in general, and anyone seriously interested in either subject should read it.

NEUROTICA : THE AUTHENTIC VOICE OF THE BEAT GENERATION: 1948-1951 with an introduction by John Clellon Holmes Published by Jay Landesman Ltd.

INTERIOR GEOGRAPHIES: AN INTERVIEW WITH JOHN CLELLON HOLMES by Arthur & Kit Knight Published by Literary Denim

EVERGREEN REVIEW

One of the most famous magazines associated with the Beats, and yet taken almost for granted in histories of the movement, was *Evergreen Review*, which started its life in 1957 and carried on for more than ninety issues. Most little magazines collapse after a few years but *Evergreen Review*, perhaps because it was published by Grove Press, survived, although its editorial policies and contents were no longer those of a true little magazine after its first five or six years of existence. It even changed its size, becoming in 1964 a large format publication, often with provocative covers and articles that picked up on all the concerns of the 1960s, from drugs, rock music, anti-Vietnam protest to Black power, sexual liberation, and much more. It did still publish some fiction and poetry, but one had the feeling that a need to shock and be fashionable took precedence over the earlier concern to print good new writing. Commenting in 1971 the journalist Bruce Cook noted that *Evergreen Review* was still in existence but added that "accretions of bile and hostility seem to have swollen it so that it now almost resembles the ponderous monoliths of American life that are attacked with such mechanical regularity in its pages: it is the revolution institutionalised."

With the above comments in mind this survey of *Evergreen Review* is not intended to be inclusive. My interest is in its first five years and a handy cutting-off point might be the 31st issue, the last one in the original paperback size. I think it is possible to see a change in editorial approach after that, though these things are never clear-cut and they alter over a period of time. I know that in 1965, when I had a couple of poems published in issue 38, the contents were still a mixture of little magazine material and pop-style gimmicks like the cartoon strips devoted to Barbarella and Phoebe Zeitgeist. But perhaps a switch of emphasis had been hinted at in issue 31 with the extract from the French pornographic novel, *The Story Of O*. Some people might argue that this was serious literature and deserved a place in the magazine but my own feelings was that it was just an attempt to jump on the bandwagon of sexual licence that resulted as censorship broke down.

It's tempting to start looking at some individual issues with the famous "San Francisco Scene" number which, as much as anything, was responsible for drawing attention to what was new in American poetry. But there had been an issue prior to that and it gave a good indication of how the editors (initially Barney Rosset and Donald Allen) wanted the magazine to reflect not just new writing in the United States but also work produced in Europe and elsewhere. In that way the Americans would be seen in an international situation which, as Rosset and Allen rightly sensed, was opening up generally. Poets, playwrights, and novelists in France, Germany, Russia, and even staid old England, were turning out interesting work and there were advances in art, music and other areas, that were worth recording in print. And the importance of politics at the time was shown by a long interview with Jean-Paul Sartre about the Russian intervention in Hungary in 1956. Set alongside a story and poems by Samuel Beckett and a translation of Henri Michaux writing about experiments with mescalin, it gave a European emphasis that contributions by Mark Schorer and James Purdy did nothing to alter.

That emphasis changed with the 2nd issue, and I'd guess that it was Donald Allen who was the prime mover in shaping the survey of activity in the San Francisco area. It needs to be said that not only poetry was included, though the issue tends to be remembered for its focus on poets. There were reports on the jazz and art scenes in the Bay region and prose by Kerouac and Michael Rumaker. And Henry Miller, seen as a kind of forerunner of the Beats, was represented with a piece about Big Sur. But the importance of poetry was made clear by contributions from Gary Snyder, Philip Whalen, Jack Spicer, Michael McClure, Allen Ginsberg, and Lawrence Ferlinghetti. The issue tried to show that the work was varied and that a few older poets (Kenneth Rexroth, Robert Duncan, William Everson, Josephine Miles) had laid the foundations for what happened in the 1950s. The selection also demonstrated that not all the work was Beat, though the inclusion of Ginsberg's *Howl* might have given the impression of a Beat issue because of the way its growing notoriety tended to overshadow shorter and less-striking poems. Properly seen, however, the contents of this number of *Evergreen Review* offered a fascinating glimpse into a world of poetry that was only just beginning to open up to a wider public. And it certainly helped draw attention to the magazine as well.

Published on a quarterly basis the 3rd and 4th issues followed on time, with the contents combining American and European influences. Poets like Gregory Corso, Paul Blackburn, and Charles Olson, who hadn't qualified for the San Francisco number, were featured, and there was more from Samuel Beckett. The Paris connection was quite strong, in fact, and work by Eugene Ionesco, Arthur Adamov, Albert Camus, and Georges Arnaud, was allocated ample space. The inference was that experimental and provocative writing needed to be promoted and links to earlier dissident writers and artists, like the surrealists, revived. This and the suggestion that theatre, music (classical and jazz), and art were linked to writing gave the impression that something exciting and dynamic was happening and not just in America.

There isn't time to examine each issue in detail but all sorts of new writers were appearing in its pages as *Evergreen Review* progressed. Robert Creeley, Denise Levertov, and Frank O'Hara, were among the poets, and John Rechy and Douglas Woolf a couple of the prose writers. Looking back, it's sometimes a review or similar short piece that attracts the attention, as with Alexander Trocchi's comments on a re-issue of George Orwell's *The Road To Wigan Pier* which showed how thinking about social and political matters had changed. For Trocchi, Orwell's faith in "the common man" was a "kind of vulgar democratic unreflectiveness" with little meaning in a world which, as Trocchi saw it, needed "the more vital level of insight which begins with a total revolt against all abstractions with which society traps, labels, and affixes status to the individual, and whose object is the self, here and now and unique and doomed in the end to absurdity in a strange cosmos." With Trocchi these days too often treated as little more than a cult figure and junkie hero it's interesting to realise that he had an enquiring mind before it was destroyed by drugs.

Most of the 7th issue was devoted to writing and art from Mexico and by the 9th Donald Allen was no longer joint editor with Barney Rosset. It could be, too, that some of Rosset's concerns were starting to have an influence on the contents of the magazine. As publisher of Grove Press he had run up against censorship problems when he brought out an edition of *Lady Chatterley's Lover* and thirty pages of *Evergreen Review* were allocated to a judge's summing-up when he overturned a postal ban on the book. There was also a long piece by Henry Miller dealing with the difficulties he'd experienced when *Sexus* was published in Norway. And though the article itself was a perfectly serious piece of writing one can't help wondering about the decision to include Mulk Raj Anands's essay on *The Spiritual Background Of The Erotic Sculptures Of Konarack.* Was it much more than an excuse to print photographs of some of the sculptures? Still, all this was balanced out by work from Snyder, Whalen, Terry Southern, John Wieners, and Seymour Krim.

I'm perhaps being unfair to Barney Rosset by suggesting that his motives in publishing some material were not always linked to artistic interests. He no doubt thought it necessary to challenge censorship and widen the areas that writers and artists could explore openly. And it wasn't as if, at this stage, the magazine was overwhelmed with sex and censorship matters. When I received my copy of issue 11 in early 1960 I was impressed by its table of contents, which included Burroughs, Kerouac, Ginsberg, Philip Lamantia, and Robert Duncan, not to mention Antonin Artaud, Sartre, and an astute review of Jack Gelber's play *The Connection,* by Nat Hentoff. The issue seemed to be right at the centre of things, and the advertisements it contained also pointed to the vibrancy of the literary and artistic scene, with listings for *Big Table, Yugen*, Auerhahn Press, Hanover Records (LPs of Kerouac, etc.) and several art galleries.

The advertisements in issue 13 were equally interesting, with *Cain's Book, The New American Poetry, The Beat Scene,* and a new magazine, *The Noble Savage,* all available. But the magazine itself was devoted to the subject of "What is Pataphysics?" The question was never answered, and had it been the pataphysicians would have denied its validity, but some idea of the general tone may be derived from the following: "Pataphysics has nothing to do with humour or with the kind of tame insanity psychoanalysis has drummed into fashion. Life is, of course, absurd, and it is ludicrous to take it seriously. Only the comic is serious. The pataphysician, therefore, remains entirely serious, attentive, imperturbable." The issue had texts by Boris Vian, Raymond Queneau, and others, and a large section devoted to the originator of pataphysics, Alfred Jarry. It was an entertaining exercise to use a complete issue to explore this theme, though some readers may have taken it less than seriously.

The magazine rolled on into 1960 and it was now appearing on a bi-monthly basis. Beats like Ginsberg, Ferlinghetti, and Burroughs, continued to contribute regularly, though sometimes the work they produced wasn't what might have been expected. Gregory Corso, best known for his poems, wrote an impressionistic prose piece about Berlin, a place he described as "a city of secrets." Some of his ideas concerning Berlin and German youth now seem dated, as does his notion of great art arising because of the non-political approach to life: "they live for the moment. They realise the eternity in the moment. This will make for a new and great art." Poets are not necessarily good prophets. Of the non-Beats, the English playwright and short-story writer, Shelagh Delaney (best known for *A Taste Of Honey*) and the Irish writer, Brendan Behan, kept the contents varied. Their names are still known but what happened to Mack Sheldon Thomas, John Williamson, and Thomas L. Jackerell? Are they still alive and active somewhere in America? The English poet, Pete Brown, was in issue 20, and though he drifted away from poetry he made a career in pop music.

The international approach has to be kept in mind and the special German issue late in 1961 was, in editor Fred Jordan's words, meant to demonstrate "how the twin burdens of the past and the present are mirrored in the best new literature of Germany." Interestingly, a lot of it contradicted Corso's assertion that the non-political would play a major part in German writing. Corso was perhaps a bit more accurate with his witty poem, *Of One Month's Reading Of English Newspapers*, in issue 22. Its sly portrayal of what English newspapers like to print (presumably because English readers like sleaze and sex) is still relevant. Reading this, and other Corso contributions to *Evergreen Review*, reminds me what an engaging writer he could be. His short play, *Standing On A Street Corner*, in issue 23 wasn't great literature but it was entertaining and amusing.

It's possibly moving away from the Beat links to *Evergreen Review*, but it's worth noting that throughout 1962 the magazine carried a series of articles about France by Joseph Barry, an American journalist living in Paris. He largely looked at the political issues raised by the Algerian War and the crisis then affecting the French nation. Forty years later a lot of people will know little or nothing about the situation in the early 1960s, but if you happened to visit Paris at the time it could be worrying to experience the atmosphere and see the police in action. And mentioning this does have relevance to the Beats as some of them made Paris their home, and if they largely steered clear of getting involved they must have noticed what was going on.

I'm still intrigued by the now forgotten writers who were published in *Evergreen Review* and who may, at the time, have appeared to show promise. In issue 26 Charles Miller wrote an account of the problems he encountered at Newhaven when he tried to enter England from France. Like Henry Miller before him, Charles Miller had difficulty convincing officials he had sufficient money to support himself in England and he was refused entry and sent back to Dieppe. The notes in the magazine referred to him as "a master mason who is now at work on a novel," and they raise the question of whether or not it was ever finished and published? Shane Stevens, in issue 27, was another writer said to be working on a novel, as were John Thomas and Michael Mason in issue 28. The world must have been full of young writers completing novels. There was a slight difference in issue 30 where Thomas Dent had a short story and was said to be writing a play. Dent was an English writer, 25 in 1963. and *Early Morning Scene* was his first published story. Did he ever finish his play and was it performed, and did he write anything else? His contribution to *Evergreen Review* was a weak attempt to catch the rhythm and lifestyle of what would soon be called "Swinging London," but it sounded too deliberately hip to be authentic. Passages like the following showed up its limitations: "But pot and sounds are the only way out. Man, often when I'm turned on I go way out somewhere else and one thing you need on a scene like mine is to go way out somewhere else, often.... " Reading that at the time made me realise how the best British writers were those like Shelagh Delaney who stuck to their own backgrounds and language.

With Trocchi, Kerouac, Brautigan, Snyder, Leroi Jones, and Joel Oppenheimer in issues published in 1963 it was obvious that the magazine was still a force to be reckoned with. Oppenheimer, incidentally, was noted as working on "a one-act musical, a movie script for a Western, and a history of war in the Western world," all of which made a change from a novel. Did he ever complete these projects? Even if he didn't he at least continued to write and publish poetry and prose for many years. William Burroughs was also still a favourite with the editors and some excerpts from *Nova Express* were in issue 29, along with an interview by Ann Morrissett. The interview was written in an idiosyncratic style so as to catch the movement and atmosphere of a Burroughs story, and at one point had him carried out by some boys, presumably to be dumped in the Seine. But a note added to the interview said, "As it turned out, this was obviously a ruse. A man purporting to be an inspector from the Nova police turned up the following week on a stool in the dim recess of a junky sanitarium called La Bohème behind the Gare Montparnasse. His voice was that of the Old Doctor."

I recall visiting La Bohème in 1962 and seeing Burroughs giving a reading and answering questions from the audience, what there was of it. The club was half empty. But it was a curious evening all round. A small jazz group played and was joined by a black musician who wandered in, got out an alto saxophone, and produced some exciting bebop. He was, I realised, Sonny Criss, a legendary figure from the Los Angeles scene of the 1940s who had come to Paris in search of work. He stayed for a time and then went back to California but his career never hit any heights and, depressed and ill, he committed suicide in 1977. Also performing at La Bohème was a Beatnik poet, barefoot, bearded, and in jeans and black sweater, who clicked his fingers, said "Yeah, man" a lot, and declaimed some third-rate poetry. The club didn't last long and it's not surprising. Not too many people had heard of Burroughs in 1962, even fewer would have cared about an itinerant bop musician, and the Beatnik poet was bad enough to drive anyone away.

I mentioned at the beginning of this article that *Evergreen Review* changed its format after the 31st issue, moving to a large publication roughly the size displayed on newsstands and in general bookshops, but it may also have been designed to allow for wider pictorial presentation, with comic-strips, cartoons, photographs, and graphics, taking on a larger role. True, there had sometimes been illustrations in earlier issues, but they were limited and usually meant to accompany an article. Looking at a much later issue, number 75 from 1970, with its cover of a naked woman in the arms of a large gorilla and its portfolio of photographs of a young couple making love, not to mention its cartoon-strip, "Frank Fleet and his electronic sex machine," makes one realise how much things had changed since the exciting days for literature of the late 1950s and early 1960s. An article by Seymour Krim and a piece about Leroi Jones were slim pickings from what was otherwise a table of trivia, and the overall intelligence and seriousness of earlier issues was long gone.

After 1963 or so *Evergreen Review* lost its role as a little magazine devoted to literature and the other arts. It could be argued, I suppose, that because of its association with Grove Press (it was like a house magazine and published many writers that Grove brought out in book form), and its relatively wide distribution, it never was a true little magazine, but I think that in its first few years it aimed to reach the kind of intellectual audience that did read little magazines. For that reason, and the range of work it published, it deserves to be placed alongside *Big Table, Yugen, Kulchur, The Outsider*, and a few others that helped shape the literary developments of the period. And, as with all magazines from the past, it's always fascinating to look through its pages and read not just the well known writers but also all those poets who perhaps never became famous or even had a book published and the novelists who only ever saw a portion of their book in print. Those forgotten names remind us that a lot more happens in writing than most histories ever tell us and that *Evergreen Review*, in its first few years at least, played an important part in promoting new work.

KULCHUR

It has been said of *Kulchur* that it was "one of the great magazines of the Twentieth century, an authoritative voice, as important as *The Little Review, The Dial, transition, The Criterion,* and *Contact.*" And the same commentator, Gilbert Sorrentino, added that he always thought of *Kulchur* "as the critical wing of *Yugen;* that is to say, *Kulchur* seemed to me what *Yugen* might have become had Leroi Jones had the money to continue it." There was a reason for Sorrentino making this claim and it was that quite a few of the writers published in *Yugen* also appeared in the early issues of *Kulchur.* They had, as well, been published in Sorrentino's own magazine, *Neon,* and in *The Black Mountain Review.* What Sorrentino was pointing to was the importance of such magazines to the development of the New American writing of the 1950s and 1960s and the standards aimed for. *Kulchur* was not primarily devoted to creative work and instead tried to set up a critical apparatus for dealing with a range of artistic activities. It did print some poems, stories, and short plays, but most of its pages were filled with articles and reviews.

Kulchur had its origins in the Greenwich Village scene of the late 1950s. Marc Schleifer, a young poet and journalist active around New York at the time and whose work was in *The Beat Scene, The Village Voice*, and *Swank*, decided to start a magazine to publish some of the vital writing then in circulation. His first issue, in Spring 1960, featured Ginsberg, Burroughs, Charles Olson, Paul Bowles, and Diane di Prima, a line-up which might be seen as fairly typical for the period. But what was significant about *Kulchur* was that it emphasised what can best be described as critical prose. Olson's piece was theoretical about such matters as perception and projection, and the noted jazz critic, Martin Williams, and the film critic, Richard Kraft, both contributed essays. Schleifer may have been interested in the Beats, but he clearly wanted a magazine that would offer a wider view of intellectual activity in New York. Donald Phelps, a writer difficult to classify (cultural critic perhaps best describes him) was also given space to expound on what he referred to as "the muck school of American comedy," meaning *Mad* magazine, Lenny Bruce, and the like. Phelps made the point that it represented much of American life better than politer forms of humour did. I doubt that Phelps is remembered by many people, but his quirky magazine, *For Now*, which largely published his own work, was always worth reading. And his book of essays, *Covering Ground: Essays For Now* (Croton Press, 1969) provided a wide ranging survey of literature, films, and politics. He was a genuinely independent voice. A major part of the second issue of *Kulchur* was given over to Leroi Jones's *Cuba Libre,* his long article about a visit to Cuba just after Fidel Castro had swept to power. Castro was then a hero of the American Left and the piece not only indicated how much Jones was impressed by him but, significantly, Schleifer's own political interests. His poem in *The Beat Scene* refers to the Spanish Civil War, the Cuban Revolution, and similar matters. And Schleifer would shortly go to Cuba. Phelps, Olson, and Paul Bowles cropped up again in the second issue, along with Gregory Corso, Fielding Dawson, and Paul Goodman, writing about Wilhelm Reich, whose theories of "orgone energy" had aroused the suspicions of the American Government and led to him being imprisoned. Like Jones's article on Cuba, Goodman's piece reflected some of Schleifer's own radical concerns.

I've detailed some of the contents of the first two issues because of what happened next. A wealthy woman, Lita Hornick, had become interested in *Kulchur* and, early in 1961, she became its publisher, with Schleifer continuing as editor. Or that was the idea. According to her, "Schleifer edited *Kulchur3* and then took off for Cuba without telling me where he was going or how long he would be gone." She also said that the issue "was more political than literary in orientation," though it's frankly difficult to know why she thought that. Ideas about what constitutes "political" do differ, but I don't recall that I thought of this issue of *Kulchur* as political. It did strike me as culturally radical, in some ways, in terms of the range of topics it covered and its focus on what was often called an "alternative" or "underground" area of artistic activity. To get a magazine in 1961 which published Kerouac, Huncke, Burroughs, Snyder, Ginsberg, and Leroi Jones (all of them in the third issue) was quite exciting and allowed readers to see what was going on outside established areas of writing. There were also provocative essays, with Paul Bowles writing about kif and Donald Phelps investigating the world of pornography. It was a strong issue, even if Lita Hornick questioned its literary intentions.

Schleifer had obviously lost interest in *Kulchur* and the fourth issue had Gilbert Sorrentino as guest editor and marked a change in the direction the magazine would take. A long article about life in a mental insititution (credited to Harry Black but actually by Hubert Selby), a similarly lengthy one about the Oz series of novels (fifty or so, beginning with *The Wonderful World Of Oz* in 1909), together with essays by Robert Duncan and Ed Dorn, and film and book reviews, emphasised the critical tone and there wasn't a poem in sight. Lita Hornick said that the issue "was much more concerned with literature and poetics than were previous issues, and was much more to my taste." And Sorrentino later recalled that it was a conscious decision to "bar all poetry and fiction from the magazine and devote its pages to criticism and commentary." He also remembered that it was Lita Hornick's initial intention to provide the money for publication and oversee production and distribution of *Kulchur* and that she claimed not to want to interfere with editorial policy. But her comments about the contents of the fourth issue being "much more to my taste" were an indication of the way she was thinking, and she was soon to play a more dominant role in determining what the magazine published. People who control the purse strings usually do want to have a say in how things operate.

Marc Schleifer was still shown as editor in both the fifth and sixth issues, though with a note saying that he was on "leave of absence," and Joel Oppenheimer stepped in to guest edit the fifth. That the policy about publishing poetry and fiction was still uncertain was evident by the inclusion of an excerpt from a novel by Louis Zukofsky (understandably never published in full if the excerpt is typical) and a poem by Kenneth Koch. But articles and reviews predominated, with Frank O'Hara writing about art and Leroi Jones looking at the black experience. The snag with guest editors is that a continuity of concerns might not be established if the individuals involved have widely varying tastes and interests, but Oppenheimer was very much involved with the New York scene and his contributors, and what they wrote about (poetry, art, music, theatre, dance), largely fitted in with what had previously been published in *Kulchur*.

According to Lita Hornick, Marc Schleifer's continued absence meant that she had to edit the sixth issue, and she chose to devote over thirty pages of it to what she referred to as "Louis Zukofsky's great play *Arise, Arise.*" I have to admit that I've never been able to get to grips with most of Zukofsky's work and the play didn't excite me in 1962 and still doesn't forty years later. It seems to have been written in the 1930s and I wonder if it was ever actually performed? I somehow can't imagine it attracting a large audience if it was. Lita Hornick perhaps showed better judgement by getting Frank O'Hara to write about various artists and Julian Beck to sing the praises of the Living Theatre. There was an interesting piece by Denise Levertov about the British poetry scene in which she provided information about Gael Turnbull's Migrant Press (she called Turnbull "a sort of living bridge between American and British poetry") and now-forgotten British magazines like *Satis* and *Outburst* which were concerned to forge a transatlantic link. Levertov particularly referred to Roy Fisher and his long poem, *City,* which at that time was probably more understood and appreciated in America than in Britain. Fisher was outside the British literary establishment framework and in the early 1960s his work circulated mostly in American magazines and British "underground" publications. He was, much later when his talents had been widely recognised, published by Oxford University Press, but had a reputation only among non-establishment writers and readers when he was written about in *Kulchur*. That some importance was attached to his work was demonstrated by the fact that several pages were allotted to *Hallucinations,* described as a supplement to *City*. And the following issue of *Kulchur* had an essay by Turnbull about Fisher.

Lita Hornick was now Managing Editor and Schleifer's name had been dropped from the magazine. She was, in theory, still not directly involved with what *Kulchur* published and a number of departmental editors (Leroi Jones - music; Frank O'Hara - art; Gilbert Sorrentino - books) had complete autonomy about what they selected for publication. They were also expected to contribute articles and reviews themselves. Like all theory this didn't stop things happening and Sorrentino was later to complain that Lita Hornick had increasingly "begun to take a hand in editorial decisions affecting the contents of *Kulchur*. Pieces appeared without having been seen or approved by any editor. Writers who had very little to do with the tone or position of the magazine were asked by Mrs Hornick for contributions." All this, according to Sorrentino, weakened *Kulchur*, but her view was that she was simply trying to broaden the contents to take in the whole spectrum of avant-garde activity and to present "an area for a diversity of opinion." This kind of arguing among editors of little magazines was not unusual, especially when some of them, like Sorrentino, had definite ideas about what ought to be published. He considered that the magazine should have "retained its original focus" but that Lita Hornick "wanted to discover her own writers and ranged all over to get them." It's not rny intention to provide an issue by issue account of the contents of *Kulchur*, largely because to do so would take up too much space. It's better to look at some of the highlights while also providing a history of the policy changes affecting what was published. Leroi Jones and another black poet, A.B. Spellman, kept the jazz coverage lively, with interviews with Lester Young and Marshall Royal and numerous record reviews. One of the most fascinating of the jazz articles was Gilbert Sorrentino's *Remembrances Of Bop In New York, 1945-1950*, a long personal memoir of what it was like to be growing up at a moment when Bop was in the ascendancy and, as Sorrentino put it, "the entrance into the general world of culture, although at the time, I wouldn't have believed it. When I was 14, culture meant going to the opera and doing your homework every night." I don't think Sorrentino's piece ever circulated widely among jazz fans, most of who wouldn't be likely to read a magazine like *Kulchur*, but it was one of the most vivid descriptions of what might be called the social atmosphere of bebop that I've ever read. Jazz historians can document the musical developments in detail but Sorrentino's personal survey caught the mood and made the excitement of the late 1940s come alive.

Sorrentino may have written some good articles for *Kulchur* but when the eleventh issue appeared in Autumn, 1963, he had quit his job as Book Editor and was listed as a Contributing Editor. Reading his account of his involvement with *Kulchur*, and how the magazine developed, does make me think that his views were affected because he wasn't able to shape the contents to his own liking. He had strong opinions about what he considered important, but so did Lita Hornick and it would be unfair to say that issues after 1963 were lacking in quality. Sorrentino himself continued to write for *Kulchur* for a little longer and his article about Hubert Selby was in the thirteenth issue in 1964, along with work by Ginsberg, Richard Brautigan, and Douglas Woolf, which showed that poetry and fiction would have a place in the magazine. It can only be assumed that Lita Hornick, now firmly in the editorial chair, made the decision to use these poems and stories. Her memoir of the 1960s certainly gives that impression. I have to insert my own memories of *Kulchur* from the point of view of a reader in Britain who looked forward to each issue and always found much in them to read and absorb. I can't claim that everything the magazine published appealed to me, but that's not an unusual response when looking at any publication. And there were always articles and reviews that balanced out the less interesting (to me) material. I recall short pieces by Walter Lowenfels about people he'd known in Paris in the 1930s, a long conversation between Robert Creeley and the English poet, Charles Tomlinson, and an article by Edward Dorn about Trocchi and Burroughs. I'm being selective in naming these pieces and personal preferences and interests obviously play a part in determining what stays in the mind over a forty year period. As *Kulchur* progressed its contents changed and different groups and individuals came to the fore. I'm not sure if anyone, apart from literary historians, now remembers the "Deep Image" group (poets like Jerome Rothenberg, Robert Kelly, and David Antin) but they had some currency in avant-garde poetry circles in the 1960s and their work was noted in *Kulchur* and elsewhere. And the New York poets, with Frank O'Hara in the lead and closely followed by Ted Berrigan, Ron Padgett, Joe Brainard, and others, were also given space to expound their ideas and opinions.

I think it needs to be noted that the reviews in *Kulchur* were always worth reading, if only as a guide to what was new. But beyond that they offered quirky and sometimes fairly harsh comments on poets who might have expected to be treated kindly. Gerard Malanga, writing about Gilbert Sorrentino's *Black And White*, described it as a "book to be scanned through and not read." And Sorrentino, reviewing May Sarton's *To Mix With Time*, said it was "the worst volume of poetry to be published so far this year." Of course, reading little magazines many years later shows how they were often used as weapons in all kinds of literary battles, and that the feuding and fighting was very much part of the wider artistic scene in New York. *Kulchur* was, after all, a determinedly New York publication and Lita Hornick wanted it to reflect the changes in the cultural situation in the city. There were dangers inherent in such an approach and Gilbert Sorrentino may have identified them when he claimed that later issues of *Kulchur* became "fuzzy, off-centre, and fashionable." And If I can intrude a personal opinion, I have to admit that I thought

Kulchur less essential after its third or fourth year of publication. It seemed to lack focus and although I still read it, if only to keep up with what was happening, it was less exciting in terms of the writers it printed.

Leroi Jones was still quite an influence on *Kulchur* and it was planned that he would edit an anthology of "younger poets" which would be published by Kulchur Press. Later, it was decided that the anthology would not be a separate book and would appear as the twentieth issue of the magazine. This idea was then abandoned because, as Lita Hornick said, Jones had "become completely involved in black politics" and no longer had the time to devote to poetry. But Lita Hornick herself was also feeling the pressure of other involvements and though it wasn't intended that way the twentieth issue, published late in 1965, was the final one. She later said that there "was no reason to feel that the magazine's energies were depleted," but I would guess that it may have become obvious to her that it was beginning to lose its reason for existence and the contents were far less challenging than in earlier issues. It was wavering uneasily between creative and critical work and some of what was published seemed self-indulgent on the part of the writers rather than stimulating to the readers. Perhaps I'm wrong about this, and personal preferences again played a part in how I reacted to the final few issues of *Kulchur*, but I can't say that I agreed with Lita Hornick's description of an exchange of letters between Ted Berrigan and Ron Padgett as "wildly funny writing." Considering what *Kulchur* had done in the past it was wasteful to devote almost thirty pages to a weak private joke.

Despite what I've said about its decline I think it's true to say that it was an important magazine. The mixture of long articles, reviews, comment, some creative work, and unclassifiable bits of writing, struck me as being what a true little magazine ought to be about. And the range of subjects covered, including poetry, theatre, music, dance, painting, and much more, pointed to the way in which everyone connected with *Kulchur* during all its stages of development thought in broad terms about the importance and influence of the arts generally. The creation of a dialogue between all areas of artistic activity was clearly seen as something desirable, and there were few other magazines of the time which tried to do just that.

One final comment. What happened to Marc Schleifer, the original editor of *Kulchur*? A note in Fred McDarrah's *Kerouac And Friends* says that Schleifer "was born Jewish, later became a Moslem, changed his name to Suleiman Abdullah Schleifer, and moved to Cairo, Egypt. He later was chief of the NBC Bureau there and now teaches at the American University in Cairo."

NOTE

Readers are referred to Lita Hornick's *Kulchur: A Memoir,* and Gilbert Sorrentino's *Neon, Kulchur, Etc* - both included in *The Little Magazine In America: A Modern Documentary History*, edited by Elliott Anderson and Mary Kinzie, published by Pushcart Press, Yonkers, New York, 1978. Both pieces contain a great deal of information about *Kulchur* and its contents.

JACK KEROUAC'S JAZZ SCENE

Writing in *Escapade* in December 1960, Jack Kerouac ran through a long list of jazzmen he considered of importance at that time. He got a few of the names slightly wrong (Al Macusik instead of Hal McKusick, for example), but generally demonstrated that he was aware of what was going on in the jazz world, and that his enthusiasm for the music was as great as it had always been. If there is one thing that constantly comes through in his books it is the fact that he understood and loved jazz and the music of the big bands of the 1930s and 1940s. And it does need to be made clear that the two were heavily interconnected in the period that was Kerouac's most active in terms of influences and interests. This covers a roughly twenty year timescale, 1935 to 1955, give or take a year or two either way. One of the advantages of examining the music in question is that it has been well documented on record, so it is possible to listen to the bands, soloists, and singers, that Kerouac frequently mentions. And, by doing so, to understand how his writing reflected the sounds and the moods of particular periods.

But let's go back to the beginning, to the years when the young Kerouac was starting to take notice of the bands, musicians, and singers. In *Maggie Cassidy* there is a passage where Jacky Duluoz and friends visit the Rex Ballroom. There is nothing really glamorous about the place, but to them it seems exciting and different. They see "lights playing polka dots around the hall" and catch sight of "the sudden group of jitterbugs with long hair and pegged pants." One of the jitterbugs tells them, "Oh Gene Krupa is the maddest drummer in the world! I saw him in Boston! He was the end!" In Kerouac's description of the scene there is the buoyancy of initiation into the seemingly-magical world of dancehalls, jitterbugs, and heroes like Gene Krupa. Now, it is true that, in his reaction to the dance-band music being played in the ballroom, and the reference to Krupa, Kerouac was doing little more than registering what many sixteen-year olds would have thought and felt at the time. But this is, of course, what gives his writing its appeal. It refers to both the personal and the general. And so it neatly hints at things to come, in this case a fascination with jazz fans, their enthusiasm, and their language.

Still, it was quite a long way from jazz, even allowing for Krupa's name being used. Krupa was, in 1938, just launching a band of his own after three years with Benny Goodman and he had been lucky enough to be in at the birth of the swing craze. In the words of George T. Simon, Krupa was "quite a showman...with his gum chewing and his hair waving and his grimaces and his torrid drumming."[1] It was more than probable that Kerouac read Simon's articles about Goodman, Krupa, and others, as he was a leading commentator on the music scene between 1935 and 1955. Simon was employed by *Metronome* magazine, and as Dennis McNally remarked of Kerouac and his friends, "The whole gang went to Lowell's City Auditorium to hear Harry James, bought *Metronome* with the gravity of stockbrokers purchasing *The Wall Street Journal*, and disputed fine points with the subtlety of diplomats."[2] *Metronome* was an influential jazz and popular music journal in the Thirties and Forties. It helped spread the word about bands, musicians, singers, and their records, to the small towns of America, and its annual polls, in which readers voted for their favourite performers, were an indication of popular tastes.

Radio was, of course, a major factor in shaping these tastes, and Kerouac's reminiscences of the period are full of references to radio programmes. To quote George T. Simon again, "big bands headlined numerous top radio series."[3] one of the most popular shows was *Make Believe Ballroom*, which used recordings to create the atmosphere of a dance-hall so that people could clear the furniture to one side and then shuffle around their living rooms. Other programmes (*The Fitch Bandwagon*, for example, and those sponsored by Camel, Old Gold, Raleigh-Cool, and Chesterfield) featured live broadcasts by top bands such as Glenn Miller, Woody Herman, and Tommy Dorsey. Kerouac would have heard these broadcasts and so picked up on the different styles in evidence, the talents of the soloists, and the qualities of the singers. It needs to be remembered that what the bands were mostly playing was popular music and not out-and-out jazz. The swing bands did have a wide range of material at their disposal, and the better ones - Goodman, Shaw, Barnet, Dorsey - included first rate soloists in their ranks. But a glance through discographies, or better still a sampling of the actual records, will soon indicate that they churned out commercial material much of the time. Novelty numbers abounded, as did routine arrangements of popular songs. Some of the songs were of superior quality, but there were hundreds which were soon forgotten. Does anyone recall *In A Little Hula Heaven* or *Our Penthouse On Third Avenue*, (both recorded by Tommy Dorsey in 1937), and how about *There's Honey On The Moon Tonight* (Gene Krupa 1938) or *You're A Sweet Little Headache* (Benny Goodman 1938)? Nostalgically, these discs do have a certain amount of charm, and Kerouac could well have heard and enjoyed them, but only the most dedicated collector of old dance-band records would bother trying to find copies.

So, in the late-Thirties, what Kerouac was listening to was essentially popular music with a degree of jazz colouring. And the jazz was primarily of a white big-band kind, because it was the white bands which tended to get the publicity and the peak radio times, plus the bookings for theatres and dance-halls. It was possible to hear black bands on the radio, but far easier to tune in to the white ones. Kerouac's experience of black big-band music, and especially jazz, was limited in the Thirties, as it was for most people of his age growing up in towns like Lowell. Even black teenagers often found it more convenient to hear music by Artie Shaw or Benny Goodman than by Count Basie or Duke Ellington, especially if they lived outside the big cities. Here's Kerouac himself, describing what he was hearing: "At the last minute I'd stand undecided in my room, looking at the little radio I just got and in which I'd started listening to Glenn Miller and Jimmy Dorsey and romantic songs that tore my heart out...My Reverie, Heart And Soul, Bob Eberle, Ray Eberle..." Miller's band was definitely one of the more commercial of the time, and so was Jimmy Dorsey's. As for the singers mentioned, they were competent vocalists in the big-band context, but neither had the individuality to assert themselves sufficiently to succeed in the way that, for example. Frank Sinatra did after he'd served his apprenticeship with Harry James and Tommy Dorsey.

There are other references of relevance in *Maggie Cassidy*, and one curious aside in which a character called Pauline Cole is said to have later sung with Artie Shaw's orchestra: "Some day she'd sing for Artie Shaw, some day little gangs of coloured people would gather around her microphone in Roseland Ballroom and call her the white Billie." Unless Kerouac fictionalised this character completely (which is doubtful, considering his normal working methods), and in view of his liking for names which played on the originals, it could be said that he is referring to Pauline Byrne (coal burns) who, in

1940, recorded a handful of songs with Shaw. She was never well known, though she had a good reputation with other singers, and at least one of the songs she sang with Shaw's band (Gloomy Sunday) had links to Billie Holiday. Kerouac also says, "the roommates of her hard-knock singing days would go on to be movie stars," and that could tie in with the fact that Shaw and his musicians appeared in the film *Second Chorus*, though Pauline Byrne had then left the band.

Kitty Kallen and Helen O'Connell, both band vocalists, are mentioned, and then, in the final pages of the book, some names creep in which suggest that Kerouac's move to New York brought a broadening of his jazz awareness. He tells, as Jacky Duluoz, how he is introduced to "Lionel Smart" (Seymour Wyse), who recommends Count Basie's band, and so "its rush to the Savoy, talks on the sidewalks of the American night with bassplayers and droopy tenormen with huge indifferent eyelids (Lester Young)." To be fair, Kerouac also refers to Frank Sinatra singing *On A Little Street In Singapore* (hardly a great song), Glenn Miller at the Paramount, and Artie Shaw. But Basie and Ellington and Lester Young had entered his thinking, and it's at this point that he begins to touch on the kind of sounds which gave a foretaste of what was to come with the bop revolution of the 1940s.

Basie's band was, in the late-Thirties and early-Forties, one of the more influential, at least insofar as musicians and more-knowledgeable fans were concerned. As one jazz historian put it: "For the perceptive, the hip, and the aspiring jazz musician, appearances of the Count Basie orchestra became the most exciting events of those years."[4] And tenorman Lester Young became the idol of numerous young saxophone players, and of the small, but growing army of hipsters. His personal behaviour, as well as his musical approach, caught the imagination of these dissidents, and he became a kind of "underground" hero. A fictional treatment of Young in this role can be found in John Clellon Holmes's *The Horn*, demonstrating that other Beats besides Kerouac were impressed by him. In 1940, Kerouac was aware enough of Young's importance to have interviewed him for the *Horace Mann Record*, something he refers to in *Vanity Of Duluoz*, where he also recalls "Lionel Smart" insisting that he listen to Lester. And in his *Escapade* article about jazz Kerouac mentioned that he and Seymour Wyse had collaborated on an article, "Lester Young is ten years ahead of his time," which they'd sent to *Metronome* without success. To stress that Wyse was his guide in those days Kerouac said in another *Escapade* piece, "The Beginning of Bop," that Young was an important figure and that there was a "strange English kid hanging around Minton's who stumbled along the sidewalk hearing Lester in his head."

Kerouac's tastes in jazz were clearly expanding, and in *Origins Of The Beat Generation* he recalls visiting Minton's Playhouse when Young, Ben Webster, Charlie Christian, and Joe Guy were playing, which suggests that he was one of a small group of genuine enthusiasts. Minton's was a "seedy box on One Hundred Eighteenth Street. It was owned by a peripheral musician named Henry Minton, who had been the first black delegate in New York's famous Local 802."[5] Some time in 1940, Minton asked Teddy Hill, a onetime band-leader, to become manager of the club, which he did, organising a small house band (Thelonius Monk, Nick Fenton, Joe Guy, Kenny Clarke), and running the place as an after hours hangout for musicians and the hipper fans. Within a few weeks of its opening Minton's had become the place to jam, and jazzmen, known and unknown, frequented it to relax after their jobs with the big-bands and in bigger clubs had finished for the night.

All accounts agree that Minton's, and another Club called Clark Monroe's Uptown House, were the places where bop was born, and Kerouac must have been in a position to evaluate the new music as it developed. He did say (in *Origins Of The Beat Generation*) that, in 1944, he still "didn't like bop," though he was obviously listening hard, because he added that he first heard Dizzy Gillespie and Charlie Parker playing together at the Three Deuces, another club which catered to the cognoscenti. But I don't think we need place too much emphasis on Kerouac's admission that his first experience of pure bop, as opposed to the mixture of swing and bop he would have heard at Minton's, had left him a little confused. Many people felt that way initially, and that includes a large number of musicians. The music at Minton's often included some early bop ideas, but recorded evidence shows that they were within an established framework and that the experiments were tentative enough to seem to be personal eccentricities rather than major changes in jazz. But by 1944/45, when Kerouac was visiting the Three Deuces, and presumably other clubs on 52nd Street, bop had blossomed, and the kind of group that Parker and Gillespie led made little or no concession to anyone unable to adjust to their musical revolution. One either took the music to heart or left it alone. And that it could baffle even musicians is evident from this account by drummer Dave Tough of a visit to a 52nd Street club: "As we walked in, see, these cats snatched up their horns and blew crazy stuff. One would stop all of a sudden and another would start for no reason at all. We could never tell when a solo was supposed to begin or end. Then they quit all at once and walked off the stand. It scared us."[6]

Kerouac did come to terms with bop and, by the middle 1940s, was involving himself fully in the hipster milieu of New York. He probably saw the new music as reflecting the mood of his friends and paralleling the social and artistic theories they were expounding. The 1945-47 period was when bop established itself. Billy Eckstine's big-band, wilder and far more daring than any of the white swing bands had ever been, was spreading the word, and in New York, Los Angeles, and other cities, small groups of boppers were coming together to take their music into the clubs. On record, too, the new jazz was gaining ground. A number of small companies - Savoy, Blue Note, Guild, etc -were recording bop groups, and even the established labels, such as Victor, started to take chances with the new sounds. I'm not suggesting that there was a complete acceptance of the music. Bop was always a minority interest, and it was never accepted by the public in general, even though there was a short-lived commercialised bop craze around 1949 which resulted in a few bop references being used in popular songs. *Bop Goes My Heart*, sung by Frank Sinatra, is one example. But even though Charlie Parker was a great jazz innovator, and looked on as a god by the hipsters, most people had no idea who he was. and cared even less.

In *Origins Of The Beat Generation*, Kerouac states that "by 1948 it was all taking shape," and while this can be seen as referring to the general development of his involvement with Ginsberg, Cassady, and the rest, it's significant that he went on to bring in a number of jazz references. "Symphony Sid's all-night modern jazz and bop show was always on," he writes, and "It was the year I saw Charlie Bird Parker strolling down Eighth Avenue in a black turtleneck sweater with Babs Gonzales and a beautiful girl." Then he adds, "In 1948 the 'hot hipsters' were racing around in cars like in *On The Road* looking for wild bawling jazz like Willis Jackson or Lucky Thompson (the early) or Chubby Jackson's big-band while the 'cool hipsters' cooled it in dead silence before formal and excellent musical groups like Lennie Tristano or Miles Davis."

In this handful of references Kerouac neatly evokes a range of jazz styles from the late Forties. Symphony Sid, incidentally, was a disc-jockey who specialised in playing bop and related music. Babs Gonzales was a bop singer and noted character around the scene. His book, *I Paid My Dues*, is a racy account of his own participation in the activities of the 1940s, and puts forward the highly debatable claim that he was the "creator of the be-bop language." Willis Jackson was a tenor saxophonist with a penchant for hard-blown performances. Dennis McNally records that Kerouac took John Clellon Holmes to a bar with a juke-box and enthused about Jackson's *Gator Tail*.[7] Lucky Thompson was a far better jazzman, and though Kerouac doesn't do him justice by linking him with Jackson he could play with great vigour. At his best, however, he used a rhapsodic style which had a warmth and invention, and an individual sound, which made him stand out. He often played alongside bop musicians, but was not a bopper himself. Still, one can understand why Kerouac thought of him expressing the mood of the hot hipsters. Chubby Jackson, one-time bass player with Woody Herman, was definitely an extrovert, and his shouted encouragement to the other musicians can be heard on recordings of the time. He had a short-lived band of his own around New York, and it's probable that Kerouac heard it in the jazz clubs. It displayed more drive and enthusiasm than finesse, but again it's easy to understand why Kerouac associated it with the hot hipsters.

Pianist Lennie Tristano never reached the front ranks of the jazz fraternity, but he did have some critical success as the leader of a small group of white jazzmen who played in what was thought of as an extremely cerebral style. Tristano did, in fact, make some early gestures towards 'free form' jazz, and his recording of *Intuition*, dating from 1949, created something of a minor sensation among the intellectuals who liked jazz. John Clellon Holmes, reminiscing in the interview published as *Interior Geographies*, referred to Tristano as "a mostly forgotten genius of the jazz piano,"[8] and elsewhere he said, "One of our passions just then was the work of pianist Lennie Tristano, who was, perhaps, the most avant-garde of the younger jazzmen of that year, and who, a month before, had recorded the first attempt at total, free form, atonal improvisation, a record called

Intuition, not yet released, but played occasionally by Symphony Sid on his all-night radio show."[9] It's of interest to also mention the reference to Lee Konitz, an alto-saxophonist associated with Tristano, which occurs in *Visions Of Cody*. Kerouac's semi-humorous description of Konitz playing as "if the tune was the room he lived in and was going out at midnight with his coat on" catches some of the complexity of his style. Miles Davis is a familiar enough name, but it's sometimes forgotten that, in the forties, he was often linked with the so called "cool school." Working with Charlie Parker's group, he had not attempted to compete with the extrovert playing of Dizzy Gillespie, Fats Navarro, and other bop trumpeters, but had instead fashioned a style which allowed him to operate mainly in the middle register of his instrument. In 1949 and 1950 Davis teamed up with arranger Gil Evans to record a number of highly influential sides which avoided the freneticism of bop and aimed more towards tight arrangements, relaxed improvising, and a generally calm and thoughtful air. Kerouac's reference to his appeal to the cool hipsters is accurate, and jazz historian Marshall Stearns, discussing such types, said, "the proper pose when listening to a Miles Davis record was one of despair."[10]

On The Road also deals with this late-Forties period and inevitably gets around to bringing in jazz of various kinds. There are several brief references to records that jazz fans of the period would have been familiar with, among them Billie Holiday's *Lover Man*, Lionel Hampton's *Central Avenue Breakdown* and Red Norvo's *Congo Blues,* the latter featuring Charlie Parker and Dizzy Gillespie. Curiously enough, Kerouac invents the name of the drummer, calling him "Max West," whereas it was actually J.C. Heard. "Max West" may well have been made up from the names of Max Roach and Harold 'Doc' West, two other drummers who were active in the 1940s. One of the more significant references is in the scene where Dean Moriarty visits Sal Paradise's relatives in Virginia: "They ate voraciously as Dean, sandwich in hand, stood bowed and jumping before the big phonograph, listening to a wild bop record I had just bought called *The Hunt* with Dexter Gordon and Wardell Gray blowing their tops before a screaming audience that gave the record fantastic frenzied volume." This particular performance was long by the standards of the day (it lasts around eighteen minutes and was originally issued on several 78rpm discs) and was recorded at a concert in Los Angeles in 1947. It especially spotlighted Gordon and

Gray, two popular tenormen on the West Coast, but also had solos from other bop stalwarts like Howard McGhee, Sonny Criss, and Hampton Hawes. Its determined, almost wild atmosphere is expressive of much of the feeling of *On The Road*. The same urgency and excitement come through, and the suggestion (in both music and writing) that it was necessary to "Go." That very word, used in the forties as an exclamation of approval or encouragement, can be heard shouted from the audience throughout *The Hunt*. And in referring specifically to this record Kerouac was quite clearly conscious of what he was doing. It caught the tone of the times perfectly and, as John Clellon Holmes put it, "listen there for the anthem in which we jettisoned the intellectual Dixieland of atheism, rationalism, liberalism - and found our own group's rebel streak at last."[11] Kerouac perhaps didn't have Holmes's precise intellectual appreciation of what the music represented, but he recognised intuitively that it matched Dean Moriarty's mood, as well as the frame of mind of many of his other friends.

Later in *On The Road* there is an intriguing comment on George Shearing, the blind English pianist who had settled in the United States in the Forties, and who had a fair amount of popular success when he formed a group which specialised in playing quiet, relaxed jazz. The music was light, often using well known popular songs as a basis for improvising which was largely confined to a chorus or two of attractive embroidery. It was, in other words, an innocuous form of jazz, pleasant and undemanding. But Kerouac had obviously heard Shearing - a skilled musician and quite capable of producing good bop style playing prior to his popular period. As he says, "those were his great 1949 days before he became cool and commercial."

One of the best known jazz references in *On The Road* occurs when Sal and Dean go to a night club to listen to Slim Gaillard, "a tall thin negro with big sad eyes who's always saying 'Right-oroonie' and 'How 'bout a little bourbon-oroonie." Gaillard was not a bop musician, despite being linked to the music and using bop musicians such as Gillespie, Parker, Howard McGhee, and Dodo Marmarosa, on his records. He had been active in jazz since the 1930s, and the duo Slim and Slam, which teamed Gaillard with bassist Slam Stewart, had produced discs which, because of their novelty appeal, reached a fairly wide audience. But Gaillard's influence as a hipster hero relates to the mid-Forties and after. He made a large number of records for minor labels on the West Coast, some of which attained an 'underground' status. At one time, Gaillard's music, along with that of another cult figure, Harry "The Hipster" Gibson, was banned by a number of radio stations on the grounds of bad taste, supposed drug links, and encouraging anti-social behaviour. The 1940s were, as Robert Creeley once said, "the time of the whole cult of the hipster,"[12] and though Kerouac doesn't label Dean Moriarty as one he makes it clear that he shared some of their characteristics and certainly their musical tastes.

Before leaving *On The Road* I want to briefly discuss the passage where Sal and Dean listen to "a wild tenorman bawling horn across the way." (This is the section of the book which appeared, in slightly different form, as *Jazz Of The Beat Generation* in *New World Writing* in 1955). The 1940s were peak years for saxophonists of the kind described by Kerouac. There were jazzmen like Dexter Gordon and Gene Ammons who could play good jazz and arouse audiences to fever pitch. And Illinois Jacquet and Arnett Cobb were noted for hard blowing while still retaining a measure of worthwhile jazz content in their music. But there were also dozens of others, mostly now forgotten, who were never major jazzmen, but had some connection with jazz. As Leroi Jones outlined it in his aptly titled story, *The Screamers,* "All the saxophonists of that world were honkers, Illinois, Gator, Big Jay, Jug, the great sounds of our days. Ethnic historians, actors, priests of the unconscious."[13] Jones shows how jazz and rhythm and blues intermingled, just as jazz and big-band music had in the 1930s, by including Illinois Jacquet and Gene Ammons ("Jug") with Big Jay McNeely and Willis Jackson ("Gator"), and it has always struck me that Kerouac in the *On The Road* passage, was more likely writing about a rhythm and blues style saxophonist than about an authentic jazz soloist such as Dexter Gordon or Wardell Gray. Some of the sweat and power of rhythm and blues comes through in his prose. The action takes place on the West Coast, and recordings from the 1940s by local artists like Big Jay McNeely and Big Jim Wynn do match in music what Kerouac describes in words.

The early 1950s found Kerouac still actively involved with jazz in terms of listening to it and writing about the musicians. *The Subterraneans* is supposedly set in San Francisco, but the events it describes took place in New York, a switch being made for legal reasons. A bop tenorman, "Roger Beloit," is one of the characters, and Kerouac says, "or, while listening to Stan Kenton talking about the music of tomorrow and we hear a new young tenorman, Ricci Commuca, Roger Beloit says, moving back expressively thin purple lips, "This is the music of tomorrow?" Beloit is actually Allen Eager, a noted tenor-saxophonist of the 1940s who, in the early 1950s, had fallen on hard times, like many bop musicians. His cryptic comment about the supposed "music of tomorrow" is understandable in that the new young tenorman Ricci Commuca (real name, Richie Kamuca) played in a style perfected several years previously by people like Eager, and with Lester Young as a major influence on them all. If one listens to Stan Kenton's *This Is An Orchestra*, recorded in late 1952 and probably heard often on the radio in 1953 when the action of *The Subterraneans* takes place, it is possible to hear him talking about Kamuca in enthusiastic terms, and generally suggesting that his orchestra was playing "the music of tomorrow," which was the sort of statement Kenton was prone to make. Kamuca, incidentally, was a good jazzman, but it's possible to understand Roger Beloit's comments given his circumstances.

There are other jazzmen in *The Subterraneans*. Charlie Parker is there, and Gerry Mulligan who, in 1953, was enjoying success with a series of records featuring him with trumpeter Chet Baker. The fact that the group didn't have a piano player was considered unusual at the time, and tracks like *My Funny Valentine, Walking Shoes* and *Bernie's Tune* would have been played regularly on record programmes. So would Stan Kenton's *Yes,* which Kerouac mentions as highlighting the voice of Jerry Winters, female vocalist with the band in 1952. Her Christian name was actually Jerri, but that's a minor point. He also refers to Jeri Southern, whose recordings of songs like *When I Fall In Love* and *You Better Go Now*, though not jazz, were popular with some jazz fans. She had the same smoky quality as Jerri Winters, June Christy, Chris Connor, and others who Kerouac described as "the new bop singers." That he was following jazz trends closely is obvious from the names he mentions, and the 'cool' tendency of the 1950s was becoming apparent.

When he came down from his sojourn on Desolation Peak in 1956 one of his first acts was to visit a jazz club, as recounted in *Desolation Angels*: "So we go out and get drunk and dig the session in the Cellar where Brew Moore is blowing on tenor saxophone, which he holds mouthpieced in the side of his mouth, his cheeks distended in a round ball like Harry James and Dizzy Gillespie, and he plays perfect pretty harmony to any tune they bring up - he pays little attention to anyone, he drinks his beer, he gets loaded and eye heavy, but he never misses a beat or a note, because music is his heart, and in music he has found that pure message to give the world...."

The saxophonist named was Milton "Brew" Moore, a white musician who, like Allen Eager, had appeared on the scene in the 1940s with a style derived from Lester Young. He was, in fact, reputed to have made the statement that "anyone who doesn't play like Lester is wrong." Moore was never a well-known jazzman, though he was quite active in the New York area in 1949/50. By the mid fifties he had drifted to San Francisco. He was unusual for a jazz musician, not because he drank, but because it seems he liked to drink a lot of beer, something which Kerouac picked up on when he described him in action, just as he picked up on Moore's physical appearance when playing; photographs bear out the accuracy of the description. Moore's performances could be variable, often due to his drinking, but Kerouac does capture some of the wistfulness that was in evidence when he was at his best, as well as the fact that he played with a great deal of swing. In some ways Moore paralleled Kerouac's prose. He could be gentle, almost sentimental, and then good humoured and lively and, also like Kerouac, drink brought about his death. He spent his last years in Europe, and died after a fall, probably when drunk. If, as someone once said, "all poets have broken hearts," then both Moore and Kerouac bore out the truth of that assertion. It does seem true to say that musicians like Allen Eager and Brew Moore appealed to Kerouac because of an inherent quality in their music that was also present in his prose. Larry Kart described it as "a meditative, inward turning linear impulse that combines compulsive swing with an underlying resignation - as though at the end of each phrase the shape of the line dropped into a melancholy "Ah, me," which would border on passivity if it weren't for the need to move on, to keep the line going."[14]

I started this essay by referring to something that Kerouac wrote in 1960. Jazz at that time was only just beginning to move beyond what had been developed in the Forties and Fifties, so Kerouac wasn't faced with the problem of having to say whether or not he liked anything that was radically different. He was essentially still dealing with music that was a natural extension of what he had known and loved since the mid 1930s, and from the evidence of his writing there is nothing to suggest that he went much further than that. The 1935-1955 period was, as I suggested earlier, the key one insofar as he was concerned, with the death of his idol, Charlie Parker, in 1955, almost bringing an era to an end. I haven't attempted to be totally comprehensive when detailing Kerouac's references to jazz, and I'm aware that he names many other musicians in his novels, articles, and poems. There's a poem about Dave Brubeck, for example. And a mention of singer Anita O'Day in *The Town And The City*. The "New York Scenes" section of *Lonesome Traveller* brings in John Coltrane and the little known Don Joseph and Tony Fruscella, as well as altoist Charlie Mariano. *Vanity Of Duluoz* covers the swing bands again, with Jimmy Lunceford, Charlie Barnet and many more, accurately placed in the time scale and often described in a way that evokes the kind of music they played. The point is that Kerouac's interest in jazz was something which influenced him in the sense of propelling him to write and to attempt to inject an improvisational feeling into his prose. "I want to be considered a jazz poet," he said, and though arguments will always exist about how far it's possible to parallel music in writing, it has to be accepted that jazz was clearly important to him. With this in mind we can see, from what was said in his books, how the music provided a background to the events that he describes. It could even be suggested that the best way to read Kerouac is with the music of the particular period he is discussing providing an accompaniment to the movement of his prose.

NOTES

1. George T. Simon.*The Big Bands*, Macmillan, New York, 1967. Page 306

2. Dennis McNally. *Desolate Angel*. Random House, New York, 1979. Page 27

3. Simon. Op.cit. Page 56.

4. Ross Russell. *Jazz Style In Kansas City And The Southwest*, University of California Press, 1971. Page 142.

5. James Lincoln Collier. *The Making Of Jazz*. Granada Publishing, New York, 1978. Page 348.

6. Marshall Stearns. *The Story Of Jazz*, Mentor Books, New York, 1958. Page 159.

7. McNally. Op.cit. Page 106.

8. Arthur & Kit Knight. *Interior Geographies: An Interview With John Clellon Holmes*, The Literary Denim, Warren, 1981. Page 28.

9. Ann Charters. *A Bibliography Of Works By Jack Kerouac.* Phoenix Bookshop. New York, 1975. Page 110.

10. Stearns. Op.cit. Page 158.

11. John Clellon Holmes. *Nothing More To Declare,* Andre Deutsch, London, 1968. Page 199.

12. Donald Allen, editor. *Robert Creeley:Contexts Of Poetry Interviews* 1961-1971. Four Seasons Foundation, Bolinas, 1973. Page 46.

13. Leroi Jones. "The Screamers" in *Tales*, Grove Press. New York, 1967. Page 76.

14. Larry Kart. "Jack Kerouac's 'Jazz America' or who was Roger Beloit?" in *The Review Of Contemporary Fiction,* Vol 3, Number 1, Summer 1983. page 27.

Kerouac's novels have appeared in various editions, but his scattered writings, such as the *Escapade* columns and *The Beginning Of Bop* are best located in *Last Words & Other Writings*, Zeta Press, 1985. A general awareness of jazz history will help in an understanding of Kerouac's love of the music. George T. Simon's *Simon Says: The Sights And Sounds Of The Swing Era, 1935-1955* (Arlington House, New Rochelle 1971) is a selection of material from *Metronome* magazine, and provides a good guide to the kind of bands and singers Kerouac would have been familiar with. The best histories of the bop movement are Ira Gitler's *Swing To Bop* (Oxford University Press, New York 1985) and *Jazz Masters Of The* 40s (Macmillan, New York, 1966) though Leonard Feather's *Inside Be-Bop* (JJ. Robbins & Sons Inc of New York, 1949) has the genuine period atmosphere. An insight into the world of the New York clubs can be gained from Arnold Shaw's *The Street That Never Slept* (Coward, McCann & Geoghegan, New York, 1971), and Shaw's *Honkers And Shouters: The Golden Years Of Rhythm & Blues* (Macmillan, New York, 1978) documents the importance of the tenor saxophone to the music of the 1940s and early 1950s. The 1950s are covered in Ted Gioia's *West Coast Jazz: Modern Jazz In California 1945-1960* and David H. Rosenthal's *Hard Bop: Jazz & Black Music 1955-1965* (both published by Oxford University Press. New York, 1992).

The lives of individual jazz musicians indicate why they, as well as their music, influenced the Beats. Ross Russell's *Bird Lives!* examines Charlie Parker's life, as does Robert Reisner's *Bird: The Legend Of Charlie Parker* (Citadel Press, New York, 1962), while Frank Buchmann-Moller's *You Just Fight For Your Life* (Praeger, New York, 1990) tells the Lester Young story. *A Lester Young Reader*, edited by Lewis Porter (Smithsonian Institute Press, Washington, 1991) also contains some useful information. Stan Britt's *Long Tall Dexter* (Quartet Books, London, 1989) is about Dexter Gordon. First hand accounts of the jazz life in the 1940s and 1950s can be found in Babs Gonzales' *I Paid My Dues* (Expubidence Publishing Corp. East Orange, 1967), Art Pepper's *Straight Life* (Schirmer Books, New York, 1979), Hampton Hawes' *Raise Up Off Me* (Coward, McCann & Geoghegan, New York, 1973), and Dizzy Gillespie's *Dizzy: To Be Or Not To Bop* (WH Allen, London, 1980).

There have been only a few attempts to write about bop in novels and short stories. John Clellon Holmes's *The Horn* (Andre Deutsch, London, 1959) has fictionalised portraits of Lester Young, Dizzy Gillespie and others, and Ross Russell's *The Sound* (Dutton, New York, 1961) is a colourful account of the life of a Charlie Parker type musician. Alston Anderson's *Dance Of The Infidels*, a short story in the collection *Lover Man* (Pan Books, London, 1961) is convincing about the 1940s mood.

WHAT'S YOUR SONG KING KONG?

There was a time when glossaries of "hip" slang were an almost essential addition to any novel that dealt with jazz or its related sub-worlds. Clarence Cooper's 'The Scene', published in 1960, contained a listing of "the jargon used on the scene", and similar books often had some kind of notes giving much the same sort of information. Mr Cooper's list appeared to be fairly accurate, as befits an author who was not only coloured but had paid his dues as an addict. Many others, however, were not only inaccurate but often so exaggerated that they were useless as works of reference. But then the books they accompanied were hardly worth bothering with, either.

The idea of dictionaries or glossaries of the colloquialisms of jazz and its connected life-styles - the "vernacular of the streets", as Bird in one of his pontificating moods described it - is not new. Cab Calloway's *Hepster's Dictionary* appeared in the Thirties. There was, too, Calloway's record, *Jive*, which outlined the basic of jive talk, as it was then known. The snag is that slang changes so fast it's impossible to ever be totally accurate. One also has to take into consideration the fact that publications like Calloway's were essentially aimed at the "squares", the real hipsters hardly needing a book to tell them which expressions to use. The whole point of slang is, of course, to have a private language that will baffle outsiders. Studies of the Victorian underworld can be quoted to show how this trend is usually linked with a criminal or socially outcast group. Thus, American Negroes, faced with a hostile white society, created an idiom of their own. It was and is a creative language. Unlike the borrowed slang of white hippies it has a genuine spontaneity, forced on it by the need to stay one step ahead. The same is true of slang associated with narcotics users.

In a sense, then, all one can do with slang is to compile listings of outdated expressions and explain them in terms of their philological and social histories. The attractions of this for a student of language are obvious. To a student of jazz an interest in "hip" slang can prove valuable because of the musical background suggested by many of the words and phrases.

There have been few serious attempts to deal with the problems of analysing "hip" slang. True, one or two of the accepted reference works on slang in general do include some of the better-known "hip" words. (It should be noted that I'm taking liberties here by using the word "hip" to denote that area of slang associated with jazz). But there are few books concentrating on "hip" slang in particular. Robert S. Gold's *Jazz Lexicon* is a scholarly exception to this rule. And Clarence Major's *Dictionary Of Afro-American Slang* (International Publishers, New York, 1970), though not limiting itself to "hip" or musicians' slang, is clearly of great relevance. It is this latter work that has triggered off these reflections on the subject.

Mr. Major points out that "beneath the novelty or so-called charm of this mode of speech a whole sense of violent unhappiness is in operation," and he goes on to quote Robert S. Gold: "It is by ignoring the sociological side of the coin that the slick magazines have been able to caricature and patronise the colourful jargon of jazz." He obviously approves of this comment and there is a great deal of truth in it. One could also mention that those jazz fans ignoring the sociological side of the coin are, unconsciously or not, helping in the attack on the true vitality of jazz jargon.

A dictionary is more concerned with the meaning as opposed to the origin of the word, but a slang dictionary should try to bring in both points, otherwise it becomes little more than a glossary to be used as an aid to understanding other books. Mr. Major perhaps falls down on this score. For example, he quotes to "pay dues" as meaning "to have hard luck; to suffer as a result of race prejudice, to come up the hard way." What he doesn't tell us is where the phrase originated and why it should be in use amongst Afro-Americans. It is, no doubt, based on musicians' terminology for paying one's union dues, and refers to the fact that if you don't pay your dues you don't work. In other words, paying dues is a necessary but disliked fact of existence, musical or otherwise.

Having mentioned "hip" several times already, it's worth having a look at the word in the context of Mr. Major's book. He describes its meaning as "sophisticated, independent and wise; in fashion; alert and courageous." Fair enough, when it comes to current usage. But he hasn't gone below the surface, and nowhere tells us where the word came from. The usual jazz analysis has offered an explanation based on opium smoking habits: "The derivation of the word 'hip' from the callous on the hip of the regular opium smoker who lies on one hip while he balances his equipment on the other, is explained in

Cab Calloway's 'Jive'.
Now to study jive and be hip
Tell you what you gotta do
You gotta turn right over on
the other side.

This record gives an example of how a key word in jazz jargon ('hip') derives from drug user's slang." (Charles Winick: 'The Taste of Music: Drugs, Alcohol and Jazz', *Jazz Monthly*, October and November 1962).

Personally I've always thought that Calloway was doing no more than referring to the flip side of the disc, and I'm still not convinced there are other implications in what he says. On the derivation of the word "hip" it's worth quoting the following by Charles Fox which cropped up in an exchange of letters in *The Listener* some months ago: "Readers still determined to track down 'hip' and 'hippy' should glance at the Times for 19 July, 1969. In an article 'Americanisms that may once have been Africanisms,' David Dalby points out that the Wolof tribe of Senegambia have a word 'hipi'. meaning 'to open one's eyes.' Furthermore, to quote Dr. Dalby, the American use of cat to mean 'person,' as in 'hepcat' or 'cool cat,' can be likened to Wolof 'kat' used as an agentive suffix after verbs; 'hipi-kat' in Wolof means 'a person who has opened his eyes.' Dr. Dalby goes on to suggest equally plausible origins for 'dig', 'jive' and 'jam session' ('jaam' is Wolof for 'slave') all of which makes even more sense if read alongside Paul Oliver's recently published monograph, *Savannah Syncopators* (Studio Vista, 1970), for Mr. Oliver uncovers the closest musical parallels with jazz and blues in exactly the same part of West Africa. OK? Or as the Wolof – 'pace' Dr. Dalby -say, 'waw-kay'?"

Naturally, a work like Mr. Major's cannot possibly go into such detail about every word or phrase in its pages. The variances of opinion as to the origins of "hip" show how bulky a truly analytical work would be.

But instead of generalising, let's carry on with a more involved look at one or two expressions that will be known to jazz enthusiasts. "Out-of-sight" is listed and it is suggested that it is a 1950s colloquialism meaning "extremely exciting or revolutionary (idea or person or thing)". Readers of 19th century American literature will, however, know that it was a New York slang expression before the turn of the century. Stephen Crane's *Maggie: A Girl Of The Streets*, first published in 1892, has its characters frequently describing agreeable places and situations as "outa sight." It would be interesting to know if the term did originate amongst white New York slum-dwellers and whether its revival in the 1950s amongst Harlem Negroes is a curious example of slang travelling in a different - white to black, rather than black to white - direction than usual.

Bop devotees may find the explanation of "O-bop-she-bam" difficult to accept. (I've shown it as Mr. Major does, though the jazz version is "Oo Bop Sh'Bam," as per the Dizzy Gillespic disc). Anyway, we are told that it's an "existential jazz phrase; perhaps a mystic effort to comment on the inscrutable in the black man's social, moral, and spiritual condition in the United States, or simply another way of talking 'to' that 'sense' of mystery often referred to as God." I should perhaps add a passage from Mr. Major's introduction to his book: "I use the word 'existential' in one way only: to stand for my belief that there is no meaning in life except that which is imposed upon it. We are social animals."

This definition of 'O-bop-she-bam' is a little too contrived for me, and I would incline more to thinking of the term as a sound only, relating to the music of the period when it originated and with a touch of dada-like humour added. After all, one recalls Ross Russell's comments on Bird's *Klactoveedsedstene*:

"It was rather baffling. I talked to different people about it. I remember I asked a psychiatrist if he could read anything in it; he couldn't. I found a man with a background of philology. I thought maybe he could come up with something; and he couldn't. Then, I finally got around to asking some of the cats, and they said, 'Why, it's just a sound, man.' And that's what it is." (Quoted in *Bird: The Legend Of Charlie Parker*, MacGibbon and Kee. 1963).

This kind of explanation seems more logical than Mr. Major's. He tries too hard to steer clear of simple answers and this sometimes leads him into exaggerating the social implications of slang words. I'm also tempted to suggest that he would probably have asked Russell whether he got the opinions of white or black cats. His deep black consciousness is fully understandable, but one senses that he's playing down the humorous side of slang so as to escape the possibility of sliding into an Uncle Tom role. One can understand this, too, but the intellectual solemnity evident in one or two places has its own funny side. And it smacks of trying to keep up with the Jones boys of the white academy.

Some jazz nicknames are mentioned, but the less obvious ones are never clarified. We are not told why Lester Young was called "Pres," or why Leon Berry was called "Chu." And although the obvious "Hawk" for Coleman Hawkins is listed, there isn't a reference to "Bean," his other nickname. "Fats" is merely shown as "jazzman." without examples – Domino, Waller, Navarro. The latter could easily have been tied in with another piece of slang - "girl," meaning "a male homosexual" - and a classic bop record (*Fat girl*) would have illustrated its use in the Forties. The more one considers nicknames, the more one realises how informative they can be about musicians' personalities.

One can carry on analysing and contesting the suggested meanings of slang words. Even dealing with them in retrospect is hardly the simplest of tasks, especially when the influences arc as varied as they have been in America. And, as Mr. Major points out, "the crux of many slang expressions is submerged at an unconscious level that hasn't been penetrated by logic."

This article was not intended as a review of Mr. Major's book and I've merely picked out a handful of items that are of relevance to readers of a jazz magazine. But it's fair to add that the *Dictionary of Afro-American Slang* can be used as a handy supplement to those books directly concerned with jazz. Anyone seriously interested in the music needs to know something about its social background and the factors that often determined the musicians' attitudes towards their art and audience. A knowledge of the language of jazz - and of the Negro ghetto in general - can help us to understand these factors.

Oh yes, "What's your song King Kong?" -what does that mean? According to Mr Major, "how do you feel?" It's a form of greeting along the lines of "What's your story morning glory?" (not listed, incidentally) and he dates it from the Forties when such phrases were popular. A recorded example of this kind of thing? Andy Kirk's *47th Street jive* (studio version, Ace Of Hearts AH 160; airshot, Caracol CAR 424). with June Richmond trotting out "What's your plan Charlie Chan?" and others of the same ilk.

THE NAMES OF THE FORGOTTEN

All works of art are not produced by a handful of major poets, painters, musicians, or whatever, and at any time there are always hundreds of others active and often creating worthwhile, but overlooked, contributions to their chosen area of activity. It ought to be the duty of a critic to recognise those contributions, though too many take the easy way out and concentrate on a few famous names. This is certainly true of jazz writing, with the result that numerous musicians are virtually forgotten. The name of Tony Fruscella may not mean much unless you have a specific interest in the modern jazz of the 1940s and 1950s, but the facts of his life, and his few appearances on records, say a great deal about the period and the musicians he worked with. A fascinating jazz "underground" comes to life when his activities are examined, and it offers, as well, a comment on the society in which Fruscella and his contemporaries sought to function.

Fruscella was born in Greenwich. Village in 1927, though his family belonged to the Italian-American working class of that area rather than to the bohemian element. His childhood years are largely undocumented, but he was brought up in an orphanage from an early age and seems to have had little exposure to music other than as it related to the church. However, he left the orphanage when he was about fourteen or fifteen, started studying the trumpet, and came into contact with both classical music and jazz. He appears to have been quick to develop his skills and was soon playing in public. When he was eighteen he went into the army and gained more experience by playing in an army band. It was around this time that Fruscella also encountered the new modern sounds of the day and the post-war years saw him mixing with the many young, white New York jazzmen who were devoted to bebop and cool jazz. They had an almost-fanatical belief in the music and had little time for anything else. William Carraro recalled: "We'd jam at lofts, or flats in old tenement houses on Eighth Avenue, around 47th or 48th Street. The empty rooms were rented for a few hours, and the musicians and the 'cats' that came by just to listen would chip in whatever they could afford at the moment to help pay the rent. Brew Moore, Chuck Wayne and many other names-to-be came by."

One of the musicians who participated in these sessions was an alto-player by the name of Chick Maures and, in 1948, he and Fruscella recorded for a small label called Century, though the records never appeared commercially until thirty years later. They are fascinating documents in terms of what they say about jazz developments. Of course, by 1946 bebop was well-established and the music shows the influence of the famous Charlie Parker quintet of those days. But the tricky themes played in unison by the alto and trumpet also suggest an awareness of the kind of approach favoured by pianist Lennie Tristano and his disciples Lee Konitz and Warne Marsh, who were cooler and more careful in their improvising. And Fruscella's trumpet playing, though superficially akin to that of Miles Davis, had its own subtlety and warmth. Fruscella was more melodic than Davis.

But what happened after the heady days and nights of the late1940s? Fruscella and the others no doubt continued to play when and where they could, and a few even got to work professionally. But paying jobs, especially those involving jazz, were often hard to come by. Bob Reisner, a writer around Greenwich Village in the early 1950s, recalled that Fruscella never seemed to have a permanent address:

"Short marriages, short stays in hospitals and jails, and he invented the crash pad. He walked the streets, an orphan of the world but with incredible dignity. He never accepted anything for free. He would cook and clean and play music if you put him up."

The chaotic nature of Fruscella's life wasn't improved by his use of alcohol and drugs. He wasn't alone in this. Chick Maures, his companion on the 1948 record date, died from a drugs overdose in 1954, and Don Joseph, a trumpeter who was not unlike Fruscella in his playing and was close to him as a person, had a career that was marred by drug addiction. Both were wayward to the point of self-destruction. Bob Reisner once got them an engagement at the famous summer festival at Music Inn in the Berkshires, but Fruscella, when asked by a polite listener what he would play next, replied "We want whiskey Blues", and refused to carry on until a bottle was provided. And Joseph somehow managed to insult the son of the owner of the place. Bassist Bill Crow, who was around New York at the time and later wrote a fine book, *From Birdland to Broadway*, about his experiences, remembered Fruscella almost losing them a rare job in a club with his response to a customer's invitation to have a drink: "Well, I'm already stoned, and the bread is pretty light on this gig, so would you mind just giving me the cash?" Crow said that he "loved the way Tony played in a small group", but noted that he didn't fit into a big-band format. His low-key style needed a small group and an intimate club setting to allow it to flourish.

It's perhaps indicative of Fruscella's life-style, and his liking for a bohemian environment that Beat writer Jack Kerouac knew him in the 1950s. In his "New York Scenes," a short prose piece included in *Lonesome Traveller*, Kerouac writes:

"What about that guy Tony Fruscella who sits crosslegged on the rug and plays Bach on his trumpet, by ear, and later on at night there he is blowing with the guys at a session, modern jazz." Kerouac also mentioned Don Joseph in the same piece: "He stands at the jukebox in the bar and plays with the music for a beer."

There were a few moments of near-glory in Fruscella's career. In 1951 he was hired to play in Lester Young's group, though the job lasted only a couple of weeks and no recorded evidence of it exists. It would seem that Fruscella was ousted from the band due to some sort of rivalry which may have involved a form of reverse racism. Pianist Bill Triglia, who worked with Fruscella over the years, tells the story:

"Fruscella was a white fellow and very friendly with Miles Davis and used to jam with him. He played with myself and Red Mitchell a lot. He had a beautiful sound. He didn't play high, he didn't play flashy, but he played beautiful low register, very modern. When Kenny Drew left and some jobs came up, John Lewis was playing with Lester. According to what I heard, and Tony Fruscella was a good friend of mine, Tony used to get drunk with Lester. Lester loved him. He didn't play the same style as Lester, but it fit nicely, it was a beautiful contrast, but John Lewis didn't like Tony. Tony said he didn't like him because he was properly white, I don't know, but John Lewis tried to get somebody else on. The next job they had Lester's manager didn't call Tony Fruscella and he was so hurt, because he loved Lester, you know. He wanted to stay with him, he was a young fellow and very tender."

It was just after this experience that Fruscella again recorded some tracks which, like those from 1948, didn't appear until many years later. In February 1952, he joined forces with altoist Herb Geller, tenorman Phil Urso, pianist Bill Triglia, and a couple of others, to produce some music which ought to have been heard at the time and drawn some attention to Fruscella. Instead, it simply disappeared into the vaults and Fruscella and his companions carried on struggling to play their music and earn a living. Critic Mark Gardner noted that, although the 1950s were, for many, years of affluence, the good times did not necessarily arrive for musicians, "especially those who had rejected the commercial sop dispensed over the airways and via the jukeboxes." Gardner also said:

" Jazzmen adapted, as they always have, and found places to play the way they wanted - in basements and cellars, seedy bars, strip clubs and coffee houses. Surroundings were uncongenial but unimportant. The main thing was that in those varied environments where the patrons were either alcoholic/moronic or intellectual/revolutionary, nobody told you how to play or what to play. If you were looking to dig what was happening you went to the Open Door in Greenwich Village or wangled an invitation to pianist Gene Di Novi's basement or to where Jimmy Knepper and Joe Maini lived. The people who passed through these underground pads and dives were the jazz underground The life of prosperous, middle-class America was far removed from those basement jam sessions, those rehearsals and gigs in down-at-heel corner bars. Musicians, natural sceptics, turned their backs on McCarthyism and the rest."

A little steady work did come along now and then, and in 1953 Fruscella was hired to play with Stan Getz's group. Some poorly-recorded excerpts from a broadcast from Birdland do exist, and on "Dear Old Stockholm" Fruscella demonstrates all that was best in his playing as he shapes a solo that is relaxed, warm, melodically coherent, and in which the use of spaces between the notes is as important as the notes themselves. Some listeners might think there is a resemblance to Chet Baker in Fruscella's sound - and he did play with Gerry Mulligan's group briefly in 1954 - but it is only slight, and Fruscella very much had his own ways of constructing a solo. There are interesting comparisons to be made between Baker's 1953 recording of "Imagination" and Fruscella's version from the same year. Admittedly, Baker's was a studio recording with the disciplined format that implies, whereas Fruscella's was from a live session at the Open Door and has a relative looseness, but even so, there is greater depth in Fruscella's playing. As Dan Morganstern said of it: "It is music very much of its time - a time of scuffling, an inwardlooking time, a blue time."

The recordings from the Open Door - and, yet again, they came to light only years later - are valuable not only for the way in which they allow us to hear Fruscella soloing at length, but also for the window they provide into the modern jazz world of New York. The Open Door was a bar and restaurant frequented by jazz musicians and which they soon began to use as a place for jam sessions. Dan Morganstern remembered it as a "haven for jazz people with no money. It was a weird place. When you walked in off the street, you entered a room with a long bar that had a Bowery feeling to it. At one end of this bar stood an ancient upright piano, manned most evenings by Broadway Rose, a fading but spry ex-vaudevillian her hair dyed an improbable shade of red. She knew a thousand old songs and cheerfully honoured requests. From the bar, right next to Rose, a creaky door led to the huge, gloomy back room, sporting a long bandstand, a dance floor which was never used, and rickety tables and chairs." Bob Reisner, a free-lance writer who some years later produced a couple of short, but lively memoirs of the 1950s and also wrote a funny book about graffiti, hired the room for Sunday afternoon concerts at which Charlie Parker sometimes appeared, but other, spontaneous sessions took place, and drummer Al Levitt recalls musicians like Herb Geller, Gene Quill, Jon Eardley, Milt Gold, and Ronnie Singer, dropping in to play. Geller did go on to make something of a name for himself on the West Coast in the late-1950s and is still around, but most of the others made only occasional appearances on record and those mostly in the 1950s. And the casualty rate amongst them was high. Quill was badly injured in a road accident and spent the rest of his life virtually immobilised, Singer committed suicide, and Eardley had an up-and-down career due to drug addiction.

The music produced by Fruscella at the Open Door, mostly with tenorman Brew Moore and pianist Bill Triglia, sounds relaxed almost to the point of casualness, and it is played without any concessions to non-jazz tastes. Using a few standard tunes from the jazz and popular music repertoire (the popular music of the pre-rock period, that is), the emphasis is on improvisation, and Fruscella shows how inventive he could be in such a setting. He never repeats ideas and always sounds poised, no matter the tempo. He was presumably fond of the ballad, "Loverman," using it at the Open

Door sessions and also at an engagement at Ridgewood High School in New Jersey which must have taken place around the same period (1953). "A Night in Tunisia," the classic tune from the bop era, also crops up at both places. There are moments on the ballad performances when Fruscella can sound pensive, almost hesitant, but he skilfully uses that mood to shape his solos and his emotional sound complements it. It needs to be noted that the Ridgewood High School recordings, presumably made by one of the musicians or an interested fan were some more that only went into general circulation twenty or so years later. Bill Triglia appears to have been the man who organised the group's appearance. Interestingly, some other live recordings from the same period and with Triglia again in the group feature Don Joseph and a good alto-saxophonist, Davey Schildkraut, who was in Stan Kenton's band in the 1950s, recorded with Miles Davis, but then drifted from sight. Memoirs of the New York scene prior to 1959 or so place him in the centre of a lot of the activity at the Open Door and elsewhere.

1955 was probably the peak year in Fruscella' s short career and he was featured on a couple of recordings by Stan Getz and was also invited to make an LP under his own name for the Atlantic label, a well-established company. Fruscella chose Bill Triglia to accompany him on piano and he added tenor-saxophonist Allen Eager, a musician who had been highly thought of in the 1940s, when he was amongst the leading bop players, but who was, by 1955, slipping into a shadowy world of occasional public appearances and even fewer recording dates. With Phil Sunkel, another little-known trumpeter, acting as composer-arranger, Fruscella came up with some of his finest work, especially on "I'll Be Seeing You" and the attractive "His Master's Voice," on which he uses some of his classical background to fashion an engaging Bach-like series of variations. Fruscella and those who admired him no doubt imagined that this album would help him widen his reputation, but it soon slid from sight and was remembered by only a few enthusiasts. The mid-1950s were reasonable years for some jazzmen provided they could be identified with bright West Coast sounds or the hard bop forcefulness associated with black New York. Fruscella's music, like so much good, white New York jazz of the 1950s, didn't fit into either category.

What happened to Tony Fruscella after 1955? Very little, it seems, if the reference books are anything to go by. He probably still played at jam sessions and perhaps even did some club work in obscure places, but the "dogged will to fail" that Bob Reisner saw in him, and his drug and alcohol problems, must have held him back. And the 1960s were lean years for a lot of jazzmen, as pop music took over in clubs, dance-halls, and on the radio. His kind of music, quiet, reflective, and requiring sympathy and understanding from the listener was hardly likely to appeal to many people. It never had, it's only fair to say, but things got even worse in the 1960s. After years of obscurity, Tony Fruscella died in August 1969, his body finally giving up the struggle against barbiturates and booze. Bob Reisner, in a touching elegy written for a jazz magazine just after Fruscella died, said: "If I were an artist, I would paint Fruscella in the Renaissance manner. A side portrait of him bent in concentration over the horn which produced the flowing and delicate music. The usual background landscape would be strewn with a couple of wives, countless chicks, barbiturate containers, and empty bottles. His artistic life, however, was in sharp contrast. He was completely austere and disciplined. There was not a commercial chromosome in his body."

This short survey of Fruscella's life is scattered with the names of the forgotten. What did happen to Don Joseph and Davey Schildkraut? Where is Allen Eager these days? And a whole world of New York jazz of the 1950s comes into my mind when I listen to a few of the records by Fruscella and others. Where are Jerry Lloyd, George Syran, and Phil Raphael and Phil Leshin? Jerry Lloyd was around in the 1940s and 1950s and recorded with Gerry Mulligan, Zoot Sims, and George Wallington, though he never became well-known and worked as a cab-driver even when he was featured on records with such artists. George Syran was on an album with Jon Eardley which also featured trombonist Milt Gold, and the two Phils worked with Red Rodney in 1951, but what else? And what happened to that fine tenor-saxophonist Phil Urso, who soloed on Woody Herman records in the early 1950s, was with Chet Baker's group a few years later, and then seems to have faded into obscurity around 1960. There were so many who had only a brief moment or two in the spotlight. Not all of them were necessarily as ill-fated as Fruscella. Bill Triglia, who figures so prominently in the Fruscella story, seems to have still been alive in the 1980s, though hardly in the forefront of jazz. Nor would it be true to say that all the musicians mentioned were victims of an unjust or uncaring society. When there were casualties they often came about through personal waywardness and self-indulgence rather than from any form of oppression. Some jazzmen may well have felt that their music was misunderstood and neglected, but that's hardly an excuse for taking drugs or drinking heavily. Dan Morganstern may have got nearer the truth, about the early 1950s at least, when he said it was an "inward-looking time." Were drugs a part of that inwardness or simply just a social fashion?

But a lot of musicians probably just gave up playing jazz, or even playing any kind of music, and some possibly turned to commercial sounds in order to earn a living. Compromises are often necessary if one wants to eat. The point is, though, that all those I've named, and more whose names are mentioned when people reminisce, deserve to be remembered for their contributions to jazz, even if those contributions were small ones. We do the artists and ourselves a disservice when we neglect the past. A form of "organised amnesia" takes over, as is so often evident when one listens to those radio stations which purport to cater for a jazz audience but which mostly present a non-stop procession of bland sounds. There is little or no historical sense in what they do, and certainly no place for a fine, forgotten musician like Tony Fruscella.

When Charlie Parker died in 1955 the New York tabloids had a field day. "Bop King dies in Heiress' Flat" shouted one of the headlines and details followed of how Parker, just prior to his death, had made his way to the "swank 5th Avenue apartment" of Baroness Kathleen Annie Pannonica Rothschild de Koenigswarter . It was a story likely to attract attention as it mixed allusions to race, class, jazz, sex and drugs in a manner that readers at the time would have seen as convincing proof that their suspicions about the subversive nature of jazz, and especially bebop, were justified.

But who was Pannonica Rothschild (known as "Nica") and how was it that she knew someone like Parker? She was a member of the English branch of the Rothschild family and had been born in 1913 to parents who were obviously wealthy but who didn't just limit their activities to making money and maintaining large estates. Her father had a keen interest in the natural sciences and, according to David Kastin, is now looked on as "one of the pioneers of the modern conservation movement." He was an expert on fleas and amassed a collection of 30,000 specimens and published 150 scientific papers. Her mother had been a national tennis champion in Hungary, knew several languages, read Proust, and dabbled in politics. Nica also had an uncle who, like her father, was interested in the natural world. He was something of an eccentric and had a private zoo that included zebras, kangaroos, emus, and other species. Kastin says that the scholarly articles he published "established Walter Rothschild as one of the leading zoologists of his age."

Nica's father still had to play a part in running the Rothschild bank even if his heart was with his other interests, and he suffered from bouts of depression and committed suicide in 1923. Her mother took over running the properties they owned and looking after the family finances. Nica's brother, Victor, had a traditional education, going to Harrow and Trinity College, but she was educated at home and had to conform to what Kastin describes as "stringently enforced schedules." The facts of her upbringing are interesting in terms of their possible effect on her later behaviour.

Victor was a talented amateur pianist and was destined to lead a varied life. Kastin describes him as: "a research director of the

Cambridge zoology department, a member of MI5 (the British secret service), Winston Churchill's personal envoy to President Roosevelt, a senior executive at Shell Oil, the chairman of N.M. Rothschild & Sons, the head of Britain's Central Policy Review Staff (a.k.a. the Think Tank), and the suspected 'fifth man' in the clique of Communist sympathisers known as the Cambridge spies." His interest in the piano had led him to jazz and friendship with the noted pianist, Teddy Wilson. It was Victor who first introduced Nica to jazz.

Her education had been widened when she spent a year in Paris in the late 1920s and then toured Europe. Back home she mixed with other debutantes, frequented London night-clubs, and indulged her liking for fast cars. A London musician got her interested in flying and by the time she was twenty-one she had her own plane. A trip to France brought her into contact with Baron Jules de Koenigswarter and, after a quick romance, they were married in New York in 1935. A couple of children soon followed. When war broke out in 1939 Nica and the children were in France but she was told by her husband to go to England and then to America where they would be helped by the Guggenheims, "another of the great Jewish financial aristocracies." After ensuring that the children would be looked after Nica headed for North Africa where her husband, a supporter of De Gaulle, had joined up with Free French forces. She worked as a translator and decoder and later drove ambulances in Italy.

After the war the Baron became part of the new French government and had diplomatic posts in Norway and Mexico. It's probable that, by 1949, the marriage was unstable, with Nica searching for something that would add meaning to her life. The Baron was contemptuous of her liking for jazz and she started visiting New York where she renewed her acquaintanceship with Teddy Wilson and met other musicians. In 1951 as she made her way to the airport to return to Mexico she called to see Wilson who insisted that she listen to a recording of Thelonious Monk's *Round Midnight*. Kastin quotes from an interview in which she recalled what happened: "I couldn't believe my ears. I had never heard anything remotely like it. I made him play it to me twenty times in a row. *Round Midnight* affected me like nothing else I ever heard." And he adds that she missed her flight and extended her stay in New York by a couple of weeks so that she could experience more of Monk's work.

By 1953 Nica was living permanently in New York and had separated from her husband. When the jazz writer, Nat Hentoff, asked her about breaking with the Baron and her children, as well as virtually giving up the kind of social status and way of life that many would envy in order to mix with mostly black and often impecunious jazz musicians, she responded by affirming her love of the music: "It's everything that really matters, everything worth digging. It's a desire for freedom. And in all my life, I've never known any people who warmed me as much by their friendship as the jazz musicians I've come to know."

Throughout his account of Nica's life Kastin breaks off to offer his analysis of events and developments in the arts. To set the scene for her arrival in New York he outlines how bebop came about, what the Beat writers aimed for in their poems and novels, and where Jackson Pollock and other abstract expressionist painters were heading in their search for new forms. It's a narrative that holds fairly closely to what has become a fairly standard history of artistic changes post-1945, with a so-called "culture of spontaneity" taking precedence over other areas of activity. To be fair to Kastin he doesn't go overboard for this version of events and he notes that the musicians, artists, and writers he refers to weren't always "promoting the same aesthetic agenda." It's a sensible qualification to make because generalisations about movements in art or music or literature can often be seen as faulty when looked at in detail.

As Nica involved herself with the New York jazz community she did meet with a degree of suspicion on the part of some musicians. They wondered what she wanted from them, and inevitably in what tended to be a male-dominated environment it was suggested that she was sleeping with this or that jazzman. Kastin says that gossip columnists like the notorious Walter Winchell commented on her liking for being in the company of black musicians, and society types sneered at her taste for visiting run-down places where bebop could be heard. Kastin doesn't refer to it in detail but in the early-1950s bebop was considered subversive, with its practitioners mostly junkies. This was when the McCarthyite hysteria was at its height and not only communists were thought of as threats to the American way of life.

It has to be accepted, though, that the use of drugs, particularly heroin, had spiralled in the late-1940s and early-1950s, and that it was a major problem among the beboppers. Kastin points out that the

Mafia became heavily involved in developing markets for heroin once the supply lines opened up again following the end of the Second World War, and he suggests that black communities were targeted most of all. But he gives other reasons for the increased use of heroin: "Heroin's ascendancy during the bebop movement can also be seen as both a symptom of the bebopper's marginalised role in the pop music mainstream and an emblem of hipness worn (along with berets, shades, and goatees) by a generation of black jazz modernists who were challenging the vestiges of minstrelsy they associated with their big-band predecessors. For their white cohorts, the drug became a way of symbolically connecting to their musical heroes."

Kastin talks about the drugs problem among the New York modernists because Nica, like anyone observing the musicians, couldn't help being aware of it. And some criticism was levelled at her for the way in which she appeared to respond to the situation. There were suggestions that she should have done more to persuade people to stop using heroin, and a fictional character clearly based on her in a short story by Julio Cortazor appears to obtain drugs for an addicted saxophonist. She was, perhaps, sometimes over-tolerant of the behaviour of certain musicians, and tended to excuse their personal failings by referring to the music they produced, but experience taught her to be wary. Discussing addicted musicians and their problems she said: "I used to think I could help, but no one person can. They have to do it alone. I had to find out for myself that one has to stay away from them. Addiction makes them too ignoble, and you can't be safe around them."

It is known that she helped a great many musicians by giving them money, buying food for their families, and sorting out the chaos surrounding the cabaret cards they needed in order to work in clubs in New York. A criminal conviction meant that a musician could be denied a card. This was particularly disastrous for blacks who often couldn't find alternative employment in the recording studios and elsewhere. Not only musicians were affected and the card system applied to anyone working in a club as a waiter, cook, or whatever. Kastin raises the interesting point that when it was first introduced the idea was to apply some form of control to unions, such as the one organised among waiters, which were said to be communist dominated. Its most notorious use, however, seems to have been when musicians, singers, and other performers were involved.

Needless to say, it was wide open to abuse by the police and a payment into the right pocket often meant that a card would be issued even if the person concerned had a conviction or two.

I mentioned earlier that Charlie Parker died in Nica's suite at the Stanhope Hotel in New York, and that, along with complaints about noise as she entertained various musicians, led to her being asked to leave, a process repeated when she moved to the Bolivar Hotel. Parker's death and the accompanying publicity also caused her husband to sue for divorce and custody of the children. And the Rothschild family, with a few exceptions, closed ranks on her. They may have been rich and famous but courting publicity in the manner that contemporary celebrities do was not part of their thinking. For them, the only time your name should appear in the press was when you were born and when you died. Nica's life seemed to contradict much of what they had been taught to believe was the correct way to behave.

Her links to Parker were, in fact, relatively limited when compared to her devotion to Thelonious Monk. A major part of Kastin's book deals with her relationship to this enigmatic character. There's no doubt that Monk had problems and Kastin says that he inherited bi-polar disorder from his father. But sustained use of drugs over many years also affected his mental condition. At various stages he was diagnosed as schizophrenic, suffering from a chemical imbalance, and with manic tendencies. He was given shock treatment and subjected to psychotherapy which verged on the farcical. Nica's endeavours on his behalf were, at times, almost heroic, especially as he was responsible for her being evicted from a third hotel. In due course it was agreed that having her own place was the best option, and with the help of her brother she bought a large house that had previously been owned by Joseph von Sternberg. It soon became known as The Cathouse due to Nica's fondness for cats, and it was also open house for any number of jazz musicians.

Thelonious Monk's life after the early 1970s was a near-tragedy. He spent time in a private clinic, with the fees paid by Nica, and he left his wife and settled in The Cathouse, though not because of any sexual liaison between Nica and him. He simply needed to get away from the domestic arrangements that applied at home. It was during this period that he virtually stopped playing the piano and started to retreat into near-silence. He died in 1982. Nica was by that time in her late-sixties, but she continued to befriend musicians and visit the few remaining jazz clubs in New York and she was contacted by some younger members of the Rothschild family who had become intrigued by hearing about her and her adventures among the jazz fraternity. She died in 1988.

Nica had written a memoir, but it has never been published and the manuscript is in the possession of the Rothschild family along with numerous tape recordings she made of the musicians who stayed at the Cathouse. Kastin says that her five children continue to reject requests for interviews about their mother, and even refused to help a cousin, Hannah, when she made a documentary about Nica. Another young relative, Nadine, was luckier when she wanted to publish *Three Wishes*, a collection of Nica's photos accompanying the three wishes that she'd invited her musician friends to make. It's an intriguing book and I can't resist quoting a couple of the wishes made by the bebop pianist Barry Harris: "A room with a Steinway and a good record player, where I can be alone with all the Charlie Parker and Bud Powell records," and "The end of all soul, funk, and rock'n'roll jazz."

The reluctance of the Rothschilds to give interviews, and a certain amount of reticence on Nica's part when talking about her family background and life, has meant that David Kastin has written a book that is as much about New York and its bebop musicians as it is about her. Perhaps that's the way it should be because her devotion to the music and the people who played it was legendary. There are a few minor errors. Wardell Gray is called Grey, and Jackson Pollock somehow comes out as Pollack several times. When Kastin discusses the Julio Cortazor story, "The Pursuer," I mentioned, he says that it's "set in New York's 1950s jazz underground," but it's actually located in Paris.

A final point. Several musicians, including Monk, named compositions for Nica ("Nica's Dream" is one of them, as is "Pannonica") and there is currently a CD available which brings together recordings by Monk, Doug Watkins, Kenny Drew, Gigi Gryce, and others, paying tribute to her. Nica; *The Jazz Baroness* is available on Saga 531 093-0.

NICA'S DREAM: THE LIFE AND LEGEND OF THE JAZZ BARONESS by David Kastin. W.W. Norton & Company. 272 pages. £18.99. ISBN 978-0-393-06940-2

THE HIPSTER

"I mean, this was the time of the whole cult of the hipster, which is a forties designation, the crew is defined then, the whole thing of being 'hip' or 'with-it' - a lot of the ideas, that is."

(Robert Creeley, in an interview in WHERE/1, Detroit, 1966)

There was a story going the rounds many years ago about two hipsters who had just emerged into the street after hours spent at a long and hectic jam-session. One of them looked up at the sky, and said, "Man, dig that crazy moon," and the other replied, "Man, that isn't the moon, that's the sun." They walked down the street, arguing about whether it was the moon or the sun and eventually decided to get an outside opinion on the matter. They stopped a passer-by. "Hey, man," said one of the hipsters, "Is that the sun or the moon up there?" and the passer-by replied, "I don't know, man, I'm a stranger around here."

It's a nice story and, in its own small way, it does spotlight a basic hipster attitude. The hipster was not, despite the extravagant claims made for him by a writer like Norman Mailer, a revolutionary. He was not interested in changing society, or even indulging in the time-honoured pastime of antagonising the middle-class. He wanted his own world, one in which the problem of mixing with the squares would be non-existent, and part of the plan for achieving this situation was the concoction of a form of humour which required, if not a definite knowledge of hipster jargon, at least an appreciation of the hipster ethos before it could be fully understood.

Another part of the hipster's movement away from the mainstream of society was the adoption of a form of jazz which required an almost single-minded devotion from its supporters. "I moved in a group which thought that music began and ended with be-bop; anyone who thought differently was a square," wrote the American poet and novelist Gilbert Sorrentino of his teenage years in New York during the 1940s. He went on to say," To be called a square in those days was to be square in music only; which, in a strange sense, was much worse than being generally square." The hipster was not initially interested in condemning people for their social or political opinions. Such matters were simply outside his world, but the musically square did sometimes come into contact with him and he reserved his contempt for them. Often he didn't even bother to use the word "square." A slight shrug of the shoulders, and a weary "Oh, man," would be sufficient to dismiss the opposition. The hipster language was laconic at best and one step removed from inarticulacy at worst. Anatole Broyard summed it up in an article published in *Partisan Review* in 1948: "There were no neutral words in this vocabulary; it was put up or shut up, a purely polemical language in which every word had a job of evaluation as well as designation. These evaluations were absolute; the hipster banished all comparatives, qualifiers, and other syntactical uncertainties. Everything was dichotomously solid, gone, out of this world, or nowhere, sad, beat, a drag."

We have to be wary, though, of falling into the trap of seeing the hipster as a kind of post-1945 superman. The truth is a little more prosaic, and it's clear that a large part of the bop audience was made up of working and lower-middle class people who, for various reasons, found themselves alienated from the prevailing established social and cultural (including popular culture) climate. To quote Gilbert Sorrentino again: "Be-bop cut us off completely, to our immense satisfaction. It was even more vehemently decried as 'nigger music' but even to the tone-deaf it was apparent that it (the music) didn't care what the hell was thought of it - jazz had broken itself free of the middle-class world's social conception of what it should be. It gave no quarter and asked for none. It was probably, more than at any other time in its history, including the present, absolutely non-popular, and its adherents formed a cult, which perhaps more than any other force in the intellectual life of our time, brought together young people who were tired of the spurious."

There is no doubt that bop did have an intellectual appeal, though not necessarily to those who would be considered "intelligent" or "intellectual" by the establishment. If my own memory serves me right I can't recall encountering many university-educated or generally middle-class types around the bop clubs in this country. Neither did jazz as a whole, and be-bop most of all, have the acceptance among the intelligentsia that it later enjoyed. In the late 1940s and early 1950s the sons of the middle-class tended to strum washboards in amateur revivalist bands. Their attitudes always seemed to me to imply a basic contempt for the music itself as if it were just "jolly jazz" and went down well with beer and weekend bohemianism.

It's interesting to note that the hipster first appeared on the scene as a definable type in the middle- 1940s when the war effort was having a dual effect of disrupting society because of the mass movement of much of the male population, as well as the employment of women in factories, and yet forcing a kind of cohesiveness because of the necessity for everyone to make sacrifices and pull together. In popular music, and in jazz (much of which was then played by big-bands), the various pressures made themselves felt in several ways. On a purely physical level, many of the older musicians were drafted into the services, while on a musical level there was a swing towards the patriotic, sentimental, and nostalgic. The hipster, who was often young enough not to feel any involvement (physical or mental) in the war, reacted to all this by creating his own world. There's an interesting record by the now-obscure singer and pianist, Harry 'The Hipster' Gibson, which is illuminating in this respect. It's called *4-F Ferdinand the Frantic Freak* and was recorded in 1944. 4-F was American army terminology for having failed to make the grade in a medical and Gibson (whose other records included *Who Put the Benzedrine in Mrs Murphy's Ovaltine?* and *Zoot Gibson Strikes Again*) relates how weird Ferdinand is, both bodily and mentally. The final verse informs us that he was last heard of in Greenwich Village where he's doing "all reet," a term often used by another hipster entertainer, Slim Gaillard. On the whole the tone of the record is one of admiration for Ferdinand, a character who has obviously found a way out of the draft and square society. It makes an enlightening contrast with such discs as *A Slip of a Lip Can Sink a Ship* (Duke Ellington), *I Want a Grown Up Man* (Stan Kenton), *People Like You and Me* (Glenn Miller), and *I Don't Want to Walk Without You* (Artie Shaw). The sentiments expressed in the lyrics of those clearly reflect the general mood of the period.

A relevant point about Gibson is that he, like Gaillard, did attract a certain amount of attention from people working in the arts on the West Coast. There would appear to have been a fair amount of somewhat flamboyant hipsterism in California during this period and it was illustrated in the titles of some of the records made for the numerous small labels active then. Slim Gaillard specialised in his own "vout" language and recorded a number of sides which utilised it. *Vout Oreenee* is a good example and *Travelling Blues* sounds like hipster's eye-view of the United States. Other artists recorded such titles as *The Voot is Here to Stay* (Ivie Anderson), *My Voot is Really*

Vout (Dinah Washington), and *Flight of the Vout Bug* (Lyle Griffin).

Following its initial appearance on the jazz scene hipsterism developed along several different lines. One, and it's possibly the line that had most influence, was that of the intellectual hipster. There had been indications of intellectualism in the early hipsters (the horn-rimmed glasses were a surface manifestation of the trend), but around 1948 it became more pronounced. Mike Zwerin, trombonist and writer, put it neatly: "Another kind of learning started for me that summer (1948). It was my summer with Charlie Parker, although I never did meet him. Bird made it hip to be an intellectual. His interests in reading, classical music, and other similar things, changed the style of hipsterism. If he knew about certain writers, or listened to Beethoven, that was enough to start many hipsters of the day doing these things. I can't say he started me reading, but he certainly accelerated my interest in literature." And Gilbert Sorrentino said: "Bop, for me, was the entrance into the general world of culture, although at the time, I wouldn't have believed it. When I was 14, culture meant going to the opera and doing your homework every night."

It is this type of hipsterism which has, on the whole, been featured most in literature, a tendency that appears quite natural considering the attraction bop had for young writers and intellectuals who couldn't fit into the culture of the establishment. References to bop can be found in the writings of Kerouac, Ginsberg, John Clellon Holmes, and numerous minor poets who were linked to the Beats.

A second type of hipster was the genuine bop enthusiast who did not necessarily take a great deal of interest in the other arts. It might be worth noting at this point that I'm writing from a British perspective and I don't think that, in the late-40s and early-50s, many intellectuals in this country were involved with bop. There wasn't an artistic "underground" of the kind that sprang up a decade later. Still, the single-minded bop hipsters did overlap with the intellectual hipsters and with a third category that might, for want of a better phrase, be called pop-hipsters. There was a short-lived attempt to popularise bop around 1949/50, with record companies and big-band leaders jumping on the bop bandwagon. Records such as Charlie Barnet's *Bebop Spoken Here*, Babs Gonzales's *Professor Bop*, Dave Lambert's *Hawaiian War Chant,* and Gene Krupa's *Bop Boogie* (with lyrics which spoke of "the latest kind of jive, the hipsters call it bebop," this at a time when many bop musicians were starting to withdraw into the "cool" stance of the early-1950s) were typical of the period. In Britain, Tito Burns's *A Lesson in Bop* and Alan Dean's *My Baby Likes to Bebop* aimed to attract the attention of the pop-hipster. It was a time when *Life* magazine discovered bop and a British bandleader quoted the Elizabethan "Hey nonny-no" phrase as justification for his vocalists chanting bop sounds. Titles such as *Bop Kick* and *Little Boy Bop Go Blow Your Top* appeared on records by comparatively commercial artists, and Woody Herman's *Lemon Drop* (a very good big-band bop disc) was often heard on a popular record programme like *Family Favourites.*

So-called bop clubs opened in many towns and cities, though if the British experience is anything to go by most of them had little or nothing to do with bop. Records often substituted for live music and varied wildly from Start Kenton to Frankie Lane. I remember leaving one club in disgust after a conversation with one of the "hipsters." It turned out that he didn't like jazz.

The pop hipsters turned what had been a minor cult which depended in many ways on its exclusiveness for its existence, into a teenage craze and so gave it the kiss of death. The relationship between bop musicians, who often had a kind of rapport with the genuine hipsters, and the audience began to alter, and the hipster sometimes withdrew from the scene rather than mix with the new crowd. The latter made more of the clothes and the jargon than they did of the music. True, the original hipsters had not been averse to using a special language and dressing in a certain way (drape suits, etc.) but they were dedicated to bebop itself. One of the few books that successfully captures the mixture of dedication and dandyism practised by the hipster is Ross Russell's *The Sound*, a novel which, whatever its literary faults, got nearer to the mood of the bop era than anything else that has appeared in print.

I've said very little about whether the bop musicians themselves were hipsters, but I think it's obvious that they often were. Nat Hentoff, an observant jazz writer, said: "Jazzmen have always been an 'in' group - with many additional 'in' and 'out' subdivisions among them according to race, age, and musical style - and never more than in the first years of modern jazz." And the stories that abound about the behaviour of many bop musicians back up what Hentoff says. I can recall seeing various "hip" musicians around the London clubs in the

1950s, and years ago a friend told me about working with a talented trumpeter who was among the first British boppers in the late-1940s and who continued to lead a kind of hipster lifestyle. Perhaps the worst effect of hipsterism among both musicians and enthusiasts was the increase in narcotics addiction. This was almost inevitable if the withdrawal from society implied by the hipster ethos was carried to its extreme. The saxophonist Jimmy Giuffre remembered: "When I was in Woody Herman's band, eight were on at one time. They thought it was hip and they were putting on the squares." And trumpeter Red Rodney, who had been in the Herman band and also worked with Charlie Parker, said: "That was our badge. It was the thing that said, 'We know, you don't know.' It was the thing that gave us membership in a unique club, and for this membership we gave up everything else in the world." Woody Herman himself had observed how the hipsters behaved and thought that they were like the Regency dandies in their desire to be part of an exclusive group.

It was when drugs were involved that the hipster turned criminal, or at least of a state of mind where his presumed exclusiveness justified his abusing ordinary decencies and social habits. It was no longer a case of dismissing the squares because they didn't like bebop. The attitude had changed to condemnation because of the way they lived and how they generally thought. The hipster became a con-man. Bob Reisner ran The Open Door, a jazz club in New York in the early - 1950s, and later wrote about his experiences: "The Open Door audience was made up primarily of hipsters. They were so cool they scared me stiff, but I loved them. I disguised my admiration and fear by being a hard businessman. If they didn't have a buck, they didn't get in. Seated by the door with a roll of tickets I would be subjected to every ploy imaginable. 'Like, dad, I just want to see someone a minute,' or 'I want to use the John a second,' or 'I have a message for one of the cats on the stand,' or 'I have my mouthpiece with me and I want to sit in and blow.' My answer was always no. A real con type would try to breeze right by and I'd block his path and then he'd pay, but he had to put me down. With the greatest hauteur he would say in a swinging effeminate way, 'Oh, tickets. Is that the scene, baby? A dollar? Oh, all right, man, here's an ace, give me a ticket.' Then he'd walk contemptuously in."

Things were beginning to change by the 1950s as social conditions altered and jazz went through a comparative period of popularity. Many of the original hipsters had disappeared, some perhaps falling victims to drugs, others possibly disillusioned as bop lost its edge, and more than a few just moving on. Staying a hipster forever was hardly likely to lead to a truly meaningful existence. Hip ideas filtered into certain areas of intellectual life and Kerouac's *The Subterraneans* throws light on some of the characters who seemed to epitomise hipsterism in the early-1950s. Anton Rosenberg (Julian Alexander in the novel) was a painter and musician, and a heroin addict, who initially attracted Kerouac's attention with his "cool" stance. But Rosenberg's hipster-like sense of exclusiveness soon showed itself in his dismissal of Kerouac's writing. The novelist's enthusiasm clearly clashed with Rosenberg's laid-back detachment.

The Beats generally were too boisterous to ever qualify as hipsters, even if they did use some of the terminology and had a close interest in jazz. Kerouac and John Clellon Holmes, for example, had both listened closely to bebop in the 1940s and continued to follow jazz developments in the 1950s. But they were working writers and, in any case, neither of them was by inclination likely to adopt a hipster approach to what they did. It's a personal view but it seems to me that the one person who did at times reflect some hipster characteristics in his work was Robert Creeley, in his early poems at least. Both the language and the tone had something of the cool hipster feeling to them.

The jazz lifestyle continued to provide a basis for the hipster ("for me it was bebop or bust," said the pianist Walter Bishop when asked about his dedication to music in the 1950s) but it was becoming obvious by 1960 or so that words like "hipster" and "hip" had lost their 1940s and early-1950s connotations. They'd been incorporated into general parlance and were used simply to indicate that someone or something was fashionable or smart. Anyone could be hip, which meant that no-one was.

The hipster story is perhaps peripheral to the Beat experience but it does have relevance to it. Many of the Beat writers, together with others like Creeley and Gilbert Sorrentino, were influenced by jazz and in particular by bebop and the commitment it inspired. They may not have been hipsters themselves but they certainly shared some of the same interests with those obscure but fascinating characters.

CENTRAL AVENUE BREAKDOWN

'It was one of those mixed blocks over in Central Avenue, the blocks that are not yet all negro.'

That brief quote from Raymond Chandler's *Farewell, My Lovely*, first published in 1940, and using Los Angeles as its background, brings in a reference to one of the main places where jazz and rhythm-and-blues flourished on the West Coast. Chandler's book was obviously published before America entered the Second World War, a period when major social upheavals occurred in the USA generally and in the big cities in particular. And it indicates that certain areas were becoming associated with specific ethnic groups and, consequently, their music. My main concern in this article is to talk about at least some of the music, but it may be of value to sketch in a little more of the social milieu.

When the USA was drawn into the war in 1941 following the Japanese attack on Pearl Harbor two things of relevance to the West Coast soon happened. The first was that, in the wake of near-hysteria resulting from the Pearl Harbor disaster and the seeming imminence of a Japanese invasion of California, Japanese-derived citizens living on the West Coast were rounded up and interned. I don't propose to enter into an analysis of the effects of this action, but it should be mentioned that in recent years there have been attempts in films and books to show that it was not always carried out with the best of intentions, and that other Americans were not slow to take advantage of the sudden influx onto the market of Japanese-American businesses, land, etc. It can, of course, be argued that even if some people hadn't deliberately used the situation sheer market forces would have automatically ensured that the areas formerly occupied by the Japanese-Americans would have been taken over by other groups. This was especially bound to happen in a war situation as the sudden growth of war industries and related services brought about a demand for labour. It's of interest at this point to quote Paul Oliver on the subject of black migration to the West Coast:

'Detroit's phenomenal growth as a result of the developing automobile industry was echoed on the West Coast during the Second World War with the rapid expansion of the defence factories. When the factories were opened to Negro labour in the early 'forties thousands of coloured families poured into California to start a migratory trend which has continued to the present day. The figures tell their own story. In 1930 there were 81,000 Negroes in California. During the next decade their numbers increased by half as much again and the 1940 census showed a Negro population of 124,000 in a total of six and half millions. The war years saw a dramatic increase with over half a million Negroes on the Pacific Coast by 1950 and nearly all of them in California.'

Oliver went on to stress that the majority of the Negroes settled in urban areas, in particular Los Angeles and San Francisco. And that most of them came from the Central South West and especially Texas. In addition to those Negroes who actually settled on the West Coast there must have been thousands of others who went there on a temporary basis either in search of well-paid work or as members of the armed forces.

It is, perhaps, interesting to reflect on why it took the war to push up the Negro population of California. Elsewhere in the United States boom periods-the First World War, and the best years of the Twenties, for example- had encouraged blacks to move to such places as Chicago and Detroit in search of work. But as Oliver's figure demonstrates it is only in the post-1940 period that California experienced an influx of coloured families. I would guess that the fact that the West Coast, prior to the war, did not have a large amount of labour-intensive industry had something to do with blacks not moving there. Agreed, the Twenties and Thirties were not exactly good years for blacks anywhere, nor for many whites, but some Northern cities did hold out the promise of jobs, even if they were insecure and poorly paid. It would also seem true to say that, in the Thirties, certain restrictions were applied to those wanting to enter California. Readers will probably recall the famous scenes in the film of *The Grapes Of Wrath* when families with less than a certain amount of basic funds are turned back at the state line. If such restrictions, and a general dislike of impoverished newcomers, affected whites one can imagine what it was like for blacks, many of whom would most likely not own even the old trucks and broken furniture that some whites had. That American entry into the war brought about a demand for black labour justifiably led to a suspicion that coloured families were only welcome when white society needed them.

Of course, some blacks had always been needed, particularly in Los Angeles where a concentration of film and recording studios attracted show business types who, if not performing themselves, wanted to be entertained. Los Angeles had always attracted singers and musicians, and there was a jazz tradition in the city from the twenties onwards. But blacks were very much second-class citizens, and segregation applied with a vengeance well into the Forties, as the following makes clear: 'As late as 1949, ubiquitous pianist-vocal coach Eddie Beal and a white male composer friend he was working with went to hear Count Basie at a short-lived Hollywood Boulevard spot known as the Cotton Club. They were informed that they must sit at separate tables. In Hollywood that law was unwritten and subject to 'arrangement' between club owners and enforcement agencies. In adjacent Glendale, the ordinance was on the books. Black musicians had to apply for police permits to be within the city limits after 6 p.m. or be subject to arrest. At 2 a.m. squad cars escorted artists with permits from their places of employment to the LA. line.'

Despite the various problems that blacks encountered the increased coloured population of the Forties inevitably led to parts of Los Angeles becoming, in a sense, their playgrounds, where music flourished. And if the actual amount of activity increased so did the variety of influences which were absorbed into the general framework. Jazz, of course, is a more sophisticated music than the blues, and is thus more susceptible to influences and fashions with a national base, so it's not easy to pick out a style from the Forties which can be said to have been typical of the West Coast. In fact, it was only in the Fifties, and then primarily as a result of white influences, that an approach which could be said to have had certain easily identifiable characteristics was evolved.

Still, I'll persist with the notion that jazz in California often had a sound of its own which derived from the social atmosphere of its environment. (I'm talking about the 1945-1950 period). There is, I think, evidence in books, written by jazz-influenced writers which suggests a 'different' feeling applying on the West Coast. Jack Kerouac's *On The Road* is a classic example in that it takes its characters from one coast to the other, and back again, and manages to suggest that two different cultures apply. True, Kerouac's natural ebullience, and his tendency to play down that bad side of things, helps soften the harsh tone of life in New York, but it does still come through, just as it does more powerfully in John Clellon Holmes' *Go*, a novel which parallels Kerouac's in some of its incidents and characters. Perhaps the best book, however, to get to grips with the difference of life-styles of the two cities - Los Angeles and New York- is one written by a man who was a key figure in the post-1945 development of jazz in California. Ross Russell's *The Sound*, clearly based on Charlie Parker's life (in its basic outline, at least) clearly indicates that New York was seen as a harsher place, a hostile, if stimulating, environment in which poverty, criminality, and bleakness coloured most lives. What essentially comes through is that the Los Angeles scenes have a stronger community feeling to them, and that this possibly stemmed from the smaller scale of the place, or perhaps, its being split into various areas, each with its own neighbourhood feeling, as well as from the climate, both natural and cultural. This is not to play down the very real problems of segregation, unemployment, poverty, etc. which also applied in Los Angeles, but rather to suggest that they were, perhaps, easier tolerated, if only because the scale was smaller. And it would be naive to ask if the natural climate didn't also help alleviate some of the distress? Or the provincial tone of the city? From Russell's fictional descriptions of the characters and locations one gets the feeling that they are, in some ways, operating within a clearly defined community context. In comparison the characters in New York appear rootless and form a drifting nucleus of hipsters, pushers, musicians, hangers-on, and the like, whose only community is the one they themselves comprise. And to a certain degree this is not all that different from the impressions of Beat life that seep out of such novels as *Go* and *On The Road*. In New York the characters are often isolated from all but their immediate friends and associates. On the West Coast they appear to relax and even spread out into the wider community.

To return to the West Coast jazz scene, though. By the mid-Forties the network was a fairly extensive one. To quote Patricia Willard: "Dexter Gordon and Wardell Gray were a formidable front-line many nights at the Down Beat on Central Avenue at 41st Street. At closing time they moved up the Avenue apiece to Jack's Basket, a bring-your-own-bottle-and-buy set-ups/fried chicken restaurant/after hours club where the music cooked till dawn ... Central Avenue had more jazz clubs, before and after hours, than any other street or neighbourhood in Los Angeles-Alabam, Lovejoy's, Down Beat,

Memo, Last Word and Clark Hotel Bar, Plantation Club and Savoy-plus the Elk's Auditorium at 40th where the big bands played dances, the Lincoln Theatre between 22nd and 23rd with musical stage shows, and the after-hours clubs which intermittently had live music but catered to musicians and their friends - Backstage and Brother's".

Clubs obviously came and went in rapid succession, with police harassment always a major problem. But this didn't stop enthusiasts opening new ones. Trumpeter Howard McGhee and his wife ran (albeit briefly) The Finale, a club which spotlighted Charlie Parker when he spent some time on the West Coast. Parker's impact needs to be looked at in detail, in fact, if we are to fully understand the nature of the modern jazz scene in California. By 1945 bop had been accepted in New York, and record companies such as Savoy and Guild, were issuing discs by the newer jazzmen. Elsewhere in the United States small groups of musicians were listening to the latest sounds, tying them in with their own experiments, and slowly developing the mature bop style. But Parker and a handful of other New York-based jazzmen were the key names and the acknowledged leaders of the bop movement. If one wanted to hear bop at its best one had to hear them live. So, by late-1945, club-owner Billy Berg, whose premises in Hollywood were the first in the area to have a racially-mixed audience policy, was keen to bring in some of the East Coast stars. The story is that he asked singer-pianist Harry 'The Hipster' Gibson (an entertainer whose jive-talk performances made references to narcotics and other deviant behaviour) who he should hire, and was told that Parker and trumpeter Dizzy Gillespie were the obvious choices. They arrived in Los Angeles in December 1945, bringing with them a small group made up of New York modernists. When the group appeared at Billy Berg's a local tenor-man, Lucky Thompson, was added to it, most likely because Parker, when in the throws of extreme addiction, was unreliable in terms of arriving on time or even turning up at all.

The usual manner of dealing with the Parker/Gillespie stint at Berg's, at least until recent years, had been to describe it as something of a disaster, both commercially and musically. But the opposite seems to have been true, certainly insofar as the music was concerned. Ross Russell's opinion is that, 'Despite capacity crowds opening week, and, dwindling but adequate attendances in the ensuing seven weeks, the booking was a loser for Billy Berg. He was not unduly concerned, having waxed fat during the war years, and it was difficult to book bop attractions into California night clubs for some time to come. The explanation lay not with the number of patrons, but in a new lifestyle. They belong to the first generation of anti-alcohol, pro-pot culture. Their habit was to order a single beer or iced coffee-at a maximum two-and these drinks were nursed through the evening. They stayed to hear set after set of the exciting music, adjourning to the men's room between sets to turn on their own brand of dry psychedelic.'

When Parker was in California he made a number of recordings, and although I don't intend to discuss them in detail, it is worth referring to those stemming from concert appearances with a group assembled by impresario Norman Granz. Granz's concerts, world famous in later years, began their life in Los Angeles, and took their name from the hall in which they were first held-the Los Angeles Philharmonic Auditorium. The first concert was a benefit for youths arrested during the notorious 1943 'zoot suit' riots in the city which occurred when servicemen, annoyed at the flashily-dressed civilians seemingly having all the money and girls, began to beat up anyone dressed in the long drape jackets and pegged trousers which were the hallmarks of the hipsters of the period. The concert proved a success, and Granz soon began staging others on a commercial basis. His usual plan, at least in those early days, was to use a number of local jazzmen along with visiting musicians who were, perhaps, resting in the city between jobs or possibly just having a night off. Many big bands of the day used Los Angeles as a base, so there was always a large number of jazz men available for pick-up groups for concerts or recording sessions. So, for concerts staged from mid-1944 through 1946, Granz used trombonist J.J..Johnson (travelling with Benny Carter's band), Willie Smith, Nat 'King' Cole (then working the Los Angeles clubs and fast making a name for himself as a singer though still active as a pianist), Lester Young, just out of the army and trying to re-adjust to civilian life. And both Charlie Parker and Dizzy Gillespie worked for Granz during their Los Angeles visit. Incidentally, it's ironic to note that, although the concerts became famous under the title Jazz at the Philharmonic, Granz actually lost the use of the hall after over-enthusiastic audiences jived in the aisles and indulged in other activities that were frowned upon by the city authorities. Jazz in the Forties was far from being the respectable music it is today.

By the time Parker moved back to New York in early 1947 after an eventful West Coast sojourn which, musical activities apart, resulted in his being committed to Camarillo State Hospital, there was a healthy nucleus of young modernists in the Los Angeles area. Prominent among them were tenormen Wardell Gray and Dexter Gordon whose saxophone 'battles' were highspots of the musical life of Central Avenue. The instrumental 'battle' was a key item in jazz in the Forties, and Norman Granz capitalized on it by pairing off various musicians, the most popular probably being Illinois Jacquet and Flip Phillips. But on the West Coast Gray and Gordon were the masters, their 'battles' being noted not only for their excitement value but also for their musical qualities. Many tenor saxophone exchanges could degenerate into a mere trading of honks and squeals, or crowd-catching quotes, but Gray and Gordon always maintained a high level of control of invention, even when performing at a fast tempo. There are a number of records which illustrate their work with each other, ranging from a Ross Russell-organised session which produced a studio version of *The Chase*, their most famous number, through to early-Fifties items from concerts. Gray died in the mid-Fifties, a victim of drugs problems, and Gordon had more than his share of personal problems before making a comeback in recent years, but their recordings together still stand out as highspots of the bop era.

Public concerts of a jazz-session type seem to have been extremely popular on the West Coast, if the recorded evidence is anything to go by, and this possibly backs up suggestions I made earlier regarding the flamboyancy of the California jazzmen. Besides Norman Granz's efforts there were those of Gene Norman, whose activities extended from modern jazz to Dixieland and blues. Norman was originally a disc-jockey presenting a nightly show on Station KFWB and a series of concerts at the Shrine Auditorium and the Pasadena Civic Auditorium, as well as briefly running a club-the Hollywood Empire-which for a few months in 1949 featured such artists as Louis Jordan and Roy Milton. His activities in the jazz world included concerts which featured Wardell Gray, Dexter Gordon, Howard McGhee and Sonny Criss, but he was also responsible for the first California appearance of the legendary Dizzy Gillespie big-band of the late-Forties. A recording exists of part of this concert, and the electric atmosphere, and the intensity of the music, testifies to the enthusiasm with which both musicians and fans approached the event. Photographs taken at the time show Gillespie, a cult figure among bop fans, wearing the 'uniform' (dark glasses, or horn-rimmed ones, drape suit, beret, striped tie, and so on) and surrounded by a crowd of admiring, and similarly attired hipsters.

Charting the rise and fall of jazz on the West Coast isn't always easy, particularly in view of the fact that one isn't always quite sure just when certain musicians were at their most active. According to Ross Russell, 'The high point was reached in the spring of 1946, and after that wartime prosperity subsided into a saner, squarer mode of life. The big-spending GIs had gone, marginal night-clubs were closed, and music jobs grew fewer.' There is a musical reference to this easing off of the surface prosperity of the war years in Jimmy Witherspoon's *Skid Row Blues*, in which the singer bemoans the fact that the police have cracked down on the clubs, and things are generally tighter: All the hip cats on the corner, they don't look sharp no more, 'cos all the good times is over, and the squares don't have no dough'.

Recorded in November 1947 in Los Angeles for the Supreme label, one of the numerous small companies which sprang up in the mid-Forties and collapsed soon after, it aptly captures the tone of the times, and outlines how the cessation of wartime activities, and the resultant cut-backs, knocked the heart out of the false boom economy which, for a brief period, had enabled musicians, singers, hipsters, club-owners and the rest, to ride on the back of servicemen hungry for a good time, and well-paid civilians with few luxury items to spend their money on.

So far I have discussed modern jazz activity on the West Coast, but I don't want to give the impression that it was isolated from other musical forms. Many musicians worked in several fields at one and the same time, especially if they were professionals and had to adjust in order to earn a regular living. And, in any case, much jazz has often had links with dance-band music, and with urban blues. I mentioned Jimmy Witherspoon and he's clearly a good example of someone whose range covered both jazz and blues. A tenorman such as Maxwell Davis crossed easily from jazz into blues and back again, working with Jazz at the Philharmonic and also being heavily featured on numerous rhythm-and-blues records. All this brings us to the interesting fact that many of those artists who helped develop the Forties rhythm-and-blues sounds initially wanted to work with swing-style bands in which instrumental soloists had a key role. Johnny Otis is a good example, and some of his earliest discs are, in fact, by a 17 piece orchestra playing fairly orthodox jazz arrangements. Economic circumstances, plus the changing tastes of the audiences, may have forced R&B artists to tour with smaller groups than they actually preferred, but they invariably tried to ensure that some aspects of the jazz sound - saxophones, and jazz-based rhythm sections-were retained. As Otis puts it:

'By 1950 we had established what was a hybrid form that had come into its own. Roy Milton, Joe Liggins and I have often discussed this. Now, all of us came out of a big-band environment and we all aspired to the big-band sound. I had a big-band. Roy played with Ernie Field's band, and so on. When the big-bands died, and we found we couldn't function in that context anymore- in the mid to late-40s when we had to break our bands down-when we played a blues-type thing with three horns, it had a different character. Let me see if I can explain what I mean: see, Roy Milton is a blues singer and when he got his band together to play a little gig somewhere, he didn't use two guitars: he used three horns, a bass, guitar and drums. The horns were important to him because he had come out of the big-band Swing era - he was used to that sound - and they were important to me for the same reason. I still wanted my five reeds, four trumpets and trombones. I wanted to hear that in my ear. But I couldn't have that, so when I got my first job after the big-band broke down, at the Cricket Club, I then had a baritone, a tenor, a trumpet and a trombone. So I had a brass section-a trumpet and a trombone-and a reed section - a tenor and a baritone.'

This translation of the big-band sound into small-group terms coincided with, or perhaps just paralleled and helped shape, another development, that of 'jump music'. Going back to the influx of Negroes into California, and the consequent growth of clubs and bars to cater for them, it is obvious that musical forms appeared which reflected the changed world of black people. Many of them had come from Texas, Arkansas, and Oklahoma, where rural blues styles already existed, but once in the city the music took on some of the characteristics of their new way of life. One commentator has stated that the new styles were 'moulded by resentment rather than resignation ... dedicated to revelry rather than rumination,' and there is a great deal of truth in those statements. And it was not only that the lyrics changed-as indeed they did - but that the rhythmic impulse of the music altered too. Charlie Gillett described it in the following way: 'Typical jump combos featured a strong rhythm section of piano, bass and drums and usually had a singer and a saxophonist up front, with sometimes a second man added. Between them, the various instrumentalists emphasised the rhythm that a boogie pianist had achieved alone with his left hand, and the process of transcribing the effect to several instruments the difference between each beat was emphasised more in jump rhythms - or blurred-in shuffle rhythms. Several different regional variations of the style developed, in New York, on the West Coast, in the mid-South (St Louis/Memphis), in New Orleans, in Chicago and on the Eastern Seaboard.'

Gillett went on to point out that three West Coasters - T-Bone Walker, Roy Milton and Amos Milburn - were among the earliest of 'jump music' specialists, and it's worth taking a closer look at each of them. Walker had a long background in the blues, and to a degree in jazz, having played with Ma Rainey, Blind Lemon Jefferson and Les Hite's band. He switched to electric guitar in the late-Thirties and settled in California around the same time. His rise to popularity took place in the Forties, as urban rhythm-and-blues developed to cater for the tastes of new audiences and the impulse of a new era. Walker's style as a guitarist and singer was as much put of the jazz tradition as the blues, and in fact some of his early records - *I'm still in love with you* is one example-are almost ballad-like in their mood and construction. As a singer Walker had a somewhat bland voice, one which I personally feel had limitations when linked to his penchant for slow and medium-slow tempo performances, but there is no doubt that he was very popular, and that a few of his discs achieved the stature of classics of their kind. *Stormy Monday Blues* is one such item, its lyrics outlining the week as it would be experienced in the black ghettos and indeed in most working-class areas of the United States:

They call it stormy Monday, but Tuesday's just as bad (repeat)
Wednesday's worse, and Thursday's also sad.
Yes, the eagle flies on Friday,
and Saturday I go out to play.

Walker like Louis Jordan, often appealed outside purely black areas, and probably for the same reasons. His voice was blander and clearer than those of many R&B artists, and his groups less-inclined to play raucous riffs or his saxophonists indulge in hard-driving solos. A key tenorman on many early Walker records was Bumps Myers, who, like Maxwell Davis (also featured with Walker in the Fifties), had a strong reputation as a musician able to cope with most popular forms, ranging from straight jazz sessions to stomping blues or the more relaxed things which were part of the guitarist-singer's staple diet. On Walker's discs he tended to rhapsodise behind the vocals, and occasionally take a smooth, relaxed solo. The cryptic *Wise Man Blues*, recorded in Hollywood in 1947, is worth listening to in this respect.

One other factor which possibly helped Walker appeal outside black communities, and would certainly have helped with regard to getting his discs broadcast, was that his lyrics were frequently innocuous. Many R&B and jazz vocal performances of the period were more than risqué by the standards of the time, and certainly enough to ensure that they were unlikely to be used by disc-jockeys working for white stations. We don't need to move out of our West Coast context to find examples. Crown Prince Waterford's *Move your hand, baby* (recorded in Hollywood, 1947) and Helen Humes' *Drive me Daddy* (1946) had, I would guess, little currency outside the ghettoes. The lyrics on the Humes disc are especially explicit, whilst at the same time using their imagery with a fair amount of humour and invention:

All I need is real good driving,
just ignite me with your key,
just ease down on my clutch,
and let my motor run free.
Now keep me going, baby,
'cos I'm never out of gas,
just as long as you can drive me
is as long as I can last.

A comparison of the above with most of Walker's lyrics will make it clear that he played it fairly safe. Helen Humes, on the other hand, was noted for her salty vocals, and a 1950 concert at the Shrine Auditorium produced her classic *Million Dollar Secret*, with the following lines bringing a roar of approval from the audience:

Now I've got a man, he's 78,
and I'm just 23.

Everybody thinks I'm crazy,
but his will's made out to me.

Not all the lyrics of R&B songs were built around sex, though that subject, and drink, did provide much of the stimulus for the many singers. But in the lyrics one can often sense a real desire to record the kind of street life that clearly typified much of the black experience. Crown Prince Waterford's *L.A. Blues* is interesting for the way in which it provides a view of how the city was seen in the Forties:

Some call it the land of sunshine
Some call it old Central Avenue.
(repeat both lines),
I call it a big old country town
where the folks don't care what they do.
If a man can make it in Los Angeles,
he can make it anywhere
(repeat both lines),
But you've got to have a used Cadillac car,
yes, boys, and you can't stay square.

T-Bone Walker's songs sometimes had words which exploited topical themes - *Bobby Sox Blues* is an obvious example-but they rarely had the cynicism that is evident in Waterford's and which was probably more typical of city life. I have deliberately spent some time discussing a handful of songs because it seems to me important to establish how the urban blues artists appealed to their audience. And before leaving the subject I'd like to mention just a couple more tracks which are interesting because of their vocal content, but also because of the way in which they blended a number of musical styles. Recorded by a group led by tenor-man Buddy Tate, then working with the Count Basie band in Los Angeles, it mixed several Basie musicians with some local ones, and added singer Jimmy Witherspoon. But the two items of particular relevance actually feature vocals by Charlie Price, an altoist from Basie's band. The sardonic tone of *Balling from day to day* neatly complements its sad tale of a man who used to hang around with a fast-moving crowd, but whose money is now all gone so he's friendless. *The things you've done for me baby* is even more cynical, its lyrics referring to the 'hero' of the song not having to work because his girl provides for them both:

At night when I lay sleeping
You're always on the street,
saying, lay something on me, John,
'cos I got a man to keep.

Backing up Price the band plays a mixture of swing material with some blues influences, and occasionally even a few bop phrases. In other words, a cross-section of what was then current, and popular at various levels, in 1947.

Roy Milton, the second West Coaster mentioned by Charlie Gillet, was a more exciting performer than Walker, though less successful in bridging the race gap. Milton had moved to California in the Thirties, but it was only in the mid-Forties that he surfaced from the sea of musical talent in the Los Angeles area. He did have some contact with white audiences, in that he had a dual musical personality, but his recordings concentrated on appealing to his fellow-blacks: 'Milton played regular hours at a white club and he played white music: all the Tin Pan Alley songs, and then after hours he went out to Watts and played for the black people there.' It is difficult to imagine that the forceful rhythm, insistent riffs, and rasping sax solos would have much in them for sophisticated whites. Even a relatively relaxed item like *Night and Day* (not the popular song with the same title) has a fairly heavy rhythmic base, and a buzz-toned saxophone, which took it out of the popular field and into a race one. 'Race', incidentally, was the word used in the Forties to describe black popular music as opposed to that produced for whites. Billboard magazine ran a separate chart for black hits, and Milton's *R.M. Blues* was number one on it in 1946, with the band itself being voted number three in the 'Year's top band in race records' section of the Billboard annual poll.

Milton initially recorded for Art Rupe's Juke Box label, then formed a company of his own, but returned to Rupe (whose label was now Speciality) in 1947. From a collector's point of view there is a great deal of confusion regarding Milton's recorded output in the Forties, certain titles being cut for both his own label and Rupe's, and sometimes even in circulation at the same time. Anyone interested in such matters will find that the ups and downs, triumphs and failures, and occasional shady dealings, of the various small record companies and their operators, make for fascinating reading, and throws light on the social and economic conditions of the period. The mid-Forties were boom years for independent labels, many of which lasted only a matter of months and perhaps issued no more than a handful of 78's. War economies had resulted in a shortage of records at a time when people had money, and the inclination to buy them. The large companies could not keep up with the demand, nor could they come up with the kind of music that was wanted by the new black urban audience. So, local companies sprang up to cater for the immediate needs of people in specific locations. The situation was, in theory, that anyone with sufficient resources could hire musicians (often willing to work for less than union scale) and a studio, record a few sides, and then get a major company with its own pressing plant to actually turn out the records. But it didn't always work that way. A shortage of shellac during the war meant that companies were allocated only so much, and thus were reluctant to use too much of it to produce discs for other outfits. And even if they did agree to print the discs the small operator was then faced with immense distribution difficulties. Art Rupe once recalled that his first Juke Box side - The Sepia Tones *Boogie No.1* - had a print of six or seven hundred (he ordered a thousand, in fact, but didn't get the full amount) initially, and he ordered more as he sold them. He personally delivered the discs to shops in Los Angeles, in particular Gold's Furniture Store which had a large record department *Boogie No.1* finally sold around 70,000 copies, most of which were distributed in Los Angeles, San Francisco, and some larger urban centres in Texas. I mentioned earlier in this article that Texas provided many of the people who moved to California in the Forties, and it's probable that a fair amount of cross-reference, in terms of cultural influences, applied between the two states. There is an interesting reference to this in the work of the little known Zuzu Bollin, a singer in the 'jump' style who recorded in Houston in 1952. One of his songs says, 'Well, it's so long Texas, California here I come', and the reference is that the Coast, if not exactly the promised land, does offer something better than the Lone Star State has so far come up with.

The Houston link crops up in connection with Amos Milburn, whose *Chicken Shack Boogie* was a major race hit in 1947. Milburn was "discovered" while playing in Texas and a promotional trip to the West Coast resulted in him being offered a recording contract with Aladdin Records, a label which survived longer than most independents and recorded a wide variety of jazz and rhythm-and-blues. Milburn had a strong boogie style, and his clear-toned voice calling out over the rolling rhythm laid down by the section as a whole, made for an immediately identifiable and exciting sound. Like many R&B singers he used, no doubt in response to the tastes of his audience, numerous songs which dealt with drink and its related problems. *Bad, Bad Whiskey, Just one more drink, Let me go home Whiskey,* and *Milk and Water* (summing up what happens when you indulge too much) are typical, and one can easily understand why they appealed to people who most likely spent a fair amount of their time in bars, and who saw alcohol as a means of escape from the ghetto, and the social limitations that colour, a lack of money, unemployment, and other similar factors, could encourage. It would be possible to construct a whole catalogue of Forties and Fifties blues items which used booze as their basis, some of them seriously, others more humorously, as for example Jimmy Liggins' *Drunk* which was recorded on the West Coast. Jimmy Liggins and his brother, Joe, were Art Rupe artists, and popular with black audiences. Joe Liggins did manage to occasionally get through to whites, too, and his *The Honeydripper* was one of the few authentic urban R&B items, other than those produced by Louis Jordan and T-Bone Walker, which was released in the United Kingdom in the Forties. It appeared as a 78 on the old Parlophone label.

The drinking songs point to one aspect of R&B which always needs to be given high priority in any consideration of the importance of the music. By the late Forties it had easily replaced jazz as the main musical diet of the urban blacks. (Personally, I would argue that out-and-out jazz, as opposed to dance-music, never was widely popular with either whites or blacks, but I'll not press the point here). The reasons for its popularity are complex, though one stands out. To a largely unsophisticated audience the main aim of music is that it should have some functional value. It should be suitable for dancing, for accompanying socialising at parties and in bars, and for providing a background at home or at work. It should also contain a fair amount of material which is easily assimilated in terms of melodic content, simple lyrics, and so on. In the Thirties some jazzmen, along with dance-bands, had provided this kind of musical fare, with black audiences also turning to blues singers, whether of an urban or rural kind, for additional sustenance. The big-bands were, of course, very popular with both whites and blacks, as were their singers such as

Jimmy Rushing. But jazz had grown more complex by the mid-Forties. The young revolutionaries of the bop world had an appeal to the intellectually inclined among both blacks and whites, but it would be wrong to suggest that they had more than a limited impact on the majority of Americans, of whatever colour. And this was especially true of the mass of working people. So, as the big-bands died, and jazz became more slanted to the intellectuals, the ordinary blacks looked to rhythm-and-blues to provide their entertainment. The artists in that field did what was wanted, i.e. they played for dancing, for drinking, and for socialising. And insofar as stimulants were a part of the way of life, and the main stimulant in circulation was alcohol, then they produced songs which reflected that fact.

So, if the bop world had a subculture of narcotics, then the society constructed by working-class blacks had a subculture of alcohol. This isn't too strange, as anyone considering popular entertainers in this country (current ones like Mike Harding or Billy Connolly, for example) will realise. Alcohol has been, and still is, a key factor in the life of the working class in any society, black or white, British or American. And though it would be impossible to deny that drugs, of one sort or another, were also part of the American black culture, they were so on a relatively limited scale in the Forties, with their use in the musical context often revolving around the jazz scene. I think the actual lives of many of the performers reflected this. The jazz world of the Forties and Fifties was littered with the casualties of narcotics addiction, and although the facts of the lives of R&B artists are not always easy to come by it does seem true that they seem to have suffered less from that particular problem. I don't doubt that alcohol became a threat to some performers' careers, or that mild stimulants such as marijuana were in common use, but the heroin cult which the boppers built up doesn't appear to have had a strict parallel in the R&B field. I admit that my comments are mainly built on guesswork, and it would be valuable to have some definite information on the use of drugs by blues artists, but I remain reasonably certain that it was less of a problem to them than to their counterparts in the modern jazz world. Of course, one could point to the situation today, with drugs clearly in use on a wider scale than ever before, but with alcohol still holding its own - if only because of its acceptability and availability-as the main stimulant. After all, pubs are a major influence and provide easy centres to socialize, and the same was no doubt true of ghetto bars in black areas in the

Forties.

I mentioned much earlier in, my survey of West Coast activity that Nat 'King' Cole was working in the Los Angeles night-clubs in the mid-Forties. His influence on other black performers should not be underestimated. Cole's early work was based on a trio format of piano, bass and guitar, with Cole himself, and sometimes the group, handling vocals. I pointed out that Cole had a strong reputation as a jazz pianist-he worked with such well-known jazzmen as Illinois Jacquet, Lester Young, and Dexter Gordon- but as early as 1940 he recorded sides in what could be called a "jump" style. They were usually novelty numbers, such as *I like to riff, Call the police, Are you fer it,* and *Hit that jive, Jack,* bouncy items which had a tight rhythmic base and used lyrics built around some of the fashionable slang of the day. In the Forties quite a number of young blacks were influenced by Cole to the extent of modelling their singing styles, and the approach of their groups, on him. Ray Charles' early sides, recorded in California in 1949/1950, were often in that mould, and even went so far as to have Charles backed by guitarist Oscar Moore and bassist Johnny Miller, both of whom had worked with Cole.

Another Cole-influenced singer was Charles Brown, born in Texas in 1920, and a citizen of California from 1943 onwards. Brown was hired by guitarist Johnny Moore, whose combo soon became popular in the night clubs and cocktail bars of Los Angeles. Like Cole, the Moore group and Brown evolved a style to meet the demand of the environment it had to function in. According to Charlie Gillett, "During the war, the migration of blacks into California outpaced the provisions of special facilities for them, so that for some years they shared the night-clubs with whites. The unusual integrated audiences may have encouraged the black singers to minimise the blues content of their repertoires. In any case, 'cocktail' piano playing was common - pretty right-hand tickling with a light rhythm from bass and brushed drums." One can see that the Moore/Brown group would have been popular in situations where a heavier sound might interfere with the conversation. In addition, Brown's lyrics have a softer edge to them than, say, those of Roy Milton or Amos Milburn, and they point to a possible attempt to cross barriers and appeal to both black and white audiences, or mixed ones. Another factor in Brown's appeal, which soon spread outside California, was that his songs made references to a wide variety of places, ranging from

California to New Orleans and Chicago. In one Brown performance, *Sunny Road*, there are some neat lines which bring in the social impact of the closing down of the war economy:

Well the war is over, I'm going down that sunny road,
Well I can't get nothing in Chicago, but
just my room and board.
When I was making good, baby, you
treated me like I was a king,
Now I don't have a war plant job, and my
love don't mean a thing.

The specific reference to Chicago would not have stopped blacks in many parts of the United States, California included, from sympathising with the plight of the singer. There were other artists who worked with variants of the "jump" style, whether they tended to the club/ballad approach of Charles Brown, or the more energetic manner of Roy Milton and Amos Milburn. Floyd Dixon was an able pianist and singer, again born in Texas, and moving around a musical area which included boogie influences as well as others drawn from Brown and Louis Jordan. And Lowell Fulson was a guitarist with a deep feeling for the blues, but enough sophistication in his overall approach to enable him to cover a number of styles. His *Everyday I have the blues* is a good example of his earthy guitar blended with the alto sax of Earl Brown, and a "jump" style rhythm, to come up with a mixture of rural and urban influences.

One of the most popular singer/pianists of the Forties, and one who manipulated the Cole/Brown technique to good advantage, was Cecil Gant. His first records, made when he was serving in the army in California, billed him as "Pvt. Cecil Gant, the G.I. Singsation," an obvious attempt to cash in on the patriotic mood of the period. Gant even used Nat Cole's old hit, *Hit that jive, Jack*, singing it in a loose way which brought in some wordless improvising derived from a mixture of Nellie Lutcher and Slim Gaillard. Like other performers I've mentioned he also made direct references to Los Angeles in his songs:

I feel so lowdown,
I feel like changing towns.
Because when you get the blues in L.A.,
it really brings you down.

As can be seen, no-one ever seems to say anything particularly nice about the city, even if they did originally see California as a place where they could live a better kind of life, and the songs perhaps illustrate how a feeling of disillusionment was prevalent among blacks.

I made a brief reference to Slim Gaillard in the above paragraph, and in a way he helps to bring us back to the total West Coast scene in the Forties, and its mixture of jazz, bop, blues, and their variations. Gaillard was a popular performer before he went to the West Coast, and around 1938/1939 worked with bassist Slam Stewart in night-clubs and recording studios. But his most active period seems to have been in California from around 1945 onwards when he was caught up in the wave of eccentricity that I've previously mentioned. Gaillard typified much of the flamboyancy of the Forties, both in his manner of dressing, his songs, and his general "philosophy" of life. Bearing this in mind it's not unexpected to find him cropping up in Jack Kerouacs's *On the Road.* Like Harry "The Hipster" Gibson, Gaillard ran into trouble with newspapers, radio stations, and other guardians of the public morality, his records being labelled "offensive", and even "subversive", an interesting classification bearing in mind that, as early as 1946, rightwingers on the West Coast were beginning to hunt out examples of un-Americanism. Now, it's certainly true that Gibson’s records made fairly obvious references to drugs - *Who put the benzedrine in Mrs. Murphy's Ovaltine?* is the most-famous item - but what probably really determined the reactions of the critics was that both artists attracted a cult following, one which might be said to have been drawn from the first stirrings of an "underground," though the term wasn't then in use. The fact that Kerouac and his friends were interested shows how they understood what Gibson and Gaillard were up to. I'm not sure that Gibson deserves to be remembered other than as a curiosity of the period, but Gaillard was original in his own small way.

It is fairly difficult to describe one of his performances, but Jack Kerouac got near to being successful: "We went to see Slim Gaillard in a little Frisco nightclub. Slim is a tall, thin Negro with big, sad eyes who's always saying 'Right-orooni' and 'How about a little bourbon-orooni' ... When he gets warmed up he takes off his shirt and undershirt and really goes. He does and says anything that comes into his head. He'll sing 'Cement Mixer, Putti-putti' and suddenly slows down the beat and broods over his bongos with fingertips barely tapping the skins as everybody leans forward breathlessly to hear; you think he'll do this for a minute or so, but he goes right on, for as long as an hour, making an imperceptible little noise with the tips of his fingernails, smaller and smaller all the time till you can't hear it any more and the sounds of the traffic come in the open door. Then he slowly gets up and takes the mike and says, very slowly, 'Great-orooni . .. alorooni ... fine-ovauti ... hello-orooni ... bourbon-orooni ... how are the boys in the front row making out with their girls-orooni ... orooni ... vauti... oroonirooni."

There's nothing on record which captures Gaillard in such extreme form, but there are plenty of examples of his flair for the bizarre. Two recent LPs offer material mostly recorded on the West Coast in the Forties, with Gaillard indulging in a mock-African chanting, complete with asides in hip-talk and comments on his favourite foods. He's also likely to shoot off into imitations of announcers on Spanish-American stations (complete with plugs for local car salesrooms), popular singers, and so on. And although it dates from a slightly later period than the one we're dealing with, his version of *How high the moon* surely deserves a special place in any list of all-time offbeat records. According to Gaillard you can find potatoes on the moon that are the size of the Hollywood Bowl. How do they peel them? With bulldozers, of course. It's a weird world he inhabits, one in which the imagination has full play, and Sunday afternoon jam-sessions feature billions of tenor saxophones. On a Forties disc, *School Kids Hop,* Slim says he's going to school to study "chemisterini and vout." Other Forties records - *Santa Monica Jump* and *Boogin' at Berg's*- show how he was operating firmly in a Californian context. It's easy to see how he became a hero to the West Coast hipsters, his flamboyancy and semi-surreal mockery being completely attuned to their sensibilities. It's a pity that when, in the Sixties, the hippies rediscovered the late 'Lord' Buckley (whose first record was a monologue dubbed over a 1946 Lyle Griffin track, *Flight of the Vout Bug*, a typical Los Angeles title) they didn't also bother to find out about Gaillard. His eccentricities would surely have had great appeal, though perhaps they would have been considered too extreme by the more-serious devotees of flower-power philosophy. And Gaillard's tendency would, no doubt, have been to satirise the hippies, something they didn't take kindly to. One can quote various stories about him, some of them no doubt owing more to legend than reality, but my own favourite is of the time when he arrived a week late for a club engagement. By way of an excuse he presented the manager with a medical certificate which read, "In my opinion this man is perfectly sane."

I've ranged far and wide in this short survey of the West Coast scene of the mid and late-Forties, and I'm aware that I've been less than fair in my coverage of a number of important and influential blues artists. But my main aim has been to try to give a general picture of at least some of the musical activity of the period, and so to show that Los Angeles, in particular, had its own traditions and vitality. I do firmly believe that there was a different atmosphere on the West Coast, partly resulting from the flamboyancy I've frequently referred to (and it would take another article to explain fully how that flamboyancy developed), and partly from the social and musical factors which prevented the development of the kind of divisions sometimes apparent in New York, Chicago, and other major American cities.

In conclusion it's necessary to point out that many of the musicians and singers I've mentioned faded from sight as the Fifties emerged. Rhythm-and-blues went into a decline in the Fifties. Generally it has been accepted that the rise of rock-and-roll affected black blues artists tremendously, and it was around the mid-Fifties that many of those I've mentioned began to slide into obscurity. Some blacks did manage to adjust enough to survive, but Roy Milton, Amos Milburn, Charles Brown, Joe Liggins, and others like them, were neglected even if they did continue to record or play club engagements. Their liking for "jump" rhythm, jazz-inclined saxophone soloists, and similar influences, put them beyond the tastes of audiences interested in what Charlie Gillett described as "a simple 2/4 with the accent on the back beat" and lyrics which tended to make adolescence the keystone of all experience. No-one is going to pretend that R&B artists sang songs which contained gems of poetry, but they were often far more imaginative than anything that came out of the rock-and-roll era. And one always felt that they were aimed at men and women, both in terms of the contents of the songs and the way in which they were performed. With rock-and-roll the singers sounded as it they were aiming at boys and girls, which of course they were. It was the beginning of a mass youth culture which hadn't existed in the Forties. So there was little room for R&B artists who needed a sense of identification with the community as a whole. An era had passed.

SOURCES

Raymond Chandler, *Farewell, My Lovely.*Penguin Books, Harmondsworth, 1975. Page 7.

Patricia Willard. Sleeve notes for *Black California*, Savoy SJL 2215.

Ross Russell. "West Coast Bop," *Jazz & Blues*, London, May 1973. Page 10.

Mark Gardner. "Bop City," *Melody Maker*, London, 27th March 1971.

Johnny Otis. Quoted in Pete Welding's sleeve notes for *The Original Johnny Otis Show*, Savoy SLJ 2230.

Arnold Shaw. *The World of Soul,* Paperback Library, New York, 1971. Page 135.

Charlie Gillett. *The Sound of the City*, Sphere Books, London, 1971. Page 152.

Art Rupe. "The Specialist: Art Rupe talks to Ian Whitcombe," *Blues Unlimited*, Bexhill-on-Sea, October/November, 1973. Page 8.

Jack Kerouac. *On the Road*, Andre Deutsch Ltd, London, 1958. Pages 175/176.

ADDITIONAL READING

It should be noted that I have not tried to be complete in the following list. The books and articles listed are items which I referred to when writing the article, and there are others which will have information of relevance to the subject. But the ones listed are, I believe, of particular value.

Ira Gitler. *Jazz Masters of the 40's*, Macmillan, New York, 1966.

Leroi Jones. *Blues People,* William Morrow, New York, 1963.

Charles Keil. *Urban Blues,* University of Chicago Press, London 1966.

Ross Russell. *The Sound,* E.P. Dutton & Co. Inc., New York, 1961.

William Claxton. *Jazz West Coast*, Linear Productions Inc., Hollywood, 1954.

John Tynan. Teddy Edwards: Long Journey, *Down Beat*, Chicago, May 24th, 1962.

Martin Williams. Dial Days: A Conversation with Ross Russell," *Down Beat*, December 3rd and 17th, 1964.

Mark Gardner. "Interview with Roy Porter," *Jazz & Blues*, London, July/August and August/September, 1971.

Mark Gardner. "Interview with Melvyn Broiles," *Jazz & Blues*, February & March. 1972.

Bob Porter & Mark Gardner. "The California Cats: Interview with Sonny Criss," *Jazz Monthly*, April and May, 1968.

Johnny Otis. "Interview with Roy Milton," *Blues Unlimited*, June/July, 1974.

Doug Seroff. "Roy Milton and Miltone Records," *Blues Unlimited*, September/October, 1975.

Johnny Otis. "Interview with Pee Wee Crayton," *Blues Unlimited*, April/May, 1974.

Johnny Otis. "Interview with Jimmy Liggins," *Blues Unlimited*, October/November, 1974.

John Broven. "A Rap with Johnny Otis," *Blues Unlimited*, April, 1973. "Interview with Charles Brown," *Living Blues,* Chicago, May/June, 1976.

Johnny Simmen. "Maxwell Davis," *Coda,* Toronto, November/December, 1973.

In addition, there are a couple of my own articles, which may be of interest in that they deal with aspects of the West Coast scene:

1. Jim Burns. "Bird in California," *Jazz Journal*, London, July, 1969.

2. Jim Burns. "Let the good times roll." *Jazz & Blues*, February, 1972.

RECORDS

Again, I make no claim to completeness with my listing. There will be numerous LP's by individual artists which will contain tracks of relevance to any survey of West Coast activity in the Forties, and to have listed them all would have taken up far too much space. What I have tried to do is give details of a number of compilations which provide reasonable surveys of either jazz or R&B artists working in California, together with a handful of items by some of the more important individuals.

Black California, Savoy SJ L 2215. One of the finest albums of its kind on the market. It contains material by Helen Humes, Slim Gaillard, and many others.

Wardell Gray: *Central Avenue,* Prestige P-24062.

Wardell Gray & Dexter Gordon, MCA 510127 C. *Central Avenue Breadown*, Volumes 1 and 2, Onyx 212 and 215.

Helen Humes and Ivie Anderson, Storyville SLP 804. Forties tracks by the two artists, both of whom mixed jazz and blues to good effect.

Jazz at the Philharmonic, 1944-1946, Volumes 1 and 2, Verve 2610 020 and 2610024.

The Best of Gene Norman's Just Jazz, Vogue LAE 12001.

Groovin' High, Hep 15. West Coast recordings from 1945/1946 by little-known big-bands.

Nat King Cole, Capitol SC 052 80 804. Los Angeles tracks from the mid-Forties.

Slim Gaillard, Hep 6 and 11. Mid-Forties tracks from the West Coast.

Slim Gaillard, Polydor 545 107. Includes the famous tracks from Charlie Parker.

Slim Gaillard, Jazz Astrology, 30 JA 5196. More West Coast tracks.

T-Bone Walker, Music for Pleasure MFP 1043.

T-Bone Walker, Capitol T 1958

Cecil Gant, Flyright LP 4710 and 4714

The Original Johnny Otis Show, Savoy SJL 2230.

West Coast Blues, Kent KST9012. Items by Roy Hawkins, Pee Wee Crayton, etc.

Central Avenue Blues, Ace of Spades 1001. Items by Milburn, Crayton, Walker, etc.

California Blues, Polydor International 423 242. Items by Lowell

Fulson, Floyd Dixon.

Everyday I have the blues, Speciality SPE/ LP 6601. Items by Fulson, Ray Charles, Lloyd Glenn, etc.

Joe & Jimmy Liggins, Speciality SNTF 5020.

Amos Milburn, Route 66 KIX-7. There are two other LP's by Milburn currently available, Riverboat 900.266 and United Artists UAS 30203.

Floyd Dixon, Route 66 KIX-1.

Charles Brown, Route 66 KIX-5.

Ivory Joe Hunter, Route 66 KIX-4.

Roy Milton, Riverboat 900.264.

Roy Milton, Speciality SNTF 5019.

Little Willie Littlefield, K.C. 101.

Buddy Tate, Black Lion 2460 172. Contains the tracks with vocals by Charlie Price.

Blues Jubilee, Vogue LDM 30220. West Coast tracks by Dinah Washington, Jimmy Witherspoon and Helen Humes, including the latter's *Million Dollar Secret.*

Pete Johnson, After Hours AH 1202. Some tracks feature Crown Prince Waterford, one of them being *LA. Blues.*

Dinah Washington & Betty Roche, Top Rank RX 3006. The Washington tracks were recorded in Los Angeles in the mid-Forties, and include *Pacific Coast Blues*.

Jimmy Witherspoon, Polydor International 423 241. Includes *Skid Row Blues*.

LET THE GOOD TIMES ROLL

ONE of the saddest aspects of jazz is the intolerance shown by many of its devotees towards other forms of music, and even towards styles of jazz itself which lie outside the immediate area they happen to be interested in. One can see this attitude at work in the reaction to big-bands (it intrigues me that the announcers on radio programmes invariably fail to mention Alan Dell's excellent 'Big Band Sound' when listing the week's jazz shows) and the result is, of course, that a lot of good music gets neglected. But perhaps it isn't only jazz fans that are guilty. Blues followers often seem to be uninterested in jazz. Big-band fanatics dislike small groups. Collectors of so-called quality popular music, such as that produced by Frank Sinatra and the like, find jazz and blues and many big-bands hard going. These are all generalisations, I agree, but there's an element of truth in each and I can personally name individuals who would happily admit to the prejudices I've mentioned. What they appear to overlook is the inter-action that must exist between all the forms of music referred to.

With these thoughts in mind, what does one do when faced with a musical style with elements in it likely to arouse strong comment from all sides? I'm thinking of rhythm-and-blues, and looking back over the years it strikes me that, one way or another, it has had a hard time. In the early Fifties the modern-jazz audience often dismissed it as being crude and musically vulgar. It was beyond the pale according to many big-band and popular music (in the Sinatra sense) fans. And as for the blues buffs, well as Charles Keil wittily put it: "The criteria for a real blues singer, implicit or explicit, are the following. Old age: the performer should preferably be more than sixty years old, blind, arthritic, and toothless (as Lonnie Johnson put it when first approached for an interview, 'Are you another one of those guys who wants to put crutches under my ass?'). Obscurity: the blues singer should not have performed in public or have made a recording in at least twenty years; among deceased bluesmen, the best seem to be those who appeared in a big city one day in the 1920's, made from four to six recordings, and then disappeared into the countryside forever. Correct tutelage: the singer should have played with or been taught by some legendary figure. Agrarian milieu: a bluesman should have lived the bulk of his life as a sharecropper, coaxing mules and picking cotton, uncontaminated by city influences."[1] The average rhythm-and-blues artist, with his slick clothes and slick songs, would hardly appeal to a fan of the "real blues," and as for the instruments they used in their bands - electric-guitars and tenor-saxophones - they were enough to send shivers of rage down the backs of most of the "authentic music" brigade.

Keil admits to exaggerating his case when dealing with the purist policy towards the blues, but I don't think it can be denied that a lot of blues material appeared on record in the post-war years for the benefit of a primarily white audience, and the black buyer tended to prefer the more urbane sounds of rhythm-and-blues. This was certainly true of the late-Forties and early-Fifties, and in this context it's of value to quote the somewhat apologetic words Mike Leadbitter wrote about his researches into the Houston-based label, Freedom: "However awful some Freedom sides sound to a white blues lover's ears, it has to be accepted that they signified what the black buyer wanted and thus their importance cannot be ignored. The only guide to what the public felt was good or bad at the time was what was issued and what was sold. These records were not produced for white ears and they should not be condemned out of hand for this reason (as they have been). The popular Texas style is well portrayed on Freedom and later on Macy's and Peacock; even to a lesser extent on Bob Shad's historic recordings for Sittin' In which featured many Freedom artists. Ensemble vocals, slow weepy ballads, sax led big-bands with flamboyant piano and guitar solos were the order of the day. Many of the influences were Texas men themselves - the already mentioned Amos Milburn, Roy Brown, Floyd Dixon, Charles Brown, T-Bone Walker, Pee Wee Crayton contributed most to this early sound. Outside influences were undoubtedly Wynonie Harris, Albert Ammons, Bull Moose Jackson, Lionel Hampton and Sonny Thompson."[2]

Several of the names that Leadbitter mentions will be familiar to a "straight" jazz audience, and this in itself should hint at the interaction between the styles referred to earlier. It's true, too, that earlier manifestations of rhythm-and-blues - as found in the singing of Jimmy Rushing, Joe Turner, Walter Brown, Jimmy Witherspoon - were accepted by most jazz listeners, partly for their own qualities, partly because the singers worked with good jazz units. As the music developed, though, it fell out of favour in jazz circles. The reasons arc varied. Jazz itself had changed and, at the same time, rhythm-and-blues took on more of the appeal of popular music, at least as far as the Negro was concerned; the accent was on the beat, on vigorous solos that helped build up the excitement, on stage presentation, and on lyrics that dealt with aspects of ghetto life. It shouldn't be assumed that an irrevocable split took place between the two styles, but what did happen was that a major portion of the jazz audience lost contact with elements in black popular music that could, and did provide much of the vitality required in jazz. This article is not an attempt to prove that last point, and what I'm mainly interested in doing is sketching out a brief survey of some rhythm-and-blues in the hope that it will at least focus a little attention on a neglected area of music. My comments are subjective, in that they're conditioned by my jazz interests and tastes, and for this reason alone I've tried to quote other opinions wherever possible so that the reader can follow up what I've said and thus form his own point of view.

Obviously the birth of rhythm-and-blues can be traced back through standard jazz and blues history, but as a definable form it seems to have had its origins in the free-swinging, hard-blowing music of Kansas City and its surroundings. As Leroi Jones pointed out: "The 'shouting' blues singers like Joe Turner and Jimmy Rushing first were heard literally screaming over the crashing rhythm-sections and blaring brass-sections that were characteristic of Southwestern bands . . . These Southwestern 'shouters' and big blues bands had a large influence on Negro music everywhere. The shouter gave impetus to a kind of blues that developed around the cities in the late thirties called 'rhythm and blues', which was largely huge rhythm units smashing away behind screaming blues singers. The singers and their groups identified completely with 'performance', but they still had very legitimate connections with older blues forms."[3]

Jones refers to Joe Turner and, in many ways, he epitomises the history of rhythm-and-blues, from its beginnings in the Thirties through to its amalgamation into the style known as rock-and-roll in the Fifties. It's fascinating to play Turner's 1941 recording of 'Wee baby blues', with Art Tatum's band, and then his 1946 and 1957 versions of the same tune. The first two are predominantly jazz based (though the 1946 track is edgier, harder-blown, perhaps slanted more towards a rhythm-and-blues tone), but the latter stresses a heavy and rigid beat, the "doo-wah" vocalising in the background, and the honking tenor. If you want to take the lesson a little further, and hear how the tune was commercialised (in the sense of being made palatable to the teenage rock-and-rollers) then Little Richard's 'Early one morning' is worth digging out. Not that this disc is particularly bad, but to my ears it lacks the subtlety and spirit of Turner, and has a stylised excitement that the singers of Big Joe's generation never fell into. Little Richard himself was one of the better rock-and-roll performers and had a solid blues and gospel-based musical background. His early-Fifties recording, 'Get rich quick', showed him to be working in a conventional rhythm-and-blues setting (riffing saxes, and a gutty tenor solo by Fred Jackson), but by the time he recorded such splendid rockers as ‘Tutti-frutti' and 'Keep on knockin'' a strong gospel influence was obvious. These tracks perhaps lacked the instrumental qualities inherent in many of the better rhythm-and-blues discs, and the lyrics fell far short of those used by Turner and Witherspoon, but they were exciting and had an authentic quality not found in the great mass of late-Fifties rock.

Staying with the subject of gospel influences for a moment, it's clear that the vocal techniques practised by many preachers did spill into rhythm-and-blues. The call-and-answer patterns, and the falsetto yells, crop up on numerous discs made in the Forties and Fifties. And the influence carried forward into rock-and-roll. Little Richard wasn't the only singer whose work showed more than a passing acquaintance with black church music. Listen to Gary (U.S.) Bond’s 'Copy cat', for example, and you'll hear how the singer screams his comments over a constant background of chanting female voices, rather in the manner of a preacher leading his congregation. It's fascinating as well to note that a singer like Joe Joseph who, in 1954, recorded 'Sleepwalkin' woman', a track in the formative New Orleans rock-and-roll mould, had also produced gospel sides under the name of Brother Joshua. And (just to round off the question of influences) in 1945 he appeared in the studio, under the sobriquet Cousin Joe, backed by Leonard Feather's Hiptet! 'Larceny hearted woman', from the latter date, has the kind of lyrics, and the instrumental tone, of the records made by Hot Lips Page during this period and the singer sounds not unlike Page. In discussing this disc - and jazz collectors might like to note that it has an excellent baritone solo by Harry Carney - I've deviated from the gospel aspect of rhythm-and-blues, but it seems to me essential to point out, if I can, the constant interplay between various styles.

Returning to the early rhythm-and-blues artists, however, we need to accept that Joe Turner, though of major importance, wasn't the only singer working in this line. My brief reference to Hot Lips Page will hopefully draw attention to the fact that his group managed a blend of blues and rhythm which turned out to be very attractive; 'Big 'D' blues' and 'They raided the joint' are two good examples, and the lyrics of the latter have the same ironic references to drink and its effects that one finds in many rhythm-and-blues songs. Walter Brown, singer with the Jay McShann band, might also be quoted as an early starter. He had a wiry-voiced vitality and his 'Hootie's ignorant oil', yet another look at the booze problem, with the singer shouting out the words over a rolling boogie beat, is a forerunner of such rhythm-and-blues classics as 'Drinkin' wine-spo-dee-o-dee' and 'Bloodshot eyes', in tone if not completely in style. It is essentially good-time music, designed for bars and parties rather than for any thoughtful or local (in the manner of the old-time country blues artist) purpose.

Saxophonist/singer Eddie Vinson, a star of the Cootie Williams band and later a leader in his own right, added something to the developing style with his powerful vocalising on tunes like 'Is you is or is you ain't my baby' and 'Things ain't what they used to be'. Vinson needed his big voice to carry him through the shouting Williams band-backing and his alto playing was similarly direct and open. One can hear the same aim in Earl Bostic's alto solos. Bostic, of course, made a hit in the Fifties when he came up with bouncy versions of 'Flamingo', 'Harlem Nocturne', and others, but even as early as 1945 he was prone to use tunes with a simple melody line - 'Tippin' in' is one of his records from this period - and he had an immediately identifiable sound and a penchant for putting across his ideas without mincing effects. The lesser-known Charlie Q. Price also played alto solos full of bluesy effects. Price sang, too, and wrote songs in the relaxed, rhythm-and-blues style popular on the West Coast in the Forties. His 'Ballin' from day to day' is a curious little number, almost full of pathos in places, whereas 'The things you done for me, baby' is brutally frank about the relationship between the singer and his woman. Not all urban blues material spotlights lyrics of any depth but Price's do try to dig a little below the usual clichés.

Louis Jordan, like most of the people mentioned so far, had a jazz background, having played with Chick Webb's band during the 1930's. He recorded with his own group from 1938 on, and many of his early discs utilised the approach that has been associated with such performers as Cab Calloway and Slim Gaillard, i.e. a mixture of jazz/jump music/novelty-vocals. Jordan hit the big-time in the middle-Forties when his 'Choo Choo Ch'boogie', 'School days', 'Let the good times roll' and others proved popular with both black and white audiences. His tightly-arranged music and seemingly innocuous lyrics caught on with white listeners, and his good-time attitude, humour, and blues-laced soloing with black record buyers. When considering his success with whites it's probably also relevant to mention that Jordan, unlike many other blues singers, had a clear tone and one could always understand him. And I think it's necessary to admit that Jordan's act pandered to white notions of Negro eccentricity: "Unquestionably, he played into white prejudices regarding the 'funny' customs, 'colorful' modes, and 'peculiar' outlook of Negroes."[4] On the credit side, however, the music nearly always had a strong jazz content. Jordan took the lion's share of the solo space and you can hear a demonstration of his not negligible talents on 'Buzz me'.

Another of Jordan's hits was 'Open the door, Richard', and this brings in a further element in popular entertainment that was drawn into the rhythm-and-blues melting pot. Originating from a comedy routine used by Dusty Fletcher and John Mason, 'Richard' told the story of a man staggering home from a night out and realising that he's lost his key. This triggers off a series of asides on his landlady, his room-mate, work, and other topics, with the band chipping in every now and then to chant out the song title. Fletcher's own version had him backed by a Jimmy Jones group and Big Nick Nicholas's tenor is heard to good advantage throughout. I don't think Fletcher can be classed as a rhythm-and-blues artist proper - as far as I know he worked mostly in vaudeville - but his kind of situation-humour certainly had a lot in common with the style (get out Louis Jordan's 'Saturday night fish fry' if you need convincing) and would no doubt have appealed to the same audience. This is true, as well, of such artists as Nat 'King' Cole and Harry 'The Hipster' Gibson. (I'm referring to Cole when he was in his combo period, of course). Cole's 'Hit that jive, Jack' had the right mixture of bounce, ensemble vocal, and brief instrumental solos that later cropped up on numerous rhythm-and-blues discs, and such Gibson efforts as 'Handsome Harry the hipster' and '4-F Ferdinand the frantic freak' spotlighted him shouting his 'hip' lyrics over a rolling rhythm. Neither Cole or Gibson (or Slim Gaillard, who belongs in the same category) fit into the rhythm-and-blues classification in any strict sense, but they do demonstrate the power and validity of jump music in black popular entertainment.

I referred to "jump music" in the last paragraph and I was using the term in a loose way to denote those small units specialising in happy, easy-swinging sounds. In the history of the definitive years of rhythm-and-blues the term has a more exact meaning. Charlie Gillett, author of the best book on rhythm-and-blues and early rock-and-roll that has yet been written, describes it thus: "Typical jump combos featured a strong rhythm section of piano, guitar, bass, and drums, and usually had a singer and a saxophonist up front, with sometimes a second sax man added. Between them, the various instrumentalists emphasised the rhythm that a boogie pianist had achieved alone with his left hand, and in the process of transcribing the effect to several instruments the difference between each beat was either emphasised more - in jump rhythms - or blurred - shuffle rhythms. Several different regional variations of the style developed, in New York, on the West Coast, in the mid-South (St Louis/Memphis), in New Orleans, in Chicago, and on the Eastern Seaboard."[5]

Giilett classes T-Bone Walker in the jump category and rightly mentions that he was a comparatively sophisticated artist whose guitar style owed a great deal to jazz. Frankly. I'm not a great fan of Walker's singing, his bland voice - and often mediocre lyrics - tending to bore on prolonged listening. He also had a tendency to stick to an easy-paced rhythm on the majority of his records, though there are exceptions, such as the excellent instrumentals, 'Strollin' with bones' and 'T-Bone jumps again'. But it can't be denied that some of his discs are classics. 'Call it stormy Monday' just about sums up the week as a working-man experiences it. There's a passage in 'Snakes', a novel by Al Young, which tells how it is and brings in a reference to the Walker record. The hero of the book is talking about a local bandleader: "Joe's records for Moonbeam were big sellers around the Detroit area as well as places like Toledo, Ohio, and Gary, Indiana - solid working towns where people got their paychecks every Friday afternoon, lined up and cashed them, went home and got out their workclothes, and hit the streets that very night to party and frolic in the clubs and joints until it's Sunday again. T-Bone Walker told the whole story in his 'Stormy Monday blues."[6] Lowell Fulson, another West Coaster, refined his style as he went along, and many of his songs were not unlike Walker's. He recorded instrumentals like 'Market street shuffle' and 'Guitar shuffle' and these, with their loping rhythm, agile guitar, and riffing saxes, suggest the influence of the older man. Fulson was not just a carbon-copy, though, and had a definite sound of his own, one that - when he was recorded without saxes, etc. -seemed closer to the roots, i.e. rural blues. He had a hit with 'Everyday I have the blues' (later recorded by Joe Williams and the Count Basie band) and the disc has some fine alto soloing by Earl Brown. The jazz potential of the jump bands should be obvious, and many of their discs contain lively, if not always totally original instrumental work. Roy Milton's rocking little band featured rough-edged saxes on 'R.M. blues' and 'It's later than you think' - a song espousing the "enjoy yourself while you can" philosophy -and a wailing alto introduces 'Numbers blues', another item which chronicles a facet of ghetto life. There's a passage in Charles Simmons's 'Corner Boy' that mentions Milton, and at the same time perhaps points to how rhythm-and-blues was viewed by certain people. Jake, a young Negro whose musical tastes centre mainly on bop, switches on the radio one afternoon: "Roy Milton's Solid Senders jammed away on the frantic notes of jazz. It was one of the few square pieces that Jake went for. At four-thirty would come the cool sounds, a mingling of mostly bop and progressive jazz, with a few performers like Nellie Lutcher, Louis Jordan and Ruth Brown thrown in, who belonged to the corn-bread crowd, but were considered good listening by the guys in the know."[7]

Lowell Fulson made his name in California, but had actually been born in Oklahoma, and more than one artist followed his example in heading for the West Coast in search of fame and fortune. Not all of them achieved Fulson's level of popularity. Zuzu Bollin was a little-known singer in the Walker/Fulson style and Jepsen credits him with only a handful of discs, recorded (badly, I might add) in Dallas in 1952. One of these actually refers to quitting Texas and moving to California, which is perhaps what Bollin did. Of his records, 'Why don't you eat where you slept last night' has some hard-blown tenor and alto, the latter by David Newman, later a star of the Ray Charles band.

Many others worked in the jump style and it would be unfair to leave out Johnny Otis, Joe and Jimmy Liggins, and Amos Milburn. Otis had recorded with Lester Young, and in the Forties he toured with a rhythm-and-blues package show that was reputed to be the finest of its kind (he revived the idea for a Monterey Festival and you can hear the results on a recently-issued album). Few, if any, of his early records ever found their way into the British catalogues and it took the rock-and-roll explosion of the Fifties to bring his name to the notice of British listeners. Otis demonstrated that he could play rock as well, if not better than the rest, and his 'Johnny Otis hand jive', 'Crazy country hop', and 'Willie did the cha-cha' are amongst the best discs of the period, little heard now - though rock fans revere many inferior records - but full of bright good humour and swing. And 'Baby I got news for you' has enough blues feeling to show where Otis's roots lay. Amos Milburn's big hit was 'Chicken shack boogie', a track combining the obvious boogie rhythms with edgy saxes and a raucous vocal stressing good times for all. With Joe Liggins we have one of the few genuine rhythm-and-blues performers whose hit record 'The honeydripper' was issued here around the time it was popular in the States. Like T-Bone Walker, Louis Jordan, and Fats Domino, he had a clarity of diction, and his band a comparative smoothness of execution that perhaps eased the problem of making him acceptable to white record buyers. Listen to his 'Pink champagne' and it's possible to hear how, in this easy-swinging, token-bluesy piece, there lies the seeds of more commercial sounds. Maybe I'm misinterpreting what little I've heard of Liggins? Like many of his kind he has been badly served by the record companies and a wider selection of his discs would enable us to assess his contribution better. But there's certainly a vast difference between 'Pink champagne' and Jimmy Liggins's 'Shuffle shuck', a wild outing which spotlights a honking, screaming tenor riding high and wild over slamming band riffs. One would have to be an aficionado to like this, and it's similar in impact to some of the more esoteric moments of J.A.T.P. concerts.

I mentioned Ray Charles earlier, and although he's familiar enough to not have to go into any detail it is worth making specific reference to one or two of his early discs. He was active on the West Coast during the late-Forties and recorded in a variety of styles, from imitation Nat Cole ('I wonder who's kissing her now') to the excellent 'St. Pete Florida blues' and 'Ray's blues', both of which were rhythm-

and-blues influenced. Charles had a more relaxed approach than many others in this field, possibly because of his broader musical experience. Arnold Shaw mentions how Charles had worked with country-and-western bands and quotes him as saying: "I always loved hillbilly music. I never missed 'Grand Ole Opry'. It was honest music, not cleaned up, and it still is."[8] This interplay between rhythm-and-blues and country-and-western music - "white man's blues," as one critic has called it - needs to be documented, and I'll bring in other references to it as I go along. The connection between the two styles isn't an important one, but it does seem to me generally true that country-and-western music often relates to the life-style and social background of its practitioners and followers as much as rhythm-and-blues did. But to return to Ray Charles. 'Kissa me baby' (or 'All night long', as some releases have it) is a solid track, with a well-drilled little band - which includes Stanley Turrentine on tenor - belting out riffs behind Ray's ecstatic shouting. This disc was a rhythm-and-blues chart-topper in 1952.

So far I've dealt with those West Coasters functioning in the "jump" style, but they weren't the only ones active. Jimmy Witherspoon recorded frequently in Los Angeles between 1947 and 1954 and his discs had a stronger jazz tone. His rich voice - and I don't think it's exaggerating to say that, on something like 'No rolling blues', it had an almost noble quality - was much more expressive than many straight rhythm-and-blues singers' and for this reason - and his strong jazz connections - he's always been a little apart from them. True, Witherspoon recorded songs that were virtually rhythm-and-blues - 'Have a ball' and 'Good jumpin' ' are two such items - but essentially he was too subtle and relaxed to fit completely into the pattern.

Some of Witherspoon's discs brilliantly catch the tone of life in the Forties and early Fifties. 'Skid row blues' is a lament for the hipsters and their impoverished economic condition when the police clamped down on their hangouts and money raising activities. 'Money's getting cheaper' bemoans the inflationary spiral of the period and, though clearly designed for topicality, the lyrics still ring true today. What is apparent from both is that Witherspoon was not content to copy or merely churn out doggerel. His words had a validity that necessitated them being heard, which is something not always true of the rhythm-and-blues scene.

A little-known singer in the Turner/Witherspoon line who recorded in California in the mid-Forties was Crown Prince Charlie Waterford, one-time vocalist with Jay McShann. Surprisingly, he made discs for Capitol. I say "surprisingly" because most of his ilk were contracted to the small labels then active, and few of the major labels were prepared to record rhythm-and-blues and its preceding styles. Waterford's approach was clearly based on Turner's, though he was inclined to be a little more exuberant and this carried him nearer to the rhythm-and-blues of the immediate post-war years. Like Witherspoon, he was interested in chronicling West Coast life in his songs and 'L.A. blues' outlines the problems of making it in Los Angeles. He could also sing a good, bawdy blues, as 'Move your hand, baby' proves, and on 'Coal black baby' he throws in a spot of skilful guitar playing. Pete Johnson provides the rolling piano background on these various tracks.

The out-and-out rhythm-and-blues singer who probably followed closest in the footsteps of Turner/Witherspoon/Waterford was, I think, Wynonie Harris. He had recorded in California with such jazz musicians as Howard McGhee, Jack McVea, and Oscar Pettiford, and had taken on Joe Turner in 'Battle of the blues', but it was when he formed his own small group, and began recording in New York for King, that he established the sound he became famous for. 'Lollipop mama', 'All she wants to do is rock', 'Lovin' machine' and 'Bloodshot eyes' are classics of their kind and have been unduly neglected in recent years. With their risque lyrics, pounding rhythm, and rasping sax solos, they paved the way for a whole string of other groups and singers. It's interesting to note, too, that 'Bloodshot eyes' was a country-and-western number by Hank Penny, though Harris's virile version completely captured the tune for the rhythm-and-blues market.

Harris also recorded 'Good rockin' tonight' (almost the same as Jimmy Witherspoon's 'Good jumpin') - a concert version has him backed by Lionel Hampton's band - and 'Drinkin' wine-spo-dee-o-dee', a song which can be used to mark the milestones along the rhythm-and-blues trail. Originally recorded by its composer, Sticks McGhee, in 1946 or 1947, it was re-recorded by him a couple of years later, and it is the second version that is best known here, having been re-issued on various anthologies. More basic than Harris's, it nonetheless has the same overall feeling -that of a big-city street-corner at weekend with the parties about to start and everyone out to get drunk and have a good time. The song was revived by Jerry Lee Lewis in the Fifties, and during the heyday of the rhythm-and-blues influenced vocal-groups the Night Caps recorded a thing called 'Wine-wine-wine' which owed its existence to McGhee's tune. One way and another, 'Drinkin' wine-spo-dee-o-dee' had run the gamut of the rhythm-and-blues experience.

The sound of the Harris band was equalled in excitement by Tiny Bradshaw's, and the latter's 'Walk that mess' and 'Breaking up the house' are essentials for any collector wanting representative discs of the period. The beat is rock-solid, and the saxophone soloists try on their Jacquets. Bradshaw came up with a version of 'T-99', a song also recorded by Jimmy Nelson, its composer. Nelson was a minor rhythm-and-blues singer, active in the late-Forties and early-Fifties, whose main failing was his incapacity to settle on a style of his own. Listening to his records is often like playing a series of snippets from tracks by Joe Turner, Jimmy Witherspoon, T-Bone Walker, and even Louis Jordan. Play Nelson's 'Meet me with your black dress on', and then get out Jordan's 'Blue lights boogie', and you'll hear what I mean. There's the same relaxed group vocal, and the tunes themselves have a great deal in common. Other Nelson discs, such as 'Unlock the lock' and 'I sat and cried', sound like attempts at simplifying rhythm-and-blues, i.e. they're near to early rock-and-roll. 'Cried', in fact, has overtones of the kind of things Tennessee Ernie recorded in the early Fifties. The country-and-western influence again? The lyrics certainly aren't in the usual rhythm-and-blues pattern.

It may be of value to mention at this point why rhythm-and-blues appealed to black record buyers. With the gradual decline of the big-bands, and the increasing tendency of modern-jazz musicians to play primarily for listening, it was inevitable that the working-class Negro in particular would move to a form of music more suitable for drinking and dancing to, with steady rhythmic impetus and lyrics which, if often lacking in subtlety, were topical and of relevance to the audience's social condition. The words of Fats Domino's 1949 'Detroit city blues' do little more than exploit the name of the city and the joys of having a girl and a good time there, but they no doubt got across and provided the message wanted. In a way the idea behind this kind of song - that of making a limited experience seem desirable -is rather similar to the purpose of many British working-class music-hall songs of the late-19th and eariy-20th centuries, and the basic effect was probably the same. The listener could look around his own little world - be it the ghetto of an American city or Victorian London - and tell himself what a warm and wonderful place it could be. This would help to make a difficult life tolerable, but at the same time it could also blind the audience to the need for change. Colin MacInness, in his splendid book on the music-hall in England[9], has some pertinent things to say about this aspect of the sociological side of popular music. His comments on the limitations inherent in music-hall material can often be applied to rhythm-and-blues, and no reader interested in either subject should fail to devote some attention to his opinions.

Fats Domino's early records are fascinating studies in themselves, in that they demonstrate certain changes in rhythm-and-blues that became obvious in the early Fifties. The music was tending to harden, with riffs becoming the dominant instrumental mode. Listen to the 1953 Domino recording, 'Fat's frenzy', and you'll find yourself not all that far removed from Bill Haley; it's an accepted fact that Haley based some of his musical ideas on Domino's. The latter's success in the rock-and-roll boom - and with largely white audiences - whilst owing something to his use of conventionally-sentimental songs like 'My blue heaven' and 'Blueberry hill' (note: he also adapted Hank Williams's 'Jambalaya' to his style) was no doubt made easier by his relatively mellow voice, inhibited lyrics, and smooth band backing in which easily-identifiable riffs predominated. In the late-Forties and early Fifties few whites could accept the musical and sexual frankness implicit in a lot of authentic rhythm-and-blues, and those that could were often dissidents from the values of their society. There's a passage in Abbie Hoffman's 'Woodstock Nation' which neatly sums up the situation: "Back during the 1950's me and the guys I bummed around with when I got thrown out of school wore pegged pants, had DA haircuts, blue suede shoes, and hung around pool halls swearing and spitting a lot. The music we listened to was called race-records and then rhythm-and-blues. Vanetta Dillard singing 'Mercy Mister Percy' was the first race-record I ever heard. We dug stuff like Earl Bostic, James Moody, the Midnighters, Joe Turner, and later the Drifters and Fats Domino. It was all 45 rpm stuff which made for easy swiping, simple under-the-jacket stuff. The trouble was that very few stores carried the stuff cause Patti Page singing about porcelain 'Old Cape Cod' and Frankie Laine moaning 'I Believe' religious hymns and Tony Bennett singing funky Tony Bennett blues was all the stores knew. On the radio too there was just Symphony Sid out of Boston and later Moondog out of New York. We were two hundred and fifty miles from New York and had to rig up a roof antennae to hear ol' Alan Freed bang a telephone book on the table while he spun out the Sound. The Sound was SAXOPHONE and it was 'Unh-unh-stick-it-in-wa-doo-was'. Dances were all grunts and belts with names like the Ginny-crawl and the Roxbury Mule, and there were very few of us doing it. You just didn't do the Dirty Boogie to Teresa Brewer, no sir, and not at the Totem Pole in Newton, Mass., no man, definitely not. The whole scene except for a few of us hoods - I think that's what we preferred to be called especially if we had read 'A Stone for Danny Fisher' or 'The Amboy Dukes' - so except for us hoods and Bill Haley and his Comets the whole fucking scene was black."[10]

Hoffman is talking about the days when rock-and-roll was establishing itself as a definable form, and it's of relevance to consider the effect this change had on the lyrics. Wynonie Harris might have shouted how his baby liked to rock all night (and no-one with a modicum of common-sense had any doubt as to what was meant by "rock") but white rock-and-roll might be summed up by the lines of The Jodimars 'Now dig this', with their reference to "sipping cherry cokes, telling corny jokes," and their insistence on the fact that "if you're in your teens, and you like blue jeans, movie magazines," you'll dig this - the record, that is. You maybe would have, too, had the description fit, but it was all a long throw from the gut-level sounds of the rhythm-and-blues bands and singers. I suppose one could loosely sum it up by saying that Turner, Harris, and the rest, were performing for adults, whereas The Jodimars (and others like them) were catering for teenagers. And, as this was near the beginning of the pop-crazy years, the big-business exploitation machine got under way. White teenagers were told that they were different from their parents because it paid to have them think so. Of course, when they took the message literally - and the results got out-of-hand (see Abbie Hoffman's *Woodstock Nation*) - there was an almighty squeal from those same business interests. But that's another story.

By 1954 or so the sound of rock-and-roll was almost dominant. Joe Turner had commenced recording for Atlantic and his backings spotlighted a heavy beat and simple riffs. I seem to recall that records from Turner's "rock" period met with a lot of criticism in jazz circles, but in retrospect they aren't all that bad. I can't claim that the saw-edged tenor on 'Ti-ri-lee' is the equal in jazz terms of, say, Don Byas on earlier Turner tracks, but then it's maybe a mistake to judge these things in jazz terms. And although the words of the songs were often less than inspired, Turner's magnificent voice transcends such minor limitations. Like Billie Holiday, he could shape the most routine material to his own use.

Whilst pointing out that jazz terms are not necessarily the best for judging rhythm-and-blues and early rock-and-roll, it needs to be said that not all rock descended totally from black music. There are distinct elements of white country music in Carl Perkins' 'Dixie fried', not only in the rhythmic impulse but also in the phrasing and subject matter. The term "rockabilly" " was applied to this new form, and it's perhaps not out of place to suggest that Tennessee Ernie's 'Shotgun boogie' was an early example of the genre. Bill Haley typified parts of this approach, too. Haley himself was never a convincing rock-and-roll singer and his tenorman was invariably more adroit at building up the tension. 'See you later, alligator' (lifted from a Guitar Slim piece called 'Later for you, baby') is worth listening to in this respect, whereas in contrast 'Rock around the clock' shows how the guitar solos swung more towards country-and-western techniques. Generally speaking, the improvised solos on "rockabilly" sides were far less interesting than those on rhythm-and-blues records, though again this is a jazz-biased viewpoint. Bill Justis's 'Raunchy' is, to my mind, a hackneyed performance and fails in comparison with instrumentals recorded by such people as Sonny Thompson and Tiny Bradshaw. A Memphis rock track like Carl Perkins' 'Blue suede shoes', good as it is, might have been improved by a more determined rhythm-section and a more inventive guitar solo. And it's significant that Billy Lee Riley's 'Red hot' turned out to be one of the best of its kind, in my view because it held close to a rhythm-and-blues impulse. Fans of vintage rock-and-roll will no doubt disagree with my comments, and in vindication of my opinions I can only repeat what I said earlier - I approach these things mainly from a jazz standpoint.[11]

“The Sound was SAXOPHONE," Abbie Hoffman said, and this brings us to one of the significant factors in rhythm-and-blues that deserves a few paragraphs on its own. A strong saxophone soloist - usually a tenorman - was a necessity in almost every band, and many of them were featured as much as the singers. Sonny Thompson's 'Long gone' gave Eddie Chamblee a leading role, and Tiny Bradshaw's 'Soft' concentrated virtually exclusively on tenor work by Red Prysock and Rufus Gore. All right, neither of these discs can be said to do other than lay down a straightforward beat over which the soloists play relaxed, if uneventful lines, but they do have a large quota of good-humour and easy swing to recommend them. One's own tastes might run to the comparative complexities of a Wardell Gray or Dexter Gordon - though if one listens to their 'I hear you knockin' ' and ' 'Jingle jangle jump' one hears sounds not all that far removed from rhythm-and-blues - but this shouldn't distract from an enjoyment of other forms. And it must not be forgotten that, in the late-Forties and early-Fifties, such artists as Gene Ammons and James Moody were often thought of as working in a semi-rhythm-and-blues style as much as in jazz. We've read how Abbie Hoffman remembered listening to Moody, and both Ammons and Moody had rocking little bands that weren't afraid to let rip. Ammons had a popular hit with 'Red top' and also recorded various ballad performances - 'These foolish things' is one of the best known - that were acceptable to the rhythm-and-blues market. His big sound and melodic interpretations appealed to an audience that liked its music without too many frills. When Ammons and Sonny Stitt formed a group in the Fifties many of their tunes - 'Chabootie' and 'Seven eleven' spring to mind - were designed to catch the ears of listeners who normally tuned in to tenormen like Red Prysock.

Ammons and Moody are established names in the jazz world, so their work will be known to readers. Eddie "Lockjaw" Davies wasn't averse to recording in a near rhythm-and-blues style, too, and there's an LP of his early discs on which he stomps and squawks his way through 'Leapin' on Lennox' and 'He's a real gone guy' in a very solid manner. But it's doubtful if many British collectors have heard of Big Jay McNeeley, Wild Bill Moore, Sil Austin, Bull Moose Jackson, Paul Williams, Lynn Hope and Gene Barge. Others, like Hal Singer, Arnett Cobb, J. D. King, Al Sears, Bumps Myers and Sam Taylor, might be accepted for their solos with jazz groups, but I wonder how many of their rhythm-and-blues discs have graced the turntables of English gramophones? It's a favourite pastime of mine to take a volume of Jepsen off the shelf and glance through it, picking out the forgotten tracks by obscure tenormen, or the early sides by people now better known for their jazz efforts. Jimmy Forrest's 'Night train' is an example of the latter category, and one debates just what it sounded like.

Few records by the tenormen I've mentioned have been issued here and those that sneaked into the catalogues were more than probably ignored by the jazz fraternity. But they often have a lot in them worth listening to. I have a Sil Austin LP (recorded in the mid-Fifties) on which he charges through a programme of hard-hitting tracks, sounding like a combination Earl Bostic and Illinois Jacquet with rock backing. He calms down at times, though, and 'The Square from Cuba' has some very mellow tenor. What is consistent throughout the LP is the steady beat laid down by the rhythm. One can almost see the flashing lights and crowded dance-floor during the easy-paced 'Late show' and it brings home the fact that a musician like Austin was essentially an entertainer with a need to attract a wide enough audience to ensure him a steady income. This thought occurs also when listening to the music that Red Prysock played when he led his own group on a 1956 Mercury session. 'Rock and roll party, “Lulu” (a Dickie Wells composition) and 'Rock and roll mambo' storm along, placing the emphasis firmly on the tenor and always accenting a definite beat. Prysock does fall back on repetitive phrases a lot, it's true, but at times - as on the mambo number - he plays some stimulating, rough-edged tenor. If these tenormen could be so fiery in the studio, one wonders what it must have been like to have heard them in the flesh. I have fond memories of reading reports of sax soloists honking 87 times in succession on the same note, or lying flat on their backs at the end of their solos! And who was it who used to wander off the stand, walk into the Gents, and then make his way back to the stand again, all the time belching and squealing out the notes on his tenor? Leroi Jones captured the zaniness of those years in his story, The Screamers, with a turbaned Lynn Hope leading the crowd out of the dance-hall and down the street. As Jones said, "All the saxophonists of that world were honkers, Illinois, Gator, Big Jay Jug, the great sounds of our day."[12] Howard Rumsey's Lighthouse All Stars parodied the extremes of this honking age when they got Jimmy Giuffre to do a passable imitation of a rhythm-and-blues tenorman on *Big girl*.

Before leaving the subject of rhythm-and-blues tenor, we should take a brief look at Dizzy Gillespie's 'We love to boogie', if only because it has a driving solo by a young John Coltrane. The whole track, from the vocal by Fred Strong to the ensemble riffs, is in the rhythm-and-blues mode. It's often forgotten that Dizzy, after the break-up of his big-band, swung very close to the form, even to the extent of including baritone-saxist Bill Graham in his group. Graham had played with the Lucky Millinder and Erskine Hawkins bands and led a rhythm-and-blues unit of his own for a time. Neither should we overlook the fact that Dizzy recorded 'Money honey', a song made famous by Clyde McPhatter and The Drifters.

Looking through what I've written I'm conscious of having neglected certain aspects of rhythm-and-blues, in particular the contributions made by female singers. Obviously, the form favoured males with leather lungs but some women - Helen Humes, Dinah Washington, to name just two - did fit in easily. Miss Humes was recorded at the concert that produced Jimmy Witherspoon's famous 'No rolling blues', and her 'Million dollar secret' makes a neat companion piece, being an easy-paced, lightly-bawdy blues with a nice line in cynical lyrics. Reference to the appropriate volume of Jepsen will show that she recorded numerous tracks in the late Forties with such musicians as Maxwell Davis, Wild Bill Moore and Bumps Myers in the backing groups. Most of these sides have long since been consigned to total obscurity, but 'Drive me daddy' is typical of the kind of relaxed singing, and heavily-loaded lyrics that Miss Humes specialised in. Dinah Washington also recorded a large number of blues-influenced performances in the Forties and early-Fifties, with some incorporating obvious rhythm-and-blues sounds to ensure their appeal to the fans of that music. Her 'Blowtop blues' and 'Salty papa blues' (both also recorded by Etta Jones) are good examples, though their instrumental solos are admittedly closer to jazz than anything else. The words are typical of mid-Forties material, however, and 'Blowtop', in fact, is extremely subtle and witty in its description of "flipping out." Miss Washington had some success in the rhythm-and-blues charts in 1949 with her 'Baby get lost', and 'Long John blues', 'Fat daddy', and 'TV is the thing this year' (the latter pair with swinging Paul Quinichette tenor) were also popular.

There were numerous other female singers, of course, amongst them Faye Adams, Little Esther, Willie Mae Thornton, Edna McGriff, Etta James, Ruth Brown and Lavern Baker. Miss Thornton was the originator of 'Hound dog', one of Elvis Presley's earliest hits, and although I don't think her own version is available, 'Tom cat' has much the same gutsy sound. Ruth Brown and Lavern Baker managed to change their styles enough to make it into the Fifties rock charts and readers will perhaps recall Miss Baker's 'Tweedle dee', even though an insipid Georgia Gibbs cover-version tended to steal the limelight in England. Edna McGriff I know little about, other than that she recorded some sides with a band led by trombonist Bennie Green, plus a handful of others for minor labels. Her best-known number seems to have been 'Heavenly Father', a rather maudlin song which hardly pointed to Miss McGriff as being amongst the best of singers. To be fair, two versions of the song are on record and 1 suspect that the copy I have may be the later, perhaps inferior one. As for Etta James, well she slightly bowdlerised a song called 'Work with me, Annie', renamed it 'Wallflower', and chanted out "Roll with me, Henry." By the time Georgia Gibbs got hold of the tune, and popularised it with white record buyers, it had become 'Dance with me, Henry', and the lyrics were guaranteed not to upset anyone. It's worth noting that the Etta James rendering of 'Wallflower' has a tenor solo by Maxwell Davis, a musician who figured on a lot of rhythm-and-blues records and was also active on the fringes of jazz.

Small groups predominated in rhythm-and-blues, but a few big-bands did function in the style, if only partially. I've always thought that Lionel Hampton's late-Forties records often leant that way and a look at his discography will prove that he had quite a lot of tunes in his book which were obviously there to cash in on their popularity. Amongst them were 'Pink champagne’, 'Red top', The hucklebuck', and 'Drinkin' wine-spo-dee-o-dee'. Sonny Parker sang with the Hampton band, and the other vocalists - Irma Curry, Betty Carter, Little Jimmy Scott -frequently had the kind of highly-individual sounding voices that Negro audiences preferred. In other words they differed from the bland crooners found singing with white dance-bands at this time. Unfortunately, few of Hampton's records have been re-issued in recent years, and those that have tend to be the jazz sides. We might get a truer picture of the real sound of the Hampton band if the rhythm-and-blues tracks were made available.

Tiny Bradshaw had a big-band at times throughout his career, and both Lucky Millinder and Erskine Hawkins managed to keep large units going by the simple expedient of playing the kind of music audiences wanted.

And, in the early-Fifties, that happened to be rhythmically simple, riffily melodic swing, with big-toned tenors taking the solos. Millinder's 'Ram-bunk-shush' embodies these various factors, and Erskine Hawkins' 'Double shot' is similar. Charlie Gillett correctly points out that the rhythm-and-blues bands often used less imaginative arrangements than their jazz counterparts, and sometimes less skilful soloists, and whilst agreeing with him in principle I do think it needs to be stressed that the music produced by Millinder, Hawkins and Buddy Johnson never lacked for enthusiasm. At its best, it was vigorous and inventive; at its more routine, it was at least designed for easy listening.

The one final aspect of rhythm-and-blues that I want to mention - though for reasons which will soon be obvious I can't go into any detail - is the existence of the vocal groups. In his informative book *The Drifters*[13]. Bill Millar revealed the startling fact that some 15,000 black vocal groups first recorded during the Fifties, and this in itself precludes any fair comment in an article of the kind I've written. Still, even the most cursory sampling will turn up items of interest to anyone with an open-minded love of jazz. The Jivers' 'Rae Pearl', besides being an extremely catchy and happy performance, has a forceful tenor solo, (does anyone know who played it?) that has recommendable qualities of its own. There's The Hawks' 'He's the fat man', with a firm rhythm-and-blues sound throughout, including the rasping tenor. And the Teen Queens' 'Zig zag', a lively disc with brassy orchestral sounds and, again, the anonymous tenorman. These are a mere handful of records, drawn from my own dabblings in the available material - does the man exist who can honestly claim to have heard even one record by each of those 15,000 groups? - and there are no doubt hundreds of others of interest. Some vocal group records are, I agree, an acquired taste - the lesser groups made a fetish of the contrast between high-pitched lead and plunking bass voice, sometimes with hilarious results — and one would need to be a fanatic to sit through them all. But it does seem true enough that a fair amount of worthwhile music can be found buried amongst the dross.

Speaking of the advent of rock-and-roll, Charlie Gillett wrote, "Rock'n'roll narrowed the reference of songs to adolescence and simplified the complicated boogie rhythms to a simple 2/4 with the accent on the back beat. And once these new conventions were established, the rhythm and blues singers were obliged to either adapt to them or resign themselves to obscurity, at best playing for a local audience in some bar, and at worst abandoning music altogether."[14]

This is true, and such artists as Wynonie Harris and Tiny Bradshaw slid into obscurity. A few - Ray Charles, B. B. King - managed to maintain their popularity, and in fact move on to even greater success, by rapid changes of style to catch the popular fancy. And new singers, who at one time might have worked in the rhythm-and-blues form, came up with variations on it. Chuck Berry's 'Sweet little sixteen' and 'Johnny B. Goode' cleverly exploited the teenage side of rock-and-roll but they still relied on a good, swinging beat. James Brown revived Louis Jordan's old hit, 'Caldonia', and this time injected it with gospel or "soul" overtones. But too many rock-and-roll singers pandered to the adolescents in their audiences and the result was a slackening of the tension that made rhythm-and-blues such exciting music to listen to. The tenor fell into disfavour, and when it was used it had to take on the "yacketty-yak" sound required by rock record producers. Straight instrumentals deteriorated, too, as The Champs' Tequila', with its repeated riffs and paucity of other ideas, amply demonstrated. It's a telling experience to play some of the rhythm-and-blues sides I've mentioned and then put on a late-Fifties rock-and-roll disc.

I've given the impression of a slide in quality as rock-and-roll developed beyond its initial stages and this, frankly, is how I hear it, though I'm conscious of the fact that certain talented performers were still active, and that things picked up in the Sixties. Some readers will probably disagree with my view of events, but I haven't set out to narrate the rise and fall of rhythm-and-blues. Historical detail has been sketched in out of necessity, but my main purpose has been to draw attention to a selection of neglected records and to suggest that jazz history makes for more interesting reading and listening if considered alongside rhythm-and-blues and other black music. The time is ripe for a more detailed investigation of individual artists, and for an approach that will throw light on the minor rhythm-and-blues bands, or some of those 15,000 vocal groups. I'm not suggesting that this should take over from the critical and historical work that jazz writers already do, but it ought to be accepted that much of the music I've discussed is perfectly valid when viewed in a jazz and blues context.

Notes

1 Charles Keil. *Urban Blues* (University of Chicago Press, London, 1966). Pages 34/35.

2 Mike Leadbitter. *Nothing But The Blues* (Hanover Press, London, 1971). Page 175.

3 Leroi Jones. *Blues People* (Morrow & Co., New York, 1963). Page 168.

4 Arnold Shaw. *The World Of Soul* (Paperback Library, New York, 1971). Page 119.

5 Charlie Gillett. *The Sound Of The City* (Sphere Books, London, 1971). Page 152.

6 Al Young. *Snakes* (Sidgwick & Jackson, London, 1971). Page 85.

7 Herbert Simmons. *Corner Boy* (Ace Books; London, 1960). Page 26.

8 Shaw. Op. cit. Page 325.

9 Colin Maclnnes. *Sweet Saturday Night* (MacGibbon & Kee, London, 1967).

10 Abbie Hoffman. *Woodstock Nation* (Vintage Books, New York, 1969). Pages 22 to 24.

11 See Harlan Ellison's *Rockabilly* (Muller Ltd., Gold Medal Books, London, 1963). This is a novel about a singer making it in the "rockabilly" style and is useful for background information.

12 Leroi Jones. 'The Screamers', in the collection *Tales* (Grove Press, New York, 1967). Pages 71 to 80.

13 Bill Millar. *The Drifters* (Studio Vista, London, 1971).

14 Gillett. Op. cit. Page 195.

In addition to the books already mentioned, interested readers should find the following of value. Paul Oliver's *Screening The Blues* (Cassell, London, 1968); Bob Groom's *The Blues Revival* (Studio Vista, London, 1971); Dave Laing's *The Sound Of Our Times* (Sheed & Ward, London, 1969); Carl Belz's *The Story Of Rock* (Oxford University Press, New York, 1969); none of these deals specifically with rhythm-and-blues but all contain information of relevance to any study of the subject. The same can be said of some of the essays in *Soul*, edited by Lee Rainwater, and published by Aldine Publishing Co., U.S.A. 1970. John Gabree's 'The Roots of Rock: Rhythm and Blues' in the *Down Beat* yearbook for 1969 might also be of interest, though I don't think it says anything new or different.

Records

Individual records referred to can be traced through discographies, but there are a number of anthologies that serve as an introduction to the subject.

Specialty SNTP 5002 and 5003 ('This Is How It All Began', volumes 1 and 2) have a selection of tracks from the rhythm-and-blues and early-rock periods, including material by Roy Milton, Joe and Jimmy Liggins, Percy Mayfield, and Little Richard.

Liberty LBL 8321 5E and LBL 83327 ('Urban Blues', volumes 1 and 2) have items by Wynonie Harris, Joe Turner, Fats Domino, Smilin' Joe, T-Bone Walker, and others.

United Artists UAS 29215 ('Sound Of The City/New Orleans') has Domino, Roy Brown, Smilin Joe, etc., and ties in with the Liberty albums.

Liberty LBL 83216E and LBL 83328 ('Rhythm 'N' Blues', volumes 1 and 2) are collections of vocal group performances.

Atlantic 587094/95/96/97 ('History Of Rhythm And Blues', volumes 1 to 4) contain a wide selection, ranging from Sticks McGhee to The Drifters.

Polydor 623 273 ('Kings Of Rhythm And Blues') is a superb set of tracks by Wynonie Harris and Tiny Bradshaw.

Ember 3359 '25 Years of Rhythm and Blues Hits' also has Harris and Bradshaw, plus Sonny Thompson, Earl Bostic, Lucky Millinder, etc.

Polydor 423 242 'California Blues' has Lowell Fulson, Smokey Hogg, and others, and Specialty SPE/LP 6601 (Every Day I Have The Blues) has Fulson, Charles Brown, Lloyd Glenn, etc. Finally, Sun 6467 006 'Memphis Rock' with Carl Perkins, Jerry Lee Lewis, Bill Justis, and Billy Lee Riley.

NOTES

LA VIE DE BOHÈME

This was the first piece I produced on the subject of Bohemia, and it was written for *New Society*, a weekly publication largely devoted to sociological surveys of a wide variety of subjects. I recall writing other articles for *New Society* about alcohol problems in northern towns, the police, and a scheme to promote Burnley as a good place to live and work. The conclusion I drew at the end of the article about bohemianism now seems to me something I tagged on to suit the nature of the magazine.

IN PRAISE OF BOOKSELLERS

I think it's only too obvious that the kind of booksellers I wrote about have largely disappeared, especially outside London. The decline in second-hand bookshops is, in my view, a matter of regret. I'm told that they're no longer needed and that everything is available through the Internet. I acknowledge the virtues of the Internet when it comes to tracking down obscure titles, but they can't really replace the pleasures of browsing in a bookshop, no matter how untidy it is, and finding something unusual.

THINGS ARE NOT AS THEY SEEM

A highly personal response in that it refers to a few writers I came across without making a special study of their work. I found their books on market bookstalls and in second-hand bookshops. Recent years have seen a rise in interest in some of the writers I mention (Gil Brewer's stories for pulp crime magazines in the 1950s have even been reprinted by a university press), and I suspect that some over-rating is taking place. When this piece was first published it appeared under the name of John Dunton.

THE NAMES OF THE FORGOTTEN

Another piece by John Dunton. Its subject, the now-forgotten trumpeter, Tony Fruscella, is not well represented on record, but since I wrote about him in 1997 one or two additional items have come to light. The Japanese Marshmallow label released a CD, *Tony Fruscella: Brooklyn Jam 1952*, with material recorded at the pianist Gene Di Novi's home. The trumpeter plays in the company of Di Novi and alto-players Charlie Kennedy and Hal McKusick. And the Spanish Fresh Sound label unearthed a studio session that Fruscella recorded in 1955 with tenorman Brew Moore, pianist Bill Triglia, and others.

KURT VONNEGUT

I was asked to contribute this article to *Luciad*, a student magazine published at Leicester University. It amused me that its editor, when introducing it, clearly didn't know how to deal with it. He said that it "contains so many digressions and anecdotes that it could be entirely fictitious." None of the people and events I referred to were fictitious, and the fact that the young editor of *Luciad* wasn't sure about them seemed to me to bear out Vonnegut's contention that labour history was looked on as "pornography of a sort."

B.TRAVEN

I wrote several articles and reviews dealing with Traven's life and work, among them "Mysterious Traven" (*The Guardian*, 30th April, 1964); "B.Traven - an epitaph" (*Tribune*, 8th August, 1969); "Traven Before Mexico"(*Palantir* 20, 1982). The latter piece was published as by F.C.Dobbs, a name which Traven readers will know is that of the central character in The *Treasure of the Sierra Madre*.

HOW FAR UNDERGROUND?

I recall that when this was published it aroused some negative reactions from people who liked to promote the idea of an "underground" and didn't care for my critical view of it. I think I was seen as something of a traitor to the cause, especially as I'd been included in *Children of Albion; poetry of the "underground" in Britain* (Penguin Books, 1969) and appeared in one or two magazines with "underground" connections. But my own leanings were always towards literature and I had no interest in pop music, drugs, and vague schemes to revolutionise society. My politics were firmly centred on the Labour Party, unions, and bread-and-butter issues.

THE HIPSTER

This was originally written for *Jazz Journal* in the 1960s and I made some minor adjustments to it when it appeared in *Beat Scene* in 2011. I'm still not sure that it deals fully with what is something of a fluid subject. It may be that the original, and only true, hipsters were a small group of musicians and enthusiasts linked to New York and bebop in the 1940s. After that, the term and the types diversified so much that trying to arrive at an accurate definition is almost impossible. My attempt may at least provide a few pointers for future research into the subject.

JACK KEROUAC

When discussing the jazz and big-band music references in *Maggie Cassidy*, I mentioned a singer who Kerouac calls Pauline Cole and I conjectured that the real-life model for her may have been Pauline Byrne, who sang and recorded with Artie Shaw's orchestra. If readers refer to my article about *Maggie Cassidy* in *Beat Scene* 67 (Spring, 2012) it will be seen that I acknowledged being completely wrong, and that Pauline Cole was actually based on Margaret (Peggy) Coffey, a friend of Kerouac from his boyhood days in Lowell. Thanks to some detective work by Beat scholar, Dave Moore, it has been established that Peggy Coffey sang with the Bobby Byrne orchestra in 1946 and recorded at least two vocal tracks with Byrne for a small, short-lived label called Cosmo. She was with Byrne when his band appeared at the Roseland Ballroom in New York in May, 1946, which ties in with Kerouac's comment about Pauline Cole singing at Roseland. Peggy Coffey also sang with the Vic Roy orchestra, a local outfit in the Nashua area. I'm grateful to Dave Moore for sharing this information with me.

INDEX